Praise for *Finding Home*

"This is a fantastic read, a real page-turner, which keeps you wanting more."—*South Wales Argus*

Praise for *Life as I Know It*

"An excellent story of love, loss and forgiveness, reminding us that sometimes we don't know what's missing in our lives until it's thrown in our path."—*Woman's World*

"Cecelia Ahern territory, highly recommended."
—*The Bookseller* (U.K.)

"Fans of Sophie Kinsella will love Melanie Rose."
—*News of the World* (U.K.)

"After being struck by lightning, formerly single gal Jessica Taylor wakes up in a hospital room with a husband and four children she knows nothing about. The family is tested as Jessica learns more about her new life."
—*More,* "Books We're Buzzing About"

"Rose makes a fantastical premise seem realistic and compelling."—*Booklist*

"This phenomenal story is paced just right and all the threads come together in the end neatly for a satisfying conclusion after many twists and turns....This book is amazing; you will laugh and cry and remember the story for years to come, and it is definitely a Perfect 10!"
—Romance Reviews Today

Also By Melanie Rose

LIFE AS I KNOW IT

finding
Home

finding Home

A Novel

Melanie Rose

BANTAM BOOKS
TRADE PAPERBACKS
NEW YORK

This book is for my son James, with love.

And for Dave—my rock.

It is also for Lyn and Sam,
who will one day be reunited.

Special thanks to my beloved late grandmother Mima,
whose childhood reminiscences provided much
inspiration for this novel.

———

A Bantam Books Trade Paperback Original

Copyright © 2011 by Melanie Rose

All rights reserved.

Published in the United States by Bantam Books,
an imprint of The Random House Publishing Group,
a division of Random House, Inc., New York.

BANTAM and the rooster colophon are
registered trademarks of Random House, Inc.

Originally published in Great Britain as *Coming Home* by Avon,
a division of HarperCollins Publishers, in 2010.

ISBN 978-0-553-38687-5

Printed in the United States of America

www.bantamdell.com

2 4 6 8 9 7 5 3 1

Book design by Ellen Cipriano

finding
Home

chapter one

The rest stop was small and muddy, with only one other car parked at the far end. Spray and grit from the road had all but obscured the car's license plate and left the paintwork a nondescript khaki gray. Even the bushes were a dull brackish brown.

I poured myself a cupful of sludge-colored coffee from a thermos. It had the sickly aroma that only flask coffee has, but I closed my eyes and savored the comforting warmth. It had been a long drive south toward Boston, and the break was very welcome. When I opened my eyes again, I stared wearily out the rain-speckled windshield, rolling my shoulders back to ease the tension several hours of driving had left in my arms and neck.

As I peered out at the leaden sky, I felt a pang of jittery nerves, and I was uncertain whether I had made the right decision. The bubbly excitement I'd felt when I'd set out had gradually evaporated with the passing of the miles, leaving me feeling like a condemned woman awaiting the executioner's block. I gave myself a mental shake, pushing aside the shivery premonition that I should simply turn the car around and head back the way I'd come. I swallowed the last of the coffee. A chill had begun to steal up from the foot well and whisper across my shoulders since I'd turned off the ignition, and it was probably this that was causing my bad mood, or maybe it was simply the bleakness of the weather.

I started the engine again and left it running so that the heat crept gradually back through my veins. A truck sped past, throwing up sheets of filthy spray. The car rocked with a whoomp that made me tighten my grip on the plastic cup as I fixed it back onto the thermos and glanced around to check that all was well. The car was loaded to the ceiling with everything I had ever owned. Boxes, suitcases, potted plants, bedding, bags. Twenty-five years of accumulation was piled behind me.

A plaintive mewing came from the seat beside me, where the pet carrier containing my traveling companion, Mitsy the tabby cat, was sitting. I poked my fingers through the wire mesh and stroked what I could reach of her face, and she rubbed her furry cheek against my fingers with a purr. The touch of her warm body brought new confidence flooding into me. I could hardly believe I'd ever considered leaving her behind. Mitsy watched with huge soulful eyes as I withdrew my fingers and fumbled the road atlas open on the dashboard with renewed resolve.

"Looks like we've got a ways to go yet." I surveyed the map, following the route with my finger, tutting with irritation when I realized the highway I wanted went off over the page. I searched for the continuation of the route. "I knew I should have gotten a GPS," I told Mitsy with a rueful grin.

When I looked up again, I realized that the rain had turned thin and sleety-looking, almost like snow, and was driving hard against the windshield at an angle. "Time to go." I slipped the atlas down beside my seat and turned the windshield wipers on.

Nosing my car back onto the main road, heater humming,

lights on, and wipers swishing back and forth, I found that the traffic had thinned out considerably. It was just as well, I thought, as the sleet was thickening into large flakes of snow and increasing in ferocity. Already the grubby grass in the median strip was becoming blanketed in ice crystals, and the fields and woods that flashed by were speckled with white.

Half an hour later, the world outside the car had become a white blur. Thinking I might find a bed-and-breakfast where I could take shelter, I left the highway and took a smaller road that wound between high hedges, which gave partial protection from the billowing snow. With headlights and wipers on high now, I inched forward, hoping nothing would come careering from the opposite direction, but it seemed that all other traffic had already found refuge; I had the road to myself.

Minutes stretched into what seemed like hours. My doubts returned with a vengeance, and I realized I was perspiring with anxiety, despite the cold outside. I came at last to a crossroads, but the open space exposed me completely to the elements, and my car shuddered beneath the onslaught of heavily falling snow. The tires slipped as they fought to gain traction on the snow-covered road. The flakes that fell against the windshield were huge, obscuring the signposts, disguising the countryside, and distorting my sense of direction.

Trying not to panic, I leaned forward, hands tightly gripping the steering wheel, and I looked at the street signs. Nothing seemed to make sense. Eventually I guided the protesting car left, down what looked like the wider of the turns. I hadn't gone very far before I began to doubt my choice. The drifting snow was collecting in ditches on either side of the road, making the road almost impassable—certainly too narrow to risk a three-point turn. For better or for worse, it seemed I was stuck with my decision.

I came eventually to a stone bridge that, if I hadn't been lost in a snowstorm, might have been quite pretty. Immediately after passing over the bridge, the road began to climb quite steeply, and the car's wheels spun and whirred as I inched forward.

"This isn't good," I told Mitsy through gritted teeth. "Not good at all."

Despite the muffled slowness of my progress up the hill, it seemed to me that everything inside the claustrophobic confines of my car was gradually gathering momentum, making everything feel suddenly intense and noisy. I had the headlights full on, windshield wipers battling away, and the heater blasting a clear patch on the inside of the windshield. The engine whined and protested as it labored up the steep incline.

I was getting desperate; if I could have thrust the car forward by sheer willpower alone, then we might have made it, but just below the summit the car faltered and began to slide backward down the hill. I floored the accelerator in a desperate attempt to regain control, but the wheels spun, the engine shrieked indignantly, the car lurched sideways as it continued its downhill slide, and after a few terrifying moments of gathering speed, we slewed to an abrupt halt with one back wheel jammed against a sapling at the opposite side of the snow-covered lane.

For a moment I was frozen with shock. The car was at such an angle that I felt I was hanging backwards and to one side in my seat. Reaching forward, I killed the ignition, and things were suddenly deathly silent. Giant snowflakes fell softly against the windshield, and then I heard a sharp crack followed by the tearing, grating sound of metal ripping wood.

Looking over my shoulder, I realized with horror that the spindly snow-covered tree that had stopped my car's descent was splintering under the weight of the loaded vehicle. At any second it could give way completely and the car would continue its slide toward the bridge I'd crossed at the bottom of the hill, or worse, plunge toward the swollen river itself.

Mitsy broke the silence by howling piteously beside me. The long heartfelt yowls jolted me back into action. I shifted carefully in the precariously wedged car, unclipped my seat belt, and reached for my coat, which was on top of the pile on the backseat, but the car groaned and trembled with the movement, and I turned quickly back and sat very still, my hands clasped in my lap. The car stopped moving.

After a moment I resolved to try again, and inched my fingers toward my cell phone, which was on the seat beside the cat box, but my shaking hands only succeeded in nudging it onto the floor, where it fell with a clunk and slid under the seat, out of reach. Holding my breath, and very carefully, so as not to upset the balance of the car, I reached sideways with my right hand and lifted the handle of the pet carrier, easing the box over onto my lap. The change in weight caused the car to tremble and creak, but it didn't move. With my other hand I tried slowly pushing open the driver's door. It seemed incredibly heavy, as the angle of the car meant I had to push upward and out at the same time.

With the carrier lodged between the steering wheel and my chest, I shoved harder at the door, using all the strength in my arm and shoulder. For a moment I thought I wasn't going to be able to move it, but then it swung back; the car bucked against the tree with the sudden movement, and immediately snow rushed in, stinging the left side of my face, arm, and leg. The tree creaked against the metal of the car, protesting and cracking under the weight, and suddenly it gave way altogether and the car broke free.

For a split second the car seemed to teeter in midair. With a mighty heave, I dragged Mitsy's carrier off my chest and made a desperate leap from the vehicle just as the door swung down again. The crushing weight smacked heavily against my temple as I dived for safety, knocking me half-senseless. I landed awkwardly in cold, deep snow. Somewhere in my befuddled brain, I was vaguely aware that the car was sliding backward. It rolled away from me down the hill, snapping small trees and twigs as it went. I watched, stunned, as it slewed sideways, missing the narrow bridge, and launched itself backward with a last suicidal plunge into the fast-flowing river below.

chapter two

Full consciousness returned with the realization that I was huddled in deep snow on the shoulder of an empty road with what sounded like a cat's mewing ringing in my ears. My head hurt and my jeans and sweater were soaked through. As I shivered uncontrollably, a mixture of bewilderment and fright flooded through me; I had absolutely no idea who I was or how I had come to be here.

My mind felt sluggish and my stomach tightened with fear as I sat up and stared around me, blinking through snowflakes that were landing thick and fast on my face and lashes. I reached up to brush the cold wetness from the long hair fringing my face, and my hands came away sticky with red clotting blood. So this body was injured, I thought numbly, but why, how? What was I doing way out here freezing slowly to death in the snow?

A cat meowed again somewhere nearby. Looking around, I saw a plastic pet carrier lying close by. So I hadn't imagined the sound; there really was a cat. But what had I been doing out in the middle of nowhere in such weather and with a cat in a box?

Blinking away the moisture that was collecting on my lashes, I peered through the billowing snow, looking for any possessions that might belong to me, but apart from the partially buried cat box, the freshly fallen snow was empty of clues.

Snow beat against me, freezing on my face as I struggled unsteadily to my feet. I knew I had to get moving. Straining my eyes through the blizzard, I felt a momentary rush of hope. Could that be a cluster of buildings? I wasn't sure, but ... yes, wasn't that smoke rising from a chimney in the distance? After drawing in a cold raggedy breath, I swallowed hard, trying not to cry. Maybe the cat and I—whoever I was—could make it there.

It was eerily silent in the snow. Taking a deep icy breath, I tried to pull myself together. I couldn't leave the cat to freeze, so I fumbled to pick up the carrier, and started gingerly up the hill, slipping and sliding in inadequate boots, until I reached a footpath, ankle-deep in snow.

Soon I could no longer feel my toes. My head was swimming, and my breath was coming in short gasps, clouding the air in front of me as the snow continued to batter me—little pinpricks of icy cold stinging my cheeks, eyes, and hands like tiny bullets. Every so often an overhanging twig would snatch at me, unloading a torrent of fresh snow down my neck. My nose was running, my eyes tearing, and I was shivering so violently that my teeth were no longer chattering but crunched together in a permanent grimace. Every step was a challenge now, every breath an agony, and the weight of the cat seemed to be wrenching my arms from their sockets, creating a dull ache across my back.

And then, as I tried to shift the weight of the carrier slightly, my frozen feet shot from under me, and I pitched sideways into the snow, landing with a crash on my right side. The cat box rolled away from me into a bank of deep snow on the edge of the field. It hadn't gone far, but I was too cold and too exhausted to do more than drag myself to where it lay on its side in the thick snow and hunch my body over it.

Snow hammered against my back. I ran an icy finger along the mesh of the cage and I felt a wet nose press against me. I wondered vaguely if I should try to undo the catch on the carrier to let the animal go free; maybe then it would have a better chance of survival than it had trapped here with me. But I didn't seem to have control of my hands anymore, and it was just too much trouble when all I wanted to do was rest my aching head on the pillow of cold white softness and sleep. . . .

As I closed my eyes, a feeling of peace washed over me. I knew I shouldn't sleep here in the snow, but it was so comfortable with my head resting on my arms across the box, like floating on cotton wool. I couldn't feel the cold anymore, just a gentle emptiness. I dreamed that there was a tunnel ahead of me, somewhere where I would be safe and warm . . . warm and safe.

$\mathcal{W}hen$ I $opened$ my eyes again, there was a hazy figure floating toward me. I tried to call out to him, but no sound escaped my frozen lips. The shape came closer, swirling and swaying with the mist, and I saw that he was holding out his hands toward me.

Willing my arms to move, I reached for him. I still wasn't sure if he was real, or some ethereal spirit come to lead me into the place beyond, but as my frozen fingers connected with his, I felt a surge of pure joy run through my body. The figure pulled me forward, lifting me, and I felt weightless in his embrace. Closing my eyes, I reveled in the closeness of him, the intoxicating feeling of belonging. I wondered if I was dying or even already dead, but I wasn't afraid. If this was death, then I was ready; it was as if all my life I had been traveling alone and now in the white mist I had found my soul mate, the other half—the better half—of me.

The figure cradled me in strong arms, and I turned my face into his shoulder, wanting nothing more than to float into him, to be one with him. The rough fabric of his coat grazed my frozen chin, but I stretched my arms up and wound them round his neck, burying my face deeper, inhaling the scent of his skin, feeling my very being melt against him, into him, through him.

I felt him moving forward, taking slow measured steps through the deep drifts, his breathing deep, and as I clung to him, his warmth gradually brought me back to life. Though half-conscious, I realized from the gentle rocking motion that he was wading through thick snow, his breathing becoming increasingly labored as he battled against the blizzard with the weight of me in his arms.

Pinned against him, I tried to match his rhythm, to make my body weightless. He was strong; I could feel the muscles in his arms supporting me, his chest rising and falling methodically. My own breath mingled with his as he carried me steadily onward.

I would have been happy to stay entwined like that forever. But somewhere in the murky depths of the tunnel, I heard loud voices, and then I was jostled and moved roughly about. Squeezing my eyes tightly shut, I tried to feel him against me again, to savor once more that amazing connection of energy, but then I was being lowered and I felt hands roughly dragging at my clothing, bundling me into something soft and heavy, and then the bright white light went out and I slipped into the lonely darkness of unconsciousness.

chapter three

"*Hello . . .*"

Searing pain ran through my hands and feet. Struggling not to cry out, I opened one eye, and there before me stood an angel. She was small and slight, with a halo of golden hair tumbling over her shoulders, and deep blue eyes.

My first thought was that I was truly dead and had gone to heaven, but my pain was too deep, and I wriggled my fingers and toes in an attempt to lessen the stinging discomfort. Seeing the movement, the angel leaned toward me, her hair cascading forward as she bent to whisper to me, her voice soft and slightly husky.

"Hello," she breathed again, her lips brushing close to my ear. "Amber said you'd come."

I opened both eyes and stared hazily at her. "Where am I?" My voice seemed thin and reedy. The effort of speaking made me cough harshly, causing fresh pain in my chest and head. This surely couldn't be heaven when I hurt so much; but if not heaven, then where?

The angel had stepped back when I'd coughed and was now surveying me anxiously.

"Are you going to die?" she asked.

I considered this question, stretching my aching fingers and wiggling my toes to assure myself that the pain was real enough.

"No." I was relieved to find that I believed it. "No, I don't think I am."

"Not ever?" she pressed, coming closer again and staring so intently into my face that I wondered again for a fleeting moment if I was hallucinating. Something about the solemnity of her expression, however, made me cautious with my answer. I needed some answers myself, but it seemed that my questions would have to wait.

"Well, I will die one day.... We all will one day. But I'm certainly not going to die today, not if I can help it."

Pushing myself up on one elbow, I looked at my surroundings. I was lying on a couch in a living room with low wooden ceiling beams and leaded-light windows just visible behind partially closed curtains. There was a Persian rug on the polished wooden floor and a fire roaring in an inglenook fireplace; it seemed warm and peaceful, a sanctuary from the blizzard raging outside in the darkness.

The angel was smiling at me with a wondrous expression that made me feel slightly nervous. It was the sort of look a child might have when seeing Santa Claus actually emerging from the fireplace on Christmas Eve. I wondered if that was how I had been staring at her.

"Where am I?" I asked again, struggling into a sitting position so that the blankets flopped down into my lap. I realized belatedly that I was wearing only underwear, and hastily pulled the blankets back up. "And who are you?"

"I'm Jadie." The angel was dressed in a little tartan skirt with a cream sweater and thick woolen tights. "I'm six and a half years old." She paused for a moment, then repeated softly, "Amber said you'd come."

"Who's Amber?"

"My sister." Jadie shrugged, as if I should have known such a thing already.

"Ah. And can you tell me where I am?"

"You're in our house. Daddy brought you in. You were all cold and covered in snow, so me and Tara, we pulled your wet things off and Tara sent me to get the blankets."

"Where is your daddy now?" I asked, remembering suddenly the glorious feeling of being carried by the man in my dream. I felt myself blushing. Jadie was looking at me carefully. I felt quite guilty under her scrutiny, as if she could read my thoughts, which weren't at all suitable for a child of six and a half years old.

"He's working." Jadie inclined her head to somewhere behind me. She swallowed and cleared her throat slightly. "He only went out to clear a path to the road, and he found you, and now he's working in his study again. Daddy's always working."

"What about your mommy?" I asked, looking round as I spoke. "Is she here too?"

Jadie looked down at her toes. "Mommy's gone away. She was very sad, and then she went on an airplane with Uncle Jack."

Deciding not to pursue that further, I tried to get back onto more neutral ground. "Oh. And what about . . . er, Tara, wasn't it?"

Jadie suddenly pressed her lips together as if afraid more words might tumble out. I looked at her quizzically, then realized from a movement of air in the room that a door had opened somewhere behind me.

"You're awake, then." The voice came from behind me, making

me jump. I turned to see a slim young woman with short dark glossy hair emerging from a doorway, drying her hands on a dish towel. "I'm Tara, the housekeeper here. How are you feeling?"

She came around the couch to look at me, and I couldn't help noticing that she seemed to be sizing me up. Although she was dark, she had luminous aquamarine eyes that were as startling in their way as Jadie's cornflower-blue ones.

"Have you thawed out a bit?" she asked.

I nodded, trying not to stare at her. I swung my feet out from under the blankets to try to get up.

She put out a hand and pushed me down against the cushions. She was surprisingly strong, and I fell back, looking up at her with some embarrassment.

"You shouldn't go getting up yet." It was an apology of sorts, as if realizing she had overstepped the boundaries of propriety. "You were pretty far gone when Vince ... Mr. James brought you in. Give yourself a minute or two. I expect your hands and feet hurt. And that cut on your head is quite deep. It probably could have used a stitch or two, but I put a butterfly Band-Aid on it, so hopefully it won't leave a scar."

My hand went to my temple, and I felt the bandage gingerly before I rubbed at my still-tingling fingers. I nodded, totally confused. My lack of any sort of memory was terrifying. "I'm sorry for any trouble I've caused. I'm very grateful for your help. For a while out there in the snow, I was afraid I'd had it."

"Another half hour out in that blizzard, and you might have," she agreed. I had the fleeting impression she wouldn't have minded too much if that had proven to be the case. "Still, nothing a nice warm fire and some blankets can't put right. I've been making soup. I'll bring you some, if you like."

"I don't want to put you to any trouble ..."

"You've done that already, haven't you? I'm stuck here for the night now. The road's completely blocked, and according to the news, there is more of this weather to come. It looks like we're both stranded here, so we'd better make the best of it, eh?"

Color flooded my face at her candor.

Then she smiled, and her face lit up. "I'll go and tell Mr. James you're awake. After carrying you over the threshold like some hero out of a Jane Austen novel, he vanished off to his study."

She was about to retreat to the kitchen again when a thought struck me and I sat bolt upright in alarm. "When he brought me in, did Mr. James say anything about finding a cat?"

Tara paused and looked back at me, shaking her head. "No, he didn't say anything about a cat. Did you have one with you?"

"I think so." I wondered how much of what I remembered was real and how much had been a dream. "It'll freeze to death out there in the snow."

"Cats can look after themselves." She shrugged. "I'm sure it'll be okay."

"It was locked in a carrier. It won't stand a chance."

"We can't do anything about it now." Tara turned to look out through a chink in the curtains at the cold, dark night outside. "Maybe Mr. James can go look in the morning."

She left, and I sat morosely, rubbing at my painfully thawing hands. Jadie came and stood next to me. She gave me a reassuring smile. "Amber says your little cat will be okay. And Amber is always right."

"Where *is* Amber?" I looked around the room again for this all-knowing sister of hers.

Jadie peered at her shoes in much the same way she had when I'd asked her about her mother. "She's not here."

"Where is she, then?" I was confused, wondering how Amber could have told her anything about the mystery cat. "Is she with your daddy?"

Jadie continued to study her feet, but she shook her head infinitesimally.

Tara came in carrying a tray with a steaming bowl of soup and what smelled like freshly baked bread wrapped in a cloth. "Here you are." She laid the tray across my lap. "I thought you'd better eat in here by the fire until you've thawed out completely." She held out a hand to the child. "Come on, Jadie. Let's go and have ours in the kitchen. I'll give your father a shout."

She paused and looked from Jadie to me with a puzzled half smile. "Am I missing something here?"

"I was just asking her where Amber was, that's all."

Tara's mouth dropped open, and her face paled. I thought for an awful moment she was going to faint, and then she squared her shoulders, grabbed Jadie, and marched her out of the room. A door slammed somewhere nearby, and a moment later Tara returned alone and deposited herself between me and the fire. She gave me a hostile glare. "What's your game?" She had planted her hands on her hips and was staring at me as if I had sprouted horns. "Who the hell are you, anyway?"

I wanted to say that I didn't know who the hell I was, but this didn't seem like the right time. "Jadie informed me her sister knew I was coming. That's all. Amber told her the cat was going to be all right."

Tara continued to stare at me viciously. An awkward silence yawned between us.

"Amber *was* Jadie's sister." She took her hands from her hips and crossed them tightly in front of her chest as if to protect herself from the pain of what she was going to say. "Amber passed away two years ago. Jadie's mother couldn't cope with the grief and walked out on them a few weeks later. Amber's name hasn't been mentioned since her mother left, and Jadie hasn't uttered a single word since then. She's what they call an elective mute; no one has been able to make her talk, not her teachers nor doctors nor several different psychologists." Tara narrowed her eyes suspiciously at me. "So like I said, who the hell are you and what the devil do you think you're playing at?"

chapter four

Tara's eyes bored into me. I felt as if I'd been invited to participate in some gruesome game where everyone knew the rules but me. I didn't even know my own name. In the last few hours I had woken on a snow-filled roadside without any idea how I'd gotten there, nearly died from exposure and hypothermia, been rescued by a man with whom I'd felt a weird affinity, abandoned someone's cat in a snow-covered field, and gate-crashed a household where a supposedly mute child had informed me that her long-dead sister had been expecting my arrival.

I fought a desire to throw back the blankets, struggle to my feet, and run crazily through the snow, back to my own life, whatever and wherever that was. I suddenly felt very lost and alone, as uncomfortable with throwing myself on the mercy of this stranger as she seemed discomfited by my presence. It was odd; I knew how to speak and how to act in a given circumstance. I felt sure I could still read and write and perform the normal functions of living. I just couldn't remember who I was or how I'd gotten here.

"I don't know why Jadie spoke to me." I summoned as much calm as I could muster. "I didn't know she couldn't."

Tara continued to regard me with suspicion. I returned her scrutiny with what I hoped was an apologetic gaze, and then, for want of a better idea, I picked up the soup spoon and scooped up some of the delicious-smelling soup.

"This looks lovely. I really am very grateful to you for bringing me into your home like this." It was true, I *was* grateful.

"It's not my home. I just work here." She stuck out her chin, but the familiarity of the action had broken the spell of hostility; I was a guest again. "We'll be in the kitchen; if you want anything just call."

She tossed her head and left the room.

When she had gone, I put the spoon into the bowl and lay back, exhausted, squeezing my eyes shut for a moment. Had I arrived in a madhouse? Or perhaps I'd died out there in the blizzard after all and been brought to some strange testing place where my suitability for the world beyond was being measured. Neither possibility brought much comfort.

The awkward weight of the tray on my lap and the tantalizing scent of the thick and hearty leek and potato soup suggested something much more down to earth. I spooned some of the soup and raised it to my lips, sniffing the warm aroma appreciatively. The soup tasted as good as it smelled, and I was soon wiping the bowl with the bread. I hadn't realized quite how hungry I was until I'd started eating. After popping the last hunk of bread into my mouth, I sensed someone standing behind me. I craned my head around, still chewing, and found myself staring into a pair of blue eyes that left me in no doubt that this was Jadie's father.

He was a handsome man in his early thirties. His features were nicely symmetrical; short blond hair framed a clean-shaven face with a smell cleft in the center of his chin. His stiff posture reminded me of a Roman centurion—I decided he'd look pretty good in a short-skirted leather uniform—but I wished I didn't have a mouth full of bread, because I was fairly sure it was about to choke me.

I chewed with a dry mouth and swallowed with difficulty as he walked around the couch and directly into my line of vision. He was wearing a pair of jeans and a blue checked shirt over a white T-shirt, which on anyone else might have looked casual, but there was nothing casual about his demeanor; he seemed almost more ill at ease in his own house than I felt as a visitor. He came over to perch on the arm of the nearest chair and offered an embarrassed half-smile. I watched as he knotted his hands in his lap and leaned forward, his expression neutral.

"How are you feeling?" he asked.

"I'm much better now, thank you." I ignored the dull throbbing in the tips of my fingers and toes, and the ache in my head. "I can't thank you enough for bringing me into your home like this. I hadn't realized the weather was going to get so bad."

He nodded, apparently reassured by my answer, but I noticed he avoided making direct eye contact with me. "I'm glad you don't need to go to the hospital, because I don't think we could have gotten you out. We're completely snowed in, and, according to the weather forecast, there's more to come."

"I'm sorry to be such a nuisance." Picking up the empty tray, I leaned forward to try to deposit it on a nearby coffee table. I succeeded in sliding the tray onto the polished surface of the low table, and sat back. Realizing the blankets weren't quite covering me, I gathered them quickly to me.

He seemed not to notice. "I'm Vincent James." He half rose out of the chair toward me, his hand outstretched to shake mine.

I kept my hand knotted tightly over the top of the blankets.

What was I going to say? Should I confess I hadn't the faintest idea who I was or what I'd been doing out there in the snow? Would he think I was a crazy woman and throw me back outside to take my chances in the blizzard?

He frowned at my hesitation, and I realized I had no choice but to tell the truth. Taking a deep breath, I took the plunge.

"I'm afraid I can't remember who I am. The bump on my head has obviously given me some sort of amnesia . . . but I'm sure everything will come back to me soon."

He let his hand drop onto his lap as he scrutinized me closely with a frown of surprise. "You can't remember *anything*?"

I shook my head.

"Um," he murmured, thinking things over. His eyes drifted over me, and I watched his face as he came to a decision. "Well, whoever you are, you're welcome to stay here until the weather clears and we can find some proper help for you."

Breathing a sigh of relief, I began to relax. But then he seemed to remember his manners and reached his hand rather abruptly toward me again in welcome. Keeping the blankets in place with one hand, I stretched the other hesitantly toward his. I was holding my breath as our hands met; this was my rescuer, the man who had carried me through the snow. I don't know quite what I expected, but his handshake was dry, firm, and unremarkable. Had I dreamed the whole thing? No flashing lights, ringing bells, or electrical currents passed between us—nothing to indicate we were soul mates greeting each other. I felt strongly disappointed. I relinquished his hand and inwardly berated myself for my foolishness. It was just that after he had rescued me in the blizzard I had thought . . . What *had* I thought?

"So you have no idea what you were doing out there in that snowstorm?" he asked, intrigued now. He sank back onto the chair and glanced past me toward the kitchen. Was he looking for a means of exiting without giving offense, or was he watching for his ever-vigilant housekeeper?

"I have no idea at all." I hauled my thoughts back. "I remember coming to at the side of a road and feeling the cold eating into me. I don't know how I got there, but I do remember having a cat with me." The memory brought a new flood of anxiety rushing through me. "You don't know what happened to it, do you? It was in a pet carrier. I was trying to carry it to safety, but it was so heavy and my hands were so cold, I think I dropped the poor thing into the snow."

"I don't know anything about a cat, but I'll call some of the locals, see if anyone has seen it."

"It was in a plastic carrier," I persisted. "It'll die out there in this weather."

"I'm sorry, but there's nothing we can do now. It's still snowing heavily and it's pitch-dark outside. You should try to get some rest and not worry about it. And when the snow clears, we should get you to a hospital." He rose to his feet.

Resting my head against the back of the couch, I felt suddenly overwhelmed by the events of the day. My head was throbbing, my hands and feet still ached, and I felt bone weary.

Vincent paused. "Look, you were huddled in the snow up on Adam Jenkins's top field, next to the footpath. It's possible the cat is still there, so I'll give the farmer a call and ask if he could look for it in the morning, okay?"

I nodded resignedly.

He hesitated just before he left the room. "You can use the room my mother normally has when she stays with us. Tara will show you where it is. Get a good night's sleep. Things never seem so bad in the morning."

"Thank you," I said quietly.

He left, and I closed my eyes and tried to force my mind back. Surely, I thought, I had to be able to remember something of my past, anything at all that could give me a hint as to who I was or what I was doing in this place. But my mind remained obstinately blank, as if there were a curtain drawn across it, sealing off my former life and keeping my memories elusively out of reach on the other side.

"You've finished your soup, then." I jumped as Tara appeared, her lips pursed in what I took to be disapproval. "Vincent said you could use the guest bedroom when you're ready to go up."

I noticed she was no longer referring to her employer by his surname and wondered if she'd been listening in on our conversation. Looking at my watch, I realized it was almost nine o'clock at night. It had felt like sometime in the early afternoon when I'd woken in the snow. Where had the rest of the day gone? I rubbed a hand over my eyes and thought, Where had the rest of my *life* gone?

My hands and feet felt defrosted now, and I was about to offer to help Tara with the tray when I remembered I was still wrapped in blankets.

"You stay right there while I take this to the kitchen," she instructed, some of the earlier hostility returning to her voice. "I can bring you some magazines, or you could watch TV, if you like, until you're ready to go upstairs."

I guessed she would have liked to add, "And think yourself lucky you've been allowed to stay here at all," but she contented herself with handing me the TV remote and opening a neat mahogany cupboard in the far recess beside the fireplace before hurrying off.

The TV showed pictures of raging blizzards, cars abandoned on highways, and overworked snowplows. My gaze drifted to the narrow shelf above the TV cabinet to a row of family photos. I made out Vincent with Jadie and Tara, all three of them smiling into the camera, and another of Tara, standing in what looked like a park, her hands resting on the handle of a stroller, out of which peeked a toddler wrapped up in blankets. Whether it was Jadie or her sister, I couldn't tell, but I did understand that Tara had been part of this family for a long time.

"Could you tell me where the bathroom is?" I called, hearing footsteps behind me.

"Down the hall there at the very end, next to the room that's full of boots and coats," Tara called back.

After getting awkwardly to my feet, I hugged one of the blankets around me and followed her directions. There was an ancient oak staircase behind the couch that opened directly into the living room. Beyond that, the rest of the house disappeared around a corner, the whole house appearing to be a huge reverse L shape. I padded through the wood-paneled sitting area, my bare feet slapping on the cold wooden flooring as I passed the bottom of the staircase. The rest of the rooms led off the long arm, with a boot room and downstairs bathroom at the farthest end, opposite a back door, presumably opening onto a garden.

In the bathroom, I turned to face the small mirror that hung over the sink and stared at my features for several long minutes. Running a hand over tawny shoulder-length hair, I peered into a stranger's hazel eyes, trying to find something familiar in my reflection. My fingers traced the outline of the Band-Aid Tara had used on my cut. It wasn't too awful, despite the blossoming blue bruise surrounding it. It was an odd feeling looking at that face: I realized I hadn't expected to look like this.... Who was I, and what *was* my name?

I crept back along the length of the L, where there were three doorways. The nearest door was open a crack, with light spilling out. I peeped in to see Vincent sitting at a wide desk, his features in profile, studying a computer screen with a telephone pressed to his ear. I tiptoed quickly past. The next room had a formal dining table surrounded by elegant chairs, and the last room, the one nearest the living room, was the kitchen. Pausing in the doorway, I took in the warm domesticated scene. This was obviously the hub of the household. A modern stove stood against the far wall with a huge pot resting on top, a soup ladle protruding. A cloth-covered table still showed signs of where the family had eaten their last meal and a doll with flaxen hair lay on a chair next to the table.

"Will you come up and kiss me good night?"

I turned to see Jadie standing behind me, clad in a pair of pink pajamas and fluffy animal slippers. She walked past me to collect her doll, then turned back into the hall and headed for the stairs. She paused at the foot of the staircase and put her head on one side, studying my features. "Say you will," she pleaded.

"Well, if Tara doesn't mind . . ." I was a bit dubious. It seemed an odd request of a virtual stranger. "I don't even know where your bedroom is."

"It's next to Amber's."

"Er, right." The child seemed to think I'd automatically know where her sister's room was. "Well, maybe I'll come up in a minute."

"I've got to have my physical therapy first," Jadie said quietly.

"Your physical therapy?" I repeated, mystified. "Did you hurt yourself?"

Jadie smiled as if I'd made a joke. "No, silly, my back patting."

Before I could question her further, Tara called from somewhere upstairs, and Jadie tucked her doll under her arm and climbed up toward her.

I returned to the comparative safety of the couch. Staring into the crackling fire, I wondered what twist of fate had brought me to this curious household.

chapter five

"*I think Jadie* wants you to go up to her." Tara's voice made me jump for the second time that evening. "She's hovering by her door with her favorite book, and she won't let me read it to her."

I turned and saw Tara staring at me. She looked as uncomfortable as I felt. "I can't imagine why, but she asked me to go up and kiss her good night," I explained apologetically.

"She told you that?"

I nodded.

"In actual words?" She sat down next to me.

"Yes. She asked me just now when she came down for her doll."

"I thought that might be what she wanted, because she wouldn't let me turn off the light. She kept getting out of bed and standing by the door. I wasn't sure I believed you before when you told me she'd spoken to you. I don't understand it."

"Nor do I," I admitted. "Have you told her father she's spoken to me?"

Tara shook her head. "I didn't want to get his hopes up; the thought crossed my mind that you might be some sort of con artist, a trickster . . . I don't know."

I couldn't say I blamed her. "Shall I go up to her?" I asked.

I watched Tara struggle with herself. I could see she didn't entirely trust me, but she obviously cared for Jadie and didn't want to let her down. "I don't see why not," she said at last. "But I'll come up with you and wait on the landing where she can't see me—if you don't mind?"

"Of course I don't mind." I found myself responding immediately to the woman's softer side. Jadie was in her care. She was right not to leave her alone with a stranger.

Tara inclined her head in a gesture of thanks. We tiptoed up the stairs, the blanket draped around my shoulders like a thick cloak. Tara pointed out Jadie's bedroom door. Jadie was sitting on the edge of her bed, apparently waiting for me.

"Hi." I was feeling horribly self-conscious with Tara listening outside the door. It occurred to me that maybe I had a child of my own somewhere, and I felt a further jolt of unease, though somehow I didn't think this was the case. I perched next to Jadie on the edge of the pink quilted bedspread and looked down at her, unsure what she expected of me.

She held out the book, then climbed under her quilt and waited for me to pick it up.

"You want me to read you a bedtime story?" I willed her to talk so that Tara could hear her, but she just nodded. I picked up the book of fairy tales and read out loud a story about a princess and a wicked witch, showing her the pictures as I went.

"And they all lived happily ever after," I finished, closing the book. "Now I'm going back downstairs and you must get to sleep. I'm staying in your grandma's room tonight, so I'll see you in the morning."

She held out her arms for a hug, and I hesitated only a moment before bending forward and sliding my arms around her slight form. As I held her, I became aware of an ache deep in my chest. I hugged her close for a second or two, feeling the warmth of her body through the blanket. To my surprise she reached up, brought her face close to mine, and planted a kiss on my cheek. "Night-night," she whispered.

"Night-night, Jadie. See you tomorrow."

Tara was waiting for me when I turned out the light, and we crept back along the landing to the top of the stairs. I realized I was shaking.

"Did you hear her?" I asked, trying to keep my tone light.

Tara shook her head. "No, I didn't hear her say anything. Did she speak to you again?"

"Only to whisper good night."

We returned to the living room, where Tara gave the fire a prod with the poker, sending red sparks flying up the chimney. I watched as she put a couple of small logs on the fire and hung the tongs back on a brass stand. The activity seemed somehow familiar to me, as if I'd seen her do it before, and I felt a shiver run down my spine in spite of the extra warmth.

Tara obviously felt something too. "Who are you?" She leaned back on her haunches, studying me much as Jadie had done earlier. "What are you really doing here?"

"I don't know." I made an awkward grimace. "Did Vincent tell you that I've lost my memory?"

"He did. I wasn't sure I believed it, though, any more than I believed Jadie had spoken to you." She pulled herself up off the floor, came over to the sofa, and sat beside me. Her voice was lower when she spoke again, and full of misgivings. "It's really odd. I mean, *you* don't know who you are, and Jadie's treating you as if she already knows you." She paused, frowning. "And why has she decided to talk to you? I do believe she spoke to you, because otherwise you couldn't have known about Amber. I just don't understand why, after all this time, she chose to break her silence with you."

"Maybe because I'm a stranger," I suggested. "I had no expectation that she couldn't talk, and therefore it was a natural thing to do." I yawned, belatedly covering my mouth with my hand. "I'm sorry; it's been a heck of a day."

"Wherever you come from, you should have listened to the forecast before setting out," Tara admonished, sounding confident again now that the conversation had returned to the mundane. "Vincent decided not to go in to work today after hearing the bad weather warnings this morning, and it was only the second time he hasn't made it to the office in all the time I've worked here. Usually he leaves as soon as I arrive at seven-thirty, but they were warning of blizzards even then. You must have been crazy; when he brought you in, you weren't even wearing a coat!"

She was right, of course, and the knowledge sent fresh spurts of panic through me, rekindling the sick feeling in my stomach. I didn't want to dwell on why I had found myself out in the snowstorm with no warm clothes and no belongings; it was just too much for my tired brain to cope with.

"What does Vincent do?"

"He works in Boston, in banking. I don't know the details exactly."

"Do he and Jadie live alone—apart from you, of course?"

"I suppose you could say that, though I'm here more than he is. Vincent works long hours, and he hands Jadie over to me, Monday to Friday. He's not usually back until after I've gotten Jadie into bed. I cook his dinner and then I go home."

"You don't work weekends, then?"

"Not usually. Jadie's grandmother comes every Friday evening or Saturday morning and stays until Monday when I arrive. She looks after Jadie when I'm not here."

I yawned again, and Tara stood up. "I'll show you to your room, if you like."

Her tone was friendlier now, and I responded in kind. "Thanks. I'm hoping that a good night's sleep will clear my head and that my memory will be back by the morning." I felt like a child, dependent on strangers for my most basic needs, hollow inside and horribly vulnerable.

Following Tara back up the staircase, the blankets still draped around me, I ran my hands up the polished wood banister and felt a reassuring warmth creep through me. Something about the house itself was comforting, when nothing else was.

We passed the closed door next to Jadie's room, which I assumed must have been Amber's, and Tara waved her hand at the next room along, telling me it was the bathroom. There was another short flight of steps at the end of the corridor, over the boot room, which Tara said led to an attic room where she slept occasionally if she stayed over. The last room on the right was to be mine.

Tara flicked on the light and stood back to let me pass. The room was old-fashioned, dominated by a queen-size bed.

"Is there anything you need?" she asked abruptly as she turned to leave.

I stood awkwardly, feeling even lonelier and more displaced than ever as I stared around the room. I found I didn't want Tara to leave. "What happened to my clothes?"

"I pulled your wet things off you when you were brought in," she replied. "Your boots are drying in the boot room, and I've washed your clothes and hung them in the kitchen to dry. Do you want them now?"

I nodded, and she went off to fetch them with a cluck of her tongue and an exasperated sigh. After a moment I ventured forward, halfheartedly pulling out drawers and glancing through the contents. The room looked comfortable enough. I sat on the bed and tried to think sensibly.

I must have had a handbag with me when I'd set out. What about all the things one would normally take when going out? Surely I owned a cell phone, wallet, credit cards, driver's license . . . everything that gives a person their identity. I didn't have so much as a hairbrush or lipstick to call my own right now.

Tara returned a few minutes later carrying a pair of denim jeans and a thin sage-green sweater with three-quarter-length sleeves.

"The jeans are still a bit damp at the waist." She handed them over to me. "You can hang them over the radiator in here and they'll be dry by the morning."

"Thank you." I took them despondently, and she left me alone again. Where had I bought this sweater? I wondered as I held the unfamiliar clothes. And who had I been with? Where had I been going when I'd put it on this morning? Tears threatened at the corners of my eyes.

A floorboard creaked in the open doorway, and I turned, expecting to see Tara, but to my surprise, I found Vincent leaning against the door frame, contemplating me thoughtfully.

"Tara's just reminded me that you have nothing with you in the way of luggage. My wife left most of her things when she did her disappearing act a while back, and I've never really gotten around to sorting through them." He paused awkwardly. "Would you like to come and see if there's anything you could use?"

"That's very kind of you." I gave him a wan smile. "I'm so sorry to be such a nuisance."

"Not at all," he replied politely.

Clutching the blanket to me, I followed Vincent back along

the landing to his own bedroom, old floorboards creaking under our feet. He turned on the lights and then stood back to let me pass in ahead of him. It was a beautiful room with a four-poster bed elaborately draped with embroidered cream and red silk. The curtains at the window were made from the same material, with crimson tassels and tiebacks that matched the bloodred carpet. It looked like the king's chamber in a medieval castle, or the interior of a sultan's palace.

"Here." He pulled open a cleverly concealed door fitted within a faded tapestry that ran the length of the room. "You're welcome to borrow anything you want."

I peered into a long walk-in closet containing a whole range of women's clothes on hangers and in drawers, rows of shoes nestling tidily underneath at one end, and a man's closet at the other. I glanced questioningly at Vincent, who was hanging back, watching me.

"These would be useful, if you're sure your wife wouldn't mind." I pulled a pair of silk pajamas and a dressing gown randomly from the first drawers. Picking through his absent wife's belongings while he watched made me feel distinctly uncomfortable.

"I'm quite sure she wouldn't mind," he said shortly. "If she'd been interested in anything here, she wouldn't have been so quick to abandon us. You can keep them, for all I care."

"Thank you." At the pain in his voice, I lowered my gaze, blushing with embarrassment.

"I'm sorry if I sound harsh." He ran a hand through his hair. "It's not your fault. . . . If you need anything else, please just take it." He turned away and walked toward the door. "I hope you find your room comfortable. Good night."

Walking slowly back along the landing with the borrowed night wear clutched in the folds of the blanket, I pondered this strange dysfunctional family and wondered if perhaps there was such a thing as fate. I paused outside Jadie's room and listened to her slightly ragged breathing. Whether it was by chance or design, I didn't know, but I felt deep in my bones that there was some sort of inevitability to my being here where I had no identity and yet felt so strangely at home.

If only I had known then how strange things were going to become.

chapter six

I slept badly, tossing and turning and having dreams where I found myself wandering through the house like a lost spirit, and every creak of a floorboard, every groan of an unknown pipe, disturbed me yet again.

When I eventually opened my eyes in the cold light of morning, I felt a moment of panic. Where was I? My eyes raked the ceiling, darting from side to side. Then the events of the previous evening came back to me and I groaned, realizing that I had no better idea who I was or how I had come to be here. A sick feeling rose in my stomach, and I snuggled farther under the bedclothes, unwilling to face the day.

After a while I relaxed enough to uncurl, and I lay for a few moments, gazing around the room. It was comfortably furnished in pale greens, with floral curtains and a matching armchair squeezed into one corner. The floor didn't seem to be quite flat, and the walls sloped more at one end of the room than the other, making me wonder how old the house was. There was a dressing table standing against one wall and a sink along another, which I'd used in preference to the family bathroom the previous night, afraid I'd run into Tara or Vincent. The closet was full of clothes, but these were more everyday and in larger sizes than those in Vincent's room, and I assumed they belonged to Jadie's grandmother. The only thing I'd found of real interest was a half-empty bottle of gin, neatly hidden in a drawer full of underwear.

Eventually, lured by the strange silvery blue light filtering between the cracks in the curtains, I slid out from beneath the covers, pulled on the borrowed dressing gown, and tiptoed across the cold carpet to the window. I peered out through the frosted glass to find a snowy fairyland of white mounds, white-tipped trees, and soft stillness stretching away into the distance.

I felt a childish thrill at seeing the beautiful landscape, and despite the cold creeping around my bare feet and ankles, a warmth rushed through me as I stood, silently entranced by the scene.

A timid knock on the door made me spin around. It was only Jadie, already dressed and grinning.

"Have you seen the snow?" she breathed, her eyes round with awe.

Her excitement matched my own and I nodded, my eyes shining. "It's like a fairy wonderland, isn't it?"

She nodded enthusiastically, her blond curls bobbing. "Can we go outside and make a snowman?"

"I don't see why not. Give me a minute to get dressed and I'll be right along."

Jadie left, and I threw on the clothes Tara had returned to me the night before, wiped some of the toothpaste I'd found onto my teeth with my finger, and followed her. The house seemed quiet as I walked along the landing and stuck my head into Jadie's room. She was waiting by the window, looking out onto the landscape where the sun was beginning to glisten on the snow.

Together we crept through the sleeping house like a couple of coconspirators, stopping in the boot room to slip on coats and boots. Jadie found me a quilted gardening jacket and an old woolen scarf, which I tied around my neck as she tugged a hat over her golden hair and rummaged in her coat pocket for a pair of mittens. Then she unlocked the heavy oak door and we stepped out into the glorious silence of her backyard.

Directly outside the back door was a courtyard area and an adjoining cottage next door that was the mirror image of Jadie's house. I assumed the two homes had originally been one big house. There was a low hedge dividing the two properties, topped with snow. I was about to scoop up a handful of the fluffy frosting, when Jadie put her finger to her lips and led me around the side of the stone house to where a smooth white lawn stretched away toward a snow-covered boundary hedge.

We stood side by side on the white path and gazed at the virgin snow, a temptingly blank canvas awaiting the first brush-strokes of our boots. It felt like a good metaphor for my life: every movement, every word, a first, untainted by a past. Just the clean slate of my existence stretching enticingly ahead of me.

"You first," I whispered, suddenly unnerved by the enormity of my thoughts. Jadie didn't need telling twice. She danced across the lawn, making tracks with her boots. She turned, giggling, and I followed her, planting my feet in the squeaky coldness, following her tiny prints with my size sevens.

"Do you know how to make a snow angel?" Jadie asked when we had circumnavigated the lawn twice over.

I shook my head, wondering if my eyes were as bright as hers, cheeks pink and glowing.

Throwing herself down onto her back in an area of untouched snow, Jadie stretched out her limbs and made a waving motion with her arms, opening and closing her pink leggings-clad legs so that when she got up, she left the outline of an angel.

"I saw it on TV," she said, and beamed. "But I've never made one before. You do it now!"

Jadie squealed with glee as I threw myself into the snow next to her, waving my arms and legs before jumping up to admire our handiwork.

"We made angels," she whispered, her face aglow. "That's what Amber looks like. . . . She's an angel too."

I hesitated only a moment. "Shall we build Amber that snowman?" I asked, unsure whether I should encourage her to talk about her dead sister as if she were still here. "A big snowman with a hat and scarf?"

"Ooh, yes!"

Jadie started rolling a snowball round the lawn, and as the fluffy snow stuck to it like a magnet, it grew bigger and bigger, leaving a trail of ice-speckled grass in its wake. When the ball grew even larger, I hurried over to help push it. We rolled it to a halt and scooped up more snow from around the base, patting it down with icy fingers to make a nice smooth coat of white. Jadie made a second, smaller ball for the snowman's head, and then I took off my scarf and wound it around his neck.

Laughing, Jadie took her own hat from her head and reached up to place it on the snowman's head. The sun bounced off her blond hair, burnishing it with a sheen of gold, giving the impression of a golden halo surrounding her head. As she laughed, I glanced up at the house to see a figure watching us from one of the upstairs windows. It was Vincent, and I could have sworn he was smiling wistfully down on his daughter. I smiled up at him, and then Jadie tilted her head to see where I was looking. Her face fell, and her eyes grew round and fearful. In the same instant I heard the sound of the back door opening with a crash, and Tara came hurrying around the corner of the house, clutching a flapping cardigan to her chest.

"What do you think you are doing?" she shouted at me, grabbing Jadie by her arm and dragging her toward the house. "Are you trying to kill her?"

"We were just . . . making a snowman," I called to her retreating back. "She's fine." I jogged after Tara, who was towing a silent Jadie in her wake. "She's well wrapped up. We were just having fun."

Tara almost threw the child in through the back door before pulling off Jadie's wet coat and gloves. Jadie began to cry, big silent tears coursing down her cheeks and dripping off the end of her chin.

Tara looked up at me, her face contorted with anger. "Jadie can't go in the snow. She's sick."

"Sick?" I echoed.

As if to prove a point, Jadie began to cough—deep bubbling coughs that escalated into heaving gasps. Tara whisked her into the living room and lay her facedown on the couch, handing her a pile of tissues. And then she began to beat the child firmly up and down her back, hammering and pounding until Jadie was spitting great gobs of mucus into the tissues.

I watched, horrified, wondering what terrible harm I had done to this innocent child. Vincent had come to stand at the bottom of the stairs. He was resting one hand on the banister, watching his young daughter with a resigned stare. Then, as if realizing someone was observing him, he tore his gaze away from Jadie, and our eyes met in a moment of shared helplessness.

"Is there anything I can do?" I asked him.

Before he could answer, Tara whipped her head around. "You've done quite enough," she snapped.

Vincent approached, and for a moment I thought he was coming to offer comfort to Jadie, but he gave Tara and his spluttering daughter a wide berth. He circumnavigated the couch and kneeled instead at the fireplace, where he piled kindling, lit it, and sat back on his heels to watch as the first small flames licked upward. I went and crouched down near Jadie's pale tear-streaked face with my back to the fire, and reached out to push a tendril of damp hair behind her ear. When I looked up, Vincent had slipped away.

I took several more tissues from the box and handed them to Jadie. "I'm so sorry," I whispered. "I wouldn't have hurt you for anything." I looked up at Tara, who was still slapping and kneading. "What is it?"

"Cystic fibrosis," Tara replied through gritted teeth. "It's what her sister had as well. Jadie could get pneumonia as easily as you or I could get a slight sniffle, just like Amber did, and then, well . . ."

Suddenly everything became clear. Everyone Jadie loved, including the child herself, was living in fear that she was going to die, just as her sister had before her. I remembered Jadie's anxious face when I'd coughed yesterday, and the earnest question that must already have been forming in her mind when she had broken her self-imposed silence: *Are you going to die?*

I thought perhaps my answer was the first time anyone had been honest with her about death. If Amber's name hadn't been mentioned since she'd died, then the natural grieving process must have been severely hampered. I was no psychiatrist, but it seemed to me that if the adults surrounding Jadie hadn't been willing to talk about their loss, she might not have felt able to talk about it herself, and had squirreled away all her questions, doubts, and fears into her secret silent world. It occurred to me that she was a child trapped not so much by the physical constraints of her body but by the anxieties and poor expectations of everyone around her. I wondered who was more broken, Vincent or his child.

As I stroked Jadie's face, I let my mind wander. Maybe the wormhole that had tossed me out into this small universe had not been quite so haphazard after all. I didn't know why, but still I couldn't shift the thought that I had arrived exactly where I was supposed to be.

After a while Jadie stopped coughing and spitting, and Tara paused in her back-slapping. She pulled Jadie upright and gave her a hug.

"All right now?" she asked gently.

Jadie nodded, wiping her mouth on a tissue, and Tara planted a kiss on the child's sweaty forehead.

"I'll go and get your thick pink cardigan and your slippers." Tara rose to her feet with a chilly look in my direction. "You stay right here in front of the fire and keep warm, Jadie."

As soon as Tara had gone upstairs, Jadie turned to me and offered a hesitant smile, but there was a reticence in her expression now that hadn't been there before. I wondered if it was because now that I knew the truth about her condition, she was adding me to her list of adults who lived in a state of fear.

"You should have told me you weren't allowed to go out in the snow," I chided gently, perching on the couch next to her.

"Then we wouldn't have made the snowman or the snow angels," she said. "I never get to do *anything* fun."

"It was fun, wasn't it?" I acknowledged with a smile. "Did you used to play a lot with Amber?"

Jadie's eyes became round at my easy mention of her sister's name. She studied my face for a while and then nodded. "We still talk a lot, but she can't play now."

"How did she know I was coming?" I asked softly.

"She knows everything. I used to cry every night because I wanted Mommy to come home, but Amber says she won't come back. She promised we'd have a new mommy soon, and then you came. Are you going to be my mommy?"

My mind lingered momentarily on the extraordinary feelings I'd experienced when her father had carried me back here. I shivered involuntarily with pleasure at the memory, but I knew I was being fanciful in entertaining the concept even for a millisecond.

I could hear a telephone ringing somewhere in the house, jolting me back to reality, such as it was. I ignored it and shook my head. "I don't think so, sweetie," I replied. "Would you settle for me just being your friend?"

"If you're going to be my friend, maybe we could play some more." She looked at me hopefully. "Can we make more angels?"

I thought about it for a few minutes, then asked her if she had some paper and scissors. I had the most curious feeling that someone—an old lady perhaps—had taught me how to make a string of angels from paper. Jadie nodded happily and scrambled off the couch, going into the kitchen and returning with some scissors. "Daddy's got paper in his office," she said after handing me the scissors. "I'll see if we can have some."

After she'd gone, I belatedly remembered Tara's instruction to Jadie to stay near the warmth of the fire. I was about to hurry after her when she returned with her father in tow. He was holding a pile of computer paper and seemed a lot more relaxed now.

"Jadie's been trying to steal my paper." He eyed me over the stack in his hands. "Is she bringing it for you?"

"Well, yes." I took a couple of sheets of the paper from him. "I'm trying to see if I can remember how to make paper angels."

To my surprise, Vincent perched on his armchair and studied me with a look of delighted anticipation. "Do you think you remember how to do it?"

"Let's see," I replied, determined to rise to the challenge.

I folded the paper over, back and forth as if I were making a fan, and then I began to snip little bits of it away. I noticed as I was cutting that Jadie had crept closer to her father and was resting a hand on one of his knees. They were both watching me expectantly.

After snipping the last tiny piece away, I opened out the folded paper and held up the row of little hand-holding angels with a flourish. "Ta-da!"

"Angels!" squealed Jadie, clapping her hands in glee.

"Good grief!" Vincent's mouth dropped open. He was looking not at my masterpiece but at his daughter, in total astonishment. I suddenly realized it must have been the first time he'd heard her speak in almost two years. He looked as if he were about to exclaim further, but I shook my head slightly, afraid that if he made too much fuss, Jadie would fall silent again. He gave me a questioning glance, then took a deep breath, taking the hint.

"We used to make snowflakes with paper and scissors at school when I was little." His voice cracked slightly, and I saw him swallow. "The teacher hung them on the classroom ceiling and stuck them on the windows at Christmas."

"Here." I handed him the scissors. "I'll bet you can remember how to do it."

He picked a piece of paper from the pile he'd brought and folded it carefully, then started cutting. I watched as he snipped away, his eyes moving every so often to his daughter, who was watching intently. She looked so much like him, with her golden hair and slightly pointed chin. I wondered if she was aware that she'd spoken in front of him. I also wondered when had been the last time he had played with her, given what Tara had said about his work habits.

"What's going on?"

We looked up to see Tara approaching with Jadie's cardigan and slippers in her hand.

"We're making angels and snowflakes," Vincent answered, more calmly now, as if he was trying to pretend this was an everyday occurrence. "Watch this."

He unfolded the paper to show a beautifully made snowflake with symmetrical points and delicate filigree arms.

"Ooh!" said Jadie. "Let me try."

"I'll show you how." Vincent's voice was heavy with emotion at hearing his daughter speak again. Tara clapped her hand to her mouth and watched as he showed Jadie how to fold the paper, then handed her the scissors.

Jadie snipped happily away, seemingly unaware of the consternation she had caused. Now the floodgates were open, and although her voice was still weak and whispery, Jadie was evidently finding it easier to speak with her father and Tara present.

She unfolded her snowflake, and Vincent reached out and clasped her to him. "It's beautiful, princess. Just like you."

Tara had fallen silent and was standing stock-still, looking from her employer to her charge and then to me. I was about to smile when I realized that behind Tara's aquamarine gaze was an emotion I couldn't quite discern. Was it anger? Confusion? Or jealousy?

I shivered and looked quickly away. I was at this family's mercy, and it didn't seem like a good time to start making enemies.

Tara drew in a deep breath and appeared to make an effort to pull herself together. She plastered a thin smile on her face. "Well, time for some breakfast, I think."

chapter seven

We *were sitting* at the kitchen table, finishing bowls of cereal washed down with strong sweet tea, when the front doorbell rang. Tara got to her feet, muttering about how it was a miracle that anyone could come calling in this much snow. As soon as she left the kitchen to answer it, Vincent turned to me. He seemed to be struggling for words, and I waited, wondering what he was going to say.

"This seems to be a day for miracles," he said quietly. I glanced at Jadie, who was sitting with her mug of milky tea, but she didn't seem bothered by her father's comment. "I don't know what you did to get Jadie to speak, but I want you to know . . . Well, if there's anything you want, anything I can do, just say the word. And you are welcome to stay here until you are completely recovered."

"Thank you." I managed a smile over the lump that had formed in my throat. "I don't want to impose on your hospitality, but until the roads are open or my memory returns, I think you might very well be stuck with me. Even though neither of us knows what you should call me. . . ."

"Ah, I've just remembered another miracle." He tentatively returned the smile. "I left a message on Adam Jenkins's answering machine last night—he's the local farmer who owns the field you collapsed in—and he called back this morning to say he's got the cat you were talking about. Apparently she's alive and well."

My heart leaped with the good news. With all my possessions and memories gone, it was good to think that just up the road was a creature that might actually belong to me. She was the only link to my past. "Thank you *so* much," I said. "It really means a lot to know she's safe."

"Sorry to break up your little celebration." Tara was watching us stonily from the doorway. "Maria from next door wants to know if you are still going over for dinner this evening."

She was directing the question at Vincent, but her eyes strayed to me as I quickly sank in my seat at the table.

"I don't think it's a good idea." He seemed hesitant. "I never really wanted to go in the first place. Can't you put her off?"

"Now, that is not a very neighborly thing to say," a heavily accented female voice admonished from behind Tara's shoulder.

Tara stood to one side, allowing a buxom dark-haired beauty into the kitchen. Maria pulled out a chair and sat down, crossing her suede-booted legs with a flourish. "You must come, Vincenzo. You promised!"

"I didn't promise anything of the sort." Vincent looked decidedly awkward. "I said I'd think about it."

Maria's face fell, and for a moment I thought she was actually going to burst into tears. "But I have already begun the preparations."

I noticed Tara rolling her eyes heavenward behind Maria, her lips pursed with obvious disapproval at Maria's attempt to persuade him.

Vincent looked down at the table, his pale skin coloring slightly. "I don't want to put you to any trouble."

"It is no trouble at all. And it would be good for both me and Michael to have some adult company for a change."

"Male company, you mean," Tara muttered under her breath.

"I beg your pardon?" Maria turned smoldering eyes on Tara.

Tara shrugged, and Vincent shifted uncomfortably in his chair as the two women glared at each other. He looked across at me, and his face brightened. My presence had given him the perfect excuse to refuse the invitation. "But I haven't introduced you to our guest," he said. "This is a miracle worker who is staying with us for a while. It would be very rude of me to go out while we have a visitor."

Maria hesitated, giving me a curious glance up and down. Apparently satisfied that I was no competition for her, she held out a beautifully manicured hand. "I am pleased to make your acquaintance." She grimaced slightly, and said, "Of course the invitation includes you also."

A look flickered across Vincent's features that I couldn't quite discern, but after a moment's hesitation he nodded, turning to Tara, who was sulkily inspecting her own rather short nails. "You won't mind babysitting for Jadie, will you, Tara? You're pretty much stuck here anyway until the roads are cleared."

"I could cook for us here," Tara offered. "Then you wouldn't need a babysitter."

"But then I would have to leave my own son all alone—and I have planned to make one of my specialty Sicilian dishes," Maria countered.

Vincent sighed, and I could see he was finding the interaction between the two women tiresome. I found myself thinking that perhaps there was more to the relationship between Vincent and Tara than just the normal employer-employee one.

"What do you think?" He looked directly at me. "Would you like a night out eating homemade Sicilian food?"

All eyes were upon me.

"Er...," I spluttered awkwardly.

"Say you'll come." His handsome features broke out into a hopeful smile. "Maria's cooking is not something to turn down lightly," he said.

I avoided Tara's gaze. I had to admit I didn't much want Vincent to go next door alone with the luscious and apparently single Maria any more than his housekeeper did, but I was even less enamored of the prospect of spending the evening in Tara's company. "I would be delighted," I said at last.

"Excellent!" Maria exclaimed, though she was looking at Vincent, not me. "I will expect you at eight-thirty." She threw Tara a triumphant glance, pushed back her chair, and rose to her feet.

Tara sprang up, obviously relieved that Maria was leaving. "I'll show you out," she said shortly.

When the kitchen door had closed behind them, Vincent glanced at me apologetically. "Thank you for coming to my rescue. I hope you don't mind me dragging you over to Maria's tonight. She waylaid me while I was out clearing snow yesterday and was most insistent that I join her." He gave me a rueful smile. "I know you're not well with that head injury of yours, but you still need to eat, and she really does cook very well."

My hand went to the Band-Aid on my head; the cut didn't hurt, and I'd forgotten all about it. "It'll be fun," I said graciously. I was still euphoric with the news that the cat I'd abandoned in the snow was alive and well. "It's the least I can do."

"I hope you won't think of the evening as a chore. You have already repaid any kindness by helping my daughter to find her voice."

I looked at Jadie, who seemed busy cutting enough small bits of white paper to make her own indoor snowstorm. She was engrossed in her task.

As if she realized our eyes were upon her, she glanced up. "Why is Tara mad?" she asked.

"It's nothing you need to worry your pretty head about," Vincent said, and hastily made for the door. His daughters ability to speak seemed to have quickly lost its appeal for him with her first awkward question, and I could see why she had retreated behind a wall of silence, if this was how he had reacted to any questions she'd had after the death of her sister. "I must get back to my work"—he glanced apologetically at me—"if you'll excuse me."

We listened to the sound of his feet disappearing down the passage.

Jadie looked more pointedly at me. "Why is Tara mad?" she asked again, and after a pause where she seemed to be trying out a newly discovered word, she added, "What's an 'adult company'?"

I sighed and wished Vincent would come back and rescue me. It wasn't my place to explain things the child's father would not, but I worried that if I didn't answer, she might disappear off into her silent world once more.

"I'm not entirely sure why Tara is mad," I replied carefully. "But I think Maria meant she wanted someone of her own age to talk to. It must be very lonely living way out here."

She contemplated my answer, then lowered her breathy little voice. "I'm not lonely," she said. "I talk to Amber."

I saw that she was watching me closely. "Is it all right for me to talk to Amber?" she asked, her eyes fixed anxiously on mine. "I don't think Daddy or Tara would like it."

She was probably right. She had realized that the subject of Amber was out of bounds, and, perhaps not wanting to upset her father or Tara, she had withdrawn from them and lived with her sister's memory alive and well in some secret place inside herself.

I rested my elbows on the table and leaned toward her. "It's perfectly all right and normal for you to miss your sister. Thinking about Amber and talking to her inside your head just means that you loved her very much. A part of her will always be with you."

Jadie smiled. I pushed back my chair so she wouldn't see the tears glistening in my eyes, and went to the kitchen window to stare out at the white lawn sparkling under an ice-blue sky at the side of the house. The snowman was still there, wearing the colorful scarf and Jadie's woollen hat. Without turning, I felt Jadie come to stand beside me. She slipped her small hand inside mine, and I gave it a quick squeeze.

"Amber says she loves you," she said quietly.

"Look at all the mess you're making," Tara chided Jadie irritably. "Why don't you get out your coloring pencils instead and I'll throw all this rubbish away?"

"No!" wailed Jadie. "Those are my snowflakes. Daddy showed me how to do them."

Tara stared at her. "I can't believe you've decided to talk to us after all this time. If there's nothing wrong with you, why didn't you talk for the doctors?"

Jadie hung her head, and I glared at Tara, annoyed by her insensitivity.

"And don't you go looking at me like I'm some sort of heartless monster," she flung at me. "You haven't been trying to decipher her sign language for the last two years. You have no notion what it's been like, playing charades all day every day, sometimes not having a clue what it is she wants. On top of everything else we've had to cope with, it's not been a picnic, I can tell you."

I lowered my voice so that Jadie couldn't hear me: "I'm sure it must have been hard—"

"You have no idea!" Tara snatched cups and bowls off the table and turned to the dishwasher so I couldn't see her face. She loaded the machine noisily, then turned back to me suddenly. "The doctors told us Jadie's refusal to speak was an anxiety thing. Apparently it affects about one in a thousand children, and it's not because she couldn't speak. She just refused to, and the longer she went on doing it, the harder it was for her to start again. We tried everything to help her, but she's a stubborn little thing—gets it from her father no doubt." She sniffed loudly, rubbing her nose with the back of her hand. "Do you have children?"

I fell silent, considering the possibility for the second time since I had been in this house, groping inside a head that seemed devoid of memories. It was like looking at a blank wall, and I found myself quelling a sudden upsurge of panic. "I don't think so," I said at last.

A pang of sympathy crossed Tara's face. "Then you have no idea what heartache they can bring. I worked here when Amber was still with us, and Jadie was just a baby and I loved both those little girls like they were my own. We lost Amber, and then their mother left, and we've been waiting . . ."

I glanced toward Jadie, horrified at what Tara might be going to say, but she shook her head, sniffed loudly, and finished, "Waiting for Jadie to speak. And it's been hard on me and harder on her father. And then you blow in with the snowstorm, and suddenly Vincent is playing with his little girl for the first time in two years and Jadie decides to talk . . ."

She bit her lip fiercely, fighting back tears, and I stood still, unsure how to react. After a moment I unrooted my feet, walked over, and put a tentative arm around her shoulders.

"I can see how much you care for them both," I said, wishing I wasn't partly the cause of her distress, "and I can also see that you are important to both of them. They probably couldn't have coped without you all this time. I'm just here by chance, and maybe Jadie chose to speak simply because she was ready to. I'm sure it had nothing to do with me."

"Yes, well, whatever," Tara said in a strangled voice. She shrugged me off.

"Jadie, come and give Tara a hug," I said, and awkwardly turned to the child, who released the pile of snowflakes she'd been clutching protectively, slid off her chair, and came to put her arms around Tara's middle.

Tara smiled down at her through the glint of tears. I left them to it and turned to finish clearing the table, but Tara was having none of it.

"You're a guest," she insisted, breaking free from Jadie's embrace and hurrying to take the dishes from me. "This is my job."

I stood back and watched as Tara finished loading the dishwasher. Jadie, taking no chances, picked up her scattered snowflakes and took them over to the windowsill, where she held them up to the light one at a time.

"They're lovely," I told her.

She turned to me, beaming. "What are we going to do next?" she asked.

I realized that I had made myself the playmate of a six-year-old. But I had some grown-up things to attend to first.

"I'm going to see if your daddy minds if I use the telephone," I told her. "I need to call the police to see if anyone's reported me missing."

Jadie giggled. "It's funny you think you're missing, when you're right here."

"I won't be long." I shot a sideways glance at Tara, slipped out of the kitchen, and walked along the passage toward Vincent's office. The door was ajar, so I peered in. Vincent was sitting in profile, staring at his computer screen in consternation, and swearing like a sailor.

I gave a discreet little cough, and he spun around, half rose from his chair, and slammed his laptop closed with a snap of annoyance.

"The damn thing says there's no signal." He glanced across at me with a belated attempt at nonchalance. "It was working perfectly earlier this morning. I don't know how I'm supposed to keep in touch with the outside world when I can't even use the Internet." He sank back down in his leather swivel chair and tapped his fingers impatiently on the closed lid as if willing it to come to life.

"Used up all your miracles today?" I suggested glibly.

"What?" Vincent scowled at me, and then his expression cleared. "I'm sorry. I'm working on something rather important, and a lot can happen in the financial world in a few hours. It's got me rattled, but you're right, in comparison with Jadie suddenly finding her voice after all this time, it's nothing." He leaned back and swiveled the chair gently to and fro as he surveyed me curiously. "How did you do it?"

Taking his question as an invitation to come into the room, I crept closer to him and stood near his desk. "I didn't do anything," I told him truthfully. "I didn't know she couldn't talk, so when she spoke to me, I just answered her, that's all."

"You must have sparked something in her," he persisted. "Tara has spent the last two years taking Jadie to all sorts of therapists, and none of them could get her to talk. Her teachers have given up trying and just let her sit in silence. Fortunately, it doesn't seem to have affected her ability to learn, but it can't be doing much for her social skills."

He rose from his chair, which was the only seat in the room, and waved for me to sit down, but I shook my head. "I'm fine. I only came to ask if I could use the telephone. I need to contact the police and find out if anyone's reported me missing. Someone must be looking for me."

"Yes, of course." He waved a hand toward the phone. "Go right ahead."

I picked up the phone and held it to my ear. "There's no dial tone."

"What? Give it here." He leaned over and took the phone from me, putting it to his own ear. "Oh, great; the line's dead. That's probably why I can't get a signal."

"I thought you said your farmer friend had called you back this morning," I said, puzzled.

"Yes, Adam called about an hour ago, and it was working fine then. Damn! Maybe there's snow on the wires or something."

I watched as he banged the phone down onto its stand. "So now we're completely cut off." He looked around the silent room as if the concept was totally new to him. "It's an odd feeling, having no contact with the outside world."

My insides churned with renewed panic. If we were completely cut off, there was no way I could find out who I was or where I had come from. I thought he should try being in my shoes, not only severed from the outside world but stranded in a stranger's house with nothing to call my own but the clothes I was standing up in. "What about your cell?" I asked, trying to keep the desperation out of my voice.

"Cell phones don't work here. We're in a dip between two small hills and you can't get a signal until you reach the top road," he explained. "It's never really bothered me because we've got the house phone and the computer. As soon as I'm at the station or on the train to Boston, the cell service comes back. And you can get a signal up on the hill at the Jenkinses' farm."

I stared at him, feeling more trapped than ever. "I haven't even got a toothbrush." I tried to keep my voice from trembling.

"I'm not sure that counts as a life-or-death emergency," he said with the beginnings of a smile. "I'm sure Tara will be able to find you one from her store of 'just in case' items. Tara seems to live in fear of the world ending at any time and society being plunged into chaos."

"Tara seems very much part of the family," I put in tentatively. "She tells me she's been here since Jadie was a baby."

"Yes, she was doing her nursing training back then, and came to work for us a few hours every week to help fund her course. Cheryl needed someone to help when we realized both children were ill, and we gradually relied on Tara more and more. She eventually gave up her training and her job at the hospital to work here full-time. Tara might not be a fully qualified nurse, but we couldn't do without her, despite her little quirks." Vincent gave me a brief smile. "I'll ask her about a toothbrush."

I returned the smile, feeling a connection with him. He immediately broke eye contact and turned to rummage through some papers on his desk.

"Thank you." I wondered vaguely why Tara hadn't volunteered a toothbrush last night if she had a stock of things like that. But on second thought I couldn't see her putting herself out on my behalf; I remembered the feeling I'd had that there was more to her devotion to this family than just her job. Tara had already admitted to loving Jadie as if she were her own child, and she certainly hadn't liked either Maria or me getting anywhere near her employer. I wondered about the sacrifice she'd made in giving up her future as a registered nurse to stay here. The sooner I was gone the better Tara would like it, of that I was in no doubt at all.

chapter eight

$\mathscr{I}$ *excused myself* from Vincent's study and was making my way back down the hallway when a knock sounded at the front door. I expected Tara to come grumbling, or even Jadie to wander in to answer it, but there was no one. The knocking sounded again. I looked back toward Vincent's study, but he had closed his door and was obviously expecting Tara to see to it. At the third knock, I pulled back the draft-excluding velvet curtain and opened the door.

A man stood there holding a pet carrier, the cat peering out at me from behind the wire mesh. The caller was tall, maybe just over six feet, in his early thirties, bundled in a dark padded jacket, wool cap, scarf, and heavy-duty gloves. He moved from one green-booted foot to the other, trying to keep his feet from freezing. The neighboring farmer, I assumed. Behind him, a black and white collie was panting, despite the cold.

The man gave me a hesitant smile. He had a pleasant face—what I could see of it from under the cap. His cheeks and nose were reddened from the cold, and his rugged jawline was covered with what could be described as designer stubble.

"Hi." His breath made clouds of vapor in the ice-cold air. "I've brought your cat."

"You must be, um . . . ," I said, and then paused, trying to remember the farmer's name while feet pounded down the stairs behind me.

"Sorry. I was making the beds. I only just realized . . . Adam!" shrieked Tara, hurrying across the room to push me out of the way. She took one look at the pet carrier and gasped, "You can't bring that thing in here! What were you thinking? I've told you Jadie can't go anywhere near animals; it'll bring on her asthma."

There was a sudden embarrassed silence. Tara had planted herself defiantly to guard the doorway, her lips pressed tightly together. Adam hovered, undecided, still shifting his feet on the partially snow-cleared path, and I just stood, grounded to the spot as tightly as if I'd been fixed there with superglue.

Jadie appeared and pushed her way past Tara and me to look into the carrier. She reached out a finger and poked it through the mesh front of the box. The cat sniffed at her finger and then rubbed her pink-tipped nose against it.

The spell was broken as Tara yanked Jadie backward. "Don't touch it!" she yelled. "Go and wash your hands and fetch your inhaler from the kitchen. Quickly now."

Adam had begun to back away from the door, still clutching the carrier. "I'm sorry, Tara. I forgot. I was just bringing the cat back to your guest; Vincent called last night, and it sounded pretty urgent."

But Tara had followed Jadie to the kitchen and wasn't listening. I watched the man take another backward step. "Please . . . don't go." I found myself at a bit of a loss as to how to treat this stranger who had obviously walked a good distance in terrible conditions to bring the cat to me. As a guest in Vincent's house, I didn't feel that I was in a position to invite him in, but I wanted to see the cat and knew I shouldn't let him just turn right around and trudge all the way home again.

Fortunately, Vincent came up behind me and rested a hand on one of my shoulders. It was a possessive gesture, which rather disconcerted me. I knew he considered himself in debt for my getting Jadie to speak, but I was still a virtual stranger to him. I turned to look questioningly up at him. Was it possible that he too had felt something when he'd carried me here?

"Hello, Adam," Vincent said. "I don't know what pandemonium's going on in the kitchen, but do come in and warm up by the fire. Come on." He reached out to take the offending cat box. "Don't mind Tara; you know how protective she is of Jadie." He leaned right across me to take the box from his neighbor, and I felt the warmth of his body pressing against my back. He seemed to hover there for a little longer than was necessary.

"Should you bring the cat indoors?" I asked, anxious not to risk making Jadie ill after my earlier mistake of taking her out in the snow.

"I'll take it to the boot room," Vincent said. "Jadie will just have to stay away from that end of the house for now."

He peeled himself from me and turned away. Adam followed him into the house, pulling off his boots and removing his hat and gloves while Vincent carried the box off down the passage.

I watched as Adam walked over to the fire and held out his work-roughened hands to the heat. He looked different without the hat, his cheeks glowing from the cold. He smelled of hay and fresh air. His hair was a deep glossy brown curling onto the collar of his work shirt. He rubbed his hands together for a second or two, then turned slowly, straightened up, and regarded me with interest.

"Vincent tells me you can't remember who you are." It was said matter-of-factly. "I read about a man who was found wandering on a beach once and no one knew who he was or where he'd come from. He couldn't speak, though, rather like young Jadie."

"This little miracle worker has got our Jadie talking, would you believe?" Vincent cut in, coming back into the room, minus the cat carrier, and smiling at me.

"Really?" Adam looked at me with undisguised curiosity. "How did you manage that?"

I shrugged, feeling like a fraud. "I didn't do anything; she just talked to me."

"Maybe she felt there was something special about you."

Adam said it quietly, but there was a catch in his voice that made me look more closely at him.

Vincent sprang into action, becoming the solicitous host. "Let me get you a beer, or a cup of tea, perhaps?"

Adam looked at his watch. "I won't stop, thanks. Lad and I still have to go and check for missing sheep and lambs. They're struggling a bit in this snow even though I've brought most of the flock down to the near field now."

"It's a bit cold for them to be outside, isn't it?" I asked.

"They're surprisingly hardy," he said easily. "As long as they don't get buried in the snowdrifts and I can get to the ewes with some extra feed, they're fine. What I have to look out for are any newborns the mothers might have rejected or that have strayed. It wouldn't take them long to die out there in the cold, so I've brought the ewes that haven't lambed yet into the barn to be sure."

"It was really kind of you to bring the cat over for me when you're obviously so busy."

He shrugged as if struggling miles through deep snow meant nothing to him. "It sounded as if you were pretty worried about her. I thought you'd like her with you, especially when Vincent told me you'd lost your memory. I thought seeing the cat might help you to...remember." He took a deep breath, then added, "It was no problem at all. I was out this way, anyway."

"Well, it is a problem now." Tara had returned from the kitchen with a towel in her hands. "We can't keep the cat here, not with Jadie's asthma."

"I'll take her back, then," Adam offered simply. "The cat's no trouble. She slept in the kitchen last night. I've got one of the old stable cats living indoors at the moment, so there's a litter box and everything. She won't have to go outside with the rest of the farm cats."

Tara picked up Adam's coat and held it at arm's length, eyeing it distastefully. "This is probably covered with animal hair; I'll put it in the boot room out of Jadie's way."

"Don't worry, Tara," Adam said. "I'm not staying."

Vincent turned steely eyes on his housekeeper. "I know you're only thinking of Jadie, Tara, but the cat's safely at the other end of the house."

"If she gets a bad asthma attack while the roads are closed—"

"I'll get the cat," I put in hastily. I turned to the farmer. "If you're really sure you don't mind keeping her for a bit longer?"

"I told you, it's not a problem." Adam was still looking at me speculatively.

I supposed the presence of a young woman found wandering in the snow with amnesia wasn't an everyday occurrence. Leaving Tara and the two men staring at one another in a kind of standoff, I walked along the corridor to the boot room. I expected to see the cat peering at me from the carrier, but as I approached, my heart skipped and I sucked in an anxious breath. There, sitting on a rag rug on the quarry-tiled floor with the tabby in her arms, was Jadie. She had her back to me and was whispering to the cat. I heard the name Amber, but I couldn't tell what else she was saying. My first instinct was to pry the cat from her arms, but then I watched her cuddling the cat, and my heart softened. The cat was purring so loudly I could hear it from where I was standing, and Jadie was stroking its back and chatting away as if she'd been talking all her life.

A movement behind me made me jump, and I looked over my shoulder, wondering if Vincent or Adam had followed me, but unfortunately it was Tara, still holding Adam's coat. She let out a screech, dropped the coat, and lunged toward Jadie and the cat.

"Put that thing down!" she yelled. Jadie started guiltily, and the cat shot from her arms, bolting past me and Tara down the hallway in fright. Tara hustled Jadie into the nearby bathroom, and I could hear gushing water and Tara telling a protesting Jadie to hold her hands out for the soap. I turned on my heel to chase after the cat. By the time I reached the living room, Adam had already scooped the cat into his arms and was looking questioningly toward me.

"Jadie had her out of the carrier," I explained breathlessly. "She was cuddling her, and now Tara is scrubbing Jadie down." I looked apologetically at Vincent, who had visibly paled, but he seemed in no hurry to rush to check on his daughter. "I'm sorry the cat has caused all this commotion, but Jadie seems all right, honestly."

Vincent leaned a hand on the back of the sofa, then ran his other hand over his face. "It's like living on a knife edge," he confided. "We never know when she's suddenly going to become ill. It's either the risk of coughs and colds or some outside influence that could affect her breathing."

I glanced toward Adam, who was still holding the cat. I wondered what he was making of all this drama.

"Can you get the carrier?" His voice was firm, with a no-

nonsense edge to it, yet something about it made me pause. Then he said, "I'll take her back to the farm before she does any more harm."

I reached out and stroked the cat gently, my fingers brushing close to his hand. "I don't think the cat's to blame; it was Jadie who got her out of the carrier. There's no harm done."

"No harm?" echoed Tara, coming around the corner into the living room, dragging a tearful Jadie in her wake. "Do you realize what could happen if she has a really bad attack while the roads are closed like this? We wouldn't be able to get her to a hospital, and no ambulance could get through the snowdrifts—"

"Tara, she didn't have an attack," Vincent interrupted wearily. "Maybe she isn't even allergic to cats. Just because Amber . . ." He trailed off.

"Amber said the cat wouldn't hurt me." Jadie was standing defiantly with her arms crossed. "Can we keep her?"

"Don't be ridiculous!" Tara snapped. She rounded on Adam. "For goodness's sake, take that thing away!"

"I'll go get the carrier, I said, and retreated toward the boot room, glad to leave the tension behind me. We soon had the cat stowed safely away, and Adam pulled his boots back on before turning to leave. I was strangely reluctant to part with the cat, but I handed the carrier over to Adam, who promised to take care of her until I was ready to collect her. Jadie had given up demanding and was trying tears instead.

"Maybe you could come and visit her," Adam offered to Jadie kindly as he headed for the door.

"Over my dead body," murmured Tara. "Even if she appears not to be allergic to cats, think of all the other animals at your place that could bring on an asthma attack."

Adam ignored her and turned to me. "You are welcome to visit your cat whenever you like. The phone lines are down over

Becket's Wood, but I'm sure the phone company will fix it as soon as the snow clears a bit. Then you can give me a call—or just come over."

"Th-thank you." What was it about him that made me feel so tongue-tied?

Vincent got up, suddenly remembering his manners, and saw his neighbor to the door. "I'm sorry you had a wasted journey over here." He watched as Adam set off into the snow, his dog leading the way. "We'll be in touch when things get back to normal."

Rubbing my hands together as the door closed on the cold and snow, I wondered how long it would be before anything got back to normal for me. I wasn't even sure what normal was.

I found myself wondering suddenly what would happen when the snow cleared. Would I have to go to a hospital once the roads were clear, and suffer lots of probing and questioning? Would I end up on a psychiatric ward enduring endless tests? The idea didn't appeal to me, but I knew from the look on Tara's face that my welcome in this house was wearing decidedly thin.

chapter nine

After Adam left, I spent the rest of the morning playing Monopoly with Jadie while Tara cooked and cleaned and fussed over Jadie's medication. The child appeared to need endless feeding, and Tara brought her fudge brownies and a milk shake midmorning, then produced a huge meal at lunchtime with which Jadie had to take extra vitamins. I tried to offer my help, but Tara was adamant that this was her job and that I was a guest.

Vincent had returned to his study to catch up on his paperwork. It seemed that being cut off from the rest of the world didn't stop him from working.

After lunch, which Vincent took in his study, Jadie lounged on the sofa watching children's TV, and I insisted on helping Tara clear the kitchen. "Please," I entreated, "I won't get in your way. Just tell me where things go."

Tara was standing at the sink with her back to me, and I thought she was going to refuse again, but to my relief, she told me to get a dish towel and dry the things that wouldn't fit in the dishwasher. Standing next to her, I was able to gaze out the window at the yard with the snowman still standing where Jadie and I had left him. Despite the sunshine, it was still cold enough to prevent him from melting.

"Tell me about Jadie's illness," I said as I dried a large stainless steel pan. "How come she eats so much? She looks as if a gust of wind would blow her away."

"That's the nature of CF." Tara bent to scrub an ovenproof dish, her elbow darting back and forth with the effort. "Her body has trouble digesting food. She has a poor appetite and would hardly eat at all if I didn't keep offering her snacks like the chocolate brownies. It's a constant battle to keep her weight up because her pancreas has impaired function. Most of what she does eat doesn't get absorbed."

"What causes cystic fibrosis?" I asked, pausing in my drying to watch a squirrel run across the snow-covered lawn.

"It's hereditary." Tara blew soapsuds from her wrists as she scrubbed. "But both parents have to be carriers for a child to be born with it. Even then, there's only a twenty-five percent chance of a child actually having the disease."

"Surely if Amber was diagnosed with it, there must have been some sort of test during pregnancy to check whether Jadie had it too?"

Tara fell silent, and I glanced sideways at her. "Amber was late being diagnosed with it," she said at last. "Apparently she seemed fine as a baby, a bit wheezy now and then and prone to getting colds, but her digestion wasn't such a problem as it is with Jadie. She was more than a year old when Vincent and Cheryl took her to the doctors and CF was diagnosed. Cheryl was already pregnant with Jadie by then and she wouldn't have the baby tested in case she miscarried. Once Jadie was born and tested positive for CF, they asked me to come and work for them so that Cheryl could concentrate on the baby and get plenty of rest." Tara paused, holding the sponge in midair. "I don't think either of them realized how bad CF could be and how ill Amber was going to get. If they had, well..."

"If it's hereditary," I puzzled, "why didn't Vincent or his wife know they had the gene? Surely someone else in the family must have had it?"

"One in twenty-five people are symptomless carriers," Tara explained. "They live their whole lives without knowing they're carrying it, and it's only when two carriers produce a child with CF that they find out it exists in their families."

We continued in silence, both lost in our own thoughts.

"You're very protective of her," I ventured. "It's almost as if she's your own child."

"I'm all she's got." Tara wiped her forehead with the sleeve of her sweatshirt. "And I've grown very fond of her."

"But she's got her father, and there's a grandmother too, isn't there?"

"One's a workaholic and the other is... Well, you don't want to know."

I remembered the gin bottle I'd found in my room. I took the last dish from the draining board and dried it to a shine. "Where does this go?"

Once the kitchen was spotlessly tidy, she turned to put the kettle on. When she'd made the tea, she took a cup down the hall to Vincent and then returned to sit at the kitchen table with me.

"It's not that Vincent doesn't love Jadie," she said, taking a sip of the hot tea and staring at me as if willing me to understand. "I think he loves her too much and can't bear the thought of losing her. After Amber... and then Cheryl going, he became more distant. He's a good employer, don't get me wrong, but he leaves everything to me, and sometimes the responsibility is enormous."

She gave me a rare half smile. "That's why I overreact a bit some-times, I suppose. I'm sorry for getting so angry at you over the cat."

I smiled back. "Don't worry about it. If I were in charge of Jadie's health, I'd be wary of anything that could hurt her too."

We spent the afternoon making tissue paper flowers with Jadie. Jadie was an old pro at folding the tissues and tying thin green garden wire around the middle, then peeling the layers apart to make very realistic-looking carnations.

"We learned how to do this at school," she told us as we struggled with bits of tissue and Tara found vases for our cre-ations. "I like school, but it's fun being off today. Usually if I'm at home, it's because I'm not well, and then I don't feel like doing anything."

It should have been idyllic, sitting at the kitchen table with the sun streaming in and the garden stretching away, white and bright outside the window, except for the nagging fact that there was another life waiting for me somewhere else. Maybe there was another family somewhere sitting in this same wintery sunshine, grieving because they didn't know where I was or what had be-come of me. I was in limbo, waiting for something to happen, for my memory to return, for the snow to melt, or for someone to come and claim me.

I glanced up to find Vincent leaning against the kitchen door frame watching us, a smile playing upon his lips. I was about to return it when I realized that Jadie and Tara had seen him too and were smiling up at him, on both their faces an expression of love. My heart sank. I was an interloper, an outsider who had no place here. Wrenching my gaze away, I concentrated on the half-made flowers on the table in front of me and vowed not to get involved. These weren't my family, my problems, or my home; I had no right to yearn for things that weren't mine to hope for.

* * *

Soon it was time for Jadie to go to bed and for me to start getting ready to accompany Vincent to dinner next door. After managing to extract a new toothbrush from Tara's store in the small room she used when she stayed over, I went to the bathroom to take a shower.

For a while I stared at my reflection in the mirror, trying to find something familiar in the face that looked back at me, but in the end, depressed, I gave up and stepped into the shower cubicle. It was a good feeling, letting the hot water cascade down over me. I found it was impossible to protect the bandage on my temple from getting wet, but the cut didn't hurt much and I soon gave up trying to tilt my head to avoid wetting it. All my negative emotions washed away with the running water, leaving me relaxed and tingling under the hot jets. I closed my eyes, daring myself to conjure up the feelings I'd felt with Vincent when he'd rescued me, but all I felt was a light-headedness, a strange sensation of disembodiment.

It was all too easy to pretend I didn't exist, standing under the warm water as it trickled over my eyelids, ran down my nose and over my mouth, and dripped off the end of my chin. I had just tipped my head back, luxuriating in the feel of it, when the water began to cool. In a few short seconds the water turned downright cold, and I reached for the tap to turn the heat up, wondering if the hot tank was empty. The tap seemed stiff, and I began to gasp as the jets of water falling over me became breathtakingly icy.

Squinting from under the deluge, I groped again for the tap, trying to turn it off, but the water stung my eyes, so I closed them again quickly, wrenching at the tap with both hands. But the water kept pouring. Freezing cold water invaded my mouth and nostrils, filling my airways, and suddenly I could barely breathe.

Gasping and choking, I held my head away from the cascading water, my fingers fumbling frantically for the tap again. It wouldn't budge. I tried to push open the shower door to escape the icy torrent, but that too appeared jammed. With horror I found the shower cubicle was filling with dark water that was rising rapidly up around my ankles and legs, climbing swiftly up over my hips, and then under my raised and frantically flailing arms.

Pounding on the shower door with fists that were turning white with cold, I tried to call for help, but within seconds the water had risen up around my shoulders and was trying to force its way from the back of my neck over my upturned chin and into my mouth. I clamped my lips tightly together as the water lapped over my head and I took one last great gasping breath before I sank beneath the murky blackness.

For a few more agonized moments I kicked impotently at the glass door with frozen feet and hands. I could feel my hair floating up around my head as my lungs burned with the desperate urge to breathe. Everything started to go black.

"No!" I screamed, the words erupting in a cascade of bubbles, which broke the surface over my head. *"No!"*

The last of my breath had been expelled with the scream, and now I hung limply in the water. Any second my tortured lungs would take a last desperate, gasping breath and the water would flood me, claiming me for its own. As I prepared myself for the inevitable, the shower door was yanked open. Water poured out in a great torrent, and someone hauled me out of the shower onto the bathroom floor, where I lay fighting for breath.

I felt a warm towel being draped over my violently shaking body, dry hands tucking it securely around me. A second towel was placed under my head, and I lay there for a moment, too weak to move.

"You're okay now." Tara's voice was anxious. "Looks like you had the water turned up much too hot and you fainted. I'll fetch another Band-Aid for that cut of yours. Just lie still. You'll be all right in a minute."

I lay for some time staring at the black-and-white-tiled bathroom floor, trying to make sense of what had happened, while waiting for some strength to return to my limbs. Eventually I managed to sit up and pull the towel tightly around me.

Tara bustled in holding a first aid kit and kneeled next to me while she patted dry the cut on my temple and applied a fresh bandage. "You want to be careful of that for a few days," she advised. "That wound is quite deep. You shouldn't have gotten it wet."

I stared around the steamy bathroom. "Where did all the water go?"

She looked at me blankly. "I assume it went down the drain."

"There was so much of it," I mumbled. "The shower was full to the top."

I could see her eyeing me dubiously. "The tap was already off when I heard you call out and came in to find you huddled on the floor of the shower. It's lucky I know how to unlock the knob from outside the bathroom door—I've always worried that Jadie might lock herself in."

"You didn't see all the water, then?" I asked hesitantly.

She shook her head. "I saw you hunched over in the shower, and I pulled you out. I thought you'd slipped or fainted. Lucky you cried out when you went down, or you could have been in there for ages."

"I'm sor—"

"Don't apologize," she interrupted, cutting me off. "It could have happened to anyone. Just take it easy, okay?"

I nodded and let her help me to my feet, supporting myself against the sink with my free hand.

"I'm fine now. Honestly."

"You shouldn't go out tonight, you know. You look really washed out."

I would have laughed at her unintentional joke if I'd had the strength. Instead I allowed her to help me to my room, where I sank gratefully down onto the bed.

"Is there anything else you need?" She hesitated before turning to leave the room.

I shook my head. "I'll be fine in a few minutes. Thank you."

As soon as she'd gone, I pulled the quilt over me, trying to instill some warmth back into my damp, shivering body. What had happened in there? Had it all been a hallucination brought on by the heat of the shower, or was my head injury worse than I had feared? Closing my eyes, I realized that this was not the first time my imagination had run away with me; first there had been the feeling of euphoria I'd experienced when Vincent had carried me here, then the bad dreams, and now this. . . .

I sat bolt upright on the bed as another thought occurred to me. Hadn't I been trying to recapture that very feeling—the peaceful out-of-body sensation of floating in another place with Vincent—when the water had suddenly turned so cold? Little daggers of fear shot through me. Could my memory loss be part of something else, something sinister that I didn't understand?

I slid off the bed and dried myself vigorously, taking comfort from the roughness of the towel as I rubbed it hard over my skin. Soon my whole body was pink and glowing, and I put my doubts firmly to the back of my mind as I turned to the immediate matter of readying myself for an evening out with Vincent.

chapter ten

For all her possessiveness over Jadie and Vincent, Tara was providing me with everything I needed to survive. She had laid out some clothes for me over the back of the chair, presumably selected from Vincent's wife's wardrobe. I slipped into what appeared to be some brand-new silk underwear, pulled on a pair of tailored gray trousers, and buttoned the blouse and thick cardigan. Tara had brought me mascara and lipstick, and I applied both to my pale face, determined not to give in to the lingering feeling of despair the ordeal in the shower had left me with.

Downstairs Vincent was waiting for me, looking sharp in a striped shirt, a suede jacket thrown over his shoulder.

He looked at what appeared to be a pretty expensive gold watch and smiled at me. "Right on time. I like a lady who can be punctual."

I ventured a glance at Tara, who avoided my gaze as Vincent took my arm and guided me toward the front door.

"I couldn't have been ready without Tara's help." I turned to look her in the eye. "You've been very kind."

Tara held my gaze for several seconds. I could see her fighting an inner struggle between what I assumed was jealousy and good manners, before saying a rather begrudging "You're welcome."

I flashed her a quick smile while Vincent looked warily from her to me. He had probably been able to sense the undercurrent of hostility in the air between us earlier and was wondering what it was all about. I sighed at the ineptitude of this man to see what was plainly before his eyes—that his housekeeper was in love with him.

"You're sure you're up to this?" he asked as we stood in the doorway. "You still look a bit peaky."

"I'll be fine," I assured him as he turned to where Tara was hovering behind us.

"We shouldn't be too late," he said.

"I'll be waiting," Tara replied drily as we stepped out into the freezing night.

I clung tightly to Vincent's arm as we negotiated a partially cleared path through the gardens between Maria's front door and his. It wasn't far to go, which was just as well because I had on the boots I'd been found in, which weren't much better here than they had been the previous day. Once or twice I nearly fell, and Vincent had to grab me to stop me from pitching headlong into the snow-covered bushes. Each time he touched me, I half expected the pressure of his hands on my arms to send shivers down my spine, but the only shivering I was doing was from the biting cold.

As we stood on the covered porch, Vincent asked, "Do you want to make up a name for yourself before we go in? We're going to have to call you something."

Resting my hand against the wall, I chewed my lip. "I don't

know." We heard footsteps coming to the door. "I can't think of anything."

Maria opened the door, dressed in a gypsy-style skirt with a flowing long-sleeved top in a deep burgundy red. Her black hair hung loose, and she had a sparkle to her eyes and flush to her cheeks that made me wonder if she'd been drinking. With her long black hair and slightly haughty demeanor, she reminded me of Kate from Shakespeare's *The Taming of the Shrew.*

"Vincenzo!" she exclaimed as though she had been caught totally off guard by our arrival. She looked me up and down much as she had done earlier, and pasted a thin smile on her sensuous lips. "And, er...?"

"Kate," I said hurriedly, still thinking of Shakespeare. "It's Kate."

"Come on inside. Dinner is almost ready." She took Vincent's coat and my cardigan. "Please come through to the dining room."

We followed her through a mirror image of the house next door, past an imitation of the open staircase, toward the dining room, which was decked out with candles and glittering silverware. There was a large wooden salad bowl on the table and a basket full of bread. The table was set for four.

"What would you like to drink?" she asked, indicating several bottles of wine standing on the sideboard next to a cheese board groaning with assorted cheeses and decorated with small bunches of grapes. "The white is good, but I think the red is better; perhaps both, eh?"

She disappeared off to the kitchen, and Vincent poured three glasses of the red while we stood awkwardly. I wandered to the window, pulled back a corner of the curtain, and looked out through the leaded-light windows into the darkness beyond. When Maria came back, she was bearing a large ovenproof dish, which she placed in the center of the table. It smelled delicious.

"Michael! Our guests are here and we are ready to eat!" Maria called as she discarded the oven mitts and slid into the seat at the head of the table.

The door opened and a dark-haired boy of about Maria's height walked in. He was pleasant-looking, with big almond-shaped eyes set in a still-smooth oval face. I guessed he was around thirteen, and I had no doubt that he was going to be handsome one day.

"Good evening," Vincent said magnanimously.

"Hello," Michael managed, though the flush that suffused his cheeks told me that he would rather not have been helping to entertain his mother's guests.

"Michael, hand me the plates," Maria said. "I hope you are all hungry! Here, Vincenzo." She handed him a plate piled with food. "We must feed you while that skinny housekeeper of yours is not looking." She passed me a plate of pasta with meatballs. "How do you come to know Vincenzo, Kate?"

"I got lost in the snowstorm," I told her. "Vincent very kindly gave me shelter in his home."

"Ah, but your family must be so worried about you! And the phone lines are down. Have you managed to let anyone know where you are?"

I picked up my fork and toyed with the food, my appetite suddenly gone. "I'm not sure that I even have a family," I admitted.

"I know exactly what you mean." Maria threw up her hands and nodded, her eyes dark. "My own family in Sicily were once lost to me. I married an American, and my father disowned me. And then almost two years ago my mother begged my father to allow me to return for a brief visit. Until then, my parents had never even met their grandson! Now I am on my own with Michael and they want me to return permanently, but I am not so sure it would be a good thing for Michael. His life is here, and he goes to visit with his father one weekend a month, which would not be possible if we moved back to my home country."

Maria pushed a bowl of salad toward me. "And family is so important," she sighed. "At home in Sicily, the firstborn son of each generation of our family is always called Michael." She reached out and patted her son's hand proudly. "I have kept the tradition, although my husband wanted to name him after himself. More wine, Vincenzo?" Maria paused to replenish our glasses before we could refuse. "Please, help yourselves to the salad. In Sicily we always have the salad first, but it is so cold outside I thought you would like to start with the hot dish." She turned to her son. "Michael, stop playing with your food and put some of it in your belly." She turned to me. "The youngsters today don't eat enough, do they? I blame the film stars; they are all like stick insects."

I glanced at Vincent, but he was keeping his head down, piling salad onto his plate next to the pasta and meatballs and digging in. Michael seemed content to let his mother do all the talking, and we ate while Maria prattled on about one thing and another, all the time plying us with wine. After the main course and salad, she placed the cheese platter in front of us. I nibbled at a slice of Roquefort on a cream cracker—and almost gagged. The cheeses had looked so enticing, but now that I had a piece in my mouth, I realized I didn't like the taste of it at all.

As I swallowed with difficulty, the significance of what had just happened suddenly hit me. A tiny bit of the person I really was had revealed itself to me. I wanted to shout for joy.

"I don't like cheese," I whispered triumphantly to Vincent as Maria went off to get coffee. "I don't like cheese!"

He raised an eyebrow.

"It's the first thing I've found out about the real me," I explained. "Whoever I am and wherever I came from—I don't like cheese."

Vincent smiled as the significance of my discovery dawned on him. "Thank goodness you liked the meatballs, then, and didn't turn out to be a vegetarian! I told you Maria was an excellent cook."

"You were right," I groaned. "And I've overindulged big-time. I don't think I'll ever need to eat again."

"Unless the roads clear soon, none of us will eat again," Maria proclaimed as she set the coffee tray on the table. "The only shop within a reasonable walking distance is the gas station, and I don't think we can survive the winter on snack food."

I blanched, horrified that we had cleared Maria's stock of food just when she should have been rationing it.

"Don't look so guilty!" She laughed, patting my hand. "The snow will be gone before we starve. I was only joking."

She poured the thick black coffee into tiny cups and placed them on coasters in front of us. Michael, who had hardly said a word throughout the meal, got up and began clearing the rest of the table. Although I offered to help, Maria would have none of it. Soon the table was empty of everything, including the table-cloth, leaving a polished walnut surface on which Michael placed a couple of coasters for our wineglasses, coffee cups, and a large white candle in a silver holder.

Maria leaned forward, her eyes shining. "Have you ever felt the presence of a ghost in this great shared house of ours, Vincenzo?"

Vincent gripped his glass of wine tightly as he stared at the candle, and I regarded our hostess suspiciously as she gave a tinkly laugh.

"What makes you ask such a thing?" Vincent's voice held a tremor of alarm, though his eyes never left the candle.

"I thought that while we were cut off from the outside world and feeling mellow after the wine, we could tell ghost stories and frighten one another," she said easily. She turned back to the sideboard and brought out an incense stick, which she lit with a theatrical flourish before sitting back, smiling round at us.

Determined not to be dragged into it all, I drained my cup quickly and gave Vincent a pointed stare, expecting him to take the hint. "We shouldn't keep Tara waiting too much longer, I suppose?"

Vincent took another mouthful of his wine, his eyes now fixed on Maria's. "Tara's probably turned in by now. I'd like to hear what Maria has to say."

He rested his wineglass on the table. I could feel the anxiety emanating from him as he sat back in his chair. I watched as Maria smiled knowingly, refilled his wineglass, and poured more coffee into my cup.

"I've got homework, Mom." Michael got up from the table. I had the impression he'd heard his mother's stories many times before. He left the room, turning off the main light as he went, which left only two wall lights glowing dimly. Maria didn't even seem to register his absence but sat staring at Vincent in a room that looked suddenly eerie and menacing in the flickering candlelight.

"Cheryl and I often used to share a bottle of wine together in the evenings when you were late home from work or away on business," Maria said into the silence. "She was a good friend to me. I still miss her, you know."

"What has this to do with your ghost story?"

"Oh, we used to tell each other stories, Cheryl and I. I think she was glad to leave the little girls with the housekeeper once in a while and remind herself she was something other than the mother of two sick children." She narrowed her eyes at Vincent, and I wondered if I detected a hint of accusation behind the easy chatter. "Cheryl was good company. Sometimes we speculated about the house being haunted, the way the floorboards creak and the pipes groan when they settle. We fancied we could imagine a lonely spirit walking from one house to the other, passing through the dividing walls as if they were nothing more than thin air. And recently," Maria continued, "it seems that things have begun to vanish when I put them down, and later they turn up somewhere else. But Cheryl is no longer here to speculate on these things."

"I didn't know Cheryl believed in ghosts." Vincent's voice sounded hollow and nervous.

"Perhaps there were things you did not know about her." Maria's dark eyes glittered in the candlelight. "In my experience men never listen to what their wives are truly saying."

I felt Vincent stiffen beside me, but he remained silent. I could hear the accusation plainly in her voice now and wondered why Vincent was still sitting here listening to this woman implying that he had not been a good husband. I nudged Vincent's arm, wishing we could go back to his own half of the old house. I was tired, my head had begun to throb, and I didn't want to be drawn into some strange quarrel between people I hardly knew. This was not my world, and these people were virtual strangers to me. I wished I could simply get up and leave.

Vincent at last seemed to sense my unease and started to push back his chair. "I don't want to talk about my wife and daughter. It was all a long time ago. I don't see any point in dragging up the past."

Maria seemed unperturbed by Vincent's reproof. "Sometimes the past has to be properly addressed before you can make a future." She reached out and laid her darkly tanned fingers on his arm. As she peered into his eyes, I felt as though I was witnessing something private and meaningful pass between them, something in which I was not included.

The candle sputtered suddenly as if a gust of air had entered the room, and at that same moment the wall lights seemed magically to switch themselves off, breaking the spell between Maria and Vincent. The room was plunged into momentary blackness, and I gave a small yelp of fright. But the candle recovered, the flame burned brightly once more, and I watched as Maria removed her hand from Vincent's arm in a room that was now dark save for the flickering candle.

"I think the power went out." Vincent seemed to come to his senses as he pushed his chair all the way back. He motioned to the pitch-black hall beyond the dining room. "The lights are off out there too."

Maria flicked the wall switches up and down to no avail, then moved to the sideboard and returned with another candle, which she lit from the one in the center of the table. "I will take this up to Michael," she said as his voice called and footsteps sounded on the stairs in the hallway.

Vincent and I followed Maria out into the hallway, waited while she reassured her son and handed him the candle to take back upstairs. Shivering, I pulled on my cardigan. As I buttoned it, I wondered again what trick of fate had brought me to this place where so many unseen currents ran just below the surface.

"The strange thing is," Maria announced, her sultry voice echoing in the darkness as she walked us to the door and fumbled for the latch as if nothing had happened, "that Cheryl used to confide in me all the time, but she didn't even tell *me* she was thinking of leaving you."

chapter eleven

$\mathcal{V}$*incent and I* walked back across the snowy front lawn, our arms linked together as we staggered unsteadily through the slippery snow toward his front door. As my boots sought a sound foothold, I wondered how much wine I'd actually drunk and how much bearing it had had on what I had just experienced.

"The lights are out here too." Vincent frowned as we approached the shadowy darkness of his door, our breath clouding the air. "We left the porch light on, didn't we?"

I nodded, waiting while he groped for the door handle. I wasn't sure how much of his fumbling was due to the lack of light and the cold, and how much to the quantity of good Italian wine he'd consumed, but he soon had the door open, and I entered the dark house behind him with trepidation.

"Tara?" he called softly. "Tara, we're back."

There was a red flickering light coming from the dying embers of the fire, and a shadowy shape rose from the sofa, making me step closer to Vincent in fright as I remembered Maria's talk of ghosts.

"You're back?" Tara's voice cut through the gloom.

"I wish we'd never gone," Vincent mumbled as he made his way unsteadily to the sofa.

"Don't say I didn't warn you." Tara picked up a small candle and a box of matches from the coffee table, lit the candle, and handed both to me. "You know what Maria's like. She's been trying to get you over there since her husband left. Now you've fallen straight into her clutches." She smirked, obviously pleased she'd been right about the evening.

"Maria is a good cook, but she did seem to have some sort of agenda," I admitted.

"I don't doubt it for a moment. That woman's agenda has been obvious for some time." Tara shot a glance toward Vincent. "I'd suggest a nightcap, but I expect you've had enough for one evening."

"I wouldn't mind a stiff brandy, actually," Vincent said, peeling off his coat and throwing it over the back of the sofa.

I looked at him as he flopped down wearily onto the couch, looking suddenly tired and drawn. Tara obviously thought so too, because she quickly poured and handed him a glass of brandy without further comment.

"Well, I'm off to bed." Her teasing tone had been swiftly replaced by quiet concern. "I'll see you in the morning; hopefully the electricity will be on again by then."

"I'll come up too," I said hastily. "It'll be easier to see the way with both of our candles." I didn't want to admit that it was because my nerves were still jangling and I didn't want to go upstairs alone in the still-unfamiliar house in the dark.

Vincent continued to stare moodily into the fire's embers as

Tara and I mounted the stairs side by side. I was worried about leaving him down there to brood, and obviously so was Tara, because when we reached the dark landing, she turned to face me.

"He misses his wife and daughter terribly," she confided. "He never says anything, but I'm sure that's why he makes himself scarce whenever he can. Work is just an excuse to run away without actually leaving us."

I noticed her use of the word "us" with a sinking heart. It reminded me that I had no business feeling anything other than gratitude toward Vincent. "Do you think he'll ever be able to move on?"

"I don't know." Tara wiped a hand over her tired eyes. "I wouldn't have said he was the sort of man to brood, but grief does funny things to people."

We walked down the hallway together, paused outside Jadie's room to check that she was sleeping soundly, and said good night outside my room. Holding the candle in front of me, I pushed open the door and slipped inside.

It didn't take me long to jump between the icy sheets. Once in bed, I blew out the flame and stared into the darkness, going over the evening in my mind. First there had been the episode in the shower. Had I really just fainted and dreamed the near drowning? And what had happened between Vincent and Maria next door? Had Maria really been suggesting that Vincent had somehow been to blame for his wife's sudden departure? Or had I merely been responding to the unsettling timing of the power cut, the effects of quite a large quantity of good wine and the heady incense-filled atmosphere?

As I closed my eyes and drifted into sleep I really wasn't quite sure.

*   *   *

It was still dark when I awoke, and try as I might, I couldn't get back to sleep. My mind was filled with images of people and places I didn't recognize, and I had no idea whether the hazy figures that came and went were characters from my real life or if I was conjuring imaginary pictures of Cheryl and Amber. After twenty minutes of tossing and turning, I decided to go downstairs for a glass of milk. I pulled on the borrowed dressing gown, groped for the matches, and lit the candle again. Then I made my way out onto the landing, checking first that the light switch on the wall still wasn't responding, and went down the dark stairs.

The squat candle provided only a small circle of light in my immediate vicinity, and as I rested it on the kitchen table to free up my hands for the fridge door, I had the eerie feeling that someone was in the room with me. I peered into the darkness without moving a muscle. I began to wonder if I had imagined it, but then I heard the unmistakable sound of someone breathing. I squealed, and suddenly Vincent and I were staring at each other in the candlelight.

"Christ, you nearly gave me a heart attack . . . I thought you were a ghost!"

"Vincent?"

"Kate? What are you doing down here?" He turned to the table and switched on a flashlight, shining it into my face. Blinking, I pushed the light away from me so that the beam swung out across the table and struck the opposite wall. All I could make out was his dark form standing before me, but where the flashlight illuminated the table, I could see a photo album lying open.

"I couldn't sleep," I murmured

"What time is it? I must have nodded off."

"I'm not sure, but it must be two or three."

I glanced across at the album again and shivered. "It's freezing in here."

"I know; the boiler is out. I just hope Tara put enough covers on Jadie's bed."

"I'm sure she did." I pulled the dressing gown more tightly around me. "She seems very protective of her."

"Tara's a saint," Vincent agreed. "We couldn't have managed without her."

He fell silent, and I yawned, rubbing my eyes. "I came down to get a glass of milk. I hope you don't mind."

"Of course not." He opened the fridge door and took out a milk carton, handing the flashlight to me so he could use both hands to get a couple of glasses from the cupboard. I sat down at the table, holding the light over the album so I could see the pictures of a pretty dark-headed woman holding a toddler. I recognized Vincent in one or two of the photos—a younger, more carefree Vincent with his arm around the woman's shoulders, his eyes beaming down at the child with pride.

He reached across and snapped the album shut.

"I did love my wife, you know," he said softly as he cupped his hands around his glass. "Maria made it sound as if I'd been a bad husband, and maybe I worked too hard and stayed away from Cheryl too much after finding out that Amber was so sick, but I always loved her, right up until the end."

I wasn't sure how to respond. I wondered if it was more that Jadie was suddenly talking again, and that Amber's name had at last been openly mentioned, rather than that Maria had jolted him to begin this soul-searching. Maybe it had pierced the protective wall he had build around himself and made him think, What if?

I peered tentatively into his face through the gloom. "Have you seen a counselor or anyone since you lost Amber?"

He shook his head, suddenly angry. "What good could a counselor do? He couldn't bring them back, could he?"

"Them?" I queried, puzzled until I realized he must have been referring to his wife's abandoning them, as well as to Amber's death.

He seemed rattled. "I meant Amber. No one can bring her back, can they, so what's the point in seeing some do-gooder who didn't know her?" He raised his voice to a loud hiss. "No one knows what it's like, waking up every morning and just for the briefest fraction of a second thinking everything is as it was— your child is safely asleep in her bed, your wife is lying next to you, the world hasn't turned upside down and shat all over you." Even in the dim light I could see the anger and hurt in his eyes. "I was supposed to be able to take care of them, for God's sake! I was the father, the husband, I was meant to make everything all right again, and I couldn't do anything to help them."

I shook my head. "I don't know for sure if I even have a child or a husband somewhere myself, but I do know that you can't cope with that sort of loss on your own. You need professional help."

"You sound just like Tara," he sighed, the anger evaporating as quickly as it had come. "She tried to get us to see that brother of hers when Amber...you know. He's some sort of psychoanalyst, but Cheryl just shut everyone out, and then when it all become too much, she left me too. I need to ask them to forgive me." Judging by the tremor in his voice, he was close to losing the tenuous grip he'd kept on his emotions for the past two years. "I wish with all my heart that I could have Amber back for just a moment to tell her how sorry I am that I couldn't keep her safe."

He fell silent, but I realized from his ragged breathing that he was still battling to keep his emotions in check.

"When Maria asked me if I had ever felt the presence of a ghost in this house of ours, I admit I did consider the possibility of the property being haunted. I found myself wondering if—

hoping even—Maria had sensed the spirit of my little girl." He uttered the words so quietly I could barely hear him.

I was surprised and a little uneasy at this strange admission. Up until then I'd thought of Vincent as being totally rational.

Leaning forward, I found my hand resting lightly against his. All at once I felt Vincent's fingers encircling mine, and he lifted my hand to his face so that my knuckles rested against his lips. Closing his eyes, he pressed his mouth to my hand.

"I need forgiveness, Kate," he mumbled. "I wasn't there for my daughter when she needed me most, and I can't bear the fact that it is too late to do anything to change that."

"Maybe it's too late for Amber," I whispered, holding my hand very still, "but you've been given another chance with Jadie. You still have your other little girl."

He raised tortured eyes to mine and gazed at me for a long moment. Then, as if registering for the first time that he was touching me, he released my hand abruptly and gave a curt nod. Before I could say anything else, he had picked up the flashlight and walked quietly from the room, leaving me sitting alone in a stranger's kitchen in virtual darkness in the middle of a snowy night.

chapter twelve

In the morning it was snowing heavily again. I went down-stairs to find Tara furiously trying to light the fire in the living room. I watched as she struck match after match while Jadie looked on from where she sat huddled on the couch.

"Here, let me try." Taking the matches from Tara, I kneeled next to her at the hearth. I struck a match and it flared easily, and I held it quickly to the torn newspaper she had wrapped around some kindling and watched as the small flame grew. "What's the matter?"

"It's freezing, that's what the matter is." I noticed she had her coat on over yesterday's jeans and sweater, and yet her lips were still blue with cold. "We need to keep Jadie warm, and I can't even boil a kettle to make her a hot drink."

I glanced at Jadie, who was watching us quietly, swathed in blankets. She did seem even paler than usual, and a shiver of dread ran through me. If this child was too delicate to even play outside in the snow, she was going to be in trouble living in an old house that was quickly growing damp and bitingly cold. I realized that Tara's intense, almost fanatical concern for the child was horribly infectious.

"Where's Vincent?"

"He's not here. I went to speak to him about Jadie, and I couldn't find him anywhere." Her voice was anxious. "I can't understand it."

The fire was growing now as little tongues of flame licked at the kindling and took hold, warming the pieces of wood Tara had dotted about the top of the fire, until they too began to smolder.

"Come and sit on the rug in front of the fire," Tara urged Jadie. "See if we can get you warmed up."

We lifted Jadie between us to save having to unwrap her from her bulky layers, and she gave an ominous chesty cough as she moved.

"I've only just finished doing her physical therapy." Tara crouched anxiously beside Jadie, vigorously rubbing her hands. "She's so congested this morning."

"Can we make more angels?" Jadie asked me croakily as I wriggled onto the rug next to her.

"Maybe after breakfast," I said distractedly.

I was worried about Vincent. Last night he had opened up for perhaps the first time since losing his child and being abandoned by his wife, and now he had disappeared. After two years of denying his grief, it had all come bubbling to the surface. His emotions must have been raw and overwhelming. I hoped he hadn't done anything stupid.

"I've had breakfast already," Jadie said. "I had peanut butter sandwiches."

"Oh, good." I tried to instill some cheer into my voice. "Did you save some for me?"

"There's cereal and milk on the kitchen table," Tara told me as she patted and rubbed Jadie's extremities. "Help yourself."

I headed for the kitchen and poured cereal into a bowl, ate it, and then headed straight for Vincent's office. I knew Tara had said she'd already checked, but I needed to see for myself that he wasn't busying himself somewhere, too embarrassed about our nocturnal chat to see me. There was no sign of him. I looked into the boot room and the downstairs bathroom, but he wasn't there either. Retracing my steps, I went into the icy-cold dining room, and then I jogged up the stairs, trying to keep myself warm by moving quickly.

Starting at the end of the landing, I worked my way back, hurrying up the uneven staircase that led into Tara's attic room. I peered around the door at the empty room with its sloping ceiling and single bed, walked back down past my own room, the bathroom, and Jadie's room. Everywhere had a blue glow of light coming from the windows, a reflection of the thickly falling snow outside. At the door to Amber's room, I paused and listened. This would have been the obvious place for him to come if the grieving process had begun for him at last, and it was somewhere Tara might not have looked. Slowly I turned the doorknob and poked my head into the room.

It was a girly room, all decked out with pink hearts. The wallpaper was pink, the curtains were purple with pink heart shapes, and the bed was tidily made up with a pink duvet and matching pillowcases, with heart-shaped cushions strategically scattered. I noticed with a smile that even the white closet had pink hearts for door handles. There were soft toys on the bed and there was a little white dressing table with a pink cushioned stool. On the dressing table there were a couple of elastic hair bands with pink bobbles on them. The room looked untouched, like Amber was about to return any minute, I thought sadly. Her room had become a shrine.

But Vincent wasn't in there, and I began to feel afraid for him. He surely couldn't have gone out in this weather; the snow would make any kind of journey virtually impossible. I pulled Amber's door closed softly behind me and crossed the landing to his bedroom. I knocked, then inched the door open and stepped inside the red and cream tapestry-hung room. It was disappointingly empty. I checked anyway, noting that the bed looked as though it hadn't been slept in. I pushed open a door I hadn't noticed before, which led to an en suite bathroom housing a free-standing tub with brass fixtures and fittings and a shower unit in the corner with the curtain pulled tightly around it.

I stood for a moment surveying the closed shower curtain with a quaking heart. What if Vincent was lying in there—I quashed the thought before it took shape and in a decisive move stepped forward and yanked the curtain back. The shower was empty.

"Where are you, Vincent?" I demanded of the echoing room. I was about to leave the room when I spotted the medicine cabinet door standing slightly ajar. I peered at the shelves containing toothpaste, mouthwash, a razor, a bottle of ibuprofen, and a can of antiperspirant deodorant. Anxious not to be found snooping in this most private of places, I pushed the cabinet door closed and on impulse crossed to the walk-in closet. For a moment I simply stared at the tapestry wall hanging, but then I flung open the concealed door to reveal the contents of the couple's wardrobe.

I stood stock-still, staring at the rows of clothes and shoes. Gingerly I opened a drawer, just as I had the day I'd arrived, when Vincent had offered me the use of his wife's things. But the day before yesterday I had been a lost soul, just grateful for something warm to wear to bed. Today, as I ran my eyes over the neatly folded piles of T-shirts, blouses, and sweaters, I realized with a cold feeling of dread that this closet reminded me of Amber's sad little bedroom.

These weren't the dregs of a woman's belongings she had left behind in her rush to get away. This was the entire contents of a wardrobe, carefully laundered and waiting—as Amber's room was—for someone who would never return.

After a quick glance over my shoulder, I opened the remaining drawers and found much the same things as in the others: tights, panties, bras—all the personal items a woman needs on a daily basis. And then at the very back of the bottom drawer I saw something that made me pause. I drew forth a black leather handbag with a silver clasp. The leather was soft and well used. This wasn't a fashion accessory like the bags I'd seen on one of the high shelves; this was an everyday bag that looked as though it had been in frequent use. Turning it over in my hands, I chewed my lip, willing myself to open it.

The clasp flipped up with a single click, and I peered inside. I took it over to the bed and shook the contents out onto the quilt. Running my fingers lightly over them I realized I was holding my breath, and I let it out slowly. There was a lipstick, a small tube of hand cream, tissues, a comb, an assortment of loose bits of paper, a pen, and, to my dismay, a bulging leather wallet.

Taking another quick look over my shoulder toward the door, I opened the wallet and found it held about fifty dollars in bills and change, a collection of credit cards, and a driver's license . . . all in the name of Cheryl James.

I took a step backward and pressed a hand across my mouth. If I'd been going to leave home, I would have taken most of these things with me, particularly the wallet. Trembling now, I unzipped a wide compartment on the side of the bag, and there, beneath my probing fingers, I felt a slim booklet. Withdrawing it, I sank down heavily on the edge of the bed and looked at the passport in my hand. The picture of a young dark-haired woman looked back at me, the name beneath the photo proclaiming it was Cheryl James.

Sick to my stomach, I realized that without her ID, Jadie's mother was unlikely to have gone on any aircraft with Uncle Jack.

But if she hadn't gone, then where was she?

chapter thirteen

After a cold, miserable lunch, Tara, Jadie, and I huddled in front of the fire, playing a game of rummy. I had realized as soon as Tara had dealt the first cards that I remembered how to play the game, and had spent most of the time peering at my cards trying to picture when and where I might have played it before. After the discovery of Cheryl's handbag, I was even more desperate to remember something of my real life. My mind wandered, dwelling on the incongruous fact that although I considered it very strange that Vincent's wife had left without her ID and personal belongings, it seemed that I had done just that myself, landing with this family with no possessions or any means of identification whatsoever.

I was fiddling with my cards and watching Jadie spread a run of hearts triumphantly on the rug when there was a loud commotion at the front door. Tara's cards flew out of her hand and scattered across the floor.

"It must be Vincent." She scrambled to her feet and hurried to open the door, pulling the heavy curtain behind her so as not to lose the heat from the fire-warmed room. I rested my cards down and waited for her to reappear. My stomach was churning with a mixture of feelings—relief at finding that he hadn't harmed himself in some way, and a renewed fear for what might have become of his missing wife. But it wasn't Vincent who appeared at Tara's shoulder. It was someone I'd never seen before.

The man followed Tara back through the curtain, bringing with him a blast of cold air. He was an inch or two taller than Tara but had the same slight, almost elfin, build and the same dark, nearly black, hair. He pulled off his boots, showering the polished floor with lumps of dirty ice and snow, then shrugged out of a thick anorak, which Tara took from him and laid over the stair banister.

Jadie glanced over the couch at him with a nonchalant look, then returned to making a fan with her hand of cards. The man hurried over to stand by the fire, rubbing his hands together and blowing on them. I smiled at him, and when he returned the smile, I saw that, behind a pair of rimless glasses, he had Tara's aquamarine eyes too.

"You must be related to Tara." I rose to my feet. "I'm, er... Well, I suppose I'm Kate."

"I'm Colin, Tara's older brother." He held out his hand, then gave me a firm handshake accompanied by a questioning look. "You only *suppose* you're Kate? Don't you know?"

"She's lost her memory," Tara explained when she turned from sweeping out over the doorstep the snow and ice her brother had tramped in. "Kate, or whoever she is, got lost in the blizzard, and Vincent brought her in and is letting her stay."

I noticed the disapproval in her voice, and apparently so did her brother, because he shot her a questioning glance and then looked back at me with renewed interest.

"I'd offer you a cup of tea, Col," Tara continued, getting down on her knees and scrabbling about on the floor for her scattered cards, while her brother sat down on the nearest chair, "but of course there's no hot water."

"That's why I came," Colin said. "I was worried about you and Jadie. Since you didn't come home, I assumed Vincent had gotten delayed in Boston by the weather and you'd had to stay over. I knew you'd be fine, but then the power went off last night, and I wondered if you needed some support."

"That was kind," Tara acknowledged. "Fortunately, Vincent heard the weather forecast and stayed home, but now he's gone AWOL and we're worried sick. We can't imagine where he's gone in conditions like this, but apart from that we're fine—as long as we stay by the fire."

"The snow is pretty deep out there," Colin told us. "It took me more than an hour to walk here from the village, and there wasn't any sign that anyone else had passed that way. I listened to the radio before I came out, and apparently they've started to clear some of the main roads, but most of the smaller ones are impassable."

"Well, where could he be, then?" Tara slapped her cards down onto the floor.

Colin shrugged. "Vincent's a survivor. I'm sure he's fine."

"What's going on in the world, apart from the weather?" I asked hesitantly, hoping Colin was right about Vincent, and eager to hear that there was still a normal working world out there beyond the confines of this house. "We've been really cut off here without electricity or a working phone."

"The world is much the same," Colin replied, stretching

out his feet to warm them in front of the glowing logs. "But drivers have had to abandon cars and trucks in the blizzard. Helicopters have airlifted a few elderly people to the hospital. This cold snap is quite widespread. We've been advised to stay home and sit it out."

He ignored his sister's anxious look and regarded me for several moments before curiosity got the better of him. "Tell me your story, Kate. How much do you remember about how you came to be here?"

"Not very much. All I remember is waking up by the side of a road in the snow and walking for ages before Vincent found me. I have no idea how I came to be there or who I really am. It's horrible, not knowing."

"Were you able to find out anything before the phones went down?" He leaned forward, his eyes full of interest. "Has anyone reported you missing?"

I shook my head. "No, the phone lines were already down by the time I'd pulled myself together enough to think of calling the police."

He glanced at his sister, and Tara rolled her eyes. "Oh, no. I know what you're going to suggest." She groaned.

"It can't hurt," he said to her. "If I can get her to remember who she is, she'll be able to go home as soon as the roads are clear."

Tara suddenly looked hopeful, and I realized they knew each other's little ways very well. Colin had sensed that Tara didn't want me here, and she knew what he was planning to do about it.

"Is someone going to tell me what you're talking about?" I asked nervously.

"Colin is a hypnotherapist," Tara explained. "He holds a doctorate in counseling and hypnotherapy. People come to him with all sorts of problems and he uses hypnosis to take people back to their childhoods, from whence he insists all problems stem." She looked at her brother. "Is that about right, Col?"

"In a nutshell," he replied with a grin. He turned to me. "If you let me hypnotize you. I can probably unlock whatever door in your mind is jammed and open it for you. Your memories will return and you'll be able to continue your life where it left off."

I looked at them dubiously. I wanted to remember my real life—of course I did. The sooner I was able to leave this house with all its mysteries, the better. So why was I so nervous about the suggestion of hypnosis? I fixed him with a steely glare. "If you're so sure you can unlock doors in the mind, then how come you didn't do anything about Jadie's mutism?"

"Because I don't work in that field," he replied, seemingly un-ruffled by my skepticism. "My specialty is in taking clients back to a troubled childhood, and of course children aren't usually can-didates for that type of therapy. Plus, neither Vincent nor Cheryl would hear of it."

"Would you be able to do this hypnosis thing on me?"

"I don't see why not."

I thought about it for a moment while Colin and Tara ex-changed news.

What did I have to lose? I had no memories prior to a couple of days ago; nothing could be worse than this feeling of loneliness and disembodiment. If there was a chance he could resurrect all or even some of my memories, it had to be worth a try.

"Are there any side effects?" I asked when they paused in their chatting to look back at me.

Colin shook his head. "None that I know of."

"Probably because they don't remember what their com-plaints were after you've messed with their minds," Tara com-mented. She gave me a quick grin when she saw the look on my face. "I'm only kidding; Colin is a really experienced hypnothera-pist."

Colin pursed his lips at his sister. "You're making the poor girl nervous," he complained.

"I'm sorry," Tara said, and shrugged. "Look, if you want to know who you are, then Colin can probably help. He's the best there is."

"What would it entail?" I asked hesitantly.

"Because we don't know what trauma caused your amnesia, it would probably be best to take you back to a safe and happy childhood memory and work our way forward to the present." Colin was barely able to keep the excitement out of his voice as he explained the process to me.

"I can't believe I'm even contemplating this." I shivered. "I don't know anything about you."

"I assure you I am accredited." He looked me in the eye. "Honestly, I do know what I'm doing."

"He is good," Tara insisted. "I tried really hard to get Vincent and Cheryl to see him after Amber . . ." She glanced at Jadie. "You know. But they wouldn't, and then Cheryl took the easy option and walked away. If they'd talked to Colin, maybe things would have worked out differently."

I wondered again what had really become of Cheryl, and whether Tara or Colin genuinely believed there was nothing sin-ister about her disappearance, despite what Tara had just said. Even if they were completely innocent, I couldn't see how hypno-sis would have helped.

"Neither Vincent nor Cheryl had problems that stemmed from their childhoods," I pointed out. "They knew exactly what their problem was."

"I hold a doctorate in counseling as well as hypnotherapy," Colin explained. "And what Tara has told you is a very condensed description of several years of studying and practical experience. I'm sure I could have helped them if they'd let me."

And maybe if they'd let him help them, I thought with a shudder as I visualized Cheryl's abandoned belongings, whatever had befallen Cheryl might not have happened.

"Sometimes," Colin was saying, "people have to accept that they need professional help."

I stared at him, studying his features. He had a kind face and a gentle way. Even his voice was soothing, and I found myself instinctively trusting him.

"If I did let you hypnotize me," I hedged, "could Tara sit in with us?"

"I don't normally allow anyone to sit in on a session because I think it is harder for people to let go when they have someone watching and listening to what they say. But in the present circumstances, if you want Tara there and she doesn't mind, I suppose it would be all right."

"When can we do it?"

"Well, I don't know about you, but I don't have a lot on my schedule at the moment." He flashed me a disarming smile. "And by the look of what's left of that card game, you're not doing very much either."

"We've been playing a waiting game," Tara said drily. "Waiting for Vincent to return from wherever it is he's gone, and trying to keep warm while we wait for the electricity to come back on. It's like being in limbo."

"Even more for me. I can't imagine feeling any more in limbo," I said.

"Then, let me help you remember." Colin's voice was softly persuasive.

"Suppose I don't like what I remember?" I asked anxiously. "Suppose I've blocked it out on purpose?"

"You may find that is the case, but if we don't try, you'll never know."

I turned to Tara. "Have you ever let him hypnotize you?"

She shook her head and gave me a wicked grin. "No need. I'm such a well-rounded, well-adjusted person; I don't need people poking about in my brain, thank you very much."

"Don't mind Tara," Colin said with an apologetic smile.

I took a deep breath. You must be mad, I told myself. Mad, mad, mad. But after finding Cheryl's things, I was beginning to feel desperate and I wanted to go home. If going under hypnosis offered a chance of bringing my memories back, then I had to seize that chance. Biting my lip, I stared from Tara to Colin. "Okay. Let's do it."

chapter fourteen

It was too cold in the rest of the house to leave the warmth of the fire, so Tara moved Jadie into one of the fireside armchairs and gave her some schoolwork. I lay stretched out on the couch wrapped in the blankets Tara had found for me when I'd been brought in from the blizzard the day before yesterday. My head was propped on a couple of lavender-scented cushions. Tara took the second armchair, and Colin sat close to me on a high-backed dining chair.

"First I'm going to do some simple breathing and relaxation exercises with you," Colin explained in that soporific voice of his. "When you're comfortable with that, we'll move on, but only if you are ready. Your heart rate will probably slow and your blood pressure drop, which is why we've wrapped you up so you don't get too cold. If at any point you want me to stop or you need to ask something, hold up your right hand. Okay?"

I nodded stiffly, my hands clenched tightly at my sides, but as

I listened to his voice, my body gradually relaxed and my eyelids grew heavy. Colin talked me through a set of relaxation exercises, having me flex and release one part of my body at a time, and asking me to picture various soothing images in my head. The room was silent apart from the almost imperceptible sound of snowflakes landing against the window, Jadie turning the pages of a book, and the occasional sniff from Tara. I felt silly lying wrapped up on the couch, the center of attention in an otherwise silent house.

"I can't do it." I opened my eyes and peered at Colin. "I feel like an idiot."

Colin's eyes blinked behind his glasses, but his voice came back to me, calm and unruffled. "Inside your head you hold a picture of who you really are," he murmured. "Close your eyes again and look deeply into your mind."

And slowly, as I stared into the blackness inside my lids, I felt my whole body relax. My mind wandered as if on the edge of sleep, and I felt warm, cozy, and strangely safe.

"I want you to go back in time a few days to your arrival in this area," he intoned. "It is snowing and you are making a journey. Tell me, are you on foot or in a vehicle?"

I can't remember," I whispered. "There's nothing—just a white mist swirling. It's like being inside a cloud."

"That's fine, Kate, you are doing very well," droned the voice in my head. "We will go back a little further, perhaps to when you were a young adult. It is a lovely summer's day and you are happy and content. Your family is all around you. You are warm and safe. Tell me what you see now."

"Just whiteness," I said with a hint of dismay as I peered into the nothingness. "Swirling whiteness and emptiness."

"Okay, Kate, I want you to look further into your mind. Imagine there is a doorway that you need to pass through; on the other side you will see yourself as a child at a time when you were content and relaxed. When you have passed through the doorway, tell me what you see."

"I can't get the door to open; I can't get past it."

"What does the door look like, Kate? Is it a wooden door, or glass perhaps?"

"It's more like a thick white curtain, heavy and soft, but my hand just passes straight through. I can't get a grip on it."

Panic flooded through me, even more than when I'd been awake. The whiteness reminded me that my life was a complete blank. I was in a void somewhere, lost and alone, stranded between my real life and this one, and suddenly I was terribly afraid.

"Calm down, Kate. Take some deep breaths and we will try the door again."

"What's the matter with her?" Tara's voice came as if from a distance. I heard Colin reassure her, and then the curtain came down in front of me again and I concentrated my mind on seeing what lay on the other side of it.

"I want you to part the curtain with your mind, Kate. Push those folds back one by one until you have an opening you can pass through to the other side. You have nothing to fear; you are a child again and you are relaxed and happy."

"It's moving...like a heavy velvet cloak." I could hear my own voice, relieved and excited. "Oh, I think I'm through."

"Tell me what you see."

"I'm jumping with my rope on the cobblestones by the front yard of our redbrick schoolhouse."

"That's good, very good.... Can you tell me what time of day it is?"

"It's early morning. The sun is shining down on me. I can feel the warmth of it on my long hair."

"Your breathing is becoming rapid again, Kate. Are you panting because you are jumping?"

"I'm counting my jumps; the rope is whirring through the air and I am counting as I jump. And I like being called Kitty; everyone calls me Kitty."

"Tell me what the schoolhouse looks like, Kitty."

"It's in a row of redbrick tenement houses. They all look the same, with their front yards leading out onto the cobbled street. Each yard is divided by rickety wooden rail fencing, with straggly grass growing between the posts, and one or two low redbrick walls."

"What else do you see?

"Gray smoke is winding out of the highest chimney. It's billowing down on me, making me choke."

I started coughing, wrinkling my nose as I hopped and skipped over the flying rope.

"Oh, no!"

"What is it?"

"Bits of black coal soot are speckling down on my clean white pinafore smock! Mother will be angry if I get it dirty."

"What else are you wearing, apart from the smock?"

"Well, the pinafore is over my cotton dress, of course, and I've got them both tucked up into my gray drawers to keep them from snagging on the rope. I've got socks on, and my boots, of course."

"Apart from worrying about getting dirty, are you happy, Kitty?"

"Oh, yes! I love the early mornings when the dew sparkles on the cobbles and the air is still fresh—before the neighbors light their fires and then the air fills with the smell of coal smoke."

"Do you have to get up very early to play like this?"

"I rise at the same time as Mother in the bedroom above the schoolroom. I usually wash my hands and splash water on my face from the earthenware bowl that stands on the cupboard, before getting dressed."

"Who lives above the schoolroom with you, apart from your mother?"

"My sister, Alice, and my little brother, Arthur." Resting the rope down, I stopped skipping and glanced up at the top window.

"What are you looking at, Kitty?"

"Mother is waving at me. I think she wants me to come in soon."

"Why aren't your siblings down here playing with you?"

"Because I'm much older than them; I have to work all day and so Mother lets me have this time to play."

"How old are you, Kitty?"

"I'm twelve, almost grown up."

"And where is your father?"

I found myself gulping, my heart constricting with the memory. "He died."

"I'm very sorry to hear that, Kitty. Can you tell me how he died?"

Holding the jump rope loosely in one hand, I stood and stared off into space, remembering the day it had happened. I had answered the urgent knocking at the door of our cottage, to be confronted by the sight of my father being carried home by a group of local men. Father's bloody head had been hanging limply to one side. Mother had let out a wail of anguish.

"The men told Mother that Father had been making his way home from the tavern when a runaway horse thundered down the street behind him. Without even thinking, it seemed Father had stepped out into the road and tried to grab the animal's flying reins. The horse had reared up on its hind legs and brought its front hoofs crashing down on the side of his skull."

"What happened to him?"

"They laid him on the kitchen table, and Mother leaned over him, touching her cheek against his cold bloody one. She told me he was still breathing, but her eyes were wide with shock and I felt so helpless. There was nothing I could do, and the men had run off to summon a doctor."

"Would you like to tell me what happened next?"

"Father drifted in and out of consciousness. Mother applied poultices of chamomile flowers and hops to his head wound to ease the pain as the doctor had instructed her, but Father died a week after the accident. He was hailed as a hero for trying to stop the runaway horse, but my poor mother was beside herself with grief, and left with three young mouths to feed. The horror of ending up homeless filled our waking hours."

"What's she talking about?" I could hear Tara's voice somewhere in my head.

"I don't know," Colin's voice answered hers. He sounded puzzled, and I felt a flicker of fear. "Keep talking to me, Kitty." His whispery voice seemed to come from somewhere inside my head. "What are you looking at now?"

"Mother is at the schoolhouse window again. She's holding up five fingers, which means I have five more precious minutes of freedom."

"What are you thinking about when you look at your mother?"

"I'm picturing her getting ready for the day ahead. She'll be smoothing down the skirts of her long black mourning gown and twisting her hair into a neat bun at the back of her neck, securing it with a pin, as I've seen her do so many times before. She'll have to use the button hook we keep on the lace doily that lives on top of the mahogany cupboard to fasten the buttons on her leather ankle boots.

"Can you still see your mother, Kitty?"

I glanced at the window again, but Mother was gone. "No, she'll be creeping down the stairs as she does every morning to stoke the schoolroom fire into life while the younger children are still asleep in the room above, snuggled in blankets on the mattress on the bedroom floor."

"This isn't right." It was Tara's voice again. "What's she remembering? I think you should bring her back, Col."

Taking my rope again in both hands, I tried to banish the nagging voice inside my head. I jumped and counted for five more minutes and was about to wind up my jump rope when I became aware that I was not alone in the yard.

At first I thought it had something to do with the voice I had heard, but spinning around, I found myself looking into the ice-blue eyes of a boy around my own age. He had jet-black hair and he was staring rudely at me from over the fence that divided our front yard from his.

Flushing to the roots of my hair, I pulled my skirts from where they were tucked indecently into my drawers, and ran for the house.

"Kitty, tell me what you are doing now," the voice commanded.

"I'm going indoors. Go away!"

"All right, Kate. I'm going to count backward from ten, and at each count you will travel forward in time, until you are back here in the present with me. When you wake, you will remember everything that you have seen, and you will be calm and feel refreshed."

I heard someone counting backward while my mind traveled through what seemed like a long brightly lit tunnel.

"Three, two, one. Open your eyes, Kate!"

I opened my eyes to find Colin and Tara looking at me intently. I tried to sit up, but my head was swimming.

"What happened?" I leaned shakily up on one elbow.

"Do you remember anything of what you just recounted?"

Colin's eyes were bright, and his cheeks were flushed with excitement. Thinking back to the vivid dream I'd just had, I frowned, trying to make sense of it all. "Yes, I remember. But what exactly was it I was remembering?"

"I'm not sure," Colin said slowly. "But I think—and this is just a guess because I've never dabbled in this type of hypnotherapy—I think I just took you back to a previous existence."

"You're kidding, right?" I stared at him incredulously.

"You described what sounded to me like life in New England around a hundred years ago." Colin was trying to conceal his excitement, but his eyes were shining behind his glasses. "The clothing, the use of a button hook to fasten your boots, the medical treatment your father received after his head injury . . . It all adds up to a lifestyle from well before you were born."

chapter fifteen

"*Ridiculous,*" *Tara proclaimed,* getting to her feet and walk-ing to the fire as if to distance herself from me. She rubbed her hands together over the flames and turned to face her brother with a look of consternation.

"It isn't ridiculous, Tara," Colin explained patiently. "Many hypnotherapists actually specialize in regressing their clients to past-life experiences. You must have seen some of those TV shows where famous people recall past lives under hypnosis; it's quite an acceptable practice these days."

"Yeah, right." Tara sank to her knees on the rug in front of the fire. "So why did it happen to Kate when you were only trying to get her to remember her childhood in *this* life? What did you do, put her on the wrong bus?"

"I don't know why it happened so spontaneously to Kate." Colin narrowed his eyes at me thoughtfully. "It's possible she has suffered a trauma so painful to recall that under deep relaxation she returned to a time when she was happier, which just happened to be a previous-life experience."

"Or maybe it was that knock on her head," Tara said, going over to check on Jadie.

I eyed Colin dubiously. "Don't you think it's a bit odd," I said, still shaky from the experience, "that the name I'm using here just happens to be so similar to the name I had then? Isn't Kitty a derivative of Kate?"

"I believe it is. So how did you come up with the name Kate?" he asked, his eyes still gleaming.

"It just came to me," I answered truthfully. "Vincent and I were invited to the next-door neighbor's for dinner and I had to have a name. Maria's dramatic looks reminded me of Kate from Shakespeare's *The Taming of the Shrew*, so I just said it without thinking."

"Ah, how the subconscious mind works," Colin murmured almost reverently. "If only we humans could utilize more of our subconscious brain power, we would be very powerful creatures indeed."

"But what does it mean?"

"I'm not sure yet." Colin removed his glasses and began to polish them on the hem of his T-shirt. "I'd like to put you under again and see what else you recall." He paused, taking in my horrified expression. "But I think you've had enough for now." He glanced sideways at me, changing the subject, presumably in case I refused.

"How did the dinner next door go? I've always thought the lovely Maria had an unhealthy interest in Vincent."

"You don't suppose he's there, do you?" Tara asked over her shoulder as she opened a bag of chocolate chip cookies and handed one to Jadie.

"What would he go there for?" I asked. I realized the minute the words were out of my mouth that it was a silly question, and it was duly met by raised eyebrows from Colin and grimly pursed lips from Tara.

"He was in a strange mood when he got back from the dinner last night," Tara offered into the sudden silence. "What exactly happened, anyway?"

"Maria said some things about Cheryl," I said carefully, not sure how much of my unease about Cheryl's disappearance I should share. "She was going to tell us a ghost story but ended up talking about how she and Cheryl had been close friends and that she was surprised Cheryl had left without telling anyone."

"A ghost story?" Colin stood up and went to stand by his sister, holding his hands out to the fire for warmth. "Maria always struck me as a reasonably sane person—a bit excitable, perhaps, but not someone I'd have thought believed in all that stuff."

"How come you're willing to believe that I just had a past-life experience, but you're skeptical about ghosts?" I swung my legs down from the couch, glad he had latched on to that part of the conversation rather than the fact that Maria had accused Vincent of... *What* had she accused him of? Last night I had thought she was suggesting that he had not listened to his grief-stricken wife properly. Today, after finding Cheryl's things, I wasn't so sure.

"Past lives and the existence of ghosts are completely different things," Colin replied. "If you believe people can have more than one life—and as I have just said, many normal, ordinary people insist they have been here before—then you could also believe that occasionally a spirit might linger for a while after their earthly body is no longer capable of supporting life. For example, a soul might be so confused by their sudden or unexpected death that they decline going immediately to the place beyond. If that happens, those troubled souls may be perceived by the living as ghosts. A newly deceased soul might possibly even try to make contact with family or the friends he or she has left behind by appearing in dreams or willing a living person they care deeply about to feel their presence." He helped himself to a cookie, took a bite, and chewed thoughtfully. "But most souls pass peacefully to the other side and don't run about making trouble for the living, as ghost stories would have us believe."

I shrugged. "I don't know. I've always thought—I think—that when you're dead, you're dead. I have the feeling that I may have been interested in historical facts rather than ghost stories." I gave a short laugh. "Of course, this is all new territory to me."

"Everything's new territory to you," Tara pointed out. "You may as well have been born the day before yesterday, the amount you know about anything."

I was about to retort, "Well, thanks," when we heard the sound of a latch being lifted as Tara ran toward it. I waited, my heart in my mouth.

This time it was Vincent. He came in with a blast of cold air, much as Colin had done an hour or so previously, shaking snow off his shoulders and stamping ice off his boots. Tara flung her arms toward him, and I thought for a moment she was going to hug him. She seemed to come to her senses suddenly and stepped back, her cheeks blushing a crimson red, and in that moment it came to me that she'd been thinking he'd done himself some harm, just as I had.

"Calm down, Tara." A voice came from behind Vincent's shoulder. We both looked behind Vincent to see Adam, the neighborly farmer, standing awkwardly in the doorway, his hands stuffed deep into the pockets of his coat.

"Where have you been?" Tara demanded as the two men came into the living room. She slammed the door closed behind them as if to emphasize her displeasure.

"I went to get help," Vincent explained as he peeled off his coat. He noticed Colin standing by the fire, and hurried forward, holding out his hand. "Good to see you, Colin; what are you doing here?"

"I came to see if Tara and Jadie were okay alone, what with the power outage and everything. I thought you might have been stranded in Boston." Colin said, returning the handshake.

"That was good of you," Vincent acknowledged. "I've been worried about Jadie. She was coughing a lot in the night. I couldn't sleep, so I decided to battle my way over the hill to Adam's place and beg a favor. I remembered they had a generator. I hoped Adam and his grandparents might have hot water and a warm house where Jadie could stay until the main power comes back on."

"We've got a wood-burning stove in the kitchen," Adam put in. "The generator makes enough power to run the water pump and some light in the house and outbuildings, but the stove means we can cook and heat the drinking water."

"Adam has kindly said that we can take Jadie over to his place until things return to normal, with Tara to look after her, and you too, Kate, if you want to go. It's up to you."

He was looking at me strangely, as if challenging me to make the decision, and a tremor ran through me. I didn't want to leave this safe haven I'd found myself in, but I wasn't sure enough of this man to stay here alone with him. It was true he'd rescued me and I probably owed my life to him, but his wife's abandoned belongings and Maria's veiled accusations had made me jumpy.

"How would we get there?" I asked tentatively. "It must have taken you hours to walk over the hill in this much snow."

"It did take me quite a while." Vincent shuddered at the memory of his ordeal. "I spent the early hours listening to Jadie coughing, and I remembered that Adam had made it here with the cat yesterday so I thought it couldn't be that difficult to make the journey on foot. I left at first light, but I found out the hard way that farmers are a lot tougher than financiers." He glanced at Adam and grinned. "I must have looked like the abominable snowman by the time I got there. It's taken a couple of hours and a warm meal to thaw me out. We came back over in Adam's tractor. It's got a cushioned passenger seat and a heated cab."

"We can't take Jadie to a farm with all those filthy animals. Think of the allergens that must be floating about!" Tara was looking horrified. "What if she has an asthma attack?"

Jadie gave a chesty cough from the armchair by the fire, and Vincent said, "We have to take that risk. Jadie needs hot food and drinks and a warm place to sleep. She was okay with the cat yesterday, so hopefully she'll be fine with the other animals."

Jadie coughed again, this time in earnest, spitting sticky mucus into a tissue, and Tara paled.

"I'll have to do some physical therapy with her." She hurried over to Jadie's side. "Then we'll make a decision."

"I already have made a decision," Vincent said firmly. "I'm sorry, Tara. I know you only want the best for her, but I'm her father and I say she'll be better off at the farm."

Forcing myself to meet Vincent's eyes, I couldn't resist a small smile. Not because he'd stood up to Tara but because it seemed that he'd taken to heart the things I'd reminded him of the previous night. He still had the chance to take care of Jadie, and he'd waded a far distance in terrible conditions to find her a safe place to stay. He had taken control of the situation at last, and I was glad for him, despite my misgivings about his missing wife.

Tara turned her back on him and pulled Jadie into a prone position so she could pat her back. We all watched as Tara expertly worked and pounded, and we were humbled by her obvious devotion.

"I'll go too," I said, "if Adam has room. I could help Tara look after Jadie, if you'd like me to . . . Tara?"

"Yeah, why not?" Tara didn't bother looking up from her task. "You could start by packing her a few things, warm clothes and such. There are a couple of bags in my room under the bed. You can use one of those to put her stuff in."

I was surprised by her easy capitulation, but decided that maybe she wanted me where she could see me. And if Vincent wasn't intending to come with us, she would rather have me with her than alone in this house with him.

"Would you mind awfully if I came along too?" Colin said mildly. "I'm working with Kate and would like to be on hand to see how she progresses."

"Working with Kate? What do you mean?" Vincent eyed him suspiciously.

"I'm trying to help her get her memory back so she'll be able to go home when the weather improves."

"Since when?" Vincent demanded.

I heard the proprietary note in his voice and glanced sharply at him.

"I put her under hypnosis a short while ago, and she remembered some *very* interesting things." Colin smiled to himself.

"Yeah, Kate's had a previous-life experience," Tara put in sarcastically. "Would you believe she remembers being some twelve-year-old girl a century ago but has no recollections of this life at all? I mean, how bizarre is *that*?"

"It's because Kate's not really here," Jadie said between thumps from Tara. "Amber says she's just visiting us from heaven to sort things out."

I stared at Jadie with my mouth open. When I looked around I found every eye fixed upon me.

Colin broke the sudden silence by clearing his throat. "This is a psychoanalyst's dream," he breathed. His eyebrows were raised, and I realized he hadn't known until then that Jadie was speaking again. "I don't know what's more interesting, the fact that Jadie has decided to break her silence, or what it is that she has chosen to say."

chapter sixteen

After packing Jadie's things I raided Cheryl's wardrobe to get everything I thought I might need for the next day or two.

I rode in the passenger seat of the tractor with Jadie on my lap and a couple of tightly packed duffel bags at my feet. There was only one passenger seat in the tractor, so Tara had to travel ahead of us on the first trip, squashed haphazardly on top of her brother so she would be there with Jadie's inhaler, decongestant medication, and other paraphernalia, ready for the child to arrive with me.

Vincent, to my relief, chose not to join us, but to stay and make sure his house didn't freeze by keeping the fire going in the living room. Before we left, he went next door, at Adam's behest, to find out how Maria and Michael were coping and to ask if they wanted to join us at the Jenkinses' farm. They opted to stay where they were, convinced that the electricity would soon return, and insisting they were warm enough in front of their own fire.

I couldn't help thinking about Vincent as the tractor bumped and jolted over the uneven surface of the snow-covered lane.

Apart from my strange hallucination when he'd carried me to the safety of his house, had there been any spark between us? I wasn't sure. He was good-looking, certainly, but what of Tara, who was so obviously in love with him? Not to mention the missing Cheryl.

Adam drove as carefully as he could, his strong hands tightly gripping the steering wheel, but still Jadie lurched and swayed in my lap, squealing whenever the enormous wheels ran up the side of a bank of snow or bumped over a concealed object. I risked a furtive glance at our driver, noticing the firm set of his jaw, determination emanating from him as he concentrated on the path ahead.

It was warm and cozy inside the heated cab with the blizzard raging all around us outside. The tractor's windshield wipers were scraping the snow away as soon as it settled, but below the wipers the snow had gathered in a soft arc, bathing the cab in a silvery blue light. I shut all thoughts of Vincent and Tara out of my head and began to relax. I felt strangely at ease and comfortable, despite the continual bouncing of the vehicle and the lack of any attempt at conversation from our driver. Jadie too had stopped wriggling and was sitting snuggled against me, gazing at Adam's profile as he concentrated on getting us safely down the narrow lane to the farm.

When an old brick farmhouse and a huddle of outbuildings loomed through the dancing flakes, I found I was disappointed that our journey was almost at an end, and I was reluctant to go in and continue the prickly relationship with Tara, or continue with Colin's unnerving delving into my subconscious.

"Can we stay in here?" Jadie whispered, echoing my feelings as Adam brought the tractor to a halt in the front yard. "I like it in here with you and Adam."

"I like it too,' I acknowledged. "But we have to go indoors."

I turned to thank Adam, and found him watching us with a perplexed expression on his face. "Don't you girls want to get out?"

"Not really," Jadie and I said in unison. We laughed, and I gave her a hug.

Adam was shaking his head as he came around to open the door and help us both down from the cab. He lifted Jadie down first and carried her to the front door, where Tara was waiting anxiously for her. I had collected the bags and was working out how to get down from the high cab when he returned and held out a hand to assist me. I looked into his calm brown eyes and at his outstretched hand, and the world stilled again, much as it had when I'd first seen him standing on Vincent's doorstep holding the cat box out to me. Giving myself a shake, I passed him the bags and scrambled down the step. Adam gave me a puzzled look as he carried the bags to the house.

I stood in the cleared space of the yard, taking in the rambling farmhouse with its low front door framed by the thick trunk of a hibernating wisteria. Apart from the driveway, the yard was hemmed by snow-capped barns and outbuildings, from which I could hear the bleating of lambs and the answering rumbles of ewes.

"It's beautiful," I breathed. "It seems a shame to go indoors."

"You're welcome to stand here and freeze if you want to." Adam had returned from dropping the bags off. "But if you don't mind, I've got work to do." He turned on his heel and crossed the yard to one of the barns. I had a glimpse of a wall of hay bales stretching to the ceiling before the door swung shut behind him. Wrenching my gaze away, I walked toward the farmhouse, knocked perfunctorily, and entered the Jenkinses' hallway, blinking in the sudden gloom of the interior.

The hallway was paneled with dark wood, very similar in design to the corridors in Vincent's house. There were engravings in the wood, but it was too dark to see much detail, and I was drawn toward the end, where light spilled out from under a door and I could hear the murmuring of voices. After passing a closed door on my right and an ornate staircase, which seemed to bend back on itself as it swept upward, I pushed at the half-open door and found myself in the kitchen.

Tara and Colin were ensconced at one side of a long, scrubbed, pine table, and Jadie had immediately made herself at home by sandwiching herself between them. She was already drinking a glass of milk and digging into a slab of what looked like home-made cherry cake. At the far end of the table sat a frail-looking white-haired woman who was officiating with a brown earthen-ware teapot, a milk jug, and a tray of thick-rimmed mugs. She looked up when I entered.

"Tea?" she asked.

"Yes, please, that would be lovely." I considered how best to introduce myself. "I'm Kate, by the way."

The four people sitting at the table weren't the only occupants of the room. Hunched in a moth-eaten-looking armchair in front of the large iron stove, which dominated the far wall, was an elderly man, his slippered feet resting on a low footstool. He had a tartan blanket spread over his knees and a tabby cat curled on his lap. And in the farthest corner of the kitchen, in a small alcove formed between the stove, adjoining cupboards, and the wall, was an area cordoned off by a couple of wooden crates, where two tiny lambs were cuddled together in some straw.

I walked around the table to introduce myself to the man, smiling and holding out my hand. "It is very kind of you to have us all here like this."

The man glanced up. "You'll excuse me if I don't shake hands." He indicated his gnarled hands, which bent and twisted on his lap on either side of the sleeping cat. "I'm afraid they don't work so well these days."

I looked down at his hands and then at the cat, wondering if it was the one Adam had brought over the previous day. "She looks comfortable." I reached out to stroke her.

"My grandson found her up on the top field and brought her back here to the farm." The old man ran his clawed hand over the cat's back, making her purr and twitch in her sleep. "She's a darned sight more friendly than the farm cats. She's obviously someone's much-loved pet."

"I think she may be mine." I crouched down next to the old man's chair so I could look at the cat more closely, hoping to see something in her that might spark recognition.

"Don't you know if she's yours?" He was studying my face, and before I could explain further, his rheumy eyes came to rest on the Band-Aid on my forehead. "Ah, you're the lass who's lost her memory! Adam told us about you. Well, she's a lovely cat, well cared for, I'd say—not too fat like most pets these days—so if she's yours, you can be proud of her."

"Don't let your tea get cold, Bill," the old woman barked suddenly at him.

"You haven't given it to me yet, you silly old woman," Bill responded affectionately.

"I've made a fresh cherry cake," the woman continued as if he hadn't spoken. "That'll go nice with a cup of tea."

Bill grinned up at me. "Get me a cup, would you, lass? With all these people here, Betty is more confused than usual."

Rising to my feet, I took the cup Tara passed across the table, and then I stood with it, not sure how to hand it to the old man.

"Put it on this table, lass," he said, and nodded to a spindly round-topped table that wouldn't have looked out of place in a lady's drawing room. It was half-hidden on the other side of the chair, but was of a height that made it almost level with the old man's face. There was a box of drinking straws on the table, so I put the cup down and popped a straw in for him, bending it so it was near his mouth. I watched as he took a good long pull at the straw and sat back contentedly.

"Would you like some cake too?" I asked hesitantly, wondering how this couple normally managed when he was so physically impaired and his wife obviously suffered from some kind of dementia.

"It's a good cherry cake, so eat it all up." Betty was busy cutting several large slices and putting them on plates. "We've got guests, so I made a cake."

"Yeah, Betty my love, I know," Bill said patiently. "But a man could die waiting for you to part with a piece of it."

Jadie giggled, and Tara gave her a nudge with her elbow. I took a plate and positioned it next to Bill's cup, and he reached across with both hands, skewered the cake between his two twisted thumbs and lifted it to his mouth.

"Tea?" Betty barked at me as I sat next to Colin at the long table.

"That would be very nice, thank you," I said again, wondering if she'd get as far as pouring it this time.

She handed me a mug, peering at me with a perplexed frown. "Who did you say you were, dear?"

"I'm Kate." I smiled as I took the mug from her.

"Would you like another piece of cake?" she asked. "We've got guests, so I've made it specially."

"Yes, please, that would be lovely, Betty."

The cake was delicious. I wondered how she remembered the recipe, but soon realized as I listened to the chitchat around the table that Betty had been born to cook. The conversation was all about food, and it seemed that Bill merely reminded his wife which mealtime was coming up, and off she'd go, peeling, chopping, marinating, and mixing. I sat and ate my cake while Tara, who had been here nearly an hour already and had finished hers, helped the old woman begin to prepare what looked like our evening meal.

Judging by her easy movements, it seemed that Tara had been here many times before and knew her way around the kitchen well enough. Even Jadie, who had finished picking at her cake, was soon sitting at the table with a mixing bowl in front of her, stirring suet into flour to make dumplings under Betty's expert eye.

Colin and I volunteered to wash up the dishes from our snack. We stood together at a big old enamel sink in the adjoining whitewashed utility room, which had a line of laundry strung from wall to wall. We listened to the chatter wafting in from the kitchen as I sloshed mugs and cake plates about in the soapy water and he dried them. I handed him the last plate, aware he was looking sideways at me.

"You will let me hypnotize you again, won't you?" He dried the plate. "I'd like to try a different regression technique and see what we come up with."

I glanced at him suspiciously, wondering if he was planning to use me as some sort of experimental lab rat, but he looked sincere enough, so I said, "I'll think about it."

"You don't have to," he said quickly. "It has to be your decision entirely. I just thought you'd want another chance at finding out your real identity, or at the very least to visit Kitty's world again." He grinned at me. "You have to admit it's all pretty intriguing."

"It's pretty scary, actually." Drying my hands on a towel, I gave him a quick smile. "But I'll admit it's intriguing too."

"Perhaps we could ask Bill if there's somewhere quiet we could go."

I nodded, wondering again if I was crazy to give the hypnosis thing a second go. But this time, I told myself, I knew what I was getting into.

I followed Colin back into the kitchen just as a door opened behind us and Adam walked in, blowing on his work-reddened hands.

"Stock all tucked up for the night?" Bill asked as Adam took a seat at the table. "It looks bad out there."

"I've brought most of the ewes down to the small field behind the barn," Adam told him, reaching for the teapot. "The ones that have lambed in the last day or two, and the ones still to lamb, are in the shed." He glanced over to where the two orphaned lambs were up on their feet now in the corner of the kitchen. "Anyone fed those two yet?"

"Betty's making up the bottles now," Bill replied. "I thought young Jadie might like to feed one of them."

"I don't think that's a good idea." Tara rose quickly to her feet. She placed a clean mug on the table and hoisted the heavy kettle from the stove to make a fresh pot of tea. "I don't want her getting too close to the livestock."

"It's a bit late for that," Adam observed.

We turned to see Jadie leaning over the enclosure with her arms around the neck of one of the lambs.

"Oh my God!" Tara shrieked, slapping the kettle down and hurrying over to Jadie. She pulled her roughly away. "Those creatures will set your asthma off, you silly girl."

"Amber says they won't!" Jadie struggled in Tara's grasp. "I want to feed the lambs."

"Stop this nonsense about Amber," Tara panted, as she tried to restrain the wriggling child. "You can't go near the lambs."

"I want to, I want to!" Jadie shouted, fighting Tara in earnest now as Tara tried to drag her away. "You're horrible. Let me go!"

"They'll make you ill, Jadie." Tara sighed as she held her struggling charge. "I'm not going to let you make yourself sick."

"I'm not ill. I'm not. . . . Why does everyone think I'm going to die?" Jadie sobbed, still fighting.

Tara paled, and let go of Jadie so suddenly that the child went sprawling into Bill's lap. The cat leaped up with a surprised yowl, and the old man caught the child awkwardly in his stiff arms, holding her against his chest and muttering, "There, there, stop your crying, lass. Shush, shush now."

Jadie continued to wail with her face buried against Bill's green cardigan. The lambs began bleating hungrily, as they smelled the prepared bottles of milk Betty had placed on the kitchen table. Adam, having sprung to his feet when Jadie had fallen onto his grandfather, had knocked over the empty mug with a crash. He was attempting to scrape the larger pieces into a pile, and the jagged bits clanked together noisily. Tara was crying, her elbows resting on the table, her face hidden in her hands. Colin went to her and put an arm around her, and she turned into her brother's embrace.

Adam paused, resting on his haunches, wincing at the pandemonium that had erupted. He glanced in my direction, and we looked on helplessly while Jadie wailed, Tara sobbed, and the lambs bleated with increasing urgency.

Suddenly Betty's quavering voice broke calmly through the commotion. She had slid into her chair at the head of the table and was looking at Adam with a sweet smile of recognition as she poured tea into a clean mug. They might have been the only people in the room. "I've made a cherry cake. Would you like a cup of tea and a nice slice, dear?"

chapter seventeen

Jadie ended up feeding the lambs after all, with a bit of help from me. Tara wiped her eyes and begrudgingly admitted that the creatures didn't appear to be having any effect on Jadie's asthma. Sniffing, she said Jadie could do what she wanted as long as she didn't expect Tara to pick up the pieces. I kneeled beside Bill's chair and stroked Jadie's hair until she quieted down, then I explained how Tara only wanted her to be safe. Jadie wiped her tear-stained face on the sleeve of her cardigan and trotted over to kiss Tara. She murmured that she was sorry for shouting, but added that Amber had been right, because her asthma was fine.

Adam showed us how to hold tightly to the feeding bottles because, despite looking so small and frail, the lambs had mighty sucking powers, and pushed and nudged roughly at the bottles in an attempt to increase milk flow while their little caterpillar-like tails danced and trembled with pleasure. Adam eventually left us to it while he ate his cake.

"Is there somewhere quiet that Colin and I can go to, er...
talk?" I asked Adam when I emerged from the utility room a
while later with Jadie, the feeding bottles and our hands washed.

"You could use the front parlor, but it's not very warm." Adam
stood up. "The only really warm room is the kitchen." He cocked
his head to one side and contemplated me. "What are you hoping
to achieve with this hypnotherapy craziness?"

I remembered he'd been standing in the living room with
Vincent when Tara had explained to him what Colin had been
trying to achieve earlier.

"I'm trying to find out who I am, and you might think it's
nuts, but it's horrible not knowing anything about myself."

He fished in his pocket and produced a mobile phone. "I
didn't mean to make fun of you," he said evenly. "But why don't
you call the police and see if anyone has reported you missing? It
might be an easier way to find out who you are than having someone delve into your subconscious mind." He was already punch-
ing in a number. "Here"—he held out the phone—"this is the
number for our local police station. You can find out if they have
any record of someone matching your description having been
lost in the last few days."

I took the phone out into the gloomy hallway, where things
were quieter, and pressed it to my ear, feeling incredibly stupid.
Here I was talking about hypnosis as if it were the most natural
thing in the world, when probably all I'd needed to do was make
a simple phone call. I should have remembered that Vincent had
told me it was only in the area near his house that mobiles
wouldn't work.

The call was answered quickly by an efficient-sounding female
who asked what I wanted to report and then transferred me to an
operator. The operator, a man, asked for my name.

"Er, well, that's the problem, actually," I said. "I've lost my memory and don't know who I am. I was hoping someone might have reported me missing."

"What is your present location?" asked the officer.

I had no idea of the address here. I stuck my head around the kitchen door and beckoned Adam over, thrusting the phone into his hands. "They want to know your address," I said.

I stood back while Adam gave the name and address of the farm and then explained that I had been found wandering in his top field near the road two days previously. He told them I appeared to be all right apart from a small cut to my head. He listened for a moment, then turned and looked me up and down appraisingly.

"She's about five foot six, slim, light brown shoulder-length hair, kind of streaked with blond, and a bit wavy.... Er, I don't know. Just a minute..." He beckoned me over to the light spilling from the kitchen door and stared into my eyes. "Green with little brown flecks..." He paused and fell silent. I found myself gazing into his deep brown eyes, suddenly mesmerized. Minutes seemed to pass. "What? Oh, sorry," he said into the phone, looking away. "She has a light-skinned complexion, a few freckles maybe. I think she was wearing jeans...?" He took the phone away from his mouth. "What were you wearing exactly?"

"Jeans and a thin sage-green sweater—three-quarter sleeves, V-neck."

He relayed the information into the phone. "Yes, yes, of course. No, I understand."

I listened while he gave them two phone numbers and then clicked the phone off. "They can't send anyone out until the weather improves; all their departments are overstretched by the emergency conditions. I said we'd look after you in the meantime, but they've entered your details into the missing persons database and will let us know if they come up with a match."

"Thank you."

"So if you don't want to wait to find out who you are, it looks like you might have to resort to Colin's shenanigans after all." He regarded me with the hint of a smile. "Of course, you might find you are that twelve-year-old girl from a hundred years ago that Tara was talking about, in which case the police computer will probably draw a blank."

"Or I might not," I retorted. "You're as bad as Tara."

His expression softened. "I'm sorry. You're coping really well, given the circumstances."

Adam built a fire in the grate in the room he called the parlor, heaving logs in from the covered porch outside and stacking them beside the fire while the kindling took and flames licked upward. It was already dark outside, and he drew heavy curtains across the leaded-light windows to shut out the chill of the snowy night, while Tara got a duvet from upstairs and wrapped it around me, ever hopeful, I was sure, of everything coming back to me so that I would return to my own life and leave hers alone.

"You've got about an hour before dinner," Tara told me as she closed the parlor door behind Adam and her. "While you're off with the fairies, I'll make us up some beds, then help Betty finish preparing the meal."

"Leave the beds until after dinner and I'll give you a hand," I called, but she had already gone, leaving me feeling decidedly guilty again.

"Take no notice of her," Colin said, settling himself in a faded brown velour armchair beside the couch on which he had told me to lie down. "Tara loves to be busy.

"Now," he said, getting down to the business at hand, "I want you to close your eyes and relax. We're going to concentrate on your breathing like we did before. Take long, deep breaths. Let your mind go blank and your body go limp and fluid."

Colin took me through the same relaxing process as he had earlier in the afternoon, and still I could conjure up no recollection of who I was or what I had been doing sitting alone in the snow on the road. Then, quite suddenly I found I was Kitty again.

"Tell me who you are and what you are doing," Colin asked calmly.

"I'm lying on the mattress in the room above the schoolroom," I whispered, so as not to wake my sister, Alice, or my brother, Arthur, both of whom were snoring gently beside me.

"Where is your mother?"

"She has gone downstairs to fetch a jug of water for washing. It's early in the morning and I'm not supposed to be awake yet."

"Can you tell me about your mother?"

"Why do you want to know?"

"I'm interested in everything you have to say."

"Mother came from a middle-class family," I said proudly. "Grandfather made sure she had a good education, which was unusual for a young lady in the late 1800s, but then Grandfather adored her and granted her every wish—until she met Father."

"Was there a problem with your father?"

"Our father was in trade, a salesman for a wood polish company."

"Tell me more," encouraged the voice gently.

"Mother was head over heels in love with Father and would not be dissuaded from seeing him. Mother told us how Grandfather cut them off without a penny when they married, and that's why we've never met him or our maternal grandmother."

"Tell me more about your early years, Kitty."

I sighed. "Mother says Father always drank too much. Even

when I was little he started coming home later and later each evening. I used to watch Mother wringing her hands while she waited for him in the darkness. She was afraid to use up the last of the oil for the lamps, you see, in case Father had spent all his commission on liquor again. Mother knew our father would eat well at the tavern, where the food was simple and relatively cheap, but there wasn't much at home for us. Mother said she knew he really spent most of his wages on beer, while the rest of us lived on bread and hard cheese."

Something about what I had just said struck a chord somewhere else in my mind. I wrinkled my brow, trying to think what it was that I was remembering. Could it be something of my real life?

"Kitty, are you still with me?"

Colin's prompting dragged me back to the distant past, and I nodded, wishing I could dwell more on the hazy memories of the real me, but Kitty was taking over again.

"Did your mother complain about your father's absences?"

"Father's excuse for the need to spend so many hours in the tavern was that it was an ideal place to ply his salesman's trade. Mother says that more often than not he drank so much that he forgot to sell anything at all. There were times when I knew Mother went hungry so that Alice, Arthur, and I could eat, yet I know she still loved Father with all her heart, and he adored her in return."

"Now I want you to remember another important event in your life," breathed the voice.

My mind faltered, torn between two different sets of memories. Hadn't I been offered the chance of a lifetime quite recently? Something I had studied hard and longed for? But Kitty was elbowing herself to the forefront, and my mind went to the day when the minister came to call.

"Tell me what's happening," said the voice.

"It's several days after Father's funeral. Mother seems numb with grief and shock. She's pacing up and down our tiny cottage with her lace handkerchief pressed to her face; she doesn't seem to even hear Alice or Arthur crying. I'm trying to help as best I can. I've brewed tea over the fire and done all the chores, and now Mother is sitting quietly in her armchair. . . . She's weeping."

"Keep talking to me, Kitty; tell me everything you see."

"Mother is still crying. She's asking me what we are to do. She doesn't know what will become of us. . . ."

"It's all right, Kitty. Don't get upset. Just tell me what happens next."

"There's someone at the door; it's the minister who officiated at Father's funeral. The light has faded in the small room—it is late in the evening."

"Where are you now, Kitty?"

"I'm lying on my cot in the adjoining room of our cottage, the place where I grew up. The door is open and I can see everything. Mother has just let the minister in and they are sitting by the fire."

Raising myself up on one elbow, I watched in the dim light from the flickering oil lamp as the portly minister sipped at a small glass of the remnants of Father's best Madeira wine.

"There is a great need in the country for education, my dear," he told Mother gently, patting the slender hands that were clasped around the handkerchief in her lap. "You are an educated woman, and you can put that to good use. I know of a house in a poor district near here that is owned by the church; I believe it would make very suitable premises for a girls' school."

I saw Mother's face focus with interest and felt my own heart skip. I lay still, ears straining to hear his words as the elderly gentleman outlined his plan.

The family, he suggested, should sell whatever the bailiffs left to us when Father's few debts had been cleared. We should use the proceeds to set up the tiny one-room school. Our family would live in the room above the schoolhouse. It would be cramped, but at least it would provide an honest living and a home. Suddenly hope flooded my being and I felt myself smiling with relief.

Education . . . I'd had a good education in my real life, hadn't I? But where? And in what subjects had I excelled? I wished I could remember.

"What are you seeing, Kitty? Are you still Kitty? Talk to me."

There was that voice in my head again, insistent and all-pervasive. I shook my head, trying to remember what it was I was doing and where I was.

"Where are you now?" coaxed the voice.

"I'm inside the schoolhouse," I replied, looking at the familiar surroundings. "We moved here a few weeks ago and opened our doors to six of the local children. They'll be arriving for the day soon so that Mother can teach them their letters and numbers."

"What do you see inside the schoolhouse?"

"Mother has put on her bonnet and is sitting in the only arm-chair, leafing through a dog-eared leather-bound book in preparation for the day's lessons. Oh, no!"

"What's the matter, Kitty?"

"I've just seen that the coal scuttle in nearly empty." I scooped it up, hurried to the back door, and made my way down the damp flagstone path to the coal bunker, which squatted next to the privy, and began shoveling coal into the scuttle. We were fortunate, I knew, to have coal. Our little school was doing well. I glanced up as the door to the privy opened and Arthur scurried out, hitching up his breeches. He grinned at me as he made his way quickly back to the relative warmth of the house. I watched him go with a protective smile, knowing that things could have been very different for us all if the kindly minister hadn't suggested the school.

With the coal scuttle full, I had begun lugging it back toward the house when a voice stopped me in my tracks. Resting the heavy bucket down, I glanced up. There was the dark-haired boy from next door again, grinning at me over the low back wall.

"Hello," he said tentatively. "I'm sorry for scaring you the other day."

I felt myself blush to the roots of my hair, embarrassed because he'd seen me in a less-than-modest pose when I'd been jumping rope with my skirt tucked up into my drawers.

"Have you just moved in?" I asked belatedly remembering my manners and finding my voice.

The boy, who appeared to be about my age, looked down at his feet as if unwilling to admit to it, but eventually he nodded reluctantly. "It won't be for long," he explained hurriedly. "Father had to pay lots of debts when the textile mill we owned closed. We had to leave Lowell, and things are hard at the moment, but he'll soon make good again. Then we'll move back where we belong."

"It's not so bad here," I assured him. "We've not been here long ourselves, but the neighbors seem kind."

"Isn't your mother the schoolmistress?" asked the boy, leaning his arms on the top of the wall.

I nodded proudly. "Mother is very smart."

The boy's eyes widened. He seemed to consider something for a moment. Then he said solemnly, "I'm going to make my fortune, and when I'm very rich, I'm going to build a big house in the country. And then I'm going to come back and marry you."

chapter eighteen

"*I'm going to* count backwards from ten, and I want you to come forward in time with each count," said the voice in my head.

"Go away," I whispered, afraid that Mother would hear it.

"Ten," said the voice firmly, "nine, eight..."

I found myself listening to the voice as it counted down, my mind in a whirl of times and places, until I opened my eyes to find I was lying on the couch in front of the fire with Colin looking down at me, his eyes shining. "You did very well, Kate," he said. "I almost feel like I've been there with you."

"What on earth is happening to me?" I sat up and brushed my hair out of my face. "What is it I'm remembering, Colin?"

"Like I said, I think we're accessing a previous-life experience."

I shook my head, still half disbelieving but unsure what else these memories of Kitty could possibly be. "I just don't know what to think. It's so weird. I didn't really believe it would happen a second time."

"The details you give of Kitty's life are fascinating. Even your voice takes on a different tone when you are her."

"I'm sorry if I don't remember to tell you everything I see and hear." I rubbed my hands together to coax some warmth back into them.

"I think you tell me more than you realize," he said. "When you stop answering my questions directly, you still talk and gesticulate, and I can see from your facial expressions how you're feeling."

"But what does it all mean?" I studied his face earnestly. "Why do I keep remembering being this Kitty person? What relevance does her life then have to who I am now?"

"That," Colin said with barely concealed excitement, "is what we're hoping to find out."

I was subdued throughout dinner. I found myself pondering the workings of my subconscious mind as I pushed the stewed beef, carrots, and dumplings around the plate, my appetite gone.

Finally, Tara, who had been glancing from me to her brother, could contain herself no longer.

"Well?" she demanded. "Are your going to tell us what happened?"

"I am bound by patient confidentiality," Colin proclaimed loftily. "But," he added, raising an eyebrow at me, "if Kate wants to tell you, it's up to her."

"It's not like you believe me anyway," I said despondently, toying with a mound of mashed potato.

"Whether I believe that Colin has accessed a past-life experience or not, I can see that something has upset you," Tara observed. "You hardly touched your food." She leaned forward, fixing her eyes to my face. "It might be good for you to talk about it."

I realized that with Vincent absent, Tara was being far more civil to me; in fact, she seemed genuinely concerned about my well-being. I wondered if we could ever be friends.

I looked up to find all eyes upon me. Even Betty had paused in scooping a spoonful of potatoes into her husband's mouth and was waiting expectantly for my reply. Jadie was the only one who wasn't looking at me; she was watching the lambs nudge each other in the small pen, with a serene expression on her face.

"Nothing much happened." I pushed my plate away. "I remembered being the girl Kitty again, that's all." What I didn't tell them was that as Kitty, I had received a proposal of marriage from a handsome boy who had made my skin tingle with delight.

"And?" prompted Tara. "What did 'Kitty' say or do to make you look like you're only half here?"

"It wasn't what happened so much as how real it seemed," I explained uneasily. "I mean, when I was being Kitty and living her life, I felt like I was really her. If anything, that life seemed more real than this one because at least I knew who my parents were and what had happened to take my life to that point." I looked at their puzzled faces. "This life I'm living now is a mystery; I don't know who I am, where I come from, or how I came to be here."

"Are you saying you'd rather remain in that fantasy world than be here in the real one?" Tara leaned toward me, her elbows on the table.

Fighting back a wave of self-pity, I shrugged, confused. "I'm not sure I know what's real and what isn't anymore."

"A lot has happened to you in the last few days." Colin reached out to pat my hand. "You've obviously suffered some kind of trauma to have buried your recent memories so deeply. Don't be too hard on yourself."

I wondered somewhat uncharitably if Colin was so excited about the unexpected discovery of the Kitty personality that he had put to one side the idea of finding out who I really was. Several times during the hypnotherapy session I'd had fleeting memories of what might have been my own life, but each time Colin had prompted me back on track with the memories of Kitty.

"You just don't want to risk her refusing any more hypnotherapy sessions," Tara accused. "Don't try telling me this isn't the most fascinating thing that's happened in your career."

"Of course it's fascinating," Colin admitted, "but I have Kate's best interests at heart. If she doesn't want to have another treatment, that's her prerogative."

"But?" Tara prompted.

"But I think she needs to see this thing through." Colin sat back in his chair and pressed his fingertips together. "Her subconscious brain wants her to remember those past-life experiences for a reason, and maybe they will help her with the healing process in this lifetime."

"Or maybe you'll make her crazy," Tara said shortly, scraping back her chair and rising to her feet. "By the time someone comes to claim her, she'll be a basket case and won't be good for anything except locking away in a mental institution."

We stared at one another awkwardly until Betty's quavering voice broke the silence. "You wouldn't allow that, would you, Bill? Those places would finish a body off."

"No, no, you silly old woman," Bill said hurriedly. "No one's going to get sent to one of those places, not while I'm still drawing breath." He rubbed the top of her frail arm through her cardigan with the back of his wrist. It was such an intimate gesture that I glanced away, feeling like an intruder.

They were like two damaged halves of a perfect whole, neither one able to function fully without the other. I wondered if I would ever find anyone to be my other half. It also occurred to me that maybe I already had—and a picture of the dark-haired boy surveying me from the wall in Kitty's garden flickered into my mind. Of course, it may have been that I had a meaningful relationship in my real life, I told myself, but had forgotten it along with everything else.

As for Betty, I knew exactly how vulnerable she felt, the fear that came with not knowing what you ought to. She might forget suddenly what she was going to say and, like me, was utterly dependent on those around her.

I must have looked as sick as I felt, because Adam, who until now had been stoically eating, suddenly pushed his plate away and stood up.

"I'm going out to check on the ewes," he announced. "A couple of them looked like they might lamb this evening." He rested his gaze on me. "Would you like to come with me?"

I nodded, grateful for the opportunity to escape. He grabbed his coat from a hook behind the door while I bundled into mine, and he handed me a pair of his grandmother's old Wellington boots. I followed him through the utility room to the back door, and then around the side of the house to the yard at the front. It had stopped snowing at last, but the path was still deep with snow and I had trouble keeping up with the sturdy farmer, who strode purposefully ahead. There was a single light on in the yard, but as soon as Adam opened the barn doors, yellow light spilled out onto the newly settled snow.

"How long will the generator keep working?" I asked as we slipped inside and he closed the door behind us.

"We get about five hours out of it at a time." He walked slowly round the pens, checking the ewes. "I filled it with a fresh tank of gasoline and turned it on just before dusk, so it'll have enough juice to last the evening." He glanced at his watch. "It has to be shut down and allowed to cool before I can refill it, so we can't use it again until tomorrow once it conks out. But we've got a few more hours if we're lucky."

I followed him, captivated by the sight of tiny lambs lying against their mothers' flanks. Some of the ewes appeared to have had twins. Several of the mothers looked huge and round, as if they were going to pop at any minute. I watched one of the lambs feeding, nudging its mother's udder much as the orphaned lambs had pushed demandingly at their feeding bottles.

"When will the orphaned lambs need their next feed?" I asked.

"Gran's probably doing it right now," Adam said. "Gramps will remind her it's time, and she knows what to do. I'm sure Jadie will be helping if Tara hasn't packed her off to bed."

"Is there a bedroom warm enough for her?" I asked as he stopped by a pen and pulled open the metal partition to slip inside. "She starts to cough if the air is cold."

"She's going to sleep on a pullout bed in the kitchen," he said as he kneeled beside a large ewe who was lying on her side, her eyes bulging. "The stove stays on night and day and gives off plenty of warmth."

"It's lucky her asthma isn't affected by the lambs if she's going to be sleeping with them," I observed.

"I tried to tell Tara that she should get Jadie tested," he said, peering at the ewe's rear end as he spoke. "Just because Amber had asthma doesn't mean Jadie has to be the same. Tara is overly protective of her."

I watched as he scrubbed his hands in a bucket of disinfectant.

"You seem to know Tara quite well," I ventured, fascinated to see that he'd discovered two little cloven hoofs protruding from the ewe's birth canal. "Is it stuck?"

"It looks like she's been in labor for a while," Adam murmured, giving the hoofs a gentle tug. "Yes. Tara, Colin, and I spent most of our school vacations together. My mother moved away, and I went to school in the city but I came back here during summer vacations to help out on the farm. Our families have lived here all our lives; we're not newcomers like Vincent."

"Can I help?" I asked.

"Yes, come on in. You can keep her calm while I see if I can turn this little fellow around; its head is back, and when she strains she's strangling him."

I pulled the partition apart and slid into the pen, squatting down in the straw near the ewe's head while Adam worked on the lamb, easing it back inside the ewe and maneuvering it so the lamb's head came forward over its front legs. It took some time, as the ewe strained every so often, ruining all his hard work. Adam was sweating by the time he had the lamb turned to the right position.

"Good girl," I encouraged the ewe as she panted and heaved.

"Come on, you can push now." The ewe gave one final heave as Adam simultaneously pulled at the lamb's feet, and I watched, captivated, as a pair of tiny hoofs and a head appeared. The lamb slid into the world with a sudden rush and lay steaming in the straw while the mother peered around to see what she had produced.

"It's not breathing," Adam said. He picked up a handful of straw and rubbed the lamb's wet wool vigorously. "Come on, little one," he encouraged.

We waited a moment or two, and then I watched, baffled, as he suddenly picked the lamb up by its back legs, got to his feet, and swung the tiny creature around in a wide arc.

"What on earth are you doing?" I gasped.

Adam lay the lamb down, and it gave a sudden heave, sucking in a lungful of air. "Does the trick most times," he said with a grin. "Makes the blood rush to all its organs." He pushed the lamb up toward its mother's head, and we watched as the ewe struggled to her knees, nudging the baby up onto its trembling legs with her head. We sat for a moment in the damp straw watching mother and baby bonding as she washed him with her pink tongue, making him stagger about. Eventually the ewe found the strength to get properly to her feet, and the baby made its way under her flank, latching on to the swollen udder and taking its first feed.

"Gets me every time," Adam said quietly as we watched the pair together. "No matter how many times I witness a birth, it's always a little miracle."

I stayed with Adam while he completed his rounds, checking the other ewes and newborn lambs, and we had only just made it across the yard when the lights snapped off in the barn behind. I gave a quick gasp and went to grab his arm in the sudden blackness, but stopped myself at the last second, letting my hand drop to my side.

"Don't worry, I've got a flashlight," he said, clicking it on and swinging the beam on the ground before us, illuminating our way back to the door and in through the utility room. The kitchen was dark, but I could just make out a narrow camp bed in front of the stove, and Jadie's sleeping form.

"I don't know where the time went," I whispered. "Thank you for taking me with you."

"I'll show you to the room you're going to share with Tara," he said. "Follow me."

Adam guided me through the sleeping house, up the stairs I'd seen earlier, and along a sloping corridor to a door that was slightly ajar. He played the flashlight beam along the nearest of two beds. "Looks like Tara's left you the one nearest the door."

Pausing on the threshold, I stared up into his gentle brown

eyes and allowed my gaze to linger over his features. Something inside me stirred. Where had I seen that look before? I felt an incredible rush of warmth toward him. He had made my troubles vanish for a while, and I was grateful beyond words. We stood for a moment, neither of us, I felt, wanting the amazing evening to end, but then he handed me the flashlight and turned away.

"Good night," I whispered as the darkness folded in behind him.

"Good night, Kate."

chapter nineteen

𝒥 *awoke in* the morning to find myself snuggled under a huge down-filled duvet that smelled vaguely of mothballs. I was still in all my clothes. It had been too cold to do anything but take off my coat and dive straight between the covers, and now I lay listening to the stirrings of the old farmhouse, wondering what the new day held.

The bed next to mine was empty. I could hear the clank of dishes in the kitchen below and the murmur of voices, so I braced myself to slide my feet out onto the cold floor and snatch up the coat, which I pulled on as I made my way along the hallway.

The kitchen was a hive of industry. The pine table was laid with seven settings and was groaning under an enormous pile of toast; earthenware dishes full of butter, marmalade, and honey; the big brown teapot, a milk jug, and a sugar bowl; a bowl of freshly boiled eggs; and several generous bowls of porridge. Bill was bent over one of the porridge bowls, with a spoon fixed precariously in his gnarled and bent fingers.

Colin, sitting across from the old man, was eating his porridge with gusto, while Tara was mixing something for Jadie. I realized that she was preparing the lambs' powdered milk. She looked up as I appeared and gave me a smile. "Yeah, I know," she said. "But her asthma seems fine, so I thought, What the heck."

"Are you going to feed one of them?" I asked, pleased that she and Jadie were getting along again. It seemed to me that Tara spent so much time taking care of her charge's health that she missed out on spending quality time with her.

"No, you and Jadie can do it," she said with a shudder. "I'm not fond of animals, as a rule." She handed one bottle to Jadie and the other to me, and we moved the crates away so Jadie and I could sit with the lambs and feed them.

It didn't take long for the bottles to be emptied, and we spent a couple of minutes cuddling the babes and fussing over them before Tara called Jadie for her breakfast. Jadie ran off to wash her hands while I put the crates back into position, and I was about to follow her when I felt something soft and furry rubbing itself around my ankles. Looking down at the tabby cat, I realized that she obviously felt some attachment to me. I picked her up and stroked her, tickling her under the chin. She stretched out her neck, closed her eyes, and purred.

"Who am I?" I asked her softly. "Oh, if only you could talk."

After washing my own hands, I sat at the table and accepted a bowl of porridge from Betty. Bill was still struggling with his. Large globs of porridge spattered the table between him and the bowl, and I could see why Betty had helped him the night before.

"Would you like a hand, or are you okay?" I asked tentatively. I wasn't sure if pride would get in the way of his asking for help.

"I'd never say no to the attentions of a pretty young woman," he said with a grin. "If you could just put this spoon in my hand properly I'll persevere until Betty has a moment."

I took the spoon and wiped the sticky handle on a paper towel before inserting it between his fingers again. "Is that better?" I asked.

He gave an experimental swoop toward the bowl, and I sighed with relief as the spoon came up filled with porridge.

Tara pushed a mug of tea toward me, and I held it to my lips. "Where's Adam?" I asked, looking around.

"Oh, he's been up for hours," Tara said. "He was off to check on the animals when I came down to do Jadie's physical therapy."

A croaky sob suddenly erupted from the direction of the stove, and we glanced over to where Betty was wiping her eyes with a dish towel.

"What's the matter, Betty love?" Bill asked, pausing in his scooping. "Come and sit down here and have some food."

"I forgot," Betty said as she came to sit next to her husband.

"You haven't forgotten anything. You've made everyone breakfast; you've done a great job," he said softly.

"I forgot where I was, just for a minute," she said, sniffling. "I couldn't remember where I was or what I was supposed to be doing. I felt so . . . lonely suddenly."

"You know I'll always tell you what to do, you silly old woman," Bill said affectionately. "So have a nice cup of tea and you'll feel much better."

"Here," I passed Betty a cup of tea, put my arm around her bony shoulders, and gave her a brief hug. "I know exactly how you feel. It's that feeling of floundering, when you forget something, isn't it, of not having the comfort of memories to keep you on track?"

Betty nodded and leaned into her husband. "Sometimes I look up and all I see is a blank wall in front of me. I can't remember who I am or where I belong."

I watched as Bill gave her hair a light kiss. This time it wasn't the image of the blue-eyed boy in the school yard that flashed into my mind, but memories of being carried through the freezing snow in a pair of strong, protective arms. I wondered how Vincent was coping alone in his cold dark house, and felt guilty that I'd hardly thought about him since arriving at the Jenkinses' farm.

"I wonder how Vincent is doing," Tara said, echoing my thoughts. "He never was much for eating out of cans."

"I wish Daddy could see me feed the lambs," Jadie said through a mouthful of egg. "I wish we lived on a farm and we could have lambs of our own, and a cat, and I could sleep in the kitchen with them all the time. Living on a farm is so much fun."

"Don't talk with your mouth full, Jadie," Tara said automatically. She had a faraway stare, her mind evidently miles away. I thought I knew exactly where it was.

"It's not snowing this morning," I said. "Maybe the roads will soon be clear and we can go home."

Tara narrowed her eyes at me, and I knew she was thinking about my use of the word "home." I was saved further embarrassment by Colin.

"Would you like another hypnotherapy session this morning, Kate?" he asked, laying down his spoon and looking across at me. "I think we'll be here for a bit longer, so we may as well make good use of the time."

I hesitated. Where was the harm in it? And Colin was right—at the very least it helped pass the time. "All right, then, yes." I turned to Colin. "As long as you're okay with the fact that I can't pay you unless you get me to remember who I am and where I keep my purse and credit cards."

Colin smiled at the joke, but I could see he was anxious to start.

"We haven't yet come across any instances in Kitty's early life that are traumatic enough to explain why your subconscious mind keeps returning there," he mused. "The father's death made a huge impact on her life, of course, but she seems to be handling the changes to her lifestyle with fortitude." He rubbed his hand thoughtfully over his chin. "So what we need to find out is what else, or *who* else, factored in Kitty's life so dramatically that her previous life aura has remained in your subconscious mind so powerfully that, for the moment at least, it has taken precedence over your present psyche."

"It's probably just that she had a nasty bang on the head and she's gone nuts." Tara observed. She looked up as Colin made a snorting noise. "What?"

"I thought you wanted Kate to remember who she was," Colin reminded her.

"Yeah, but she's got to remember the right stuff, doesn't she? I don't suppose this Kitty character is going to know where Kate's credit cards are, is she?"

"Come on," Colin said, not deigning to reply to his sister. He held out his hand to me as I scooped the last mouthful of porridge into my mouth and pushed the bowl away.

"Don't go." Jadie looked up from where she was finishing coloring a picture. I thought she looked a bit peaky and felt a wave of anxiety wash over me, which intensified with her next words. "I've got a tummy ache."

Tara was immediately attentive. The child was paling visibly. "Do you feel sick?" She pressed a hand to Jadie's brow and frowned.

"I want to go to the bathroom."

"Okay, come on." Tara tried to take her hand, but Jadie shook her off.

"No, I want Kate."

Tara's face darkened, and I took a quick breath, unsure what to do. "You'd better go with Tara," I said to Jadie. "If you're not feeling well, it might be better for her to take you.

Jadie eased herself from her chair carefully but instead of heading to the downstairs toilet, she came and rested her head against my arm, gazing up at me with those deep blue eyes of hers. "I don't want you to go away." There was a catch in her voice.

I wrapped my arms around her and hugged her close. "I'm not going away just yet, Jadie, only to the other room with Colin. You go with Tara, and I'll be back before you know it." I learned down to plant a kiss on her sweaty little forehead, and when I ran my tongue over my lips a moment later, I found they were surprisingly salty.

Tara was watching me closely, and the scowl on her face lifted very slightly as she realized what had happened. "It's the CF," she told me, obviously glad to display her superior knowledge—to put me firmly back in my place as interloper and outsider. "It makes her skin salty like that."

Jadie was pouting. "I've still got a tummy ache."

"Come on." Tara took her firmly by the hand, and I watched as the two of them left the room.

I waited until Jadie returned a few minutes later, looking a lot better, before accompanying Colin to the parlor.

There was already a fire burning in the grate, and the duvet lying folded on the couch. I found my mind drifting from Jadie to Adam and wondering if he had lit this fire for us before he'd gone out. I wrapped myself loosely in the duvet even though it was warm in the room. Closing my eyes, I forced myself to drag my mind away from Adam while Colin ran through the relaxation techniques.

It didn't seem to take any time at all to slip into a relaxed state. I could still hear Colin talking to me, but his voice seemed faint and so very far away.

Perhaps it was because I wanted to go—wanted to see Kitty again—but it seemed that no sooner had I closed my eyes than I was opening them again in a different time and place.

"Tell me who you are," Colin asked gently.

"I'm Kitty."

"Do you know what year it is?"

"It's 1900."

"So, how old are you now, Kitty?"

"I'm thirteen years old, but I'll be fourteen in December."

"Have you seen anything more of the boy next door?"

"Yes. His name is Garrett," I replied dreamily. "I have seen him several times in the last few months."

"What have you learned about him?"

"He goes to a school for boys a little way from here. He told me that despite their fall in circumstances, his parents have made huge sacrifices to ensure he receives a good education. He is their only child."

"What do you feel when you see him?"

I felt myself blush. "At first I was nervous and a bit tongue-tied, but now I feel more at ease when he appears. I think his parents are cold and very reserved people. They think they're better than all the people who live around here, so they don't socialize with us."

"Are you still allowed time to play in the mornings?"

I shook my head. "I'm getting a bit old to play with my jump rope now. Mostly I just help Mother in the schoolroom."

"Surely you get some time to yourself?"

"School will be finishing for a few weeks in the summer, and Alice, Arthur, and I will be going to stay with relatives while

Mother spring-cleans the schoolroom. They are the only members of the family who still speak to Mother after she disobeyed my grandfather and married our father. Mother has written to them and they have promised to make us welcome at their home on the coast."

"Will you have a chance to say goodbye to Garrett before you go?"

My eyes filled with tears and I shook my head. "I don't know."

"Move on now to the day of your departure. Tell me what is happening."

"The wagon driver is here to take us, but I can't see Garrett. I was hoping to see him once more before we leave."

"How do you feel now that the driver is here?"

"I am so excited to be going!" Even as I said it, my mind went to another place, another goodbye. My parents were waving me off at a front door. I was no longer standing with Alice and Arthur outside our house with our belongings packed into a brown paper parcel tied with string, but outside a modern detached house with a car parked in the paved driveway behind me. The expressions on the man's and woman's faces were a mixture of pride and anxiety, and I turned to give them a reassuring smile as I walked toward the car.

"Keep talking to me, Kitty."

I shook my mind reluctantly back to Kitty's life. "The driver is waiting with the old horse while we kiss our mother goodbye. She smells of lavender and powder."

I lapsed into thought, watching as Alice stood on tiptoe to throw her arms around our mother's waist. There was another girl standing quietly in the shadows, and she was waving at me. I had the oddest feeling she was my sister—but not Alice. I blinked as Mother gave Alice and Arthur a quick hug, and when I peered into the shadow by the gate, the girl from that other life had gone. Then I was pushing the children up into the back of the wagon, taking care to place the brown paper parcel on the floor at Arthur's feet. As I climbed up behind them, I risked a quick glance back at the row of houses, still hoping to catch a glimpse of the strangely familiar girl, and of Garrett, of course. But to my great disappointment neither of them was anywhere in sight.

"Tell me about your journey, Kitty."

A journey. I had made a journey recently, hadn't I? Wrinkling my brow, I tried to remember what the journey had been for. Where had I been going? Why had I been traveling so far from home?

Scrunching my eyes tightly, I tried to picture where I had come from, but all I could feel were the cart's wheels lurching over the uneven ground. "The wagon is bumpy and uncomfortable. The wooden wheels lurch and sway at every rut in the road. Arthur is whimpering for Mother, and I have pulled him onto my lap to give his bare legs in his short breeches a rest from the chafing of the rough wooden seat."

"Are you happy, Kitty?"

I pondered the question. Despite the discomfort, I was excited to be going away. I found myself nodding.

"Are you nearly at your destination?"

"Oh, yes. Oh, look! I can see a glittering expanse of gray green that must be the sea far in the distance. It is the most wonderful sight in the world! And I can actually smell the sea, all salty and fresh on the breeze."

"Let's skip forward a few minutes. You are now at your destination. Tell me what is happening."

"We have pulled up outside a pretty rose-trellised cottage. There is someone coming out to greet us, a servant, I think."

I handed down the still sleepy Arthur while Alice scrambled from the wagon. Reaching back for the luggage parcel, I noticed the servant passing the driver some coins. He doffed his cap by way of acknowledgment before geeing up the tired horse. We were left standing in the dusty lane with the brown paper package at my feet as horse and wagon retreated into the distance, the driver still hunched on his bench, as silent now that he'd left us as he had been throughout most of the journey.

"Come along in now," the servant said. "The mistress is waiting to meet you."

We dusty children followed the servant through the low wooden front door into a dark hallway. Removing my bonnet, I patted at some escaping tendrils of hair. I paused until my eyes had accustomed themselves to the gloom after the brightness of the day outside, then stared at wood-paneled walls lined with delicate watercolor paintings in ornate gilt frames. A magnificent staircase swept upward, and I ran a hand along the base of the beautiful wooden handrail, marveling at the feel of the polished wood, smooth and warm to the touch; it sent shivers right through me. One day, I thought, I would live in a house like this, with wood paneling and a staircase that turned halfway up. I would be the lady of the house, and I would have a son of my own, one who I hoped would look just like Garrett.

chapter twenty

"*I am going to* count backward from ten, and then you will wake up calm and refreshed." The voice echoed in my head.

I listened to the counting, but I shook my head, resisting it. I didn't want to leave this place, not ever, because I was happy here in the house by the sea, and I had a feeling deep within me that this was the environment in which I truly belonged.

"Kate, you are now to come back with me; you are feeling calm and refreshed. Open your eyes."

"No, I like being near the sea. I want to stay here."

But I hadn't wanted to stay there, had I? Something had happened and I had packed everything up to begin a new life. There was something I had to find out, a mystery to unravel. . . .

"I am going to count again, and this time you are going to travel forward through time until you are here with me. Ten, nine, eight . . ."

I shook my head firmly and squeezed my eyes tightly shut. "No, I don't want to leave; go away!"

I focused all my energy on staying where I was, and the voice in my head grew gradually fainter and farther away.

The servant, Tilly, was turning at the top of the landing, and I waited while she threw open one of the white-painted bedroom doors.

The room looked cozy, with its sloping ceiling and big quilted bed, but I went straight to the window and looked out over the garden to the low hills, and in the distance, beyond the cliff top, was the sea, and I turned with shining eyes to my sister and brother.

"I wonder if Aunt Maude will allow us to go to the beach."

"All in good time." Tilly was standing in the doorway. "You've got the whole summer to explore. Now wash that travel grime off your faces and get yourselves downstairs to the garden for lunch. Your aunt doesn't like to be kept waiting."

We ate ravenously, our breakfast of bread and cheese a long-distant memory. Aunt Maude poured tea into delicate china cups atop a white-clothed table perched on the back lawn. I watched Arthur anxiously in case he spilled anything on the gleaming table linen. Our uncle George joined us in the garden, an amiable fellow with a plump rosy face. I watched him carefully, mindful of the times Father had come home with red cheeks after a day of drinking. But Uncle George appeared quite sober and entirely amenable, sitting in the shade in his jacket and embroidered vest, with a cravat tied neatly at his ample neck.

After introductions had been made to Uncle George, he and Aunt Maude asked after Mother's health. I sipped at the weak tea and assured them that Mother was quite well, deciding not to mention our cramped rooms above the schoolhouse, or how hard Mother had to work. Formalities completed, Uncle George went on to offer us the use of his library.

"Can't speak too highly of the importance of a good education," he mumbled between mouthfuls of scone, reaching out to pat Alice's knee. "Even you girls should know how to read and write? No good having recipe books if a wife can't read 'em, eh, my dear?"

"No indeed." Our aunt picked up the teapot. "More tea, dear?"

We went to bed early, exhausted by the journey. After wriggling and pushing, we all found sleeping space in the big bed, and snuggled under the coverlet, luxuriating in the amazing softness of the mattress beneath us.

Aunt Maude had tried putting Arthur in a separate tiny broom cupboard of a bedroom, but as soon as Tilly had gone downstairs, he'd crept into bed with Alice and me, and he slept curled up between us as he'd done for all of his short life.

Tilly woke us early the next morning and returned carrying our freshly laundered pinafores and Arthur's shirt and breeches, which she had peeled off us at bedtime the night before. "They're still a bit damp," she said as she laid them out on the dresser. "The fire in the kitchen range died down before they was properly dry, but I ran the flatiron over them this morning once I'd gotten it nice and hot again."

"Thank you, Tilly." I was trying to squash Arthur's head back under the coverlet so she wouldn't see that he wasn't in his own room. "It's very kind of you."

"Come down to the kitchen when you're dressed, then." She threw open the heavy curtains, and sunlight streamed into the room. "I've made porridge for you all." She turned with a wink as she went out the door. "And bring that squirming puppy you've got under the coverlet down with you."

As soon as breakfast was over, we ran outside to explore the garden. A cobbled path ran from the back door of the cottage between manicured lawns edged by flower beds crammed full of phlox, lupines, poppies, and other bright summer flowers.

We followed the path to a redbrick-walled vegetable garden where an archway led to its mysterious interior. Just outside the arch there was a wooden seat against the wall, surrounded by tall broad-leaved hostas and clumps of sweet-smelling lavender.

After the bareness of the narrow backyard at home, this seemed like a Garden of Eden. I sat on the bench and closed my eyes, inhaling the scents of herbs and flowers; it was heavenly.

"Kate . . . Kate!"

Someone was patting at my cheeks, sharp little slaps that made me wrinkle my brow, and I reached out to push the hand away. "Stop it, Arthur!"

"Kate, I want you to listen to me. Three, two, one; Kate, open your eyes."

I struggled to obey, and when eventually my lids peeled open, I found that it wasn't my little brother pestering me but someone else. I blinked at him, disoriented.

"Where am I?"

Colin was staring anxiously at me. He was holding my wrist, feeling for a pulse.

"Are you all right?"

With my other hand I gripped Colin tightly, comprehension returning, and with it, fear. "I'm so sorry. Kitty didn't want me to come back."

Colin's hand was damp under mine, but he was quickly regaining his composure. "Come on, sit up."

"If it's true that a hypnotist can't make someone do anything they don't want to," I whispered as I struggled to sit up, "what would have happened if I'd continued to disobey your instructions?"

I was shaking under the duvet, frightened by the hold Kitty had had over me. It seemed that she was a more determined character than I, and though I was intrigued by her life, I had no desire to live it permanently. I needed Colin to confirm that he could bring me back no matter what.

"Hypnosis is all about tapping into the subconscious mind using deep relaxation, but it's still your own mind. The subject is ultimately in control over what he or she does, but the mind has never in my experience refused to be brought out of the hypnotic trance."

"Could Kitty keep me from coming back?" I asked anxiously.

"Only if *you* don't want to come back, I think." He blew out a long breath. "As long as you want to return, you'll be able to. Don't forget that Kitty is only a hidden memory; *you* are the real Kate, living here and now."

"I'm so cold," I murmured, not entirely convinced. "I can't seem to warm up."

"You've had a scare," he explained. He gave my upper arms a brief squeeze. "You'll be okay. Don't worry."

It seemed to me that he was still in a state of shock himself after finding he hadn't been completely in control of the situation. What would he have done if I'd refused to come back the second time he'd tried to wake me? But his embrace was firm and reassuring as I leaned against him, drawing strength from his living, breathing body.

"It's strange to think you've seen right inside my head." The mental connection between us had seemed far more intimate than this close physical contact.

"Oh, but you're still holding out on me, big-time," he said. "There are a few more layers of your subconscious to be peeled back yet. We haven't even begun to find the real Kate, have we? Are you warming up a bit now?" he asked before I could reply.

I nodded, and at that moment the door opened and Adam entered, carrying a pile of logs in his arms. He stopped dead at the sight of the two of us sitting on the couch in a tight embrace.

"I'm sorry to interrupt."

Colin eased himself away from me and shook his head. "You're not interrupting. We'd just finished."

"I thought you might be cold." Adam was looking at me with an odd expression in his eyes. "I stepped into the house to get something and thought I'd check on the fire."

"Thank you. I was cold," I said. "Colin has been trying to warm me up a bit."

"So I saw," he replied drily.

I watched as Adam bent and threw a couple of medium-size logs onto the fire, giving the resulting blaze a prod with the poker so that the fire crackled and sparks flew up the chimney. The gesture seemed familiar, and I wrinkled my brow, trying to remember where I'd seen that done very recently. It had been Tara, of course, stoking the fire in Vincent's house....Or was it something I was used to doing myself, one of Kitty's daily chores in the old schoolhouse?

When the fire was blazing to his satisfaction. Adam straightened up. "I thought you might like to know that Vincent has arrived. He's in the kitchen with Tara."

"He must have worked hard, to walk through all this snow to get here," I said, confused. "I thought he was going to stay home and keep his house from freezing up?"

"There are obviously people here he was missing."

I felt myself blush under Adam's scrutiny; he meant Jadie, of course. I was just an outsider, rescued from a blizzard; Vincent wouldn't have come to see me.

Adam walked out into the hall, and I turned to find Colin staring after him.

"How insightful," Colin murmured as the door closed behind Adam. "He's not quite the he-man farmer he purports to be at all, is he?"

* * *

I found Vincent *sitting* in the kitchen with a mug of tea in his hands, watching his daughter playing with the lambs. She had climbed over the crates and was sitting in the straw with one of the lambs on her lap, where she was patiently trying to tie a doll's knitted hat onto its head.

"Hi." I pulled out a chair next to him at the long table. "I thought you were home, keeping your house from freezing?"

"It's not going to freeze over in a couple of hours. I've left a low fire burning and put the guard around the grate." He turned his blue eyes toward me. "How are you all getting along?"

"We're fine," Tara chipped in from where she was chopping vegetables at the end of the table. "Jadie hasn't been coughing too much."

"She looks . . . relaxed," he observed, glancing toward Jadie again and then returning his gaze to me. "I haven't seen her as happy as this for ages."

"You're not normally around to see much of her at all," Tara reminded him.

Vincent ignored her. "You're good for her," he said to me. "She's been different since you arrived—and I don't just mean her talking again."

"It's mostly been Tara," I said hastily. "She works so hard keeping Jadie healthy. If it wasn't for her, making sure Jadie's airways are clear and that she eats enough, Jadie might not be well enough to play like this."

"Tara wouldn't have let her come anywhere near those animals." He took a sip of his tea without taking his eyes off me.

"She was just worried they'd set off Jadie's asthma," I pointed out. I turned to include Tara in the conversation. "You've been making up the lambs' feed for her, haven't you?"

Tara nodded, but I could see she had heard and been hurt by his comments. She continued to chop the vegetables, but the sound of the knife on the chopping board was getting louder and more erratic.

Even Betty had paused in her peeling of a pile of potatoes as Tara's knife smacked noisily onto the chopping board, and I noticed Bill look up from the farming magazine that lay open on his lap.

"I want you to come home with me." Vincent appeared to be the only one not to notice the escalating noise.

"But surely it won't be warm enough for Jadie there?"

"I'm not talking about Jadie. She can stay here in the warm for a couple more days—if the Jenkinses don't mind, of course. And Tara will need to stay here to look after her. I'm talking about you."

"You want *me* to go back with you?"

Vincent placed his mug on the table and reached out his hands to take mine. "I need to talk to you about something," he said. "I should never have let you come over here with the others."

"Why not?" I pulled my hands away and contemplated him suspiciously.

Vincent glanced toward Tara and shook his head. "You're still not well, and I feel you're my responsibility. I'd just be more comfortable with you back at the house. It all happened in a bit of a rush, Adam saying Jadie could come, and then of course Tara had to be here to look after her, and I thought it would be warmer for you as well . . ."

"It is warmer," I agreed.

He glanced at Tara again and lowered his voice. "Has Colin been trying to put you under hypnosis again while you've been here?"

"Why?"

"I just wondered if it was doing any good, that's all."

What was he afraid of? Was he really feeling responsible for me—or was he more worried about something I might remember during the sessions with Colin?

When I didn't respond to his question, Vincent picked up his mug, leaned back in his chair with his drink held aloft, and took another sip of the tea. "Maria invited me over to her place again last night."

"I'll bet she did," Tara growled from the other end of the table, "knowing you were there on your own."

"She was just being neighborly," Vincent said shortly. "She thought we could conserve candles and food by spending the evening together."

Tara snorted and attacked the vegetables afresh.

"We talked about Kate, mostly," he continued. He looked pointedly at me as if there was something else he wanted to say but had thought better of it.

"Was it Maria's idea that you should come and get me?"

"Sort of, I suppose." He lowered his voice so that I had to lean forward to catch his next words. "Maria and I both think you would be better off back at the house with me."

"Don't you think Maria's imagination might be running a bit wild, what with being snowed in, the electricity off, and everything?" I suggested carefully, thinking of the woman's untold ghost stories and her veiled accusations about Vincent's wife. "Maria seems a bit high-strung."

"It's more than that," he insisted, fixing me with his mesmerizing blue eyes. The urgency I read in his expression made me shiver. "You'd be better off at my place. Kate, I'm asking you to trust me on this."

chapter twenty-one

I shivered under Vincent's stare. Why did he want me to go back with him so urgently?

"Well, what do you say?" Vincent prompted. "Will you come back with me?"

I looked around the kitchen with the big wood stove warming the room, Jadie playing in the corner, Betty and Bill watching quietly, and Tara throwing me increasingly hostile looks. I wanted to stay here, but was I in any position to dig my heels in? Vincent had saved me from probable death and I felt like I owed him.

"I . . . I don't know," I muttered. "It is comfortable here."

"*Please* say you'll come back." He put his hand over mine.

"I don't want to get involved with Maria," I said. "I've got enough of my own problems." Not to mention questions that needed addressing about my past, I thought darkly.

"What's going on?" Colin said, appearing suddenly in the doorway and obviously sensing the tension in the room.

"I've come to take Kate back with me." Vincent's voice was firm.

"What about Jadie and Tara?" Colin asked, seating himself at the table.

"Just Kate," Vincent said.

"Can I ask why?"

"Maria doesn't like being quite so cut off from everyone after all," Vincent explained smoothly. "There are some strange things happening in that house and she seems to think having Kate back there will make everything all right."

Colin looked searchingly at me. "Do you want to go?"

"I'd rather stay here." I avoided Vincent's eyes. "Despite everything, I think I should continue with the hypnotherapy sessions."

"You're not still pressing that hypnosis thing on her, are you?" Vincent demanded of Colin. "She's confused enough at the moment without you interfering."

"You think dragging her back to freeze at your place would be better for her?" Colin asked.

"You're all mad, if you ask me," Tara chimed in. "She'd be better off in a hospital getting proper help."

My stomach lurched at the thought. We were cut off by the weather from the police, doctors, and social workers, but as soon as the roads were clear, I knew that things might be very different. Although part of me was desperate to know who I really was, I was also fearful to leave this place in which I'd found myself cocooned. The three of them were staring at me, waiting for a decision.

"Excuse me." I scraped back my chair on the tiled floor. "I need time to think." I grabbed the borrowed coat and hurried past them all to the back door, where I slipped my feet into the boots, opened the door, and escaped onto the snowy path beside the house. I leaned my back against the closed door. Then, slipping and sliding along the frozen snow, I made my way to the yard and stood gulping deep icy breaths of fresh air. I could smell the animals and hear them moving around in the barn, so normal and real. They didn't have to worry about who they were, where they'd come from, or what might happen to them next.

The barn door opened and Adam stepped out into the yard. He stopped midstride when he saw me, and a strange expression crossed his face—not quite a frown, not really a smile, but rather a look of recognition. I thought as I studied him that he really was good-looking under the hideous wool hat, his complexion tanned from a life spent outdoors. He held a small sack in one hand, which I found myself staring at, wondering what was in it. He seemed to realize I was looking at it, because he lowered the sack down and positioned it slightly behind one leg.

"What is it?" I moved closer to him and looked down pointedly at the bag.

"Just a young 'un that didn't make it," he said.

"A lamb?"

" 'Fraid so. There are always one or two casualties."

"What are you going to do with it?"

"Put it in the machinery shed until the thaw. Then I'll either bury it or burn it."

His voice sounded matter-of-fact and in control, but I could sense a sadness in him.

I walked along with him to a long shed where a Land Rover and an assortment of farm machinery and implements were parked, partly sheltered from the freezing temperatures. There was a raised tool bench along one of the only two solid walls, and he rested the sack where a couple of others were already stacked. Adam's dog, Lad, came out of nowhere and leaned his head against his master's knee.

"What happened to it?" I asked.

"Stillborn."

"Is the ewe all right?"

"Yes, she'll make a full recovery."

"I'm sorry," I said quietly.

"These things happen."

We stood for a few moments looking at the sacks, not knowing what to say next. I felt an urge to reach out and touch him, to tell him I understood and that he didn't have to hide his emotions and pretend he wasn't sad at the loss of that little life.

"Vincent wants me to go back to his house with him," I said instead.

Adam's head jerked around. "When?"

"As soon as possible."

"Did he say why?"

"He said something about feeling responsible for me." I said it lightly, but my heart felt unaccountably heavy.

"Do you want to go?" Adam's voice was soft. He searched my face with his deep brown eyes.

"Not really . . . I don't know. Maybe."

"You haven't even been here a whole day." He sighed. "You're welcome to stay here, you know. Gramps likes you—you're good with him. He can be a prickly old devil, very proud, but he lets you help him for some reason."

"You're amazingly good with both of them." I thrust my hands deep into my pockets. "How come you manage this place all on your own and look after your grandparents at the same time? Most people would have put either Bill or Betty in a home by now."

"I couldn't run this place without them." He turned to walk over to the hay barn, and I unglued my feet to follow. He opened the door, hoisted a bale onto his shoulder, and then set off with it held high so that I had no choice but to trot along beside him.

"Where are your parents? Didn't they want to run the farm?"

Adam strode across the yard, and I followed him through what I realized was the main entrance to the farmyard. We came to a small barbed-wire-fenced field that nestled up against the back of the lambing barn. The snow had been cleared here too, but the air was bitingly cold. There were about twenty ewes in the field, all with one or two lambs, and they huddled near the wooden planking at the back wall of the barn, where there was a feeding trough and a scattering of hay. Adam opened the field's five-bar gate with his free hand and deposited the bale on the ground before rummaging in his coat pocket for a penknife. After cutting the twine that held the bale together, he shook the hay out and retreated behind the gate with me to watch as the ewes crowded around to munch hay while their lambs meandered and frisked close by.

"My grandparents had three children, two girls and a younger boy." He was leaning on the top bar of the gate with an air of contentment, despite the biting cold wind that whistled around our heads. "Both girls eventually married and moved to the city with their husbands, and the boy, Jim, grew up to hate the farm and decided to become a mechanic. I'm the oldest son of the elder daughter, Lizzy. I spent most of my summer vacations here learning how to run the farm with my grandfather; I love the place, always have. I went to college and got a degree in agriculture and business management. When Gramps's arthritis got so bad he couldn't run the place alone, he turned the farm over to me. I'm the legal owner now. Uncle Jim comes and services the farm machinery for me, and I have two farmworkers who normally come up daily from the village to work. Gran looks after Gramps and does the cooking and cleaning just like she always has, and Gramps reminds her of what she has to do and when to do it. It sounds like a harsh life, but it's all they ever wanted; it's what they know."

"And life goes on," I said quietly.

He turned away from the sheep and looked at me long and hard. "The present is what counts. I'm not saying we shouldn't take the past and future into account, but, if you ask me, Vincent has been running away from a past he can't live with. The past haunts him and the future frightens him. And then there's Colin, who has you raking over the past because that's what he does. Only you can decide what it is you really want."

I stared back at him in surprise. For someone I'd had down as the strong silent type, he certainly knew more about what was going on in his neighbors' heads than I'd given him credit for. The fact that he'd gone to college and ended up with his grandfather's farm belied my first impressions of him as a steady unassuming farmer. His world was hard but ordered, and despite the day-to-day toil and grind, the cold and the physically demanding work, it seemed he was doing what he loved best. He was obviously smart, and he appeared to have more insight and a clearer knowledge of what the world was about than the rest of us put together.

"So you're saying I should choose between dwelling on the past, looking to the future, or being content with the present?"

He shook his head. "It's not so much a choice. We can't deny that they're all connected. Everything is a circle, like the changing of the seasons. If I don't cut enough hay in the summer, the stock starves the next winter." He fondled the dog's muzzle. "If I don't spend the winter mending the fences, the sheep escape when they're put out to graze in the top fields in spring. If I hadn't had the machinery serviced last autumn, the tractor wouldn't be running smoothly now. I do it, but I don't dwell on what's past or what the future might hold. I learn from my mistakes and then I get on with things."

Adam made everything seem so straightforward. His easy

logic seemed so uncomplicated after the intensely indebted feeling I had toward Vincent, or the fascination I was finding with Colin's hypnosis sessions.

"Thank you."

If I followed his advice, I reasoned, then I should continue the hypnosis sessions with Colin to make sure I hadn't left any metaphorical fences unmended in Kitty's past that could lead to difficulties in the present and possible disasters in the future. And maybe I should go back with Vincent and try to help him resolve certain issues with *his* past so he could begin to look forward to a brighter future with Jadie. I owed him that much, surely.

"But if you choose to go back," Adam added, straightening up, "I can't take you today. I've got to keep a close eye on one or two of the ewes who've had problems in the past with multiple births. Triplets can be complicated."

"No, of course," I said hastily.

I realized as we turned and walked slowly back through the yard that Adam was already giving me time he could ill afford. This was one of the busiest times of his year, and his farmworkers were stranded in the village, leaving him to cope alone. We paused at the lambing barn, and Lad leaped up at me, planting muddy paws on my coat and trying to lick my face.

"Get down, boy," Adam instructed, and the dog returned obediently to his master's side. He gave me a long stare. "If it doesn't snow again today, I could maybe take you over in the Land Rover tomorrow."

"Thank you." I smiled, and turned to follow the path back round the side of the house. At the back door I took a deep breath and prepared myself to reenter the fray.

chapter twenty-two

"*Well?*" *demanded Tara* as I walked back into the warmth of the kitchen. "Have you made up your mind?"

She was languishing at the table with a magazine in front of her. It was the first time I'd seen her doing anything but work. Betty was sitting near Bill in front of the stove, and Jadie was perched next to the old woman. They had a ball of wool and a pair of long needles, and it seemed Betty was trying to teach her to knit. Bill was snoozing with the cat on his blanket, and the lambs were asleep in their corner. Neither Vincent nor Colin was anywhere in sight. I pulled out a chair and sat next to Tara.

"I think I will go back to the house with Vincent," I kept my voice low, not wanting to disturb the tranquil scene, "but not today."

Tara stiffened. "When?"

I studied her face. I knew her fear of losing Vincent was eating into her, and I quavered inside. "Maybe tomorrow, but I need to ask you something first."

As if sensing my disquiet, she automatically lowered her voice to match mine. "What?"

"Have you ever thought it was strange that Cheryl left so many of her belongings behind?"

She dropped her gaze immediately. "Not really."

"It's just that when I was looking for clothes to bring here, I found her handbag." I watched her carefully, keeping my voice low. "Surely no woman would have left without her bag and her wallet."

"What are you saying?" Tara demanded.

"I don't know." I shook my head. "I just wondered if you actually saw her leave."

"She was still there when I left to go home on the Friday evening." Tara shrugged dismissively. She looked back down at the magazine, pretending to be nonchalant but still keeping her voice low so that Jadie wouldn't hear her. "When I went in on that Monday morning, Vincent informed me Cheryl had packed up and left them, that she couldn't live in a house that reminded her every second of Amber. Apparently she had crept out sometime during the night, but had left him a note. He said she'd explained that she couldn't bear to go through it all over again with Jadie and that she was leaving for the airport with a 'friend,' some old family associate called Jack."

"Did you know Jack?"

"I'd never heard of him, but I wasn't there on weekends, when they entertained."

"You were there with Cheryl all week," I pressed. "Did she seem like someone who was about to leave her family? Did she seem different on the last day you saw her?"

"She was in pieces," Tara hissed "She'd just lost her firstborn child, and she was convinced her other daughter would follow suit! How do you think she seemed?"

"I'm sorry." I glanced toward Jadie, lowering my voice still further. "I just meant, was she more different that day than in the previous few days since losing Amber?"

"Cheryl was never the same, from the moment they came back from the hospital where Amber died, to the day she left. She walked around like a shadow, never crying, just moving slowly as if she were finding her way down some dark tunnel. She didn't sleep, hardly ate. She couldn't do anything with Jadie—that was all left to me. When Vincent told me she'd left, I admit I was surprised. You know, it takes energy to plan to leave, and she just didn't seem to have it in her. But in another way it made sense; she couldn't function anymore within her own family, so she just . . . ran away from it."

I chewed my lip and thought about that, but it still didn't make sense to me. "Does Jadie's grandmother ever talk to you about Cheryl leaving?"

"I hardly see the woman; Dempsey mostly arrives after I've gone home on a Friday evening, or sometimes on Saturday morning. Vincent picks her up from the station unless she comes by car, and she goes back again Sunday night."

"If I do go home with Vincent tomorrow," I said slowly, still hesitant to be alone with him until I had a few more answers, "do you think Colin would come too? We could continue with the hypnotherapy sessions over there. What do you think?"

Tara's expression cleared with the idea of us taking a chaperon. "I think that's a very good idea."

"Where are they both?" I asked, looking around.

"In the parlor; I think they're playing a game of chess."

I made my way across the gloomy hall and pushed open the door to the parlor to find Vincent and Colin sitting stiffly in front of the fire, butting heads over a coffee table where two mugs of coffee stood beside a carved wooden chess set. The chessboard sat solidly between them like an area of no-man's-land. Their eyes were locked in combat as Vincent lifted one of his pieces and moved it into position. From the amount of "fallen" pieces at Colin's side, I guessed he was winning. Colin moved another of his pieces and sat back.

"Check," he said triumphantly.

Vincent glanced up at me, his expression intense. "Did you make a decision?" he asked.

"Yes, I will go back with you."

Vincent looked down at the board, moved his queen with a dramatic flourish, and grinned at his opponent. "Checkmate!" he said triumphantly.

"But I was hoping you'd come too, Colin, so we can continue with the hypnosis sessions," I added quickly. "And we can't get a ride back until tomorrow."

Vincent visibly deflated.

"Looks like I'm challenging you to a rematch," Colin said to Vincent as he leaned back in his chair with a grin.

Vincent stared at him as if weighing his options. "So be it," he said at last. "And may the best man win."

We ate lunch at the long kitchen table. Then I helped Tara clear everything away so that Betty could relax.

Vincent was anxious to return home before dark. He assured me the journey on foot was much easier now that the tractor had cut a path through the snow-covered lane, and he set off again directly after the meal. I walked with him to the front door, where he took my hand in his and gazed, long and hard, into my eyes.

"Promise you'll definitely come home tomorrow," he said.

"Barring more blizzards or some emergency," I replied.

"I will feel much happier when you are back where I can keep an eye on you until your memory returns, or at least until proper help arrives." He reached out to brush a tendril of hair out of my face. It was a tender gesture, reminiscent of how I'd seen Bill touch Betty, and I stood still, searching his face apprehensively. Slowly he leaned toward me, his eyes locked on mine.

Inexplicably nervous, and thinking guiltily of Tara, I took a step backward, and he stopped short, narrowing his eyes as if trying to figure out what it was I wanted.

"You'd better get going," I said. "I'll see you tomorrow."

He turned abruptly, and I watched as he made his way across the yard, a lonely figure muffled in a hooded blue ski jacket and snow boots.

As soon as he had gone, I wandered back into the kitchen, my thoughts in turmoil. Colin leaped to his feet when he saw me and pulled out a chair. Betty and Bill were snoozing in their armchairs by the stove, the lambs were asleep, and the kitchen was peaceful.

"What do you think about having another hypnotherapy session now?" he asked. He had clearly been waiting for Vincent to leave, and while I was slightly uneasy about what had happened that morning when I'd so nearly been trapped in the past, I was ready to have my mind taken off the rather confusing emotions I was experiencing in the present. If I was being strictly honest with myself, I was also itching to find out what had happened to Kitty and her siblings in the house on the coast.

I accepted a mug of coffee from Tara, who had relaxed perceptibly now that Vincent had gone, and I sipped it slowly, thinking about all the possible repercussions of giving myself over to Colin's ministrations once more. Jadie clambered onto the chair next to mine and placed a piece of drawing paper and pencils on the table in front of us. I watched as, with her tongue protruding between her lips in what I'd come to recognize as deep concentration, she started to draw the outline of a figure. It wasn't a bad picture, as six-year-old's drawings go, I thought with a smile. Jadie had drawn the head and body reasonably in proportion, with wild orange hair fanning out from the circle that was the head. She gave the figure a smiley face, a pink dress, and two lines that looked like wings crossing behind its back, then sat still to survey her work.

"You've got to guess who it is," she said.

I stared at the picture with a sigh. I was pretty sure it was going to turn out to be a likeness of Jadie's lost sister, and I flicked a glance toward Tara, suddenly uncomfortable.

"Er, is it you?"

Jadie shook her head, her eyes shining, seemingly delighted that I'd gotten it wrong.

"Okay . . . is it an angel?"

"No. Guess more."

I took a deep breath, avoiding Tara's gaze. "Is it . . . Amber?"

Tara's head shot up, and she pursed her lips in disapproval.

"No, it's not Amber," Jadie said easily.

"Who, then?" I asked in surprise.

"It's you," Jadie said with a shout of glee at having outwitted me. "It's you being Kitty. Look, that's your jump rope right there. See? You're jumping."

My mouth dropped open and I gawked at her in astonishment. What I'd taken to be wings was the jump rope passing behind the figure's head and back.

"How did you know about—" And then I realized that although she'd ostensibly been quietly doing her schoolwork when I'd been put under hypnosis the first time, back in her own house by the fire, she had probably been listening to every word.

"Honestly! The ideas you and Colin are putting into that child's head," Tara tutted, passing Jadie a glass of milk and a cookie.

And suddenly, because Jadie was obviously so comfortable with my trips into the past, and even the stoic Adam had seemed to think there was nothing wrong with it, I felt somehow vindicated.

Colin watched as I drank the last of my coffee, and when I'd rested the mug down on the table, he peered hopefully over at me. "Well?"

"Let's do it," I said with sudden resolve. "But promise me you'll bring me out of it when you think I've had enough."

"Absolutely," he said, nodding.

"You stay here with Tara, and I'll see you later." I smiled at Jadie. "Be a good girl."

As I lay on the couch and closed my eyes, I realized that it was getting frighteningly easy to access the innermost workings of my mind. Colin only had to run through the relaxation technique, say the few key words, and I was gone, racing backwards in time like a child eager to shed the restrictions of the schoolroom and go out to play.

"Tell me what is happening, Kitty." It was a week or two after our arrival at the cottage by the ocean.

"We have asked our aunt and uncle if we might walk the mile and a half to the sea. I'm following Alice and Arthur along the dusty road to the high sand cliffs that overlook the gray-green sea. It is a beautiful summer's day, and Alice and Arthur are skipping ahead."

"Describe everything to me, Kitty."

"Alice and Arthur are carrying napkins stuffed with bread and cheese for our lunch, and the pockets of Arthur's breeches are bulging with tiny sweet apples collected from our aunt's garden. I'm carrying the heavy earthenware jar of apple juice that Tilly gave us to drink." I stopped talking to watch Arthur stoop to poke a large snail he'd spotted at the side of the track, and I felt a rush of affection for my little brother. He was a handsome child, his hair darker than mine and Alice's, but I could still see the reddish hues gleaming in the sunshine. Alice and I kept our pale freckled faces shaded by our sunbonnets, which was just as well, since I could already feel the heat of the sun beating down on my back through the thin cotton of my dress.

In no time at all, it seemed, the tree-lined road petered out ahead of us and the world fell away, leaving a wide empty horizon. We hurried ahead excitedly, then stopped and gasped in awe as a vast expanse of glittering gray water came into sight.

"What are you seeing? Keep talking to me, Kitty."

"The ocean is ahead of us; it is so beautiful and so huge! It stretches all the way to the horizon. There are seagulls swooping in the sky overhead, calling to one another. We've left the fields behind and are crossing the open grassy slope to the edge of the sand cliff. Oh my goodness, it's a long way down."

"What is happening now?"

"We are following the cliff path along, looking for a suitable place to climb down. Ah, here we are. Now we are clambering down the slope to the beach below; I wish this jar wasn't so very heavy."

We all sat down on the rocky sand to pull off boots and stockings, then, with the others following my lead, we hobbled over the painfully hard pebbles to the sea's edge to wait for the next wave to wash over our bare toes.

The water was deliciously cold, but the stones were hard and painful on the soles of my feet. After a moment or two I wandered back up the beach to sit and sort pebbles into sizes. There were some shells too, which Alice and I collected in our apron pockets. As I turned over a particularly pretty shell in my hand, I had a sudden recollection of having done this very thing before. But this was our first time at the seaside. Wrinkling my brow, I tried to think. Why did I have the distinct feeling I lived in a place near the ocean?

"What are you doing now, Kitty? Don't forget to talk to me."

"We're going to have our lunch," I said, pushing the puzzling memory away. "We're eating the bread and cheese and the apples, and at last the apple juice jar is almost empty, so it will be easier to carry back."

The afternoon sped by, and it was only when a dark cloud drifted over that I looked up and realized how low the sun had sunk in the sky. The tide had turned, and a light breeze was picking up, so we hurriedly pulled on our stockings and boots and started to make our way back up the beach. The temperature had dropped, and soon the first spots of rain started as we approached the place where we had descended from the cliff path.

Arthur and Alice started to climb, but as the rain increased, their boots slipped against the quickly dampening earth. I knew I had lingered too long; we were going to be late back, and our aunt and uncle would be worried about us.

I pushed Arthur from behind, while Alice scrabbled laboriously upwards ahead of us, showering us with sand and small stones. When I looked down, I saw that the tide had come rushing up over the bank where we had just been sitting.

"It's all right, Kitty. Take deep breaths and stay calm. Keep telling me what you are feeling and seeing."

"I'm frightened. We are having trouble climbing the steep cliff. It is muddy and I'm afraid the others will slip and fall. If any harm comes to them, it will be my fault. My aunt and uncle are relying on me to look after them, and for the first time in my life I'm not sure I can keep them safe. The waves, which were previously breaking several feet from the cliff, are now foaming and crashing directly below us."

Arthur began to cry as his boots scrabbled for a foothold. Every so often a shower of loose sand and stones flew down from where Alice struggled above us. I tossed aside the empty apple juice jar to free my hands, wedged my boots firmly into a jutting area of compacted sand, and pushed Arthur upward with all my might.

My vision became blurred with a mixture of rain, tears, and perspiration from my effort. A sea mist, which had come down when the rain had begun, swirled around us, making it even more difficult to see where we were going.

"Relax your shoulders, Kitty. Keep talking to me and everything will be all right."

"I will never ever forgive myself if anything happens to the children because of me."

We continued to slog laboriously upward, and it seemed an eternity before Alice at last scrambled over the lip of the cliff and reached down to help Arthur up over the brink. By the time I'd hauled myself onto the grass, the rain was slanting across the open space to lash at our hair and clothes.

For a moment we lay panting on the wet grass, our hearts pounding from exertion and fear. Then there came a deep ominous rumble from below us, and the earth seemed to shake beneath our bodies.

I pulled Arthur and Alice away from the edge just as a section of the cliff face detached itself and hurtled down toward the beach far below, throwing up a cloud of mud and grass and stones.

After a moment we crawled to the jagged newly formed edge and peered down. Debris from the cliff was being sucked and pummeled by the pounding surf, turning the sea a murky mottled brown. Arthur was shaking, but Alice was staring at the scene below with a strange, almost serene look in her eyes.

"Come away, Alice!" A knot of foreboding had formed in my stomach. I pulled at her arm, but she seemed strangely reluctant to tear her eyes away from the swirling water below. "Come on. It's not safe; we must get back."

"It's calling me," she murmured, leaning dangerously close to the jagged edge. "I feel like if I slipped, the water would catch me and keep me safe."

"Stop it!" I pulled her arm hard, and she fell back with a jerk onto the wet grass. I gave her a hug. Her thin body was trembling beneath her wet clothing, increasing the panic in my chest. I had to get the children home and dry as quickly as possible.

"Talk to me, Kitty. What are you doing now?"

"The cliff has fallen away below us; we are still perilously close to the edge."

"Are you and the other children all right?"

I could feel someone holding me, trying to stop me from shaking. "Yes, yes we are." I realized with relief that this was truly the case. We were safe for now. But the sense of foreboding was still with me, eating into my bones as surely as the cold wind that whipped along the cliff edge.

chapter twenty-three

When I came to, Colin handed me a tissue. He was sitting beside me on the couch patting my hand, and I rested my face against his shoulder, feeling completely drained. When we returned to the kitchen, Tara took one look at me and put the kettle on the stove.

"What on earth happened?" she asked.

I filled her in on how Kitty had been visiting her aunt and uncle in the house on the coast. I knew she didn't believe a word of what I was telling her, but I felt a strange compulsion to tell her everything. I shivered as I recounted how the cliff had fallen away virtually under the children's feet.

"We could all have been killed," I whispered.

Tara came around the table to sit next to me and took my hand in hers, much as her brother had done a few minutes earlier. "You do know it isn't real, don't you?" She searched my red-rimmed eyes with hers. "I don't know where you're recalling the story from...a film, or a book you once read perhaps? Maybe because you've lost all memory of who you really are, your mind has filled the void with some other person's life story, that's all. It didn't really happen, Kate. You weren't really there."

The kettle boiled, and Tara made me a mug of hot sweet tea, which I sipped slowly, letting the warmth of it seep right through me. "I don't know what to think, but Colin believes what I was seeing was real, don't you, Colin?" I asked.

He nodded. "I'm certainly convinced we have accessed a previous-life experience. The details are too accurate. Of course, we don't know what you do in your present life—it's possible you are a history buff—but most people would not be able to describe Kitty's life as you have. And I believe the emotions you're feeling as Kitty are real too."

"You're just confusing her," Tara accused him. She rose to fetch a newly baked carrot cake, which she turned onto a plate and put on the table to cool. "Look at the state of her! I thought hypnotherapy was supposed to make people feel better about themselves, not worse."

"Sometimes a person has to relive a previous bad experience so they can understand it. They have to come to terms with what happened before they can move on emotionally." Colin heaped sugar into his tea and stirred rhythmically.

"But you're talking about real incidents, real problems from someone's childhood," Tara said. "What you're doing with Kate is making her recall something that didn't really happen to her and making her believe it is somehow all true."

"I believe her memories are real," Colin insisted. "I agree that she's probably remembering them now because her accident has temporarily erased her short-term memory, but I'd stake my reputation on these being genuine recollections of a previous life."

They glared at each other while I hunched down in the chair with the mug warming my hands. I was wishing I wasn't the cause of their disagreement, when Adam stamped through from the utility room and into the kitchen, trailing muck and straw, a newborn lamb nestled in his arms.

He stopped and looked at us questioningly, and Betty tucked her ball of wool into the seat cushion of the armchair and rose unsteadily onto her thickly stockinged legs. She held out spindly arms for the lamb, and Adam deposited the sorry-looking babe into his grandmother's care. At the sight of the lamb, Jadie was off her chair like a shot and hovering at the old woman's elbow.

"What's the matter with it?" Jadie asked, poking her nose close to the lamb's face.

"The mother had triplets," Adam replied, sitting in one of the hard-backed kitchen chairs and pulling off his boots. "She might just about manage two, but this third lamb is too tiny and won't get its share of the milk."

"Can I have it?" Jadie turned pleading eyes on Adam. "For my very own? I promise I'll feed it every two hours and look after it properly."

"Don't be silly, Jadie." Tara came over to look at the lamb. She rested a hand on Jadie's shoulder. "We'll be going home as soon as the electricity comes back on."

"I'll tell you what," Adam said, looking Jadie in the eye, "why don't we say the lamb is yours and you can take care of it while you're here? When you go home, Gran and I will look after it for you, and Tara can bring you over for a visit whenever she has time." He glanced up at Tara. "What do you think?"

"I don't see why not," Tara allowed. She crouched down so she was on the same level as Jadie. "You'd better think up a name for it, then."

Jadie flung her arms around Tara's neck and kissed her cheek. "Thank you! I'm going to call her Woolly."

Watching Jadie interacting with Tara, I was happy to see

them slipping out of their old routines. I worried that Tara had looked upon her care of Jadie as another chore to add to the daily tasks of cooking and housekeeping. Now that Jadie had decided to talk, all sorts of new emotions were being explored and verbalized. Yesterday Jadie had expressed her anger at Tara, and today she was looking at her full of love.

"I suppose I'd better make up a bottle for it." Tara wrinkled her nose. "Come on, Jadie, let Betty take care of Woolly. You can fetch the powdered milk and help me make it up."

Glancing up, I saw that Adam was watching Jadie and Tara too. He had a strange expression on his face that I couldn't quite work out—affection, maybe. Possibly regret? He looked tired and drawn, and I remembered he'd been up early and had missed breakfast with the rest of us, although he had come in briefly for his lunch.

"You look tired. Is there anything I can do?" I asked him. "Would you like a cup of tea?"

He tore his gaze away from Tara and Jadie, and rested his eyes on me. "You look pretty washed out yourself. But, yes, a cup of tea would be good." He turned to Colin. "What have you been doing to the girl? She looks like she's been put through the wringer."

Colin glanced at me, and I nodded my consent for him to fill Adam in on what I'd told him while I'd been under hypnosis. While Colin recounted the story, I poured Adam a mug of strong tea and set it on the table in front of him. When Colin had finished, Adam gave me a strange searching look.

"What?" I asked.

He gave himself a little shake and picked up his mug. "Nothing. I think I'm just a bit overtired. You know that saying, it feels as if someone walked over your grave? Colin's story had me imagining things, that's all."

"Don't you start," I said with a nervous laugh. "I'm relying on you to keep us all grounded."

"In that case," he said with a smile, "you can pass me a slice of that cake."

The next morning Adam had gone out again by the time I came down to help make breakfast. Tara and Betty had beaten me to it for the second morning running, and the table was already filled with food, drinks, and preserves, so I sat next to Bill and helped him with his porridge again. He'd dropped his spoon the moment I'd walked into the kitchen, and I wondered fleetingly if he'd done it on purpose.

"Thanks, lass," he said as I worked the spoon back into his hand. He bent his head toward my ear. "If you're hell-bent on going back to the Jameses' house with young Colin, promise me you won't take any nonsense from either of them; I don't hold with all this meddling in the past. But you're a sensible girl." He paused to make direct eye contact as if to make sure I was listening to him. "Just remember you're welcome here at any time."

"Thank you." I smiled at him with more assurance than I felt. The thought of going back to Vincent was forming little knots in my belly, but Colin would be there too, I reminded myself.

After breakfast Adam popped his head through the kitchen door and announced that he was available to drive me back to Vincent's house.

"The lane is just about passable this morning," he told us, "and it's thawing all the time. According to the radio, most of the major roads have been reopened, so hopefully the electric company will have sent out repair engineers and we'll have the power back on soon."

I felt an unexpected shiver of foreboding run through me. Real life was waiting just around the corner. Soon I would find out who I really was and move on from this place and all the people in it.

Adam hardly spoke on the journey over to Vincent's cottage. It was a much easier and quicker ride than in the tractor, but the Land Rover still bumped and jolted over the slushy, rutted track, and even when we turned into the lane, there were piles of ice and snow to negotiate. Colin, much to my dismay, asked to be dropped off in the lane so he could walk the last section of the journey back to Vincent's.

"I take a brisk walk every day under normal circumstances," Colin told us as Adam sat with the engine idling while he hopped out into the slushy lane. "I need the exercise after being cooped up indoors for so long. Don't worry, I won't be far behind you. I'm a fast walker."

As Adam gunned the engine, I turned to see Colin happily inhaling the icy air as he swung his arms in a weird warm-up routine, his breath circling his head in a cloud of vapor.

"Takes all sorts," Adam commented drily as we continued on our way. "I wonder sometimes if psychologists have to be partly crazy to be able to empathize with their patients."

Lad, who was sitting next to me, panting doggy breath into my face and drooling saliva over my shoulder, barked as if in agreement with his master, and I bit back a laugh as I swayed backwards and forwards with the motion of the vehicle.

The cottage looked different with the melting snow partially revealing a neatly tended front garden beyond a small wrought-iron gate. The Land Rover slowed to a halt, and I picked up the duffel that was lying at my feet, opened the door, and stepped out

onto the glistening wet surface of the lane. It was as if I were seeing the cottage for the first time. It was old, with sagging lintels
and roof beams. The two identical front doors and low hedge that
Vincent and I had negotiated in the dark three nights ago were
the only indications that the property was now divided into two
homes. I called my thanks to Adam for the ride, but he was already turning the vehicle in the driveway and heading back the
way we had come. I swallowed a pang of disappointment and
turned to run my eyes over the stone facade, the leaded-light windows, and the low dark oak front door. A pile of snow to the right
of the door grabbed my attention, and I scraped it away with the
toe of my boot to reveal a house name engraved onto an ancient
wooden plaque. It read "Kigarjay."

"Kigarjay." I rolled the word on my tongue. I was just thinking it was a nice-sounding name, when the door opened suddenly
and I looked up to find Vincent standing in the doorway beaming
at me. "You came back."

"I said I would." I followed him through the curtain into the
polished gloom of the interior.

He peered over my shoulder. "Where's Colin?"

"He decided to walk." We stood awkwardly looking each other
over.

Vincent was dressed warmly in a casual sweater and jeans, his
fair hair swept back and neatly combed. I was wearing a pair of his
wife's trousers with an open knitted jacket over a thin sweater. I
wondered if he and Cheryl had ever stood together in these exact
clothes. Did I remind him of her?

He touched a hand to his hair. "You're earlier than I expected.
I just came downstairs. I thought I'd try an ice-cold shower before
breakfast."

His reference made me shudder, remembering what had happened to me a couple of days earlier.

I realized he must have seen the shudder, because he was looking at me questioningly. "Tara did tell you about the little idiosyncrasy with the shower controls, I assume?"

"What do you mean?"

"Well, obviously there is no hot water now anyway, but if you use the shower in the main bathroom, you have to turn it in the direction opposite from normal. Otherwise, just when you think the water is getting a little cool and try to turn up the heat, it goes freezing cold instead." He knitted his brows together and gave me a searching look. "I reminded her to warn you. She did tell you to be careful, didn't she?"

chapter twenty-four

As I recalled the panicked look on Tara's face when she'd hauled me out of the shower, I suspected her jealous prank had gone somewhat further than she'd intended. Deciding to let the matter drop, I shrugged. "There was no problem when I used it last."

Vincent looked relieved and changed the subject. "I haven't lit the fire." He went to the fireplace and hunkered down in front of the empty grate. "I'll get it going now. Have you eaten yet?"

"I had an early breakfast."

He wound some old newspaper around some slivers of wood. "Once the fire's going I thought I'd walk down to the gas station for some hot coffee and sandwiches for later. According to Maria, the Patels are being very entrepreneurial; apparently they've set up a breakfast station for the villagers until the power comes back on."

I perched on the cold damp couch and watched Vincent pile

kindling onto the grate. When he had a good fire going, he got to his feet and went off to get his ski jacket and boots.

"I promised Maria I'd fetch a hot breakfast for her and Michael this morning. I was hoping to be there and back by the time you arrived, but I don't suppose it will take all that long. I don't want to risk using the car until the roads are in better shape, but I'll be as quick as I can. Will you be all right here on your own, do you think?"

Vincent had barely been gone ten minutes when there was a knock at the front door and Colin walked in, grinning happily at me.

"Now, that's what I call a bracing walk!" He smiled at me from behind glasses that had misted up with the cold. He stamped his feet and looked round the deserted house. "Where's Vincent?"

"He's gone to fetch breakfast. He said he'd be back as soon as he can."

Colin pulled off his boots and blinked at me. "But we had breakfast already."

"Well, Vincent hasn't, and apparently neither have Maria and Michael. I don't think he realized we'd be here so early."

Colin crossed to the smoldering fire and held out his hands to the newly kindled warmth it was giving out. I went to stand beside him, and when he glanced up, it was with a hopeful smile. I knew exactly what he was going to suggest before he even opened his mouth.

Letting out a long sigh, I turned to face him. "I need to find out who I really am, Colin. These hypnosis sessions have only tapped into my memories of Kitty—whoever or whatever she is. Maybe she's a previous incarnation of my soul, or perhaps she's merely the residual memory of a story I once heard, but we have to try to bypass her and find something out about the real me." I fixed him with a stern gaze. "Can you do that, do you think?"

Colin grinned. "I'll do my best."

"We probably don't have much time. Vincent will be back soon.

But Colin was already crossing to the couch, arranging cushions and holding up the blankets, which had been left folded there. "You're getting so adept at slipping into a trance, it won't take long to put you under. I'll bring you out of it in good time so you'll have a chance to collect yourself before the lord and master returns."

And I found that Colin was right. I lay on the couch with both of our coats and the blankets thrown over me for warmth, and with the smell of the fire belching wood smoke out into the cold room.

"Tell me who you are," said the voice in my head.

"I'm Kitty, of course."

"Is there anyone else there, Kitty? Another persona perhaps; someone I haven't yet met?"

I looked around the little schoolroom, remembering the happy years I had spent here and the children who had passed through our doors. I thought of the hours I'd invested in organizing the threads for the girls' sewing lessons, and the figures I'd scrawled onto their slates as they'd struggled with their number work. And I thought of the scramble each morning to be up and dressed, the fire lit, and the coal scuttle filled. The place was normally a hive of industry, with Mother hearing the pupils read, and Alice fetching our daily jug of tepid milk from the milkman and stowing it in a cool recess in the north wall. Even Arthur had his duties, filling the coal scuttle and stoking the fire for our tea.

"There's no one else. I'm here alone."

"I need to speak with someone else, Kitty, someone who lives closer in time. Look inside your head and tell me who you see."

"I see myself, the teacher's daughter. There's no one else. I'm the one who takes the children out into the yard on a sunny day. I am the one who gets the children into a neat line for the bathroom and then referees a wild game of tag, after which I shepherd the pupils back indoors for a story."

"Why are you in the schoolroom all alone?"

"Mother has taken Alice and Arthur out on an errand. It's my birthday, and I think they are giving me time by myself."

"And how old are you?"

"Sixteen."

"Well, happy birthday, Kitty. Now, can you tell me how you feel?"

I felt my cheeks blush crimson. "I'm excited because I'm waiting for someone."

"Who are you waiting for, Kitty?"

"I'm waiting for Garrett. He comes home every year to spend Christmas with his family, and he always stops by to see me on my birthday. I'm very nervous; it is a whole year since I've seen him. He may have decided not to come."

"I want you to run forward a little way in your mind, Kitty. Let's say there is a knock on the door and you have gone to open it. Tell me who you see."

"It's Garrett. . . . At least I think it's him. He has grown so tall and he's wearing a dark gray suit and tie I haven't seen before. His hair is parted on one side of his head and combed down. He seems apprehensive."

I paused, looking this new man Garrett up and down shyly.

"Don't go quiet, Kitty; you have to keep talking to me. Tell me what happens next."

"Garrett is standing with his hands behind his back, and he seems uneasy about something. I'm afraid that he's here to tell me he no longer wants me to wait for him."

Garrett smiled nervously at me. "Happy birthday, Kitty. I've brought you a present." He took his hands out from behind his back and showed me a parcel wrapped in brown paper.

Returning the smile, my eyes on his, I took a deep breath. What I wanted most—had always wanted most—was for him to sweep me up in his arms and bury his face in my neck, showering me with kisses like the heroes in the novels in my aunt and uncle's wonderful library. I wanted him to tell me that he'd missed me and that he loved me more than anything.

"Are you going to open it?" Garrett asked.

I eyed the package with interest. I'd never had a properly wrapped present before. "It really is for me?"

"Of course it's for you, silly. It's your birthday."

"Talk to me, Kitty," said the voice. "You must keep telling me what you are seeing and feeling."

I ignored the voice and turned to Garrett, my eyes shining. "Thank you."

He nodded, and stood stiffly while I pulled off the string and tore the brown paper away to reveal a beautiful cameo brooch.

"Oh, it's lovely!" I breathed, feeling the brooch warm in my hands. It was an exquisite piece—the face of a young woman in profile carved in shell and set against an amber background, in a gilt rope-twist surround.

"It's been in my family for years. I'd like you to have it, Kitty."

Gazing up into his expectant face, it dawned on me that this was a very special gift indeed. If I accepted this, I was accepting him. Although we had made that childhood promise to be together one day, now that I was sixteen and a woman, he must have come to ask for my hand in marriage.

"Kate!" said the distant voice, insistent now. "Tell me what is happening."

"My name is Kitty," I whispered irritably. "I have opened a gift from Garrett; it is a beautiful cameo brooch."

Garrett reached out, took my hand, and dragged me from my solitary perch by the window, pulling me toward the wooden bench where the pupils sat for their lessons. One of the children had discarded a writing slate there, with the chalk still dangling from its string. Before Garrett could pick it up to make room for us, I spotted the date formed in a neat childish hand in the top right corner, my birthday: December 13, 1902.

This is it, I thought as we hovered by the bench, my hands clammy with excitement. He's going to tell me he loves me and ask me to marry him. The warmth of his hand burned into mine as I gazed hopefully into his blue eyes. I could feel my heart pounding in my chest at his touch. Everything inside me yearned for him to kiss me.

"Say you'll wait for me, Kitty," he said, pulling me down beside him. "I will try to come back and see you during the summer break."

"You're going?" I asked numbly.

"I've been accepted as an apprentice to a business in Boston. It is the chance to improve my family's fortunes that I have been hoping for. But promise you'll wait for me, and I will write to you as often as I can."

"Of course I'll wait," I said, feeling my eyes fill with tears. I held on to his hand as if I might never see him again. "I'll wait forever, if that is what it takes."

Garrett gently extracted the brooch from my trembling hand and pinned it with infinite care into the space where the lace collar of my dress ended at my throat. He gazed into my eyes, and again I thought he was going to lean forward and kiss me. For a brief moment he allowed his fingertips to linger on the soft white skin of my neck, and I thought I would burst with desire at his touch. But then he drew back, looking embarrassed, and took a fob watch out of his jacket pocket.

"Your mother will be back shortly," he said, getting to his feet. "Your reputation will be in ruins if she finds me here alone with you. I ought to go."

"Will I see you again before you leave?" My fingers went to the brooch at my neck as I spoke, sealing his caress into my soul.

He shook his head. "My parents want me to spend Christmas with the relatives who are funding my apprenticeship, and with whom I'll be staying for the next couple of years. My training begins immediately. I'm sorry, Kitty, but this is goodbye . . . for now."

I watched with a sinking heart as he went to the door and strode out into the cold December afternoon, and then the door clicked shut behind him and I was alone in the schoolroom with the brooch, a piece of crumpled brown paper clutched in my hand, and the cold hand of fate encircling my heart.

"Kitty, you must continue talking to me," said the voice firmly. "Tell me why you are distressed."

"Garrett has gone away. He didn't say for how long. I think it will be years while he makes his fortune, but he has asked me to wait for him."

"Everything is going to be all right," soothed the voice. "I'm going to start counting down from ten, and I want you to travel with me until you are back here in the present."

I nodded, but I was reluctant to go because I knew, deep in my heart, that for the briefest of moments, in another place and another time, I had found the man I loved.

Opening my eyes, I found Colin looking at me with an anxious expression.

"Are you okay?"

I blinked, stretched, and wriggled into a sitting position. "Yes, I think so."

"What do you make of it all?" he asked.

Shivering, I pulled my coat closely around me under the blankets. "What do you mean?"

"You don't think Garrett could be leading our Kitty on? Maybe he isn't ever going to really marry her."

I stared up at him askance. "As a psychoanalyst, are you supposed to put ideas like that into my head? Aren't you supposed to wait for me to draw my own conclusions?"

He had the decency to look mortified. "I know it's unprofessional of me to try to interpret your memories for you, but your sessions aren't like any other I have ever presided over. I feel like we're investigating Kitty's life and trying to see what relevance it has to your life today."

"I know," I agreed, "and I have to admit I was wondering the same thing about Garrett. He seems so intent on bettering himself, getting back to the wealthy and privileged world he came from before his parents lost everything. But Kitty is such a strong character, isn't she? I have the feeling she would wait for a very long time to be with the man she loves."

"So you do believe Kitty is real, then?"

"I confess I would very much like to believe it—as long as believing in Kitty isn't at the expense of finding out who I really am." I pulled the blankets up to my chin and frowned. "Do you *truly* think that's what I'm remembering, Colin—that I really was Kitty before I became . . . whoever I am today?"

"What else could these memories be?"

"Well, you know Tara seems to think they're just stories I've stored away in my subconscious. What if she's right?"

Colin shrugged. "Worst-case scenario is that when your memory comes back, you find this was just a film you once saw. Best-case—we find out what Kitty is trying to show us and lay her soul to rest."

"And if that soul just happens to be mine?"

"Then hopefully your soul will be at peace and you can continue this incarnation without the added complication of Kitty's problems. As I explain to all my patients if they question the relevance of digging up and going over old hurts, by remembering what happened and acknowledging it, you can come to terms with it, deal with it, and then move on with the rest of your life without taking all the old emotional baggage with you. It's a healing process."

"You make it sound simple."

"Well..." He eyed me cautiously. "There is the added problem, where you are concerned, that as far as we can see at the moment, it wasn't *this* life you experienced the hurt in. But you're right, it is simple. We just have to hope Kitty continues to give us access to her memories until we find out the truth."

"So we need to delve some more." I swung my feet down to the drafty floor. "We need to be sure of what it was that happened to Kitty, her siblings, or Garrett to understand what it is she's trying to show us."

"Which means a few more sessions." Colin nodded. "And that is going to be difficult with Vincent around. I sense that he doesn't approve at all."

I shivered again, so violently this time that Colin put his arm around me. I leaned into him, needing the warmth of his body to reassure me that I was truly alive and not some lonely spirit on a quest of my own. We fell silent as I recalled having much the same feeling a day or two ago, and I wondered if my lack of memory about who I was now was making me increasingly obsessed by the feeling that I wasn't really anyone at all.

Into the silence we heard the sound of the front door opening, and Colin and I both turned guiltily, thinking it was Vincent. The door curtain twitched to one side and a small suitcase tumbled through with a rush of cold air, coming to rest like a hand grenade in the middle of the parquet flooring.

"This is absolutely the last time I am ever driving through conditions like this," said a woman's agitated voice. She slammed the door violently behind her and backed through the curtain, presenting us with a view of blue jeans stretched tightly over a rounded rump. She was dragging a small rolling bag, which had listed to the side so that the one wheel in contact with the floor made a scraping sound.

Colin and I both sprang to our feet as she turned around. Her eyes widened when she saw us, and she gave a quick gasp. "Who the heck are you?"

chapter twenty-five

"*I'm Kate.*" I watched as she leaned on the second bag, staring uncertainly at us. "And this is Colin, Tara's brother."

"What have you done with my son and my granddaughter?"

"Vincent walked to the gas station to get breakfast," Colin told her, hurrying forward to try to take her bag before it did further damage to the floor. "I'm surprised you didn't pass him on the road."

"Gone to get breakfast?" she echoed. "What are you talking about?"

"The Patels are selling hot food, and Vincent went to get some," I tried to reassure her as she stood gripping the handle of her bag and refusing to let Colin take it from her. "The electricity went off during the blizzard and hasn't been fixed yet. The gas station is apparently selling sandwiches for those who need them."

She peered around the room suspiciously. Her shoulders dipped and she visibly deflated as if all the fight had gone out of her.

"I've had the trip from hell." She let go of the bag at last, brushed past me, and flopped onto the couch. She reached down, eased off her scuffed pumps, and rubbed at her stockinged feet. "I've made that trip so many times, yet today it was unrecognizable. I'm never doing it again. Vincent is just going to have to employ a full-time nanny."

"Shall I take your coat?" Colin asked politely.

The woman looked down at her bright red wool coat as if surprised to find she was still wearing it. "Yes, I suppose so." She shrugged out of it and handed it over.

I took in the pale blue sweater she was wearing, the jeans, and the matching blue-patterned silk scarf at her neck. Both the scarf and sweater matched her eyes, which were a watered-down version of Vincent's and Jadie's. Her eyes were lightly rimmed with laughter lines but were still her best feature. Her short spiky hair was blond and fashionably cut. I put her somewhere in her mid-fifties, which meant she must have had her son when she was quite young.

"So if Vince is off on a mission, where's Jadie?"

"Jadie's at the Jenkinses' farm," I told her, taking the seat next to her. "Vincent was worried the house was too cold for her here, and she and Tara are staying over there until the power comes back on."

"A farm? My Jadie? What about her asthma?"

"Jadie's asthma seems fine," I assured her. "The animals don't seem to have any effect on her."

"Oh my God, I didn't have to come." She leaned back and closed her eyes. "I had visions of Vincent being cooped up here with Jadie and no one to look after her. I couldn't call ahead with the lines not working, so I set out early to try and brave the roads. . . . The only reason I'm here at all is because I followed a snowplow most of the way, but in the end I had to turn off, and almost immediately the car got stuck."

The front door opened and Vincent strode in holding an insulated shopping bag. He couldn't have looked more pleased with himself if he'd had a freshly slaughtered deer slung over his shoulder. "I've got the food—" He stopped abruptly when he saw his mother. "Mom! What are you doing here?"

"It's Saturday," his mother replied shortly. "I come every weekend."

"But the roads—"

"Are a nightmare," she finished for him, "but I didn't want to leave you in the lurch, and I so love to see little Jadie. So I threw caution to the wind, and here I am."

Vincent recovered himself and bent to kiss her on the cheek. "I'm amazed you made it," he said, his earlier exuberance gone. "The highways were just reopened. They're still recommending on the radio that people avoid traveling whenever possible." He straightened up, a puzzled frown crossing his features. "I didn't see your car outside."

"The stupid car is in a ditch up the road somewhere," she replied. "You do live in the most godforsaken place, you know. I had to walk the last half mile or so dragging my bags, and my feet are killing me—you must still have been in the gas station when I passed it!"

Vincent glanced at his mother's inappropriate footwear lying discarded on the floor, then apologetically at Colin and me. "Have you made introductions?"

"Yes, yes," his mother said. "Tara's brother, Calvin, and his girlfriend, Kate, wasn't it? I'm Dempsey, by the way."

"Colin," Colin corrected mildly.

"And I'm not Colin's girlfriend," I pointed out hastily as

Vincent raised an eyebrow in our direction. "I lost my way in the blizzard and Vincent rescued me and is letting me stay here for a while."

It occurred to me that now that the roads were open enough for Vincent's mother to get in—even if she had followed a snowplow—then I could get out, but the thought didn't excite me as it should have. I had begun to feel as if my life was tied to this place. I didn't quite want my visit to end—not yet, anyway.

Vincent caught my eye and inclined his head toward the kitchen. "Come and help me make coffee. I've got a thermos full of hot water in this bag, and a pile of sandwiches." He nodded to his mother. "I'll bet you could do with a hot drink to thaw you out."

I followed him, grateful to be away from his mother's searching gaze. As soon as we were alone in the kitchen, he dumped the bag onto the table and kicked the door closed with his foot. "You don't have to go just because the roads are open." He took my hands in his and looked into my eyes as if he were reading my mind. "I meant what I said about you being welcome to stay as long as you like. You are good for us, Kate. Don't worry about Mom. She'll be so glad when she finds out Jadie is talking again."

"Vincent, I'm not sure . . ." I started, but he let go of one of my hands and pressed a finger against my lips.

"Don't spoil it, Kate. I'm happier now than I have been in two years; Jadie is talking and seems to have gained a new lease on life, Tara is more relaxed with her than I can ever remember, and I feel . . . different about everything. It's like you've cast a magic spell over us all. I know this sounds incredibly selfish, but I don't want you to find out who you were before. I want you to stay here with us."

"I feel like such a fraud," I murmured. "I haven't done anything to deserve your gratitude. I just washed up here and everything has sort of happened around me."

"Exactly," he said, smiling into my eyes. "Everything happens around you. You're special, and though I can't put my finger on it, I know this is where you are meant to be right now."

He let go of my hands and turned to rummage in the cupboard for cups.

I followed him back to the living room with a tray, and we pulled the couch and armchairs as close to the warmth of the fire as we dared.

The sandwiches were still warm as I handed them out. Vincent spooned coffee granules into the cups and produced a jar of powdered milk from the bag, along with the thermos. The fridge had long since defrosted and, despite the lack of central heating, the remaining milk had gone bad.

It was when I picked up the thermos that something clicked in my brain. I unscrewed the lid slowly, recalling having done that very thing quite recently. What was I remembering? I poured hot water onto the coffee granules in each of the cups and stirred in some powdered milk, then sat back along with the others with the cup warming my hands as I sipped at the welcome drink.

The picture of a car windshield flashed into my mind, and I wrinkled my brow, trying to catch the fleeting memory before it vanished into the depths of my mind. I was sitting in a car, in a rest stop, peering out at murky weather. But what was I doing there? Where was I going?

"Are you all right?" Colin asked through a mouthful of greasy bread. "You look like you've seen a ghost."

The memory vanished as quickly as it had come, and I gave myself a little shake. "It's nothing," I said. But the flavor of the coffee had changed, and all I could taste in my mouth was the sickly tang of flask coffee. I remembered flask coffee accompanied by the plaintive mewing of a cat somewhere close by.

chapter twenty-six

While we were eating, Vincent told his mother about Jadie's decision to start talking again.

At first Dempsey was disbelieving, then she clapped a hand to her mouth, her eyes shining with delight. "But how did it happen? Why has she decided to speak now?"

"Kate had something to do with it. I brought her in from the blizzard, and apparently Jadie just started talking to her."

Dempsey looked at me. "How did you do it?"

I shrugged. "I didn't do anything, honestly. I didn't know she couldn't talk."

Dempsey continued to press me for a little longer, before sitting back and regarding me with interest. "Well, whatever happened, I thank you from the bottom of my heart."

During the remainder of the morning and into the afternoon, I got to know Dempsey a little better. One thing became clear very quickly: The woman never stopped talking. She regaled me with stories of her younger days as a nurse in a Boston hospital and her life since her husband, a respected surgeon, had walked out on them when Vincent was thirteen. She had concentrated her energies on earning enough money to keep a roof over their heads. I had to admire her for the way she'd kept everything together and brought Vincent up single-handedly despite all the odds.

Colin and Vincent had gone to check on Dempsey's car, and after nearly two hours reported back that it would take a tow truck to extract it from the ditch. With the present state of chaos on the roads and without a working telephone, they decided it was safe enough where it was for the moment, and returned gratefully to the heat of the fire, where they stamped their feet and blew on their hands until the warmth had returned to their bones.

Dempsey showed us how to play a card game called Beanie, which was a bit like rummy. We sat around the coffee table, our cards held before us like little fans, while Dempsey told us more about her colorful life.

"I was given up for adoption as a baby when my father, a British serviceman, left my birth mother at the altar and went home to the UK in 1949." Dempsey gathered up the cards and began to shuffle them expertly.

"What was he doing here?" Colin asked, watching as she cut the deck.

"They met when he was studying in Cambridge before the war, and fell in love," she told us, dealing the next round. "He promised to return after the war and marry her, and he kept his word, returning four years after the end of the war to reacquaint himself with her. They got on well enough, though apparently he missed his home and his folks. He stayed right up until the day of the ceremony. Then, according to the story my adoptive mother told me, he got cold feet and left my birth mother standing in the church all decked out in her wedding dress."

"That's terrible," I murmured as I picked up my cards.

"What, my father leaving my mother, or the cards I've dealt you?" Dempsey smiled. "My birth mother was in the early stages of pregnancy. She probably didn't even know she was expecting me when he walked out on her."

"Why did she put you up for adoption?"

"In those days 'nice' girls simply didn't have children out of wedlock. There was no backup, no help from social services. She needed to work and couldn't keep me; simple as that."

"Have you ever tried to find her?" Colin asked, studying his hand with a frown of concentration.

"She died." Dempsey watched eagle-eyed as I laid down a run of cards. "All that I have of my ancestry is my father's name. He was a Dempsey. My birth mother never stopped loving him despite his desertion, and she named me after him."

"Have you thought of trying to trace him?"

"I've made my own life." Dempsey shrugged. "I had loving adoptive parents who brought me up and supported me while I did my nurse's training. If my birth father couldn't commit to the woman he'd thought he loved enough to save up and travel half-way around the world for, what could he have done for me that I haven't done for myself?"

Vincent, who had obviously played Beanie many times before, laid down a run of four kings and three aces, threw out his last card, and sat back looking pleased with himself. I could tell he was only partly listening to his mother. He had no doubt heard the story of her life many times before.

Colin groaned and added up the total of his cards. Dempsey and I did likewise, and she jotted our scores down on a bit of paper.

"So you met Vincent's father while you were working as a nurse." Colin prompted.

"Yes, but my parents never liked him." Dempsey dealt the

next round. "I assume you've heard the joke. 'What's the differ-ence between God and a doctor?'"

"God doesn't think he's a doctor," Colin said, finishing the punch line for her. "Although, as the holder of a doctorate myself, I could take exception to such a quip."

Dempsey laughed. "That particular doctor tired of being a husband and father very quickly. I think we cramped his style, and as the years wore on, he didn't even try to hide his string of affairs. When he abandoned me for a younger, prettier model, I could have given up and taken Vincent home to my parents, but my pride wouldn't let me." She arranged her cards and waited for me to start playing. "I found work in an art gallery and discovered I was quite an adept salesperson."

I could imagine that Dempsey, with her bubbly personality, made a brilliant salesperson. She went on to tell us how she had made a good income with fat commissions from lucrative sales. Yet despite this ability to keep both herself and her son quite comfortable all those years, she was self-effacing and seemed con-stantly to doubt herself. It seemed that she'd had a string of dis-astrous short-term flings since Vincent had married and moved out, and she had never found a replacement for her husband.

I watched her over my cards and couldn't help but compare her to Kitty's mother, who had also been left suddenly to cope on her own. Although the two women's personalities seemed poles apart—one a stickler for family values and morality, and the other taking the world as she found it—they had both coped with a sudden change in their circumstances. Both had put their chil-dren's needs before their own and had rolled up their sleeves and earned a living.

"I've been to some of those singles bars," Dempsey confided to me with a knowing glance while her son and Colin concentrated on their cards. "But most of the men are so *young,* and the older ones all have something wrong with them. Let's face it, if they're on the market in their late forties or fifties, then there has to be something wrong with them." She laid a run of cards on the table and giggled. "I went out with a police officer once, but he turned out to be married, so he had to go. I'm not into one-night stands or being the 'other woman,' and that's what the majority of them seem to want."

It was my turn again, and I picked up a card, trying to avoid Vincent's embarrassed gaze, but Dempsey hadn't finished yet. She leaned toward me and lowered her voice to a loud whisper. "I'm not sure I even work in that department anymore, if you know what I mean. . . . It's been so long."

"Mom!" Vincent exclaimed. "For goodness' sake."

"I'm just saying that I'm looking for a real relationship," she retorted defensively. "There's nothing wrong with that."

"I'm surprised you haven't met anyone through your work," I ventured. "There must be some eligible men out there somewhere."

"They're either married, set-in-their-ways bachelors, divorced with tons of baggage—you know, with grown-up kids who are programmed to hate you on sight—or weirdos who want to discuss the latest computer software or the baseball cards they've collected since they were twelve."

I laughed, but neither Vincent nor Colin seemed impressed. Colin commented, "There must have been someone, surely? They can't all be boy toys or divorced. Somewhere there must be an ordinary guy whose wife has died before her time or something, and who's searching for someone new to share his life."

Out of the corner of my eye I saw mother and son exchange a quick glance, and I felt a prickling sensation run down my spine. Vincent studiously avoided my gaze, and even Dempsey seemed suddenly flustered. She tossed the rest of her cards down and proclaimed she was going to take her bags up to her room.

"I'll give you a hand," Vincent said hastily, and the two of them scooped up the bags and vanished upstairs, leaving Colin and me looking at each other awkwardly.

"What did I say?" He collected the cards and slid them into the box.

"Either Dempsey is a very bad loser or you hit on a sensitive subject." I chewed my lip, disconcerted by Dempsey's sudden exit. I wondered if I could trust Colin, and decided I probably could. "I'm beginning to wonder if this has anything to do with the disappearance of Vincent's wife."

"What do you mean?"

"Well." I lowered my voice to a whisper. "That was a pretty violent reaction from both of them at your suggestion of a wife having died before her time. Cheryl was supposed to have run away after losing Amber, wasn't she? Only all her clothes and her personal belongings are still upstairs in their bedroom—and I mean all of them."

"Maybe she wanted to make a clean break, take nothing that would remind her of her life here. Some people can't deal with grief and simply shut it out, along with anything that might remind them of their loved one. It's not good for them to build an emotional wall, of course, but they simply can't help themselves at the time."

"But she wouldn't have left her handbag, wallet, credit cards, and ID, surely. If she was going to make a new life for herself she'd need money, wouldn't she? And she can't have left the country without the passport."

Colin looked at me. "Are you sure she left them all behind?"

"I've seen them."

We stared at each other in silence, contemplating the enormity of what I was suggesting.

"You're not just saying Vincent is lying about the whereabouts of his wife. You are also suggesting his mother knows about it," he pointed out at last. "Think what it would mean to Jadie if her father and grandmother were found to be implicated in some way with her mother's disappearance. The child has a hard enough life as it is."

"I know. That's why I haven't said anything until now, but it's worrying me," I whispered. "Do we say anything, or do we leave well enough alone?"

"I think you're probably letting your imagination run away with you." Colin drummed the corner of the pack of cards on the coffee table as he thought over the ramifications of what I was suggesting.

"Maria insinuated there was more to Cheryl's disappearance than meets the eye too," I went on. "She was surprised her friend didn't confide in her that she was thinking of leaving. And," I added, "Vincent reacted very strangely to Maria's question as to whether he thought the house might be haunted."

Colin gave me a disbelieving look. "Come on. You're not suggesting Vincent thinks his wife might be . . . ?"

"I thought at first that maybe he was hoping his daughter's spirit might be roaming the place. Maria went as far as saying that when she put something down, it would move to somewhere else. I mean, that's pretty spooky talk, and Vincent seemed struck by it. But now I'm wondering if perhaps his interest isn't only in Amber."

"Kate, could you come up to the guest room and tell my mother what you want done with your things?" Vincent was suddenly behind us.

We both started guiltily, and Colin dropped the pack of cards onto the floor. I felt my cheeks blush crimson.

"Yes, of course." I tried to keep my voice from squeaking nervously.

I followed him with trepidation toward the stairs, wondering how much he'd heard and whether Dempsey was waiting for me at the top of the stairs with a noose or a syringe filled with some sort of lethal injection. If they'd done something terrible to Cheryl, then perhaps I was going to be next, I thought wildly. I tried to get a grip on myself. So much had happened since I'd arrived here that my imagination was running amok. Such things simply didn't happen in places like this. Did they?

"I'm not sure what the sleeping arrangements are going to be now," Vincent said as he climbed the stairs ahead of me. "Dempsey went in to change the bedding, and I remembered your things were in there."

"None of the things in there are really mine. I borrowed them from Cheryl's wardrobe, remember." I wished immediately that I hadn't mentioned Vincent's wife. "I don't have anything of my own except for the clothes I was found in."

"I thought I recognized that sweater." We reached the landing, and he paused to look appraisingly at me. "You look like her, you know, although she had gray eyes and her hair was darker."

I noted his use of the past tense and felt my legs go weak at the knees. I reached out to hold the top banister for support.

"I suppose you went through the drawers in my room too?" I spun around to find Dempsey staring at me questioningly from the guest room doorway, and I remembered the gin bottle hidden among her few items of clothing.

"No, of course not. Vincent suggested I borrow some of Cheryl's things, so I didn't need to look anywhere else." I was spluttering, beginning to feel like a condemned woman awaiting the executioner's block. The thought brought me up short; this was not the first time I'd felt like that. I wrinkled my brow, trying to remember why the feeling was so familiar, so recent, like when I'd been pouring the coffee earlier, but the memory fled my mind as soon as I tried to harness it.

As I stared at Dempsey, a hand descended onto my shoulder from behind, and I gasped aloud. I think my legs would have given way beneath me if I hadn't still been tightly clutching the banister. This was it, I thought as I screwed my eyes tightly shut. I had stumbled from one half-remembered world into another, had stuck my nose in where it wasn't wanted, and now I was about to pay the ultimate price.

chapter twenty-seven

"*Are you all* right? You look a bit flustered." Vincent was watching me with an expression of puzzlement.

I took a steadying breath and willed myself to open my eyes. Peeking around, I wondered what had spooked me so badly. Was it the half-forgotten memory of some fearful episode from my real life, or was it simply that I was letting my imagination run away with me?

"I'm fine." My voice sounded high-pitched and breathless. Exhaling slowly, I tried again. "I'm fine."

He looked from my pale face to his mother's, then returned his gaze to me. "Mom, would you give us a minute, please?" he said, without taking his eyes off me.

Dempsey shrugged and walked back to her room, and Vincent tightened his grip on my shoulder. "What's going on?" he asked.

"Nothing."

He let go of my shoulder and took me by the hand, leading

me toward his bedroom so that I had to release my hold on the banister. As soon as we were across the threshold, he relinquished his hold on me, closed the door behind us, and turned to face me.

"Why are you suddenly so jumpy?"

"I'm not."

He sighed and walked over to the bed, where he sat down, looking up at me with a puzzled expression on his face. "Something has obviously upset you."

"I'm still feeling disoriented, that's all." I crossed the room and perched next to him. "I haven't known who I am for four days. I've met lots of new people, slept in two different houses, and been hypnotized so that I remember a past I'm not sure whether to believe is mine." I'd wanted to offer an explanation for my change in mood, but on reflection I realized it wasn't surprising my nerves were on edge. I didn't add: And I am wondering if you killed your wife. Although I still half believed it.

"You poor thing," he said. "I've been thoughtless, and I'm sorry. We've all been so wrapped up with our own problems. I think we've been towing you along in our wake without thinking what it must be like for you. What I said down there in the kitchen, I meant every word of it. You have made a huge difference to everyone here, and you are very welcome to stay with us for as long as you like. I don't mean to be selfish; if you want to get on with your own life, find out who you really are, then of course I'll help you in every way I can."

"Thank you." I didn't know what I wanted. And with Vincent sitting next to me, being so considerate of my feelings, I suddenly felt stupid for thinking him capable of doing anything awful to his wife or anybody else. "I think I've been letting my imagination run away with me. Tara might have been right when she said it's because I have no solid memories in my head; it's as if I've got to have something to fill the void."

"Tara is nearly always right," he agreed, taking my hand in his. "And I'm not sure this hypnosis stuff is helping. How do you know Colin isn't putting all that stuff about Kitty into your head?"

I looked at him askance. "Why would he want to do that?"

"I don't know. Maybe he's writing a thesis or something."

"It seems unlikely."

"What seems unlikely is that you are remembering a past incarnation of yourself, yet you appear to believe that."

We sat on the bed for several minutes in silence. I didn't really know what to say. I wanted to put the subject of his missing wife to the back of my mind, but it wouldn't go away, and I couldn't help but worry that he was still in pain from feeling he had let both Cheryl and Amber down.

"You know what you said the other night in the kitchen," I began tentatively, "about Amber—and you not being there for her or being able to prevent her dying?"

"I said more than I should have."

"I still think you should see someone. You can't go through life blaming yourself for your child's death."

"Why not?" His voice changed suddenly, and I pulled back, alarmed at the anguish I saw in his face. "I am at least partially to blame."

"How could you have been?" I wished I hadn't broached the subject, but now I was determined to make him see reason. "It wasn't your fault. Amber had cystic fibrosis!"

"Carried to her through *my* genes," he said.

"But you couldn't possibly have known. Tara told me that at least one in twenty-five people is a symptomless carrier who has no idea they are carrying the gene."

"Cheryl and I gave it to her, and there's no escaping it," he said flatly.

"It wasn't like you gave it to her on purpose," I pointed out.

He turned to me with haunted eyes. "But we knew before we had Jadie."

I watched as he struggled to keep his emotions in check, but his body language gave his pain away.

"I don't think we ever really accepted how ill Amber was. She didn't have the same severity of symptoms as Jadie, needing the constant physical therapy and everything. Amber seemed to have more trouble with her digestive system. . . . She could only tolerate the blandest of foods, and she was rather underweight, but other than that she was a normal happy little girl. Then she got a nasty cold, and after a couple of days it turned into pneumonia. Cheryl took her to the hospital while I was at work, and by the time I got there, she had died." He drew in a ragged breath. "Having condemned one little girl to the disease, we went on and let our next child have it too. We didn't realize until we lost Amber just what sort of life we'd brought upon them, and by then it was too late. What kind of parents did that make us?"

"I'm sure if you asked Jadie, she'd say she's glad to be here," I insisted. "She's a happy little girl."

"Happy children don't stop speaking for two years, do they?" he retorted.

"Maybe she stopped talking because she felt the same as you do—that she'd failed you or her sister in some way. It can't have helped that her mother probably reinforced the notion that Jadie was somehow at fault by leaving her like she did."

I watched him carefully for a reaction, but he merely sighed heavily.

"Cheryl took the easy way out. I'd have done the same thing. Only I couldn't do to Jadie what I'd done to her sister—not being around when she needed me most."

"You're a good father," I told him. "And just because Amber is no longer here doesn't mean you've stopped being her daddy in your heart. She'll be one of your little girls always and forever. And you'll be Jadie's father for many, many years to come. Tara isn't about to let anything happen to her, and I have the feeling your daughter is going to live a long and productive life."

He turned to me with the first glimmerings of hope. "Do you really think so?"

I nodded firmly. "She'll keep fighting. Mark my words."

"No wonder Jadie loves you," he said, with the beginnings of a watery smile. "No disease would dare take hold of her with you around to see it off."

He leaned toward me and kissed me gently on the lips. I closed my eyes, hoping for some of the magic I'd felt when he'd rescued me from the snow, but the kiss was unremarkable, a token gesture between friends. I felt a stab of disappointment. But then I opened my eyes and found him smiling at me, and suddenly it didn't matter that the kiss hadn't set fireworks off inside me, because he was happy again, and I found I wasn't afraid of him anymore. Whatever had happened to Cheryl, I was now embarrassed to have thought it might have been foul play on his part. I just wished I hadn't mentioned my suspicions to Colin.

There was a knock on the bedroom door, and we looked up as Dempsey poked her head around. She took one look at us sitting huddled together on the edge of the bed and raised a penciled eyebrow.

"Sorry to disturb," she said, "but I was wondering if you want me to help you change the sheets on the bed in the attic room. Tara won't need to stay now that I'm here, so I thought you could sleep in there."

"We'll be right out," Vincent said. "Give us a minute."

She backed out and closed the door behind her, and Vincent grinned. "This will give Mom something to think about for a few days. She's always saying I should find a new mother for Jadie."

"I wonder if she's said as much to Jadie," I cautioned. "Your daughter told me when I first arrived that Amber had said they were getting a new mommy; she asked if that was going to be me. Just because Jadie wasn't speaking for two years didn't mean she wasn't taking everything in."

He leaned closer to me. "What did you tell Jadie when she asked you that?"

"I told her I couldn't be her mommy, but that I would be her friend."

Vincent eyed me contemplatively. "Did you believe that Amber had spoken to her?"

"I believe Jadie believed it. She talks to Amber to keep her sister alive within herself. People don't leave us when they die, not if we keep them in our hearts."

"You don't think . . . I mean, it's not possible, is it, that Jadie actually sees her sister?"

My chest constricted slightly. "What, you mean like a ghost or something?"

"I . . . I wake in the night sometimes and feel she's in the room with me, watching me. I know it sounds ridiculous, and it's maybe that I want her to come to me so badly that I dream her up."

"Have you told anyone else about this?"

He shook his head miserably. "I've never told anyone before."

"Do you hear her speaking to you?"

"No. I feel her presence, but I've never heard her speak exactly. Sometimes I imagine I hear a sort of whisper, but when I strain my ears, there's nothing but the wind whistling in the chimneys and the sounds of the house settling for the night."

"It's an old house," I agreed, thinking of the noises I'd heard myself on my first night here.

"Come on," he said suddenly, taking my hand and pulling me to my feet. "My mother will be wondering what on earth we're doing in here."

chapter twenty-eight

$\mathcal{D}$*empsey quizzed me* mercilessly over my relationship with Colin while we were changing the single bed in the quaint attic room a few minutes later. I wondered if it was because she'd seen me with her son and wanted to check the status of my feelings for him, having witnessed me and Colin close together on her arrival.

"When I arrived, you and Colin looked as guilty as hell," she commented in response to my assurances that Colin and I were merely friends. She pulled off pillowcases while I dragged the duvet out of its cover. "Like you had just sprung apart from a clinch."

"I'm surprised you haven't met him before, him being Tara's brother."

"I'm not normally around when Tara's here."

I began to feed the duvet into the new cover. "Colin is an accredited hypnotherapist. He's been treating me to see if we can recover my memory." I decided not to mention that we'd both been somewhat sidetracked by a personality from the past. "Colin normally treats people with deep-seated emotional problems that stem from traumatic childhood experiences. I had just come out of a hypnotic trance when you saw us, and was feeling a bit fragile."

"A hypnotherapist?" She raised an eyebrow and gave a short laugh. "I've always wondered what it would be like to be hypnotized." She poked the corners of the pillow down into the fresh pillowcase and gave it a shake. "He *is* cute, though, you have to admit." Dempsey gave me a knowing look. "He has those pretty eyes, and he seems . . . kind and sort of dreamy, don't you think?"

I considered this for a moment and decided she was right. He did seem kind, and his eyes were definitely mesmerizing behind his glasses. I covered my confusion by giving the duvet a vigorous shake. I wasn't entirely sure how I felt about Colin. The hypnosis sessions had brought us close very quickly, as I'd had to put my trust in him so completely. I recalled the kiss I'd just received from Vincent and felt myself blush. Both men—although very different characters—seemed to have a certain hold over me.

I nodded, choosing my words carefully. "I think Colin would need to be a kind person in his line of work. His livelihood depends on gaining people's trust."

Dempsey and I finished the bed and walked downstairs to find Vincent had lit several candles in the living room. They gave the room an eerie glow, along with the flickering light from the fire. Colin was trying to read a book by holding the pages open to the dull light of one of the candles, but he closed it and sat up when he saw us.

"I don't know how people used to read in the evenings before the advent of electricity," he said. "It isn't good for the eyes."

"It looks really spooky in here." Dempsey plumped down onto the couch beside him. "I wouldn't be surprised if a spirit materialized out of the wall right in front of us." She looked around as a sudden silence fell on the room. "What did I say?"

"We went to dinner with Maria next door, and she mentioned that she and Cheryl used to speculate about the house being haunted," I said.

Dempsey started to laugh, then stopped and looked quizzically at us. "I assume you told her she was being silly?"

"Of course," Vincent said smoothly. He flicked a fleeting glance at me. "I'm sure they were just winding each other up, telling spooky tales to each other."

"I thought Maria was a good Catholic woman." Dempsey picked up a cushion and combed her fingers through the tassels. "I'm surprised she believes in such things."

"Have you felt or seen anything odd when you've been here on the weekends?" I asked lightly.

"I can't say I've noticed anything," Dempsey said with a snort. "But I'm usually so preoccupied with Jadie, I probably wouldn't notice a legion of the undead marching through the kitchen. By the time she's had breakfast and we've done the physical therapy, it's time for her morning snack and vitamins, and then I have to start thinking about lunch."

Vincent looked at his watch. "Speaking of food, there are some cans in the cupboard if anyone wants to snack on cold beans or ravioli."

"I can't believe you've had three days with no electricity!" Dempsey exclaimed, shaking her head. "If I'd known, I would have brought some food with me." She looked around the gloomily lit room. "No wonder your neighbor wants company. I mean, what else is there to do all evening with no TV and no lights or heating?"

"And no computer," Vincent reminded her. "It's astonishing how much difference electricity makes."

"I can see why you sent Jadie over to the farm," Dempsey said, nodding approvingly. "Even playing cards is going to be difficult in this light. But there are things you can do to fill the time without electricity, of course."

Colin glanced at me, and I knew that he was desperate to visit Kitty again.

"How about a drink?" Dempsey tried. "We don't need electricity to crack open a bottle of something. What have you got, Vincent?"

Vincent rose to his feet and went to the dining room. I excused myself and followed him, intending to warn him that Colin wanted to hypnotize me again. It was his house after all, and I was his guest.

Vincent was studying the label on a bottle of wine. He handed it to me as he returned his attention to the remaining selection in the cupboard.

"Am I right in thinking you and Colin are planning another session?"

"How did you guess?"

"Colin had that smug look on his face again. I don't like him messing with your mind, Kate."

"I think it's up to me whether I let someone mess with my mind or not."

"Well"—he turned his head to survey me doubtfully—"I hope you won't object if Mom and I listen in. It's too cold in the rest of the house for us to go off."

I considered this. Did I want to bare my soul in front of Vincent and his mother? Tara and Jadie had been present the first time, but that had somehow felt different. "Okay," I said slowly. "I can hardly throw you out of your own front room. If Colin is all right with it, then I won't object." I felt I should try to explain. "There's so much to Kitty I don't understand. I know she probably isn't real, but for my own sake I think I need to find out what it is she is trying to show me."

"It's your mind." Vincent became awkward again, turning his attention back to the wine. "There's, er . . . something else."

"What?"

"I told Maria I was planning to bring you back here with me, and she's invited us next door for drinks at eight o'clock. It made sense when I thought it was just going to be the two of us here on our own, so I said yes."

"Oh." I was surprised that Maria had wanted to see me again. I'd gotten the impression her agenda—whatever that may have been—extended only to Vincent.

We returned to the living room with a couple of bottles of wine and explained to Dempsey what we were going to do. She raised her eyebrows speculatively but moved into one of the armchairs so I could lie down on the couch. Vincent opened the first bottle while Colin set about making sure I was comfortable.

"Are you sure you want to go ahead with them both listening in?" Colin whispered as Vincent turned away to pour the drinks. "After what you said earlier about Vincent's wife, and then you disappearing upstairs for so long, I was beginning to wonder if they'd murdered you in the shower, Hitchcock-style."

"I can't believe Vincent's capable of murdering his wife," I said under my breath. "I think it would be best if we forgot I said anything."

"How does this work, then?" Dempsey asked as she sat back with the glass of wine Vincent handed to her.

"You have to be quiet and not talk," Colin told her firmly.

"Are you sure you want to go through with this?" Vincent asked me once more as Colin readied himself to begin the relaxation technique.

"Absolutely," I breathed as I leaned back against the cushions. "At least in the place I'm going, I have *some* memories and a past that might have made me who I am."

Colin began to talk, and soon his voice was droning like a bumblebee in my mind. I flexed my feet and let them go limp, tensed my calf muscles and then released them, squeezed my bottom down into the couch, and then worked my way up my spine and rolled my shoulders before letting them slump loosely down. Soon it felt as if the only physical things that connected me to the room were the hands that lay motionlessly next to my inert body, anchoring me to the sofa.

"Wake up, Kitty."

My eyes flickered open to find Garrett staring back at me with a look I couldn't quite discern. Brown water flowed past me, glittering in the rays of the afternoon sun. My hands were now gripping the cool sides of a small skiff.

"I've seen a good landing spot over there," Garrett said as he continued to row the skiff toward the bank. "It's a bit wild and overgrown, but I think there's a grassy patch where we can have our picnic."

It was a strange feeling. I was Kitty, and yet I was also Kate *watching* Kitty. I wanted to pinch myself to see if I was real, but Kitty's fingers wouldn't obey my instructions. I felt like a visitor who was expected to stand by and watch and listen but not actually participate in what was going on.

I tried to marshal my thoughts. Was I really in a hypnotic trance? Or was this some strangely realistic dream?

Kitty self-consciously tucked a stray strand of hair into her sunbonnet. I felt Kitty's gaze linger on her fiancé. He was wearing a navy blazer and wide-legged trousers, and I felt Kitty's flutter of pride that he was soon to be her husband. Sharing the intimacy of her thoughts seemed to meld us somehow together, and my consciousness edged closer into hers until we were one, watching as Garrett rowed the skiff expertly to the grassy bank and grabbed on to an overhanging branch, keeping the boat as close to the side as possible. I scrambled to my feet, and the skiff rocked danger-ously, but gathering up my long skirts in one hand, I made a leap for the bank. Brambles snagged at my stockings and the hem of my dress, but I didn't waste time stopping to untangle myself. Garrett was already throwing the rope to me, and I made a grab for it. After catching it deftly, I pulled the boat level with the bank. Garrett climbed out, took the rope from my hand, and looped it around the branches of a young willow tree.

Picking up my skirts, I followed Garrett up a steep bank thick with nettles and cow parsnip, pausing to gaze about me in awe. The view was wild and unspoiled, with small trees, shrubs, and areas of long grass crammed with buttercups. Pushing aside my inhibitions, I grabbed Garrett's hand ecstatically. "It's so beauti-ful! Oh, Garrett, I wish we could live right here."

We stood in silence for a few moments, hugging the moment to ourselves, while a trio of ducks quacked lazily at the water's edge and a kingfisher darted from a small tree into the brown water, surfacing a second later with a silver fish wriggling in its beak. I was excited to find this perfect place, and even Garrett's severe features softened into a near smile.

"Let's walk up that track a ways and see if there's any sign of life at the top of the rise." He strode off ahead of me while I scrambled to keep up, hoisting my skirts up and away from the tearing thistles and brambles.

We continued up through the wild meadow and along a sheep track, before coming across a couple of farm buildings with a vil-lage visible a few miles in the distance beyond. There was a pretty church set back slightly from the dusty road, a group of cherry trees dotted among the gravestones in the cemetery, and a collec-tion of small cottages nestled behind low stone walls. A horse peered at us from over the gate of a nearby field, swishing its tail to keep away the flies, but otherwise the village was quiet.

I smiled up at Garrett and slipped my hand into his. "This place is so perfect."

In an uncharacteristically tender gesture, Garrett reached out and swept an escaped tendril of hair from my face, and tucked it gently back under my bonnet, as I had done earlier. I pressed his hand to my cheek and felt a wave of emotion run through me.

Garrett stilled, his eyes searching mine.

"Is this what you want, Kitty?"

I nodded. I was twenty years old, and he had never even introduced me to his parents, but he was to be my husband, and my body yearned for his touch. He pulled me into a stable piled with sweet-smelling summer hay and we stood looking at each other, trembling at what was to come.

My body tingled with anticipation as his mouth found mine. As we kissed, his hand fumbled with my skirts, and a wave of an unknown emotion flooded through me. At the soft touch of his hand on my thigh, I quivered with delight, and slowly he lowered me onto a pile of hay and slid his body next to mine.

I gripped his hand tightly and looked searchingly into his eyes. "Tell me you love me."

"I love you, pretty Kitty," he murmured. "Say you will always be mine."

"Forever," I murmured as he moved slowly above me, "forever and always."

"*Kate!*" *An insistent voice* broke into my thoughts as I hastily straightened my skirts. "Kate, talk to me."

"Go away," I mumbled. "Go away and leave me alone."

"Kate, are you all right?" The voice was urgent, concerned. "Where have you gone?"

Someone was shaking me and tapping my face none too

gently. I tried to open my eyes, but my lids felt heavy, as if they had been stuck together with glue.

"What's the matter with her?" It was a female voice, full of anxiety. "Kate, can you hear me?"

I couldn't make my body respond to my instructions and I panicked. What was happening to me?

My mind was sifting through a number of images. There had been boyfriends before, hadn't there? When and where, I couldn't remember, but I knew with unfailing certainty that none of those brief relationships had worked out. I hadn't understood before, but now, having experienced love with Garrett, I realized that it wasn't my fault. No relationship could ever have matched up to what he and Kitty had had together.

Before I could think further, I heard a shrill ringing sound in my ears. Pictures of half-remembered people flashed through my mind, and my world went ominously blank.

chapter twenty-nine

I opened my eyes to find both Colin and Vincent leaning over me.

"That was the strangest thing I have ever witnessed." Dempsey was there too, kneeling on the floor holding one of my hands in hers. "What the heck just happened?"

I shook my head, not wanting to share the tumultuous feeling of a moment of passion with the man of Kitty's dreams, and then the fright of the second memory burning over the first. The touch of Garrett's lips was still tingling on the skin of my throat, and Kitty's tears of joy were still wet on my cheeks.

"I want to go back to sleep." I was shivering with cold and disoriented from the experience. Everything had seemed so real while I was there in Kitty's world, and I found myself reluctant to come down to earth and accept that Garrett may not have existed anywhere but inside my head.

"Try to stay awake." Dempsey rubbed my hands vigorously to

warm them. "You are here with us now, and we'll soon get you warmed up." She looked accusingly at Colin. "I've never witnessed anything like it. You do know what you're doing, I suppose?"

"I admit I've not had any previous experience with taking a subject back to a former incarnation," Colin confessed. "The first time we did this, I was trying to get Kate to remember who she really is, and we got Kitty instead."

"You're experimenting on her!" Dempsey said in disgust. "And this isn't exactly a controlled or safe environment for your 'subject,' as you call her, to be tested in."

She was becoming more agitated and I shook myself out of my torpor to peer more closely at her. There was an empty wine bottle on the coffee table behind her, standing among a pile of discarded chocolate wrappers.

"How long was I gone for?" I asked.

"Almost an hour," Vincent said beside me. "The relaxation exercises seemed to take forever, and then you just sort of floated away from us; it was an odd thing to watch."

"And it wasn't an experiment," Colin pointed out. He pushed his glasses firmly against the bridge of his nose. "I admit we might be sailing a bit close to the wind here, but it's not as if I'm documenting any of it for research purposes. I'm doing this more as a favor to Kate than anything else. Both of us have been fascinated by everything she's been reporting from her life as Kitty." He turned to me for confirmation. "You wanted to do this, didn't you, Kate? I haven't coerced you in any way?"

"No, no, of course not," I assured him, feeling better now that the unknown memory was fading. I sat forward, away from any physical contact with either him or Vincent. "I wanted to do it; I may want to do it again. It's addictive and scary, but to me it seems I'm there for such a short time." I hesitated, trying to find the right words. "I always feel cheated when I'm brought back here, when there's so much more about Kitty's life I want to discover."

"I'm not sure it's healthy." Dempsey surveyed me dubiously. "You are in a delicate state of mind already, what with your amnesia and everything. You might end up with psychiatric problems if you keep doing this time travel thing."

"You sound just like Tara," Colin told her.

"Ah! So I'm not the only one who thinks this is a highly unhealthy and unethical exercise."

"I don't think you are in any condition to pass judgment on what is healthy and what isn't," Colin pointed out. "You sat there and drank most of that bottle of wine on your own."

"It would take more than one measly bottle of wine to make me any the worse for wear," Dempsey retorted, flashing him a challenging grin. "I could drink you under the table any day."

"I don't doubt it for a moment," Colin said drily.

Vincent hurriedly consulted his watch and stood up. "Kate and I have to be next door by eight, so I think we'd better give you time to recover," he said to me, holding out his hand to help me to my feet.

"You're not leaving me alone for the evening with Dr. Jekyll here, are you?" Dempsey exclaimed in mock horror.

"I'm afraid so," Vincent told her as I steadied myself against him. "I promised Maria we'd be there at eight sharp."

"Can't I come with you?" Dempsey had a gleam in her eye.

Vincent looked dubious, but I felt relieved at her suggestion. I had been dreading a repeat of the uncomfortable evening next door, and I grabbed her arm gratefully. "I'd love for you to come with us."

She fixed her blue eyes on her son, and he capitulated begrudgingly.

"I suppose you could come along, as long as you promise to behave."

I was struck by the difference between mother and son; it was almost like a role reversal the way he tried to keep her in check. There was an underlying mischief to Dempsey that seemed to be missing in her rather straitlaced son.

"I'm so glad you're coming too." I dropped my hand to my side and smiled gratefully at Dempsey.

But she wasn't looking at me. "I'll do my best not to embarrass you in front of your neighbor, dearest," she quipped to her son. "Best behavior all around, I promise."

"We should eat before we go, I think," Vincent said, as practical as ever, ignoring his mother's gibe. "Have you decided on your choices? It's still cold canned beans or ravioli."

"Yummy," Dempsey proclaimed with a smile. "I can't wait."

The four of us tramped through the front garden to the house next door just before eight o'clock. Naturally, Colin hadn't wanted to be left out of the evening's entertainment. As soon as Dempsey had said she wanted to come, he'd asked to come too, and despite an ill-concealed reticence on Vincent's part, the host couldn't leave his guest in the cold house on his own.

Dempsey and I had ended up avoiding the canned food, opting instead to make a pile of peanut butter and jelly sandwiches, leaving the baked beans and ravioli to Vincent and Colin. We'd eaten by candlelight in front of the living room fire. It would have been cozy if the mood had been less tense. Vincent had toyed with his food and kept looking at his watch. I'd found myself wondering if perhaps there was more to the evening with Maria than just a few neighborly drinks.

As we approached Maria's front door, my stomach knotted.

Vincent, apparently sensing my apprehension, gave my hand a quick squeeze.

"Don't look so worried," he whispered as we heard footsteps approaching the door. "I know Maria was a bit confrontational last time you met, but she's not an ogre."

"There you are!" Maria beamed at us as she flung the door wide for us to enter. Her gaze went past us, and her eyes opened wide in surprise. "So you have brought guests?"

"I hope you don't mind," Vincent murmured as we followed her indoors. He introduced his mother and Colin.

"But we have already met," Maria said, glancing at Dempsey uncertainly. "Your mother and I have exchanged pleasantries over the garden fence once or twice." Her dark eyes came to rest on Colin's face. "So you must be the famed hypnotherapist."

Something passed across Maria's face that I couldn't quite discern, and I gave a shiver of apprehension as Colin reached out and shook her hand.

"You are too kind," he said. "I don't know what Vincent has been telling you, but I'm hardly famous."

Maria tossed back her long dark hair and gave a shrill laugh. "And you are far too modest." Her eyes narrowed behind the smile, and again I felt that warning flutter as the fine hairs on my arms and the back of my neck stood upright. Still wearing our coats we followed Maria down the icy hallway to the living room, where a fire was burning in the grate.

"Michael, will you fetch our guests some of my homemade fruit punch?"

The boy, who had been lying close to the fire with a book, scrambled to his feet. He moved awkwardly, as if not yet in control of his growing teenage body, his baggy jeans hanging from slim hips.

"With no electricity for the computer or his Xbox games,

Michael has been reading through all the books in the house," Maria explained. "So we have something for which to thank the weather after all. My husband enjoyed a good thriller, and he left most of them behind when he moved out. I am glad I did not find the time to throw them away." She accepted a drink from the tray Michael was holding out to her.

The boy handed out the rest of the glasses and retreated to the door, apparently preferring the cold of his bedroom to the adult company by the fire. I couldn't help but compare Maria's son to the equally handsome thirteen-year-old Garrett whom Kitty had first met in the school yard. One had been so self-assured and vocal; the other was nervous and reserved. Taking a sip of the punch, I watched as the door closed behind Michael and a flutter of something cold whispered through my soul.

The drinks seemed never-ending, interspersed with tall stories and wistful reminiscences from both Maria and Dempsey. The two women, it seemed, had much in common, with husbands who had walked out on them, leaving them to bring up sons on their own. As I let yet another mouthful of red wine linger on my tongue, my mind drifted again to the young Garrett and his determination to make something of himself, to restore his family to their former glory. The picture of a sharp-nosed woman dressed in a plum-colored gown flickered into my mind.

"I will not let you ruin his life," she hissed into my ear. "He is not to know about this child, do you hear?"

"What do you mean?" I sat sharply upright on the leather sofa. My eyes, which had drooped shut with the effects of the warm fire, several glasses of punch, and half a bottle of wine, flashed open. I elbowed Dempsey in the side with the abrupt movement, but she didn't seem to notice.

I stared around the room. "Who said that?"

Maria gazed at me, her face paling. "What did you hear?" she breathed.

"I'm merely saying that a mother's love is not to be under-estimated." Dempsey had missed the sudden tension in the room. She was slurring her words and waving her wineglass in the air inches from my face. "A man might be able to turn his back on his res...bonsibilities, but a mother will care for her child come what may."

Even through the fog of alcohol and my confusion over who had spoken, her words hit home. I glanced sharply at Vincent. My mind, which must have been wandering, half-asleep and imagin-ing all sorts of visions, was suddenly wide awake. Dempsey was lost in the past, recalling how she had been abandoned to bring her son up alone, just as Maria was doing now, but what of her missing daughter-in-law, Cheryl? If a relaxed and unguarded Dempsey truly believed what she was saying, what nonsense did that make of the story that a mother could abandon a sick little girl like Jadie to go off with another man?

Vincent's face had drained of color. He saw me looking at him, got unsteadily to his feet, crossed to his mother, and took the wineglass from her hand. "I think you've had quite enough. It's time we went home." He held his hand out to help Dempsey to her feet.

"But the evening is only just beginning."

"Mom!"

Dempsey stilled suddenly at the tone of his voice and allowed him to pull her upright. She looked anxiously around the room as she smoothed imaginary creases from her trousers. "Yes, yes, you are quite right.... Maria, thank you so much for your hospi-tality."

Colin, who had been demolishing a bowl of stuffed olives,

looked up as if only just noticing the sudden change of mood. "Are we going?"

"I believe so," I told him.

Maria looked as baffled as Colin, but busied herself collecting the wineglasses as we shuffled to our feet. "One moment," she said as we headed out into the gloom of the candlelit hallway. We stood shivering until she reappeared, smiling benignly round at her departing guests. "Here." She leaned in to kiss my cheek, and as she did so, Maria tucked a piece of paper into my coat pocket. "Something for you to look at later when you are alone."

I glanced into her dark eyes, but she was smiling again, seeing her guests out into the cold night. I followed slowly behind with Colin as Vincent guided an unsteady Dempsey back through the front gardens, and I found myself wondering what exactly had just happened in the house next door.

chapter thirty

$\mathcal{I}$ *awoke in* the morning with a pounding headache. I gingerly opened my eyes, but even the small amount of light filtering between the curtains caused me to squint and turn my head away. I lay quietly for a while, trying to work out what had happened and how I'd gotten here, but the previous evening was mostly a blur.

My mouth was dry and I was desperate for a drink of water. The normally pleasant scent of fabric softener emanating from the duvet made me feel distinctly queasy. I had just levered myself carefully into a sitting position with a view to making my way down to the bathroom, when Dempsey stuck her head around the attic door.

"Oh, so you're awake. How are you feeling?"

"Like I've been hit by a truck," I rasped. "What happened?"

"How much do you remember?"

Something in her tone made me hesitate. I recalled our sudden departure from Maria's at the end of the evening, and while I couldn't quite remember everything that had been said, I rubbed my head and decided to plead total ignorance until I'd had time to think about things in more detail.

"Not very much; I remember sitting on the couch. We had so much to drink. . . . I don't know."

"It seems you drank far too much of Maria's fruit punch." Dempsey came in and perched on the edge of the bed. She placed a glass of water on the bedside cabinet and watched as I took a grateful sip. "And I think we all had rather too much of the wine."

"You don't seem to be particularly hungover," I observed.

"Ah, but I have had more experience at drinking than you have, and of course you are probably still suffering from the effects of whatever it is that made you lose your memory in the first place. You have to pace yourself if you still want to be upright at the finish line."

"You make life sound like a sort of game."

"Who knows, maybe it is."

"Well, I'm not sure I like the way this game is turning out." I rubbed grumpily at my aching eyes. "Unless my memory returns soon, I think I'll probably go crazy, even if it turns out I'm not already."

Dempsey patted my hand as if I were a small child having a bit of a tantrum. "Look, why don't you have a nice hot bath while I make you a cup of tea? You'll feel better afterward, and then Vincent can show you what he's been able to find out about missing persons on the computer."

"Hot bath?" I echoed, puzzled. "Tea . . . computer?"

Dempsey grinned, got up, and went to the light switch by the door. She flicked it on with a dramatic flourish, and the bedroom light popped on.

"The power is back!" I exclaimed. "When did that happen?"

"A couple of hours ago." Dempsey turned the light off again.

"Vincent's making us omelettes for brunch to celebrate. Look, I'll go and run the bath. Come downstairs when you're ready."

She left, and I listened to the drone of water running in the distance. I swallowed gingerly. My insides were churning, and my head still felt like I'd banged it on a concrete block, but it was nice to be looked after.

I crawled out of bed and rested in a heap on top of the duvet, letting my nausea settle before I pulled myself upright and waited for the sound of the running water to stop. Alive was good, I told myself with a rueful smile. Alive right here and now was definitely something to aim for.

After making my way down the few rickety stairs to the bathroom, I locked the door, got undressed, and then lowered myself into the steaming water. My stomach continued to churn, but gradually the woolly feeling in my head and limbs began to wear off, and I realized that perhaps I wasn't going to be sick after all.

Now that conditions were returning to normal, I knew I should get someone to take me to the nearest hospital to investigate my head injury and the memory loss.

"*Ah, there you are,*" Vincent said as I teetered shakily into the kitchen dressed in a T-shirt, a pair of his wife's jeans, and a warm fleece sweater. "I'll do your omelette next if you're hungry."

"Good grief, you look terrible," Colin spluttered through a mouthful of stringy cheese. He pulled out a kitchen chair so I could sit down. "I think we all had far too much to drink."

"I know," I replied, wondering as I watched Colin if eating was a good idea after all. "Remind me never to drink again."

"It's affected you worst of all," Dempsey murmured. "It's likely that head injury of yours is to blame."

"You should be more careful." Colin looked me appraisingly up and down. "I need you to have a clear head if we're going to visit Kitty again."

"Oh, no." I covered my face with my hands. "I'm not sure I'm up to it today." I pictured the woman in the plum-colored gown and sighed. I hadn't even been under hypnosis when I'd conjured her up, but the punch had obviously been more potent than I'd realized, and I was in no hurry to meet with her again.

"Leave her alone," Dempsey said as she placed a mug of steaming tea in front of me. "She's suffering enough without you making her feel worse."

"What do you mean?" Colin asked, his head snapping up abruptly.

"I mean that we should be taking more care of her. She's handled this memory loss thing so well that I think we forgot that she'd had that bang to her head. We should have been more careful with what she was drinking, and I'm not sure she should be put under hypnosis again. I mean, it's not helping her present predicament, is it?"

Vincent came across and placed a plate in front of me. "It'll make you feel better if you eat something. I've left the cheese out of your omelette."

I picked up my fork slowly and prodded the soft yellow omelette, surprised he had remembered my dislike of cheese. "I didn't know you could cook." I was glad to let the subject of my memory loss and last night's excesses drop for the present. Vincent took the seat opposite me and leaned his elbows on the table so he could watch me eat.

"Mom taught me how to cook eggs and open cans when I was in my teens." He gave a nod of acknowledgment in Dempsey's direction. "It made life easier when she was working all hours and I had to let myself in from school and make my own snacks.

Omelettes have always been my specialty." He gave a grimace. "Anyway, we are a bit low on ingredients, as the contents of the freezer defrosted and everything else in the fridge has gone bad."

"Tara thought you wouldn't be much good at looking after yourself," I commented as I took a small trial mouthful of food.

"Just goes to show she doesn't know everything about me." He leaned back in his chair. "After all, there's no point employing a housekeeper and then cooking for myself."

I gave him a sharp glance, wondering yet again how he could be so totally unaware of Tara's feelings for him.

"I looked up missing persons on the Internet this morning," Vincent went on.

I sat up a bit straighter. "Is anyone looking for me?"

"Not that I could see," he said. "I didn't have as long as I would have liked before Mom shoved me out of the way to do some research of her own."

"So no one of my description has been listed as missing in the last week?"

"I'll have to look again to be absolutely sure. We could do it right after you've finished eating, if you feel up to it."

I took another small mouthful of the omelette and nodded. "Yes, thanks, if you don't mind." I still wasn't sure how I felt about being found. I felt safe here, though I still didn't entirely know who to trust.

"The evening ended very abruptly, don't you think?" Colin commented suddenly as if the conversation about the computer and missing persons had never happened. "One minute we were talking about mothers and their children, and the next we were being bundled out of the door." He turned to Vincent. "What was that all about?"

"I have no idea." Vincent pushed back his chair and made as if to get up.

Colin turned to me. "Didn't you think it was odd?"

I sighed, pushing my plate away. Although I agreed, I wasn't prepared to voice an opinion—not yet. "I really don't remember very much about it."

"Come and sit down, Vincent." Dempsey sounded nervous, and I wondered if she was afraid he blamed her for being off her guard and saying too much. She was probably well aware that he'd thought she was about to blurt out a confession about what had really happened to his wife. Or perhaps, I thought wearily, I was still overreacting and reading too much into what everyone was saying and doing.

"Have another cup of tea." Dempsey lifted the teapot and poured Vincent and me each a cup. "Everyone's feeling a bit fragile this morning, I think."

"I've got work to do." Vincent pushed the tea abruptly away. "I'll be in my office."

The teapot trembled ever so slightly in Dempsey's hand as she lowered it onto its ceramic stand. Vincent stamped off toward his study, leaving Colin, Dempsey, and me staring at one another uncomfortably.

chapter thirty-one

"*I think* I might make a piece of toast," Colin said into the ensuing silence as he rose to his feet. "I didn't realize how much I enjoyed hot food until these last few days."

"Tara and Jadie will be able to come home now, won't they?" I forced a cheery brightness. I could see Vincent's pain clearly reflected in his mother's eyes, and I wondered how many times in the past he had retreated to his office when conversations had become uncomfortable. I looked across at her. "I bet you've missed her."

"Yes, yes, of course I have," Dempsey murmured.

But her next words showed that her thoughts were still clearly with Vincent. "I think it has been just as well that Jadie was away while her father worked through his grief at last. I've never seen him as upset as this, even after Amber passed on and when Cheryl left him. He's always seemed so in control of himself."

"Everyone has to grieve in the end," Colin told her. "Shutting it out only delays the inevitable journey."

"Journey?" Dempsey echoed sharply. "What do you mean?"

"Grieving is like making your way down a dark tunnel. You could think of it as a long train with compartments leading off on either side." The toast popped up and Colin caught it deftly. "Each door represents a raw emotion that has to be dealt with before you can move forward with your life."

"I know what grief is, thank you very much," Dempsey said flatly.

Colin spread his toast liberally with margarine and marmalade. "Then you should allow yourself this journey," he said. "Desertion induces a kind of grief too. And it isn't a road that should be left too long untraveled."

Dempsey was giving Colin her full attention now, her eyes fixed on his with a sort of amazed expression. I realized that although Vincent's father had long ago abandoned her, his desertion was as raw as when it had first happened, and on top of that she had lost a grandchild and had to watch her son, daughter-in-law, and other grandchild grieve.

"By denying grief," Colin continued, taking a bite of toast and talking with his mouth full, "a person is merely left waiting at the station for the next train to take them into the tunnel, or the next, or the next. The journey has to be made in the end, but the waiting can take a terrible toll on those who remain in denial."

I was holding my breath. At any moment, I was sure Dempsey would break down and yell at Colin to mind his own business—at the very least stalk out of the room. But she remained sitting where she was, her shoulders sagging slightly.

"Is that why Jadie wouldn't speak?" she asked him, swallowing as her voice cracked with emotion. "Because Vincent, Cheryl, and I weren't strong enough to begin our own journeys, Jadie didn't know how to make hers?"

"It is possible," Colin replied. "But you can't blame yourself. You had your own grief to deal with, and it's not always easy to help others when you are struggling too."

Dempsey slowly rose to her feet and, holding on to the back of the chair for support, stood for a moment as if to collect herself before walking from the room.

"Should we go after her?" I asked.

He shook his head. "She needs some time on her own."

"But she lives on her own. She's had two years keeping everything bottled up inside."

Colin shrugged. "Go to her if you think she'll talk to you."

I hurried through the hall, glanced into the empty living room, and went up the stairs. Dempsey's room was empty, but I was pretty sure I knew where to find her. Sure enough she was sitting on Amber's bed, staring into space, and she barely seemed to notice when I sat down beside her.

"Losing Amber was the worst thing that ever happened to me," Dempsey said quietly. She covered her eyes with her hands and let out a single strangled sob.

I leaned over and put my arm around her. "Don't cry," I said helplessly. But I could almost hear Colin's voice telling me that crying was the beginning of the healing process, so then I sat quietly, while tears coursed unchecked down Dempsey's face. After a while I ventured to take up where Colin had left off. "Perhaps you need to get on that train Colin was talking about."

"You don't understand," she said quietly between sobs. "It's all my fault. Because I was adopted, no one knew my medical history. I must have been carrying the gene and passed it on to Vincent, and then Amber got it, and poor little Jadie....Oh my God, I need a drink."

"No, you don't," I murmured gently. "It will only make the journey take longer."

"I can't make the damned journey," Dempsey snapped suddenly, raising red-rimmed eyes to mine. "I don't want to. I deserve to suffer like Amber suffered. *I'm* to blame."

"Do you think drinking helps you?" I asked.

"Of course it does; I can shut out the world and forget that I'm a monster."

"If you think you deserve to suffer and want to feel the pain, then maybe you should stop taking the painkiller."

Dempsey stared at me as if I'd slapped her in the face. The tears halted as abruptly as they'd started. "You don't pull any punches, do you?" she said quietly.

I took her hand and tried to read what I saw in her eyes. "Are you ready to embark?"

"I don't know that I'm strong enough."

"You were strong enough to survive your husband leaving you and to bring up a teenage boy on your own. You're strong enough for this," I told her. "And hopefully I'll be around to help you if you'll let me."

"You won't. No one stays around."

I was quiet, wondering if I was promising too much, given the circumstances.

She took a tissue from her pocket and blew her nose loudly, and when we'd both recovered a bit, we went down to the kitchen to put on more tea. It was just coming to a boil when we heard someone at the door.

"Shall I get it?" I asked.

"Would you?" Dempsey murmured with a last sniff as she dropped fresh tea bags into the pot.

My head swam as I rose to my feet, reminding me that my hangover wasn't totally gone. I realized that Vincent had been right about eating; as bad as I felt now, it was nothing compared to how I'd been earlier. I glanced along the passage toward his study as I crossed to the front door, but he either hadn't heard the knocking or wasn't interested in seeing who it was.

Drawing back the curtain, I opened the door to find Tara standing on the step juggling a bag, with Jadie at her side.

"Hello," Tara said with a tight smile, "we're home."

"Kate!" Jadie was beaming. She flung her arms round my waist, and I held her for a moment before she released me and scampered off toward the kitchen, where I heard Dempsey's shriek of joy. Tara slipped past me, headed straight for Vincent's study.

Looking out down the garden path, I noticed the green Land Rover parked at the end. Adam was pulling Tara's and Jadie's bags from the back.

"Hello," I called when he straightened up to carry the bags toward the house.

His face broke into a warm smile when he saw me. "Hello, Kate. How is everything?"

"It's wonderful to have the electricity working again." I decided not to mention our recent emotional trauma, and stood back so he could dump the bags inside the house. "We just had a late breakfast."

"I'll leave you to it, then." He paused on the doorstep. "I expect you've got things to do."

"Jadie's grandmother is here," I told him. "It will be the first time in two years Dempsey has heard her talk."

"Give her my regards," Adam said, turning to leave. "Dempsey's one of the good guys."

"I didn't know you knew her." I wondered if Adam could possibly have known the doubts that had chafed inside my head about Dempsey over the last day, and how glad I was to hear his opinion of her.

"She likes to take Jadie for walks when she's here on the weekends and the weather is being kind," he explained. "I have to pass the end of the drive here to get to my top field, and I've bumped into them on lots of occasions when I've been out hedging or seeing to the stock. Dempsey always calls hello and we spend a few minutes chatting.

"The kettle has just boiled," I said with a smile. "Would you like to come in for a cup of tea?" I realized that I didn't want him to go. Opening the door to him had been like breaking open the locks of an institution and glimpsing the normal everyday world beyond.

"I'd love to, but Gran is expecting me back, and her whole day will be put out if we don't stick to our routine."

"How is Betty today?" I asked. "And Bill, of course."

"They're the same as ever," he replied, turning. He paused halfway down the path and looked back. "I don't suppose you'd like to come back with me and visit them both? I know you only left yesterday morning, but Bill hasn't stopped talking about you and I'm sure they would both be delighted to see you."

"Do you know . . . ," I started, and glanced over my shoulder into the depths of a house, where I knew Vincent was struggling to deal with his demons; Colin was probably working on how to continue getting Dempsey to come to terms with her grief; Tara was no doubt screwing herself up into knots, wondering what I'd been up to with her employer in her absence; and Jadie was safely home where she belonged. "I might just take you up on that. Could you wait a moment while I tell Dempsey and the others where I'm off to?"

"Yes, of course."

Peeking round the kitchen door, I found Jadie snuggled up on her grandmother's lap, telling her about her pet lamb.

"Who would have thought it?" Dempsey was muttering over and over as she stroked Jadie's blond locks. Colin was lounging at the table, his legs stretched out, cup of tea in hand, making no attempt, I noticed, to get home now that the weather had cleared and the electricity was working again.

"Sorry to interrupt," I said. "I'm going back to the farm with Adam to see how Betty and Bill are doing, if that's all right with everyone."

"Yes, of course," Dempsey said distractedly.

"I was planning to do another session this afternoon." Colin straightened and rested his tea cup on the table, his eyes searching my face. "You are coming back later, aren't you?"

I was a little wary. Intriguing though I had found Kitty's life, after last night, when I had feared that I might have strayed into her world by accident, I was beginning to doubt the wisdom of opening the door into my past yet again. I thought of Adam waiting out by the gate, and I looked longingly over my shoulder, only to find myself face-to-face with Vincent.

"I hope you'll be back later," he echoed Colin's query. "I thought we were going to go back to the missing persons file on the Internet."

Tara was hovering by Vincent's side. He seemed to have recovered from his earlier outburst and was looking apologetic.

"I thought you were anxious to find out your true identity." He fixed me so intently with those blue eyes of his that I almost wavered in my decision to skip out.

"I'm sorry." I inched past him into the hall. "I forgot."

"How can anyone forget they're a missing person with no identity, thrown onto the mercy of strangers?" Tara said sourly. "Most people would be desperate to know who they really were."

I felt torn. Tara was right. I had been so charmed by this place and these people that I had again allowed myself to be sidetracked from my desire to discover my true identity and move on with my old life, even despite my suspicions of everyone's agenda.

At that moment Jadie bounded out from the kitchen and

launched herself at me. "Come and play with me," she demanded, winding her arms around my waist.

"Later," I said, and smiled. "I think Tara and your grandma would like some time with you now."

She flashed a sulky glance at Tara and looked back at me. "I want to play with *you*," she insisted.

I hesitated, "Well..."

"For goodness' sake," Tara exploded, her eyes flashing dangerously over the child's head, "why don't you just go and stop interfering? Jadie, come with me."

Tara took Jadie by the hand and pulled her off toward the kitchen.

Shocked by Tara's reaction, I paused with my hand on the front door, my mind made up. For a couple of hours at least I was determined to get away from this house and everyone in it. I needed to take stock.

chapter thirty-two

In my enthusiasm to be away from the house, I almost knocked into Adam, who was hunkered down on the path, retying the laces of his work boots. I stood breathlessly in front of him as he straightened and gave me a questioning smile.

"Eager to escape?"

"You could say that."

He removed his hat and waved it toward the Land Rover with a small bow. "Your getaway vehicle awaits."

I clambered up into the Land Rover and fastened my seat belt as he went to the driver's side and climbed in. "Thank you for rescuing me. Things were getting pretty tense in there."

"Rescuing damsels in distress is my specialty," he said drily, and gunned the engine into life.

We traveled the couple of miles to his farmhouse in silence. I looked out the window at the changing landscape. What had previously been a white carpet with smoothly undulating dips and mounds had suddenly become a brown and green patchwork of hills and trees, ditches, hedges, and fields, where crocuses and wild daffodils gave off small flashes of brilliant color. The warm front that had swept up from the south had transformed the landscape in a matter of hours.

It wasn't until the Land Rover had swung into the cobbled farmyard and Adam had turned off the engine that he turned to face me.

"Why the eagerness to escape?" he asked lightly, pulling off his knitted work cap and turning it over in his hands. I found myself studying those hands—the skin reddened and weathered, strong fingers tapering to blunt nails. I had to stifle an urge to lay my own hands on top of his to make them better, and it occurred to me that I had never once crossed the boundary of his personal space, never come into any kind of direct physical contact with him, not even to shake hands. "Are they driving you crazy?"

"I suppose they are." I was slightly breathless at his proximity in the confined space and found myself babbling. "But I'm sure they don't mean to. It's just that I seem to be part of everyone's game plan. I am indebted to them all for taking me in and treating me as if I belong. It's just that I'm confused by what they want from me. To be honest, I'm feeling a bit smothered."

"They've been tapping into your subconscious again?" I noticed the sarcasm was tempered by the flicker of a smile.

"Something like that."

"Do you want to talk about it?"

I found that I did, very much. And I realized as we sat in the cooling vehicle that it mattered what he thought of it all. So I told Adam what I remembered about the previous evening when the woman in the plum-colored gown had told Kitty off, and how I hadn't even been under hypnosis when it had happened. I leaned against the door and swiveled to face him. "And the last time I was under hypnosis I had a sort of weird disjointed dream where

Kitty, Garrett, and I existed together." Blushing, I recalled what had happened between Kitty and Garrett in the stable by the river. Had that lovemaking resulted in a child? Could the woman in the plum-colored dress have been Garrett's mother? "I know it sounds ridiculous, but I'm beginning to wonder if I'm connected to that house in some way. There are certainly some odd things happening there." I thought of Jadie talking again, and Dempsey breaking down, of the fact that I was able to slip so easily into Kitty's world, and of course there were my worries about Vincent's missing wife. "It's strange, the way that Cheryl left."

"What do you mean?" He had gone very still.

"I mean, she left all her things behind, even her bag and wallet. I think it's very odd."

He was silent for a while, and then he looked me in the eye and I found myself mesmerized by his gaze. "Do you suspect that something happened to her? Is that what's unsettling you?"

I nodded. My heart was hammering in my chest so loudly that I almost looked down to see if the pounding was visible through my clothes. I wondered if I should have kept quiet about my suspicions. I had regretted telling Colin as soon as Vincent had put my mind at rest, but this felt different. Somehow it felt right to be sharing my thoughts with Adam.

"That and the weird feeling I have that I've been in that house before," I confessed. "I have had a couple of déjà vu experiences since I've been there. On the first night I arrived, Tara was stoking the fire, and I had this odd feeling I'd seen her do it before." I paused. "But then I felt it again when you brought the logs in for the fire in your parlor, so I thought maybe the action itself was familiar, rather than the place."

"It could simply have been a reawakening memory," he suggested. "Perhaps you have a house with an open fire wherever you live now."

It seemed like such an obvious possibility that I wondered why I had only vaguely considered such a simple explanation myself. "I felt it when I put my hand on the stair banister too, an odd feeling of belonging."

"Maybe your nerves are on edge because of the situation you've found yourself in. Just because you've had a momentary recollection of a half-forgotten experience doesn't necessarily mean anything. And Cheryl may simply have forgotten her bag; she was obviously under a great deal of stress."

"I feel really stupid." I felt myself blushing. "I did wonder earlier if what I was remembering was something to do with my real life. I suppose I've been somewhat sucked into the problems in Vincent's household. I'm jumping at shadows." I took a deep breath, trying to steady myself. "Maybe I've been analyzing everything that's happened too deeply. You're probably right. I may simply be recalling something of my real life."

His dark eyebrows furrowed into a frown. "But you don't really believe that, do you?" he probed.

"I really don't know what to believe. The images of Kitty and Garrett must have come from somewhere."

A sudden barking outside the Land Rover broke up the conversation. Adam opened the driver's door, and I could see Lad standing to attention beside the vehicle, barking with increasing agitation.

"What's the matter, boy?" Adam climbed down. "What is it?"

Lad refused to allow his master to pat his head and continued to bark. Adam swore and strode off toward the farmhouse, his dog prancing and whining around his ankles. Hurrying after him into the kitchen, I found him hoisting Bill off the floor and into his chair by the stove.

"What on earth were you doing?" Adam demanded as he tucked the blanket around the old man's knees. "Where's Gran?"

I went to the stove and removed a pan that had boiled dry and was hissing ominously. I turned to find Adam kneeling by his grandfather's chair, rubbing warmth back into Bill's twisted hands.

"What happened?"

"It's Betty." The old man could barely get the words out, he was in such distress. "She forgot she put a pan on to boil and she wandered off somewhere."

I heard the fear in his voice and felt prickles of anxiety run up and down my spine.

"I must have nodded off, and when I woke, she wasn't here. I called and called, and when she didn't answer, I tried to get up to look for her but I couldn't find my crutches, and my legs wouldn't hold me."

"I'll go and look upstairs." I turned and made for the staircase. "Betty?" I called as I went. "Betty, are you up here?"

I searched the upstairs room by room, noticing the signs written in marker and stuck to the doors so that Betty would remember where she was—"Bedroom," "Bathroom," "Adam's room"—but there was no sign of her. Adam joined me, after thoroughly checking the downstairs. His normally bronzed features were pale and drawn, his mouth set in a straight line.

"The back door's open," he whispered. "Gran must have wandered off somewhere."

We returned to the kitchen to check on Bill, but he was looking as gray as his grandson, and there were tears collecting in the corners of his rheumy eyes.

"Go after her, both of you, please. I've got a gut feeling she might have gone down to the river. She was always happiest by the water, but at this time of year, with all the melting snow, the current will be ferocious."

"Are you sure you'll be all right here?" I asked him. My mind raced with the terrible possibilities of what might have occurred to a confused old woman out alone by a raging river.

"Yes, yes, I'm fine." He made a grab for my hand with his gnarled fingers and dug his nails into the palm of my hand. "Just bring my Betty back to me . . . please."

chapter thirty-three

"*Looks like Betty's* taken her boots," I observed as I slipped into the old pair I'd used on my previous visit. I grabbed one of Bill's spare blankets from the washing pile. "Has she gone off on her own like this before?"

"Gran's always loved walking by the river. Gramps told me she always went there when things got overwhelming with the farm and the children. But she hasn't been down there for years, as far as I know." Adam was already striding from the back door, and I hurried after him.

Lad was out in front as we headed down the paved path that linked the front and rear of the house. We passed a disheveled-looking herb garden, then strode through an apple orchard full of gnarled, leafless trees.

"How far away is the river? Shouldn't we check the barns and outbuildings first?"

"If she's in one of the farm buildings, she'll be fine until we get back from the river. If she's at the river, we may not have much time."

"Shouldn't we go in the tractor?"

"It's too wet in the lower field at this time of year," he called back as he barreled ahead. "The tractor would get bogged down. It'll be quicker on foot."

I had to break into a trot to keep up with him, and the boots slopped about loosely on my feet, but my main concern was what we would do if we got to the river and Betty wasn't there.

After navigating the coarse hills on the far side of the apple orchard, we slipped through a gate into a wide sloping meadow of short wintering grass, which appeared to run down toward a thin belt of leafless trees at its lowest edge. Beyond the line of trees, a silver band of water snaked in a wide arc around the farm's boundaries. Lad surged ahead and disappeared toward the trees, barking excitedly. Adam quickened his pace, and I skidded down the increasingly muddy slope behind him until we came to the bottom edge of the field, where the swollen river chewed at the mud banks, engulfing a row of wooden fence posts that ran right down to the water's edge.

When we were close, I realized that there was a gap in the line of trees, presumably where animals waded down to drink when the water wasn't so high, and to one side of the space, under a huge weeping willow, a frail old lady sat perched on a weathered stone bench, watching the river slide by only a short distance from where she sat. Lad was already standing close beside her, resting his snout on her knees.

She glanced up when Adam approached. He put his hand on her shoulder, and I was close enough to see the recognition register in her eyes and a smile light up her features. He perched next to her and took her cold hands in his.

"What are you doing out here, Gran?" he asked gently. "You'll catch a cold!"

Betty was wearing a housecoat over her tweed skirt and thin sweater. Her stockinged legs looked like spindly sticks protruding from her Wellington boots, but despite the fact that her lips were blue with cold, she didn't appear to be in any distress.

I crept forward and wrapped the blanket I'd been carrying around her shoulders. She glanced in my direction but clearly didn't recognize me, and turned her attention back to her grandson.

"I've always loved this spot," she told him. "Your father and I used to eat lunch together on this bench when he was harvesting the river field. I'd walk down with a basketful of sandwiches and a bottle or two of brown ale, and he'd take a break and sit with me in the shade."

"I'm Adam, Gran, not Uncle Jim."

"You and your sisters used to take the dinghy out on the river when you were small. Do you remember? And once, your father had to wade in and rescue you when you let the oars float away while you were fishing."

I noticed a battered old boat drawn high up onto the bank. It was tied by a strong rope to the trunk of the ancient willow, and I thought of how Garrett and Kitty had tied their skiff to a young willow tree at what looked like a very similar spot.

"Come on, Gran." Adam tried to help her to her feet. "We've got to get you back into the warm house. Your hands are like ice."

"I like it here." Betty pulled away from him. She sounded irritated at being disturbed. "The children are all safe at school, and Bill is asleep in the kitchen; I'll follow you back later."

"You don't have a coat on, Gran," Adam pointed out, "and it's freezing out here."

"But I don't want to go."

Adam looked helplessly at me, then back at his grandmother. "I'll have to put you over my shoulder and carry you if you won't come," he warned.

"Betty," I tried, coming around to where she could see me. "Bill has sent me to tell you he's waiting for his lunch."

"Bill's sound asleep," she said defensively.

"Well, he's awake now and waiting for his lunch." I hoped I was appealing to the sense of duty that had probably been the motivating force behind most of her life. I didn't think I could bear to watch the humiliation of her grandson having to hoist her over his shoulder and drag her back to the farmhouse.

She squinted at her old gold wristwatch. "It isn't lunchtime yet; the meat won't be done."

"Come on, Betty," I said firmly. "We promised Bill we would bring you home. You can come back and sit by the river when the weather improves."

The old lady pursed her lips, but started to rise to her feet. Adam put out a hand to steady her. "Careful, Gran. We don't want you falling in the river."

She paused and peered at the dark water rushing by only a couple of steps away, and gave a strange smile. "It calls to me," she murmured, leaning dangerously close to the edge of the bank. "I feel like if I slipped, the water would catch me and keep me safe."

A cold hand reached through time and pressed against my chest. Where had I heard those exact words before? Hadn't Alice expressed that very sentiment when Kitty had drawn her away from the edge of the cliff that day by the sea? I glanced nervously at the swiftly moving current and grabbed at my throat, fighting an impulse to scream and flail my arms against the image of heavy black water crushing the breath from my lungs. *Stop it,* I admonished myself silently. I was allowing myself to become hysterical because of a random choice of words from a confused old lady. I glanced at Adam, but he was focused on drawing his grandmother safely away from the river. Closing my eyes, I pushed away the image of water pouring into my tortured lungs. For some reason, I knew the heavy suffocating pain, the terrible fear that came with drowning, the knowledge that I was dying, and the impending sense of release. I pictured myself being swept irrevocably along on the current, eyes staring blankly, hair fanning out around me like a feathered halo.

I sucked in a huge mouthful of air and Adam gave me a sharp look. "Kate? Are you okay? Can you take Gran's other arm?"

I nodded shakily, then reached out and took Betty's arm. Pushing the memory of drowning to the back of my mind, I wondered, as we slipped and skidded up the muddy slope, how this frail old woman had made her way to the bench over such terrain, and was grateful she hadn't ended up in the water.

By the time we reached the farmhouse, Betty was shivering uncontrollably, despite having the blanket and Adam's coat around her shoulders. Bill greeted us in the doorway, balanced precariously on crutches he could barely hold. I had the feeling he would have been pacing anxiously up and down if his legs could have held him.

"Betty, love!" he exclaimed when he saw her. "What have you been up to, you silly old woman?"

"I just went down to sit by the river," Betty replied as Adam lowered her into her chair by the fire. "You were snoring so loudly I didn't think you'd miss me."

"Of course I missed you." He sank into the chair opposite his wife and let his crutches drop away. Leaning forward, he sandwiched one of her icy hands between his own. "You are the most important person in my world. I thought for a while there that I'd lost you."

She gazed across at him with misty eyes. "You old fool," she whispered with a tender smile. "You won't get rid of me that easily."

Adam had to get back to work, so I busied myself making cups of hot tea and then getting the family's lunch finished with a stream of instructions from Betty. It seemed that for the moment she was content to sit with her husband and let me do most of the work, and I was grateful to be busy, as it kept my mind from dwelling on what had happened down by the river and the possibility that I had just found the very place Kitty and Garrett had come ashore on that lazy Sunday afternoon so many years before.

And if that were the case, I thought, if the river was real and the willow tree was in exactly the place I'd seen it in my dream, did it prove that everything else I'd recounted to Colin in past sessions about Kitty and Garrett *was* after all some sort of hidden memory from a previous life? Was Colin right in his belief that I was a reincarnation of a woman who had lived here a hundred years before?

chapter thirty-four

I listened absently to the old couple as I peeled and chopped, my mind a whirl of questions.

"Do you remember when young Jim hung that rope from the oak tree in the top field and got his sisters to try it out?" Betty asked Bill in a faraway voice. "And our Lizzy broke her arm?"

"Couldn't forget it," Bill growled. "I spent the rest of the day in the hospital with her."

As I listened, I felt a mixture of emotions. It was wonderful to think that they had had such full lives, rich with child-rearing and running the farm, but it was sad that they had so little opportunity to make new memories. I remembered what Adam had said about life being a circle—the past, present, and future all linked together. This old couple had been children once themselves and had grown and had children of their own, and their children had had children, and each and every one of them had thought they would be living those lives forever. Yet time passes and their bodies will wilt and eventually die and return to the ground.

"Penny for your thoughts." Bill's voice cut through my musings, and I looked up to find him watching me. I tossed the last potato into the pot with the others and rested the peeler on the chopping board.

"You look upset," he commented. "Come and sit here by me for a minute and take the weight off your feet."

After wiping my hands on a dish towel, I pulled out the chair nearest to him and swiveled it around to face his armchair. The cat spotted me and jumped onto my lap where she settled comfortably as I stroked her sleek fur. She purred contentedly as if it was something she had been used to her whole life. Betty had very abruptly fallen asleep in her chair, her mouth slightly open, false teeth protruding slightly as she exhaled.

Bill reached out to pat my knee. "I warned you not to take any nonsense from those young bucks Vincent and Colin."

It was cozy sitting in the warm farmhouse kitchen while the potatoes simmered in their pot and the smell of roasting beef filled the air. I found myself telling him about the previous evening spent with Maria, and the strange dream I'd had where the woman had told me not to tell Garrett about the child. Brushing over my confused feelings for Vincent, I admitted that I was beginning to wonder if that house had something to do with me.

"The river is here, just where I saw Garrett and Kitty come ashore in my last hypnosis session," I finished lamely.

"I don't pretend to understand what you're experiencing," Bill said slowly. "This past-life thing is all a mystery to me. I've always lived for what I can see with my own two eyes and touch with my own two hands—real solid things, like the farm here and the stock, my children, and of course my wife." He watched her fondly for a moment before returning his attention to me. "This girl Kitty and her problems have taken over your life, haven't they? Like I said yesterday morning, you have to be careful with all this meddling into the past."

He lapsed into thought for a moment before glancing up again. "Come to think of it, there was a story hereabouts many years ago about a drowning in that river. Betty knows more about it than me. She grew up here; this farm was passed down through generations of her family. This has always been the Jenkins farm." He paused when I looked up, surprised. "I came here as a farm-hand when the war in Europe ended in 1945. Betty's four brothers had all been killed in the war. She was the only surviving child. Her parents were struggling to run the farm without their sons, and I was a hard worker. I fell in love with Betty the minute I set eyes on her, and young Lizzy was soon on the way after we married in 1946. The proviso Betty's parents gave for allowing me their daughter's hand and eventually taking over the farm was that I take the Jenkins name with it. Adam did the same when it became clear that Jim wasn't interested in the farm. It's always been the Jenkinses' farm and hopefully always will be."

I was surprised to learn that the farm had been handed down through Betty's family. I just hoped Bill was right and Betty would remember something about the drowning that he had re-called. It may have had nothing to do with Kitty or Garrett, of course, but if Betty's family had been here for generations, then perhaps she knew something about the people who used to live in the house Vincent's and Maria's families now occupied.

I turned to Bill as Betty opened her eyes, including them both in the next question. "Did that drowning you recalled have any-thing to do with Kigarjay?"

I watched, fascinated, as Betty, appearing to ignore my

question, sniffed the air and checked her watch. A light came on in her eyes as she remembered where she was and what she was doing. She was grounded again and full of purpose as she rose unsteadily to her feet.

"Do you remember there being any kind of trouble connected with Vincent James's house down the road?" Bill repeated loudly to his wife as she inched stiffly past us and took down a mixing bowl from a shelf.

"The only trouble I know is if I don't get the cake made and into the oven in time." She measured flour into the bowl and mixed in eggs and milk.

Bill shrugged, and I decided to let the subject drop, but after a moment or two she paused with a whisk in her hand. "Who's Vincent James?"

"The Jameses are the current owners of Kigarjay," Bill reminded her patiently. "We had the James child, Jadie, here to stay for a couple of days, remember?"

"A child?" Betty wrinkled her brow, trying to remember. "A little fair-haired girl?"

"That's the one," Bill said patiently. "Went home this morning."

"Ah," Betty said, returning to her task.

"Kate here wants to know if there was ever any talk of a drowning connected with the Jameses' place," Bill said again.

"A drowning? Not that I know of." Betty turned her attention back to whisking the batter.

"It would have been a long time ago, before you were born, I think," I put in. "I just wondered if there was any gossip passed down about the place over the years. Bill thinks someone may have drowned."

"Can't say I heard about any drowning," Betty said. She continued to beat at the mixture, and Bill and I fell silent. The kitchen filled with the sound of the whisk tapping rhythmically against the side of the mixing bowl, the purring of the cat, and the occasional bleat from a lamb.

"There was the story my mother told me about the two deaths," Betty announced suddenly in a faraway voice, jerking me from my reverie. "She used to say that God gave and God took away, because two local people died a few days before I was born. She called it 'the miracle of giving back,' because Mrs. Green, a friend of hers, gave birth the day after she did—so after the tragedy there were two new babies in the village. Rosemary Green and I were friends for years until she went off to Australia to make a new life with her young man."

It is a mystery why people with dementia have such accurate recollections of the distant past when their short-term memory deteriorates, but at that moment I was immensely glad of Betty's long-term memory. I was desperate to know if the two people had drowned, but was afraid to ask too directly in case her memory closed down again. Then I thought of something to keep her mind focused on the right era.

"What year were you born, Betty?"

"I was born in May 1917," Betty said triumphantly. "I'm ninety years old."

"It was just after Betty's birthday in May 1945 that I came to work at the farm," Bill concurred. "The war was just over in Europe, and our Lizzy was born in the April of 1947."

"He didn't waste much time seducing me," Betty said with a giggle.

I could see that they were about to go off into a past of their own, so I quickly pulled them back to the subject I was most interested in.

"What did your mother tell you about the two deaths?" I pressed. "Were the people concerned living at Kigarjay at the time?"

"There were rumors of suicide. The people who died had been living in the big house. You know, the one the developers divided into two properties for the newcomers. It was all one when I was a youngster. It was a big old place shaped like a U with a court-yard behind. We all thought it was haunted because of what happened there, and it lay empty for years until the developers came and sliced it up. Rosemary Green and I used to gather herbs from the garden and play in the yard."

"But you never saw a ghost yourself?"

Betty laughed, her voice strong as she relived her youth, and I caught a glimpse of the vibrant young woman she had once been. "I never believed in that sort of nonsense, although some of the local boys swore they saw lights flickering in the windows on a dark winter evening, and Rosemary once said she was chased by a dark-haired man who vanished into nowhere."

I thought about the timing. Kitty and Garrett had been six-teen in 1903, so they must have been in their early twenties when they came ashore in their skiff and fell in love with the place. When Betty was born in May 1917, they would have been around thirty, if they were still alive—and if they existed anywhere other than in my imagination, of course.

"Do you know anything at all about the suicides?" I went on. "Did they have anything to do with a drowning?"

Betty shrugged. I noticed her gaze becoming hazy. "I don't re-call. And I wasn't born when it actually happened."

"Do you have any idea why the house was called Kigarjay?" I tried, changing tack.

"We always thought it was because of the birds," she mur-mured in a faraway voice. "There used to be rare birds nesting in the area: kites and garganeys—they're a type of duck, also known as summer teal. We used to have a pair of garganeys nesting in the marsh by the river. And the jays were everywhere.

"Go on."

But Betty had had enough of my questions and was pouring the cake batter.

"Do you suppose the name is a compilation of those birds' names?" I asked Bill. "Kites, garganeys, and jays . . . ki-gar-jay?"

"Who knows, lass? Maybe it's time to let the past rest. Whatever happened back then is unlikely to have anything to do with what you've been remembering."

"How *do* you remember how to cook?" I puzzled under my breath as Betty found the potatoes, drained them, and tossed them into a baking dish to brown.

She turned to give me a dreamy smile. "It was all those childhood holidays spent looking through the recipe books in Uncle's library."

I glanced at Bill, who gave a shrug. "First I've heard of it," he said to his wife. "I thought you spent your whole childhood on the farm."

"Not this time, you daft old man," Betty said, opening the oven and popping the cake inside.

"What do you mean?" I prompted, my interest sparked. But Betty was standing with a vacant expression on her face, and I knew that whatever memory she had been accessing had vanished.

"What did she mean?" I asked Bill instead.

"Damned if I know," he said.

chapter thirty-five

When Adam came in a while later for his meal, I related every-thing his grandmother had said. Betty listened to the retelling of her story with a distant stare, while Bill struggled with his food.

"The way to a man's heart is through his stomach," Betty said as she watched her grandson dig in. "That Tara girl didn't seem to understand that, did she, dear?"

Adam flicked an embarrassed glance at me and shook his head at his grandmother, but she remained oblivious to his discomfort.

Betty leaned forward and lowered her voice to a conspiratorial whisper. "We thought they were going to get married when they were old enough, but she never did like the farm. She tried, I know, but you could see she hated the animals and the outdoor life; she'd never have made a farmer's wife."

"Leave it, Betty," Bill growled through a mouthful of food. He had gravy dripping down his chin, and I picked up a napkin, hes-itating at the last minute to wipe his chin in case he thought I was treating him like a child. I felt as uncomfortable as Adam looked but was glad to have something to take my mind off what Betty had let slip. So Adam and Tara had been an item. . . .

"There are plenty of village girls willing," Betty continued, "but Adam says he doesn't have the time to date anyone. Says he's waiting for that special someone. Mark my words," she proclaimed, looking pointedly at her grandson, "you'll end up a sad and lonely man."

Bill rolled his eyes at Adam and turned his attention to the napkin poised in my outstretched hand. He winked at me wickedly. "Go on, then," he said with a sudden twinkle in his eye. "You're itching to wipe my face, aren't you?"

"I, er . . . Would you like me to?"

"Wouldn't mind if you did," he said. "I feel like a damned fool sitting here unable to get my food to my own mouth." He tipped his chin up and held my eye as I dabbed at his face with the cloth.

"Pretty girl knows how to keep a man looking tidy," he said with a wide grin. "Makes me wish I was a young man again."

Adam and I glanced at each other, and I felt myself blushing. I could see how Betty must have fallen for Bill all those years ago. I could also see, watching the old couple struggle with their food and their memories, that it probably wasn't only Adam's desire to wait for the right girl that might be making it difficult for him to consider marriage.

I looked at the napkin in my hand and again felt something stir inside my head. I'd done this before, hadn't I? I wrinkled my brow and tried to remember. There had been an elderly lady— perhaps the one who had taught me to make the paper angels— and I had cared for her. Visions of faded hazel eyes filled my head. No, I had *loved* her. I could almost smell the clean scent of soap on the parchment-thin skin on the back of her hands as she cut and trimmed the angels from the paper. Had she been my grand- mother? But the memory faded as quickly as it had come, and I turned my attention back to what Bill was saying.

After the meal Adam and I fed the lambs together and then started to wash up the lunch things in the enamel sink.

"You aren't thinking that your Kitty and her Garrett might have drowned themselves in some sort of suicide pact, are you?" Adam asked as I handed him a dripping plate.

"I just don't see Kitty as being weak-willed," I said, and shook my head, my arms immersed in bubbles while Adam dried the plates and pans. "Supposing for a minute that they aren't mere figments of my imagination, so far she's felt very determined. She lost her father at an early age, had to move into a rough area, live a life of hard work with the care of her siblings falling onto her young shoulders. Then she fell in love with a man who kept her hanging for several years. What on earth would have made her take her own life if none of that fazed her?"

Adam shrugged. "None of us knows what another person is really thinking."

"But I've *been* Kitty; I know her," I insisted, forgetting my earlier assertion that she probably wasn't real.

He fixed me with his steady gaze, and I felt something stir inside me. "You seem to have made up your mind about how you want to interpret your recollections," he said, and took the last pan I handed to him and wiped it dry.

I felt confused. "Earlier this morning I was sceptical about the whole thing, I know. But the river is here, just where it was supposed to be. And the landing area looked the same as the one I saw when I was being Kitty, even though the water was running higher today. And now there is the possibility that something *did* happen on Maria's and Vincent's property, a sudden and violent death—two deaths, in fact—that could be the cause of everything I'm seeing when I'm under hypnosis."

"There's one way to find out." Adam laid the last pan on the pile stacked to one side of the drainer. He folded the towel over the edge of the sink to dry.

"How?"

"We could take a look at the county records—later on, of course, when the weather improves."

"Or I could let Colin hypnotise me again and ask him to take me to a time of adversity in Kitty's life so we can see what happened to her."

"It's up to you. Considering that you came here to get away from the difficulty that being in that household caused you, you haven't been able to talk about anything else the whole time you've been here." Adam gave me a smile. "Why don't we go for a stroll around the farm and then I'll take you back there?"

"I'd like a walk," I said. "And I'm sorry I've been going on about Kitty—but you brought the subject up this time!" I took the hand towel he offered me. "Being here on the farm does seem to put things into perspective for me."

I could feel Adam looking at me, and as I gazed back into those fathomless brown eyes, I felt my legs weaken. Time seemed to stand still. I was Kitty again, staring into the mesmerising depths of Garrett's blue eyes as we stood in the cold schoolhouse when he'd asked me to wait for him. The towel fell from my grasp and my hand instinctively went to my neck. I could almost feel the shell carving of the woman's profile in its gilt-framed brooch nestling against my throat.

We continued to look at each other in confusion until Betty called out in her sleep and the spell was broken. Adam began to turn away, and I reached out my hand to stop him, but he moved fractionally out of reach. My hand fell to my side and I covered my dismay by stooping to pull on my borrowed boots. He bent to tie the laces of his work boots, leaving me wondering what exactly had just happened between us.

*   *   *

Adam took me on a tour of the farm, and I marveled at how quickly spring was unfolding with the thaw. There were clusters of wildflowers in the hedgerows and the beginnings of pink buds at the tips of the tree branches, which promised to burst into blossom if the sun kept shining. I tilted my face to the sun and felt its warmth seep into my bones. It felt good to be alive.

It was past four o'clock when Adam returned me to Kigarjay. Nothing had been said about the stolen moment by the sink, and I was beginning to wonder if I had imagined it, much as I had been imagining all sorts of other things since finding myself in this place. Adam didn't stay, as he needed to check the stock before it got dark, and the Land Rover disappeared up the lane as I stood on the step steeling myself to go in.

Vincent greeted me at the front door himself, for which I was heartily relieved after the confrontation with Tara earlier. He smiled, looking genuinely pleased to see me, a different man from the agitated one who had retreated to his study earlier.

"Did you have a nice time at the farm?" he asked as I followed him indoors. He took my coat from me and draped it over the back of the sofa.

"Yes, thank you, though we had some drama when Betty went missing earlier."

"No! I assume you found her?"

"Yes, we did, but it was a bit nerve-racking."

"Good Lord, I don't know why Adam keeps that old couple with him. Surely they'd be better off in a home?"

I sprang to their defense. "Being in a home would kill them. Betty wouldn't know where she was, and her whole purpose for living would cease. And Bill would go into a decline without her. His body might be falling apart, but mentally he's all there."

"Not all nursing homes are bad."

"Of course they're not," I said as I followed him toward the kitchen, "but Bill and Betty are far too independent. Their lives are too closely connected to that farm for them to be happy anywhere else. Even a healthy young person with all their faculties would struggle if they were taken away from everything familiar and dumped somewhere completely new and alien to them." I knew exactly how that felt. "For a confused old woman like Betty, it could be a death sentence."

Vincent stopped just outside the kitchen and turned to face me. He reached out and took one of my hands in his, then reached up with his other hand to rest a finger against my lips. "Shh," he said quietly. "I didn't mean to upset you again. I'm sure Adam's doing a great job. Look, I was a bit out of order earlier, and I'm sorry. I didn't mean to stomp off like a grouch and leave you with Colin and Mom."

I gave a weary shrug. "It doesn't matter."

He towed me away from the kitchen door and down the hall toward his study, presumably so that whoever was in the kitchen wouldn't hear what he was going to say.

"I've been waiting for you to come back," he said as soon as the door closed behind us. "The house seemed empty without you."

"Aren't Dempsey, Colin, Tara, and Jadie all here?" I asked, surprised.

"Well, they mostly are," he confirmed. "Tara went home. She doesn't normally work on the weekends. With the snow clearing, she was able to get away. But that's not what I meant."

I gave a sigh of relief that I wouldn't have to face Tara for a while, and waited for him to tell me whatever it was he had dragged me down the passageway for, but he suddenly seemed to be at a loss for words.

"Has Colin gone home too?" I asked at last, partly for

something to say and partly because finding out what had happened to Kitty was even more important now, and to find Colin had gone home would have been a huge disappointment.

"No, Colin asked to stay for a bit longer. Apparently he has to get back later this evening to prepare for work tomorrow, as he has a client first thing in the morning. He's waiting to see you, I think."

I stared at Vincent, surprised he had allowed Colin to stay. However, I didn't have time to dwell on the thought because another emotion had surfaced with Vincent's mention of the day ahead. Tomorrow would be Monday, the beginning of everyone's week. With the snowstorm over and the electricity back on, everything would return to normal—for everyone but me. A wave of apprehension shivered through me. I would have to start searching in earnest for who I really was.

"I don't suppose you had a chance to look more closely at the missing persons website?"

"Actually, I did." Vincent seemed distracted, as if he wanted to move on to other things. "There were one or two young women matching your approximate age and description, but they have been missing much longer than a week. There's nothing listed for anyone like you who's gone missing during the past few days."

"Oh..." I felt a little bit relieved by this piece of news. A missing wife, a ninety-year-old scandal, and a little girl who swore she spoke with her dead sister lay like pieces of a jigsaw puzzle waiting to be set into place. But above all else, how could I walk away when I wanted so desperately to know what had happened to Kitty?

"Look, you must wonder why I've dragged you here." I could hear the apprehension in his voice. "Maria wanted to tell you something last night, but then Mom and Colin insisted on coming too and she didn't have a chance—"

"I'm sorry, Vincent," I jumped in before he had time to finish. "I

really don't want to go over there again tonight." I took a deep
breath and decided to cut to the chase. "When I first met Maria, I
had the impression she was angry with you, and I have to tell you
that I've been worrying about what she might have been insinuat-
ing. Now that the roads are clear, there's nothing to stop me from
leaving here, not unless you can give me a reason why I should stay."

I sank down onto his leather desk chair.

To my surprise Vincent came and kneeled on the floor in front
of me. He searched my face with haunted eyes. "I haven't been
entirely honest with you, and I can see you need to know the truth."

"Go on," I said warily.

"The other night when we talked in the kitchen, I told you I
was hoping Maria had actually seen a ghost. I wanted the place to
be haunted. And I told you I wanted it to be Amber because I
needed her forgiveness. . . ."

I gazed at the man, and a wave of pity washed through me.
"Betty told me something today that makes me think that even if
there *is* a ghost haunting the place, it's not Amber," I interrupted
him, anxious to tell him what I knew. "Apparently there were two
deaths here more than ninety years ago, and my gut feeling is that
even if there is an earthbound spirit connected to this house, it's
far more likely to be one of them. May even have been a double
suicide. Kitty could have been one of the suicides, but, Vincent,
think about it—Amber passed peacefully away at the hospital
with her mother at her side. Why would her spirit be wandering
here? Surely you'd rather think of her as having moved on to a
better place than roaming restlessly here?"

"I'm trying to tell you," he groaned. "Kate, listen . . . Cheryl
didn't run off with another man. My wife committed suicide. She
killed herself right here in this house a few weeks after Amber
died. It's not Amber's spirit I'm so desperate to beg forgiveness
from—it's Cheryl's."

chapter thirty-six

I was still staring openmouthed at Vincent when Jadie came bundling in through the door of her father's study.

"Daddy!" she squealed excitedly. "Me and Grandma, we've made chocolate fudge. It's in the kitchen cooling down, but you can have some; it's the best fudge in the world."

Vincent looked at his daughter distractedly but scooped her up into his arms. "You're becoming quite the little domestic goddess, aren't you?" He buried his face in her neck.

"Daddy, your chin is all prickly," Jadie said, and laughed. "Are you going to come and try some?" she asked.

Vincent shot a nervous glance toward me as if he were expecting me to make a sudden announcement to Jadie, but when I said nothing, he nodded. "Of course I am, sweetheart. I wouldn't miss it for anything, especially if it's the best fudge in the world."

"And Kate too," Jadie said, holding out her hand to me. "I made it for Kate too; it's for the whole family."

"Kate isn't strictly family," Vincent murmured, still holding

Jadie and throwing anxious glances at me over the top of her head, "but I'm sure she can have some."

"Kate can have Amber's share," Jadie said. "Amber said she could."

Vincent put Jadie down and let her take his hand. I followed more slowly, trying to work out the implications of the bombshell Vincent had just dropped on me. Why had he lied? Who else knew the truth? I couldn't imagine that someone could kill themselves in their own home without the entire village finding out about it. A prime example of the efficiency of the village grapevine was the fact that Betty was aware of a possible suicide that had happened before she was even born.

I followed them into the kitchen, but there I had to steady myself against the back of a chair. I realized I was reeling with information, unsure which bits were real, which bits imagined, and which were downright lies.

Glancing around the kitchen, I vaguely registered the presence of Dempsey and Colin, but my mind was far away, sifting through facts and filing them into some sort of order. Two deaths had occurred here early in 1917, after which the place had lain empty for many years. As far as I knew, Vincent and his family were the first people to live here after the house had been converted into the two properties, and it appeared that both his older daughter and his wife had met untimely deaths since then.

I looked at Jadie, who was holding out the tray of fudge to her father, and I hoped the run of misfortune would pass her by. Was it possible, I wondered, for the very bricks and mortar of a home to absorb the energy of the people living within its walls? Could a part of the life forces of Kitty and Garrett—if it *had* been they who'd lived here then—still be here, causing a ripple effect to broaden ever outward through the passage of time?

"Are you all right, Kate?" Dempsey was taking the tray back

from Jadie and cutting out a couple of squares of the cooling fudge. "You look like you've seen a ghost. She glanced apologetically at her son. "Well, she does look shell-shocked."

Dempsey handed me a piece of the fudge and I popped it into my mouth, letting the sugar dissolve on my tongue. "Yum, that is good, Jadie," I said. "I might have to try another piece later, just to make sure I *really* like it."

Jadie giggled appreciatively, and I noticed her father resting his hand lightly on her hair, an affectionate gesture I hadn't seen him make before. Perhaps all this talk of getting in touch with Amber again—even if it had been a ruse on his part—had made him appreciate the daughter he still had. I fervently hoped so.

"I'm glad you're back," Colin spoke through a mouthful of fudge. "I was hoping we could have another session before I head home. Vincent isn't thrilled about it, but I've promised to let him sit in. Are you okay with that?"

I eyed Colin speculatively. Was that why Vincent had allowed Colin to stay—so he could watch and listen when I became Kitty again, in the hope that while I was communing with "the other side" I might be given a message for him from his wife?

Still, I wanted to find out the truth, so I nodded. "I'm definitely up for it. In fact, Betty told me something interesting that happened many years ago, which might have a connection to Kitty and Garrett. I'm actually quite anxious to visit them again."

Vincent's expression became strained, and I sighed, remembering the chess game between the two men. I was fed up with being a pawn they were fighting over. I decided it was time I became a more assertive player; Vincent and I had unfinished business to attend to.

"Could I have a word," I asked him, nodding toward the door, "outside?"

We left Jadie helping her grandmother clear up the mess they'd made in the kitchen, and we walked out to the living room, where Vincent turned anxious eyes on me.

"What are you going to do about what I told you?" He blurted before I could speak.

"I'm not sure," I replied. "It depends who else knows, whether it was covered up from the law, and if any crime was committed.".

He began to pace back and forth in front of the fire. Tension oozed with every step. "Mom knows; she was here that day. I think Tara may have guessed, but she's never asked and I haven't told her."

"How could you keep a thing like that secret?" I asked. "Surely there was an autopsy?"

"I have influential friends who arranged everything," he said in a tight voice. "A private doctor confirmed the time of death, the press was kept away, and everything was handled as quietly as possible."

"But why go to those lengths? If Cheryl's death really was a suicide, why all the secrecy?"

"Why do you think?" He stopped midstride and fixed his blue eyes on me. "Jadie had just lost her sister, and to find out her mother had purposely ended her own life would have been the ultimate betrayal. Amber didn't have a choice. She didn't want to die, but Cheryl actually made the decision to leave us. How do you think that would have made Jadie feel?"

He crossed to the couch, where he sat abruptly and put his head into his hands. I went and perched next to him, my immediate instinct to comfort him, but I felt betrayed by everything he'd told me.

"Was it all a lie?" I asked him. "All that stuff about feeling guilty and not being there for Amber—when it was really Cheryl you wanted to make contact with, not Amber at all?"

He turned haunted eyes toward me. "You can't possibly be a mother or have children somewhere you've forgotten about," he said, "or you would know that everything I told you was the absolute truth. I truly felt I had let Amber down for all the reasons I told you—but I let Cheryl down too. It wasn't just while Amber was so ill. I wasn't there when our child actually died, and I wasn't there for my wife in the weeks that followed. Cheryl felt as guilty as I did about passing the cystic fibrosis gene to Amber, but I couldn't talk about it to her. I didn't share with her that I was feeling exactly the same way she was. I threw myself into my work, and when I eventually came home each night, I closeted myself in my study. I could see she wasn't coping, but I was too much in denial to help her."

I glanced toward the kitchen door to make sure it was still closed. Vincent followed my gaze and lowered his voice still further.

"Tara told me that Cheryl needed professional help and offered Colin's services, but I turned her down. Pride got in the way of common sense, and Cheryl paid the ultimate price for my inability to show or share my emotions."

A picture of Garrett keeping himself aloof all those years flashed before me. They were so alike, the two men, both trapped by upbringing and convention, trying to build a world of material stability around their loved ones at the expense of spending time with them. I thought about Kitty's long wait for Garrett and of Cheryl desperately awaiting the return of her husband every evening. If there was such a thing as reincarnation, I could imagine that Vincent had once been Garrett . . . and if I had been Kitty, it would tie in with the deep feeling of connection I had felt when he'd carried me here.

Vincent's eyes were dull and lifeless. "I realize now that I've been doing the same thing with Jadie. She needs to know I am grieving for her sister, and yet I can't bear it when she talks about Amber as if she's still here."

"I agree with Tara about the counseling," I said firmly. "It's too late for Cheryl, but, as I told you the other night, it's not too late for you and Jadie. Perhaps you should see someone, someone you can learn to trust and express your anger and grief to. I'm sure Colin can recommend someone."

Vincent avoided my gaze again. I watched as he chewed his bottom lip as if agonizing over a decision. "There's something else, something Maria told me when I went over there the first night you spent at the farm. . . ."

"What is it?"

Vincent continued to look awkward, and I leaned back against my coat, which Vincent had laid over the back of the couch when I'd returned from the farm. Something in the coat pocket rustled, and I recalled Maria handing me a note the previous evening. Now I drew the note out and scanned it.

Kate, I have something worrying to tell you about Colin. We must talk. Maria.

A footfall on the wood floor behind us caused Vincent to start suddenly. Turning, I saw Colin standing there, and something in his expression made me distinctly uneasy.

"Ready to go under?" he asked.

chapter thirty-seven

I quickly folded the note, trying to keep my expression neutral.

"I, er... I'll be with you in a minute," I replied. My nerves, which were already on edge from Vincent's confession, jangled with apprehension. What did Maria mean? Was this something else that Vincent had been keeping from me—that there was something *worrying* about Colin?

I recalled Vincent's sudden insistence after that one night on his own at the house, when he'd apparently spent the evening with Maria, that I return from the farm with him—and his reticence when Colin had offered to come too. Looking back, I realized Vincent had never made any secret of the fact that he wasn't happy about me undergoing hypnosis. Even on the morning when I'd returned in Adam's Land Rover, Vincent had only set out for the sandwiches after I'd assured him Colin was walking back. Had Vincent believed Colin was walking all the way from the farm and that he had plenty of time to make the trip to the store and back before Colin arrived? He had certainly not seemed pleased that Colin had gotten there before him and had been alone with me. Colin was staring at me strangely and I tried to get myself together.

But just then the kitchen door burst open and Dempsey called urgently across the hallway, "Vincent! Jadie's having an asthma attack! I can't find her inhaler. Where the hell has Tara put it?"

Vincent shot to his feet, and I followed him as he ran across the hallway into the kitchen, where Jadie sat stiffly on a kitchen chair, gasping for breath.

For a moment I froze in the doorway as Vincent and Dempsey frantically emptied kitchen drawers onto the floor. I stared at Jadie in horror, noticing the bluish tinge to her lips, the look of wild terror in her eyes as she struggled to draw oxygen into her lungs.

"It's always right here on top of the first aid kit," Dempsey was panting, clearly panicked.

"I know, but it isn't here!" Vincent turned and desperately looked around the kitchen. "Go upstairs and get the one from the bathroom . . . quickly!"

Dempsey pushed past me, while I stood impotently, not knowing what to do. Then Jadie fixed her frightened eyes on mine and reached out her frail arms toward me. The child's silent cry for comfort seemed to awaken something in my brain. I went to her, pulled her onto my lap, and held her rigid, oxygen-starved body close.

"Shh. You'll be okay, Jadie," I told her, trying not to tremble beneath her. "Take slow steady breaths." The wheezing in her throat became marginally quieter, and she leaned against me, but her small body was still tense. The ragged breathing continued, and I pushed away a mental picture of her lying still and lifeless in my arms.

Colin appeared and hunkered down in front us.

"Look at me, Jadie," he instructed in his calm professional voice. "You are feeling relaxed and safe. Kate has you, and you can breathe easily now. Take a slow breath in, one, two, three; and out, one, two, three. In and out, calm and steady, there you go. Good girl."

I found I was breathing evenly in and out with Colin's instructions, and it seemed Jadie was too, because the wheezing sound was lessening and I felt her begin to relax against me.

Dempsey flew through the door with an inhaler in her hand and thrust it at Jadie, who took it obediently, pressed down the top, and sucked in a measured dose.

We all looked at Jadie, waiting hopefully.

Gradually color returned to her cheeks, her breathing eased toward normal, and she gave a little sob. "I want Mommy," she whimpered, and turned her head into my neck.

Vincent's eyes met mine over his child's head and something unspoken passed between us. He moved toward me, but then he halted as his eyes caught something on the floor. Tilting my head slightly, I followed his gaze to where a shape lay in the shadows under the table. There lay the missing inhaler, where it must have fallen at some point during the day and been nudged out of sight by an unknowing foot.

"Oh my God," Vincent sighed as he picked it up and laid it carefully on the top of the first aid kit. He wiped a hand across his furrowed brow and gave a small groan. "That's all it would take."

I sat with Jadie on my lap for some time, wondering and worrying, and stroking her hair while she dozed fitfully. The asthma attack had exhausted her, but none of us wanted to put her to bed just yet, where we couldn't keep an eye on her.

After a while Dempsey suggested we lay her on the couch, where Dempsey could sit and watch her, and Vincent seized the opportunity to make some excuse to his mother about looking up something on the computer that I must see, and dragged me back down the passageway to his study.

"What about your hypnosis session?" Colin asked after us.

But I merely held up a hand and murmured, "Later, Colin, if you don't mind."

As soon as the study door had closed behind us, I spoke. "I need answers," I told him firmly. "I want to know exactly what happened to your wife, and I want to know what you and Maria know about Colin."

"Okay." Vincent pulled out the desk chair so that I could sit down while he perched on the corner of the desk. "What do you want to know?"

"Tell me about Cheryl first. How did she do it? And," I cautioned as he hesitated, "you must be completely truthful with me."

Vincent nodded, then closed his eyes for a moment. He went very still as if he was having difficulty opening the window on a memory he had long been shutting out.

"Cheryl had a prescription for some heavy-duty tranquilizers from a doctor friend of ours. She couldn't sleep after Amber died, and if she did, she just suffered terrible nightmares." He paused and wiped a hand over his face, remembering. "On that last day, Cheryl must have waited until Tara had gone home on Friday evening. She knew Mom was coming to visit for the weekend but that she would be arriving late by train after an evening function at the gallery. According to Jadie, Cheryl did her physical therapy, gave her a bath, and read her a bedtime story. I'm assuming that when Jadie was asleep, Cheryl went into Amber's room, lay down on the bed, and took all the pills—a whole bottle of them—which she washed down with brandy." He swallowed, and

I watched his Adam's apple working up and down as he tried to find his voice. "I came in later than usual—I'd picked Mom up from the station well after eleven, and she'd gone straight to her room. I could have been home much earlier, but as with most evenings, I just didn't have the courage to face Cheryl. She'd taken to spending the night in Amber's room, and I was hoping she'd be asleep and I wouldn't have to ask how she was. I knew what the answer would have been." He turned watery eyes on mine. "How can you ask the newly bereaved mother of your child how she's feeling each day? But how could I *not* ask her? For weeks after Amber's death I prayed every evening that Cheryl would already be asleep when I came in and I wouldn't have to see her puffy eyes, or listen to her crying herself to sleep."

Vincent began to pace up and down, up and down across the room. "What sort of a coward am I? I didn't know what to do or what to say; nothing I could have done or said would have made it better anyway. Cheryl wanted Amber back; that was the be-all and end-all. So I suppose I took the easy route . . . I stayed away as much as I could."

"And when you found her?" I prompted.

Vincent stopped pacing. "I didn't find her," he said. "I listened at Amber's door, peeped in to see that Cheryl was lying there quiet and still, thanked my lucky stars she was asleep, and took myself off to bed."

"Oh God," I said quietly.

"She died in the night," Vincent said, his voice cracking with emotion. "I could have saved her if I'd gone in to check on her. But I was relieved she wasn't demanding anything from me emotionally . . . and I left her there. I left her there to die."

"But you didn't know what she'd done."

"Of course not. But it wasn't outside the realm of possibility, was it? She was grieving and unable to cope, and I shut her out."

He came and sat down on the edge of the desk again. "Mom found her; she was having trouble sleeping too, and had taken to roaming the house in the early hours of the morning. She looked in on Cheryl and saw the pill bottle on the floor by the bed. It must have dropped from Cheryl's hand and fallen onto the rug as she lost consciousness."

"I'm so sorry."

"That's what I hoped to say to Cheryl," Vincent told me, "and I need to say it to Amber as well. That's why when Maria mentioned a ghost passing between our houses and that items were being moved, I got so excited. I know its sounds ridiculous, but I wanted them to be haunting us just so I could see them both one last time."

chapter thirty-eight

𝒯*he study door* creaked open behind us, and Dempsey poked her head in. "There you both are. We've made supper, if you'd like to come and eat. Jadie felt much better suddenly and wanted something to eat."

I pictured Dempsey finding her dead daughter-in-law and helping with the cover-up at her son's behest, and wondered again at the depth of a mother's love.

Vincent and I stood, and we followed his mother to the kitchen. "I thought the food was mostly spoiled."

"We found some potatoes, onions, and the remaining eggs." Dempsey smiled as Vincent and I took our places at the table. "So we've made a potato and onion pie, haven't we, Jadie?"

"I suppose someone should have gone shopping today now that the roads are open," Vincent said vaguely as he picked up his fork. I could see he was having trouble focusing his thoughts on the here and now. He drew in a deep breath. "Never mind, this looks and smells delicious."

"I could shop tomorrow before I go home, if my car is back by then," Dempsey offered.

"I called the garage about your car today," Vincent said as he toyed with his food. "They're working through the weekend because they have a huge backlog of abandoned vehicles to recover, but they said they'd do their best to get your car out of the ditch and returned to us here as soon as possible."

"I hope I have it back in time to drive home sometime tomorrow," Dempsey said, squirting ketchup liberally onto her plate. "I have to go into the gallery in the afternoon."

"Can I have some ketchup, Grandma?" Jadie asked.

"Yes." Dempsey leaned over to give Jadie's plate three short squirts and a long flourish, leaving the child's potato pie decorated with a red smiling face.

"Tara doesn't let me have ketchup," Jadie said. "She says it's messy."

Dempsey made a tutting sound. "We really are going to have to get Tara to lighten up a bit," she said. "She's a good sort but seriously lacking in fun. Maybe now that things are a bit different around here, she'll learn to enjoy life more."

"It's not easy for her," Colin said, springing to his sister's defense. "It is a huge responsibility looking after Jadie and the rest of this household. I'll bet no one's had to worry about the shopping before; Tara would already have done it all."

Dempsey looked suitably contrite, and even Jadie piped up in Tara's defense.

"Tara helped me make up the milk to feed Woolly," she told her grandmother. "She was scared to let me go near animals at first, but I've cuddled my lamb and Kate's cat and I didn't sneeze once."

"I don't know what I would have done without Tara these past two years," Vincent acknowledged in a distant voice. "She's held things together for us."

I glanced at him anxiously, wondering if today was the first time he had really admitted, even to himself, the part he had played in his wife's death. His skin was the color of parchment and there were shadows under his eyes. He pushed his plate of food away and stood up.

"Don't you like it, Daddy?" Jadie asked.

"I'm just not very hungry, sweetheart," he managed. "Perhaps I could have it later."

He left the room, and silence fell as Dempsey, Colin, and I studiously avoided one another's gaze. We finished the meal, and Colin excused himself, mumbling something about stoking up the living room fire. I realized he was probably warming the room up for another hypnosis session but I still needed Vincent to tell me what his worries were regarding Tara's brother.

Jadie hopped down from the table and collected her coloring pencils and some paper as if she hadn't been at death's door only a short while before. I marveled at the child's resilience as Dempsey and I began loading the dishwasher and Jadie settled at the table to draw a picture.

"I'm worried about Vincent," Dempsey whispered with a glance in Jadie's direction. "He looks ill."

"Is Daddy going to work tomorrow?" Jadie asked. I wasn't sure whether she had heard Dempsey's remark or if she was simply worried about her father too.

The question reminded me of my earlier anxiety about the rest of the world returning to normal. Of course there was no physical reason for Vincent not to go into work in the morning. The roads were open, the trains mostly running again, the electricity and telephone restored. Dempsey had already said that as soon as her car was recovered, she would go off to work as well, and presumably Tara would return to take over the running of the household.

"I imagine so," Dempsey told her.

"I liked Daddy being home," Jadie said as she concentrated on coloring between the lines she had drawn. "Amber likes it too."

"You know"—Dempsey went to the table and pulled out a chair next to her granddaughter—"I wish I could talk to Amber like you do; I miss your sister very much."

Jadie glanced up at her. "Do you remember when Amber broke those eggs and you cleared up the big parts of the shells and we planted seeds in them?"

"Oh, yes, the mustard seeds." Dempsey smiled. "And Amber painted faces on the shells so the sprouts looked like green hair growing out of funny little heads."

"Can we do that again?"

"I don't see why not. I'll buy some seeds and we'll plant them when I come again next weekend."

Jadie looked up into her grandmother's face and gave her a radiant smile. I watched the two of them with a glow in my heart, hoping that Dempsey had joined the grieving train that Jadie had already boarded when she'd found her voice. Listening to them reminiscing about Amber, I realized they were traveling together. The healing process had begun, and I was heartily relieved for them.

Colin stuck his head through the kitchen door. "Are you ready, Kate?"

Jadie glanced up from her drawing. "Are you going to hypnotize Kate again?"

I paused, wondering whether to track Vincent down and demand some answers about Colin. But what could they have discovered about him that might put me at risk?

"He is," I told her decisively. "I'll see you later."

Following Colin into the living room, I found he had drawn the curtains on the dusky evening, arranged the blankets on the couch, and stoked the fire to a good blaze. The room looked cozy and inviting, and I hurried to the couch, my fears forgotten in my eagerness to learn more about the woman who was dominating my memories.

I made myself comfortable as Colin drew up an armchair and leaned toward me. He gave a quick glance around to make sure we were alone, and my heart hammered in my chest, wondering if I was crazy to be entrusting myself to him again. Visions of him calming Jadie during her asthma attack reassured me, however. He was one of the good guys—wasn't he?

"I keep thinking about what you told me about Cheryl," he whispered, causing my heart to make a sudden leap in my chest. "Are you going to tell me why you suddenly changed your mind about why a woman would leave her wallet, bag, and credit cards behind?"

I should have known it was a vain hope that he'd have forgotten what I'd told him. "What do you mean?"

"I know you told me—after spending ages with our host and his mother upstairs, ostensibly changing the sheets—that you were mistaken and everything was all hunky-dory. Well, I've been wondering as I've watched the interaction between Dempsey and Vincent if there isn't more to it. She's protecting him, isn't she?"

I sighed. I had been right not to underestimate him. Maybe this was at the root of Maria's and Vincent's worries about Colin. Maria had changed her attitude toward Vincent after they had spent that second evening together, when I'd been at the farm, and now I wondered whether Vincent had told Maria the truth and they were both afraid that Colin would find out that Cheryl had killed herself and spill the beans, which, as Vincent had feared, would almost certainly affect Jadie.

"Will you keep it a secret if I tell you?"

"I may not be able to if Vincent murdered his wife."

"He didn't murder her; Cheryl committed suicide," I said at last.

Colin leaned back in the chair and linked his hands behind his head as he absorbed this piece of information. "How did he manage to keep something like that quiet?"

"Friends in high places, apparently."

"They'd have to be pretty darned high up to keep that under wraps."

"And totally convinced there was no hint of foul play," I agreed.

"But cover-up or no, Vincent hasn't come to terms with it, has he? He's pretty desperate to get in touch with her, isn't he?"

I nodded.

"I had a gut feeling it wasn't just his daughter's spirit he was hoping to find roaming between the two houses," Colin muttered.

"*Just* his daughter?" I echoed.

"I meant from his point of view," Colin explained quickly. "I'm not detracting from the sheer tragedy of losing a child, just saying that what Cheryl did—choosing to leave him—is probably what he can't live with."

"No," I agreed. "You're absolutely right."

He sighed and gave me a sad smile. "There's no actual evidence of any ghostly goings-on next door, I suppose?"

"Not that I know of, apart from a throwaway remark or two of Maria's."

"Okay. Well, I think we'll have to leave that little mystery alone for now. Close your eyes and we'll see if we can find Kitty again."

"I need to find Kitty at a time when there was something momentous happening in her life," I murmured. "I found out from

Betty that someone else may have committed suicide in this house long before Cheryl was even born. I need to find out if it was Kitty, and if so, what happened to make her unhappy enough to take her own life."

"What's going on?" My eyes shot open at the sound of Vincent's voice, and I struggled up onto my elbows to look guiltily at him.

"Kate made her own decision to let me put her under again," Colin said defensively.

"You should have waited," Vincent muttered. "I wanted to be here to make sure . . . everything was all right."

"I told you you could sit in if you wanted to." There was still a defensive tone to Colin's voice. "What do you think, Kate?"

To be honest, I wasn't sure what to think anymore, but I did know I wanted—needed—to see Kitty again.

"Please stay," I said to Vincent as I lay back down under the covers. "One way or another I have to see this thing through to the bitter end."

chapter thirty-nine

Vincent settled himself in a chair by the fire as Colin nodded and began the relaxation ritual I had come to know so well. Soon I was imagining my body and soul separating in streams of rainbow-colored bubbles, floating outside each other so that I was weightless and invisible in space.

"I want you to go back to a time when you were Kitty. You are at an important milestone in Kitty's life, a time when she was struggling with something momentous."

I felt myself tugged backwards through time, and when I opened my eyes I was lying in a sagging wooden bed with a woman sitting in a high-backed chair at my side. It was the woman in the plum-colored dress I had dreamed about. She was holding a damp cloth, which she used to wipe my forehead, dipping it every now and then into an enamel bowl of water at her side.

"Tell me who you are," said the voice in my head.

"I'm Kitty and I hurt," I wailed. "I don't want to do this."

"Where are you, Kitty? Describe your surroundings to me."

I looked wildly past the wooden corner posts of the big double bed to the bare walls of my temporary home.

"I'm in a strange room," I answered. "I don't recognize where I am."

"Is Garrett there with you?"

"No, he doesn't know about this. Someone has gone to get the midwife. Garrett's mother is here with me. Oh no. Oh, it hurts so much!"

"Are you ill?"

"No, not ill; it's the baby. It's on its way—"

I broke off as I doubled up to clutch at my belly. Garrett's mother patted my hand perfunctorily.

"It'll be all right, dear," she murmured. "We all go through it. Take a few deep breaths and get ahold of yourself."

I was gritting my teeth. "I'm sure something is wrong."

"The midwife won't be long," the woman assured me. "She'll be here anytime now."

Looking at Garrett's mother sitting so primly by my side, her back erect, clothes neat, hair smoothly tucked in a severe plait, I couldn't imagine her writhing in the agony of childbirth.

"Kitty!" called the voice in my head. "I understand that you are hurting, but you must keep reporting back to me."

"I'm wondering how Garrett's mother ever went through this." I let out a sigh of relief as the contraction eased away.

I must have spoken aloud, because the woman took my hand and gave it a light squeeze. "We all do, dear; there's no other way."

The bedroom door flew open and a woman wearing a long gray dress with a white collar entered the room, a cap on her head.

"I'm Mrs. Drayton, dear." She was tying a white apron around her waist as she crossed to the bed to take a closer look at me.

"I want Garrett," I pleaded weakly as another contraction took hold of me.

"Remember what we discussed. He can't be saddled with a child out of wedlock when he's just making a name for himself in the city. You don't want to ruin his life, do you, dear?" Garrett's mother was getting to her feet, leaving me with the midwife.

"Now let's see how far along you are."

I groaned again as the contraction increased, spreading across my lower abdomen and the small of my back; holding me in its viselike grip.

"Kitty, I want you to skip forward in time until after the baby is born," the disembodied voice instructed firmly. "The labor is over and you are holding a tiny baby in your arms. Tell me if it is a girl or a boy."

The room shimmered, and I was looking down at the dark-haired bundle in my arms. "It's a boy!" My labor pains were forgotten with the joy of holding my newborn son. "He's so perfect."

"Is he all right?" asked the voice.

"Yes. The midwife said I have a healthy little boy."

"Where is Garrett?"

"He's still in Boston. Garrett's mother has brought me to stay with friends of hers in Lowell."

"Will you tell him about the child?"

"Garrett's mother has said I can tell him later, when he has made his fortune and is ready to marry. I don't want to hold him back—and Garrett's mother has promised we can return for the child when we are wed."

"Okay, Kitty. I want you to travel forward in time to the first time Garrett hears about his son. He is right there in the room with you. Tell me what is happening."

Again the room shimmered, and this time when I opened my eyes I was in a different place. I looked around, recognizing the tapestry-hung walls.

I gave a deep sob. "Garrett is very angry. After I returned from

Lowell, I received news that Jaygo, our lovely son, had succumbed to a fever and died. My heart was broken at the news, but I remained true to my word and have kept our child secret from Garrett these past years. His mother said it was the right thing to do. And Garrett has made something of himself now, has bought land and built several properties."

"And are you married?"

I watched my new husband pace back and forth across the bedroom, and nodded through my tears. "We have married at last, but I am twenty-eight years old and I fear I may not be able to have another child."

"And now you have told Garrett about the boy?"

"Yes. He is inconsolable. He is going to his mother to demand an explanation, and relations are strained between us. He says he thinks his mother never believed he would marry me." I lowered my voice to a whisper. "Apparently she wanted a more highly born wife for her only son."

"Do you still see anything of your own family?"

"Mother passed away nearly two years ago. She refused to speak to me after my confinement. She made it clear I had brought disgrace to the family, but I still see Alice. She is unwell."

"What is wrong with her?"

"The problem is all in her head."

"Tell me."

"Alice and Arthur continued to visit my uncle and aunt on the coast; they went every year, as I used to until I moved to Boston to work." I pictured the house by the sea, the house I had dreamed of owning. Looking around my bedroom in the home Garrett and I shared, I marveled at having been fortunate enough to build a house so similar.

"Talk to me, Kitty. What does this have to do with Alice being unwell?"

"Oh, she's such a silly girl. She was always trying to get our mother's attention. She made up some terrible story about Uncle George. Apparently Mother was extremely angry after my aunt and uncle had been so good to us over the years. Alice and I were both disowned by our mother before she passed away—I because of the child I bore out of wedlock and Alice for the wicked story she told."

"What story was that?"

I hesitated, not wanting to say it out loud, but the voice became insistent, and I worried that my new husband would hear it.

"She made up a fib about Uncle George touching her inappropriately," I whispered awkwardly. "Alice is a bad, ungrateful girl."

"How old is Alice now?"

"She's twenty-two, six years my junior."

"Had Alice ever said anything like this about Uncle George before?"

"No. But she told Mother that it had been going on for several years. Alice tells me she didn't understand before that it wasn't her fault, but now that she's older, she understands."

"And you don't believe her?"

"Of course not! Our aunt and uncle were always so kind to us! It's a terrible thing to say. A fib like that could ruin Uncle George's reputation."

"Will you support her if she comes to you for help?"

I looked across at Garrett and sighed. "Alice is no longer a child. I have my husband to consider now and my child to mourn. If she wants to be silly, it's up to her, but I simply don't have time for her tantrums."

"I want you to return to me now, Kate." The voice sounded as if it were echoing down a long tunnel. "I am going to count down from ten and I want you to travel back and awaken when I snap my fingers on the count of one. Do you understand?"

"I don't want to leave Garrett. He is hurting so badly. Can't I stay here a while longer?"

"You will still be with him, Kitty; it is Kate I want to come back with me now."

Still I was reluctant to go. I recalled the glorious feeling of nestling my face into my newborn son's sweet-smelling neck and inhaling the scent of him. Once, in the brief time we had spent together, Jaygo's eyelids had flickered open as I gazed down at him, and he'd peered sleepily up at me with his baby-blue eyes. Not a day had passed that I didn't think of him. A tremor of grief ran through me at the terrifying reality that I would never see him again, and then the numbers were counting down in my head and I found myself floating irrevocably back through the tunnel of time.

"Three, two, one," said the voice. "Open your eyes, Kate. You have a visitor."

I opened my eyes slowly, and there was Jadie, standing looking down at me with her blue eyes fixed intently on my face. I wriggled up until I was in a sitting position, our heads on a level, and as soon as I was settled, she slipped her small hand into mine.

"Don't be sad." She smiled at me. "I've been waiting for you right here all this time."

"What do you mean, Jadie?" Colin asked.

I noticed Vincent was still sitting quietly in his chair by the fire, but he made no move to interrupt or intervene.

Jadie lowered her eyes, and I knew Colin probably wouldn't get an answer.

"I think you should go and find your grandma." Colin sounded strangely irritated but added more gently, "There's a good girl. I need to talk to Kate."

Jadie turned questioning eyes to me, and in truth I didn't

want her to go. I realized she was still holding my hand, and when I didn't release her, she smiled and climbed onto my lap, leaning her blond head against my sweater.

Colin sighed, shifting impatiently in his chair. "Go upstairs now, Jadie. It was very kind of you to wait for Kate to wake up, but I promise you she's all right. These things she remembers under hypnosis happened a very long time ago. You don't have to stay with her now."

But I was still feeling empty and emotional. It might not have been me giving birth in the physical sense but some part of me had been there, sharing Kitty's tumultuous emotions. I'd felt the joy of holding her newborn son in her arms, the agony of separation, and the terrible depth of her grief; I wasn't ready to let go of Jadie just yet.

"Can't we discuss this another time?" I begged Colin.

He shook his head. "To garner proper benefit from these sessions we have to work through your latent memories while they are still fresh. If you go rushing off now, it will all have been for nothing."

"No it won't." I hugged the child tight, inhaling the scent of her. This could never be counted as nothing. I glanced up at him. "Can I ask you something?"

He nodded and took the seat beside me.

"Do you really believe reincarnation is possible?"

His gaze flicked toward Jadie. "This isn't a suitable conversation to be having in front of a six-year-old."

I tightened my arms around Jadie, knowing full well that he was right and that what I was imagining was probably nonsense. It was just so hard to let go.

"I think Colin's got a point," Vincent chimed in softly.

I sighed, releasing my hold on the bundle in my arms. "Why

don't you go and find your grandmother, Jadie?" Reluctantly I shifted the child from my lap. "I need to talk to Colin for a few minutes, and it must be way past your bedtime."

Jadie pouted but ran off up the stairs to find Dempsey.

"Why are you asking such a question now?" Colin asked.

"Because," I murmured, feeling foolish, "I have the strongest feeling that Jadie could be the reincarnation of Kitty's lost son."

chapter forty

To *my surprise,* Colin didn't laugh at me, and I avoided Vincent's gaze as I waited for Colin to answer.

"I was always prepared to entertain the possibility that the human soul survives the death of its host body," Colin said. "What I've seen and heard during these sessions has pretty well confirmed that. Otherwise, how could people under hypnosis recall a previous-life existence?"

"You don't think it's just my head injury or the amnesia causing confused memories to surface, as your sister believes? You don't think I'm crazy?"

"If it had only happened once, then that might have been a possibility," he allowed, shifting his weight on the sofa next to me. "But as I explained before, many normal sane people claim to have experienced the same thing. There is California: a psychologist I've read up on who has recorded years of hypnotherapy sessions and written several books on the subject. According to the thousands of people he has put under hypnosis, souls reincarnate in the same geographical location with a small "family" of souls as well as a wider group of fellow souls to work through problems encountered in previous lives. If you believe in karma, then you'll understand that what happens in one life is supposed to affect another. Lessons have to be learned and wrongdoings have to be righted."

"You mean to tell me that people reincarnate with the same entities time and time again until they get things right?"

"Yes, more or less. Apparently we reincarnate with a soul mate as a partner or special friend, with lesser-known souls playing some of the smaller roles."

"You make it sound like we're all the cast of a play!"

"In a way we are, I think."

I stared at him, not sure if he was joking.

"The psychologist's theory, backed up by numerous subjects questioned under hypnosis, is that if problems in one life are not addressed and remedied, then those same entities will choose to reincarnate in a different role to experience life from all viewpoints."

"If what you're saying has some truth to it, could a person come back as a member of their biological family?" I pressed. "I mean, could we be our own ancestors?"

"That appears to be unusual. According to subjects asked these questions under deep hypnosis, it seems it is more beneficial to us as souls to reincarnate in genetically different bodies with varied biological characteristics to get the most benefit from each life experience."

I stared at him dubiously. For someone I believed to be of sane mind and belonging to a recognized professional body, he certainly had some zany ideas. And yet, far-fetched as his theory seemed, it was also a comforting thought that death was merely a release from our earthly bodies, not the end of our being.

I glanced across at Vincent to see him sitting forward in his chair, his gaze fixed on Colin. I could see the hope shining clearly in his eyes, and my heart went out to him. As Kitty I had felt the devastating grief at the loss of a child and knew at last something of what Vincent was feeling.

"So are you saying that when someone dies, their soul inhabits another body?" I asked.

"Good heavens no!" Colin exclaimed. "My understanding is that when a body dies, leaving the soul without an earthly vessel, the essence of that person, the pure electrical energy that is their eternal self, transcends to another plane. People call it, variously, heaven, Valhalla, nirvana, Tao, the happy hunting grounds. . . . It doesn't matter what it's called; it is the waiting area between lives where we meet up with departed loved ones, evaluate our previous-life experience, and plan out our next incarnation on Earth. When we are ready to reincarnate, we join the biological entity of our choice as a baby in the womb."

I thought of Betty and how she'd reminded me of Kitty's sister, Alice. "If I entertain this 'cast of characters' theory, could someone who had been my previous life's younger sister have been here for more than ninety years already?"

"You're talking about Betty, aren't you?"

I realized I'd been right about Colin taking everything in. He hadn't missed a thing while he'd sat in the Jenkinses' kitchen with his feet up, enjoying their hospitality.

"Maybe," I said in confusion.

"What makes you think she might have been Alice?" He was looking at me with the same air of quiet fascination as the first time I'd come around after finding myself as Kitty.

"It was something both Alice and Betty said about the feeling they got from being near water. They both said that it called to them—that if they slipped, they believed the water would catch them and keep them safe. And Betty mentioned spending holidays looking through recipe books in her uncle's library, but Bill knew nothing about her having been anywhere other than the farm. I wondered if she was remembering something from a previous life ... a life perhaps as Alice."

"Interesting." His eyes took on a faraway stare. "Souls are apparently supposed to reincarnate with a kind of amnesia so they don't remember previous-life existences or what their tasks are each time. If they recalled bits of a previous life—other than in a controlled environment under hypnosis, of course—it would not only be frightening and confusing, but would rather defeat the purpose of making the right choices this time around. It would be like having access to the answers of an exam before getting the questions."

"Could Betty be recalling emotions from a previous life because of her dementia, do you think? If those stored memories can be accessed through hypnosis, then what's to stop them from surfacing through illness or injury to the brain?"

"Are you still talking about Betty?" He was eyeing me shrewdly, and I felt myself blush.

"I did wonder about my own amnesia maybe being the catalyst to remembering Kitty's life so clearly," I confessed. "If any of what you're saying is true, then it's a possibility, isn't it?"

"It seems there are myriad possibilities," Colin said reverently. "I certainly wasn't a particular disciple of that California doctor's claims until I met you. I found it best to keep an open mind on matters of the soul. In my line of work it's easy to get sucked into other people's fantasies ... but what happened to you under hypnosis has changed everything."

"But what about the timing and Betty being so much older than me?"

"His hypnosis subjects reported that there is no time in the place between lives. No past and no present, just eternal existence, purity of thought, and a quest for perfection. If Earth time has no meaning, and your meeting with Alice again now is part of your destiny, it might not matter that she may have been here sixty Earth years before you."

"So maybe I should start looking out for other characters from my past lives," I said with a smile, trying to make light of his disconcerting revelations. "You could have been Kitty's mother-in-law, for all we know."

Colin didn't return the smile. He was still staring at me with a clinical interest, and I felt a little bit like a lab rat again.

"Have you recognized anyone else from your life as Kitty?" He asked lightly, but I suspected he was taking careful mental notes of everything I said. I thought again of Jadie reminding me so vividly of Kitty's newborn son, and I told him how I'd felt when I'd woken and found her watching me. Then there was Vincent. I glanced across the room at him. He was so like Garrett in his characteristics.

"You mentioned a soul mate," I continued carefully. "Do people always reincarnate with their soul mate?"

"I'm pretty sure he asked his subjects that question. Most of his subjects believe it is usual to reincarnate with a soul mate, usually as a spouse or someone very close to you. Soul mates each have their own karma to work through, of course; sometimes they may only meet up briefly in a life to help each other through a certain problem. Other times they might spend a lifetime together." He fixed me with an inquisitive eye. "Do you think you may have met your soul mate?"

"Even if I were to give credence to such things, I'm not sure I'd know my soul mate if I met him." I avoided Vincent's gaze as I recalled the unconditional love Kitty had felt for Garrett and the feeling of belonging and joy I'd felt when Vincent had rescued me from the snow.

"Are you all still in here?" Dempsey appeared behind the couch.

She seemed agitated, and Colin, Vincent, and I looked up, jolted rudely back to reality.

"Is Jadie all right?" Vincent asked.

"She's fine. She's all ready for bed. She said you were being boring and talking too much." She turned accusing eyes toward me. "She asked me what 'reincarnation' was."

"I'm sorry. That was my fault. I should have sent her off earlier." I scrambled up from the couch. "She takes everything in, that one."

"I need to talk to you." Dempsey was casting me meaningful looks. "There's something I think may be important."

"Yes?"

She shot Colin and her son a swift glance as she headed off toward the stairs. "We should get Jadie settled for the night and then we'll talk."

"I'll get my things together and go, then," Colin said. He rose to his feet. "We'll talk about this again later, Kate."

After I had kissed Jadie good night, the older woman drew me back down the landing to her room. I watched from the doorway as Dempsey picked up something that looked like a newspaper clipping from the dressing table.

"Come in." She motioned me over with a wave of her hand. "I found this." She unfolded the clipping on the bed as I came to stand beside her, and her eyes watched me anxiously.

" 'Local psychologist in suicide spat.' " Reading the headline, I frowned. "Does it give a name?"

She shook her head as I sat down on the bed and read the short article twice through.

A local psychologist has denied any wrongdoing after the verdict of suicide was reached by the coroner in the case of

Mary Penny-Brown at the court yesterday. Miss Penny-Brown was the third patient of the doctor, who has not been named, to die under suspicious circumstances in the past few years.

I looked up at her with a feeling of dread. "Where did you get this?"

"I found it on the floor of the study," Dempsey said shakily. "It must have fallen out of Vincent's pocket. I'm really sorry, Kate, but I have the feeling that the psychologist in the article might be Colin."

chapter forty-one

$\mathscr{I}$ *smoothed the* newspaper clipping with my hands while I mulled over its implications. Was this what Maria and Vincent had been trying to tell me? Was this why Vincent had wanted me back from the farm and Maria had invited us for drinks? I remembered Maria's look of dismay when she'd answered the door the previous evening to find Dempsey and Colin standing behind us, and then the hastily scribbled note she'd thrust into my coat pocket as we left.

Vincent had not been happy about the hypnotherapy sessions from the outset. But was that because he'd seen this article, or was it because of what had happened to Cheryl? And how much did Maria know?

"I'm going to have to talk to Colin," I mumbled, realizing as I sat on Dempsey's bed that until this evening when Vincent had come clean about what had happened to Cheryl, I hadn't entirely trusted Vincent's mother either.

I took a deep breath. "I know about Cheryl, Dempsey."

Dempsey made a small noise in her throat, and her eyes flicked to the drawer where I'd spotted the gin bottle on my first night here. She cleared her throat and found her voice. "What are you going to do?"

"It's all right, Dempsey. I'm not going to say anything. I wouldn't do that to Jadie. But I do need to know if Colin was involved in any way. He wasn't the doctor who prescribed Cheryl's medication, was he? He didn't have anything to do with her suicide?"

"I'd never met Colin before I arrived here yesterday morning." I watched as Dempsey swallowed nervously. "I don't know who gave Cheryl those pills, but I do know that Maria's husband was a doctor. Vincent and Cheryl and Maria and her husband, Jules, were good friends. And they were a similar age, both husbands professionals, both wives stuck out here alone with their children. They had a lot in common. It's not beyond the realm of possibility that Jules was the one who prescribed the medication for Cheryl's nerves. He came quickly enough when Vincent went over in a panic after we found what Cheryl had done. I'm pretty sure Maria's husband wrote the death certificate and arranged to have the body removed without fuss."

"Did Maria know about it?"

"No, she was out of the country with her son. I believe her marriage to Jules was becoming rocky and she was trying to build bridges with her estranged family in Sicily. By the time she returned, Cheryl had been buried and Vincent had dreamed up the story that his wife had left him. Vincent decided that Jadie must never know the truth and that the fewer people who knew about it the better."

"Where is Jules now?"

"I don't know. He and Maria split up about six months later. We thought Maria would return to Sicily, but she stayed here."

Dempsey gave a hollow laugh. "It doesn't seem that Maria was any luckier with her doctor husband than I was with mine. Michael is about the same age as Vincent was when his father walked out. It's funny how history repeats itself."

"I'm going to have to talk to Maria, and then have it out with Colin about this article," I said firmly. "If you ask me, it's high time *these* particular ghosts were laid to rest."

Leaving Dempsey sitting on her bed, I made my way back along the landing and down the stairs. Creeping quietly, I slipped along the hall and out through the back door.

It was dark in the back garden, but enough light spilled from the lighted windows for me to skirt the low hedge that divided the two gardens and make my way to where I guessed an identical back door opened onto Maria's downstairs hallway. Passing a small hall window, I saw Maria standing near her boot room, and despite the darkness, she must have seen me, because when I reached the back door, she was already standing there, holding it open, waiting.

With her long black hair cascading across her shoulders, she made a striking figure. "Come in," she said, motioning for me to slide past her. "You read my note?"

"Yes. What was it you wanted to tell me about Colin?"

Maria led me to her kitchen, waved me to a high stool that stood at the central island, and took the second stool for herself. "Would you like coffee, or a glass of wine, perhaps?"

I shook my head. "I can't be long. I haven't told Vincent or Colin I'm here."

"Ah."

"Tell me what you know." I placed the article about the suicides on the counter in front of her, and she acknowledged it with a nod.

Maria poured herself a glass of red wine and sipped it thoughtfully.

"On Thursday evening when you were at the farm, I asked Vincent to come over for a drink. I confess I wanted to get him on his own to confront him about Cheryl's hasty disappearance, which has always troubled me greatly. I had waited a long time for this opportunity. Until the snowstorm came and forced him to stay home, Vincent was making himself a stranger to me." She looked at me from under dark lashes. "I was tidying some papers prior to his visit, and I saw the piece about the suicides. It was right on top of the pile and folded back so that the article could not be missed. It was very strange, almost like a message from beyond." She gave a shudder before continuing. "I left the paper on the table so that Vincenzo would see it. I wanted to gauge his reaction, you understand? But instead of talking about Cheryl, he became distressed and said the article must be about someone named Colin and that he should fetch you back from the farm."

"Did you suspect that Cheryl may have killed herself?" I asked quietly. "Is that why you left the article there for Vincent to see?"

I noticed Maria's hand was shaking, and she rested the wineglass down on the counter. "I was not happy about the way Cheryl left," she said at last. "When I returned with Michael from visiting my parents the week she disappeared, I asked Jules—my husband—if he knew anything about my friend leaving so suddenly, and he said he knew nothing. I had no reason to doubt him." She turned the glass and toyed with it, watching the crimson liquid swirl slowly round. "I asked Vincenzo about it, of course, but he insisted Cheryl had abandoned him, and he would not discuss the subject further. He became distant and seemed always to be at work. He and Jules no longer socialized, and without Cheryl I became bored and lonely. Six months after Cheryl left, Jules walked out on me." She shrugged. "I would have gone home to Sicily, but Michael refused to go. He sees his father regularly, and his school and friends are not far away."

"But that was eighteen months ago." I wished I'd accepted a glass of wine after all as I folded my hands awkwardly in my lap. "Why didn't you press Vincent about Cheryl sooner, if you were worried?"

"As I said, he was always at work. Even before she vanished, Cheryl had complained that she hardly saw her husband. She felt so alone, and Vincenzo was never around." Maria lifted the glass to her lips and took a long sip. "But then the snow came and Vincenzo was stranded at home. I saw him clearing the driveway and asked him to come for a meal. He was uncomfortable, but he was weakening under my pressure, and then when I stopped by to make sure he would not go back on his word, you had arrived and so I had to invite you also." She made a tutting noise with her tongue as if to emphasise how inconvenient my appearance had been, but she gave me a smile. "I couldn't ask Vincenzo directly with you, a stranger, in tow, but I wanted him to know I was not happy about the way he had treated Cheryl or the way she'd left."

We stared at each other in silence for a moment or two. It was all beginning to make sense now. "And after he had seen the newspaper article about the suicides, did you manage to confront Vincent about Cheryl?"

Maria nodded. "Vincenzo was already agitated about you, and when I pressed him once again, he sat clutching the newspaper against his chest and just broke down and confessed that Cheryl had taken her own life."

We fell silent again, and then I managed, "Do you think Vincent had anything to do with his wife's death?"

Maria shook her head. "No. I knew Cheryl and I know Vincenzo. My friend was beyond reason after Amber passed away, lost in a dark world of her own. That is why I was so surprised when I returned from Sicily to find her gone. I didn't think she had the strength to leave."

I thought of what Tara had said about it taking energy to plan to leave and how she'd thought it unlikely that Cheryl would have done so.

"That Cheryl killed herself makes far more sense to me than the story that she had run away," Maria confirmed. "I believed him."

I stood up. "I think I had better get back."

Maria put a darkly tanned hand on my arm as if she was going to say something else, but at that moment the front doorbell sounded loudly, making us both jump.

"Wait here," she said, holding up her hand.

A moment later she returned with Vincent at her heels. He looked agitated, but when he saw me, his expression softened.

"Kate! We wondered where on earth you'd gone. Thank God I've found you. Colin called upstairs to say goodbye and we couldn't find you anywhere. Mom was acting all cagey and I thought you might have . . . left us."

"She came to see me, Vincenzo," Maria told him. "I have told her about the newspaper article and about Colin." She paused. "You should have told her yourself."

"I tried," he said, turning apologetic eyes toward me. "I wanted to tell you, but you were so set on this hypnosis thing. And there is no proof the article is actually about Colin."

I frowned, confused. "Why did you think it might be about him? The article doesn't give a name."

"It seemed too much of a coincidence," Vincent said. "Colin had appeared on our doorstep and put you under hypnosis, and then Maria showed me this article . . ." He looked away. "I was afraid for you, you know—after what happened . . ." His voice cracked with emotion and he swallowed before continuing, "After what happened to Cheryl."

"Nothing is going to happen to me," I told him gently. "I may have lost my memory and have made some sort of connection with a troubled character from my past, but I'm strong, Vincent."

A warm glow came over my body at the sudden, sure knowledge of it. The fleeting memory of a relationship gone sour and the need to make a new life for myself sprang into my mind. I furrowed my brow and stared unseeing at the Italian tiled kitchen floor and willed myself to remember. A family mystery, that's what there had been. Something I had promised to discover for someone important, whom I had lost. A feeling of sorrow filled my being. I had lost someone dear to me, but I had refused to crumble and let the bereavement pull me down. I was stronger than that. I had picked myself up and moved on with the intention of investigating a family secret.... Moved on ... but to where? Where had I been going?

I put a hand to my head as I tried to remember more. What was the mystery I had to uncover? When and where had that happened? And who had I been?

"Are you all right?" Vincent raised his troubled eyes to scan my face. "You look rather pale."

I shook my head, happy that my memory was gradually returning. I might only be recalling fragmented bits of my real life, but each piece of the jigsaw puzzle contributed to a tantalizing whole.

"I'm absolutely fine," I told him, focusing my mind back to the present dilemma. "But I think we should confront Colin and see what he has to say."

chapter forty-two

"*Where have you* been?" Colin grumbled when we entered the living room. "I didn't want to leave without saying goodbye and making an appointment for you to come and see me at my office."

"What can you tell me about this?" I came straight to the point, unfolding the clipping and handing it to him.

Colin looked surprised but took the now rather dog-eared piece of newspaper and read it through. He glanced up, his eyes anxious behind his rimless glasses. "Where did you get this?"

"It doesn't matter. Is the article about you?"

Colin sank down onto the sofa, and both Vincent and I walked around so we were facing him, our backs to the crackling fire.

Dempsey came down the stairs complaining the Jadie couldn't sleep and that she'd had to sit with her, but stopped short when she saw me and Vincent facing Colin down.

Colin turned to look at her. "You may as well hear this too, Dempsey," he said with a sigh.

Vincent's mother perched herself on an arm of the closest armchair and waited expectantly for Colin to speak.

"This article is about me, but it's not what you think."

I tried to hide my dismay. Was he going to tell me next that he'd driven the unfortunate Mary Penny-Brown to suicide? Had he taken her back to another supposed existence and driven her insane in the process? I recalled Tara warning that her brother might drive me crazy with the regression-hypnosis, that I could end up in an institution. I thought she'd been joking.

"All psychologists deal with unstable people," Colin went on. "The nature of our work involves taking on clients at the lowest ebbs in their lives. Statistics can always be swayed to look a certain way." He looked at each of the three of us in turn. "I firmly believe all people should be given help. Potentially suicidal patients whom other psychologists have turned away, condemning them as lost causes, come to me. Most face their demons and recover in time to become healthy members of society once more, but on three occasions—spread over several years, I might add—patients of mine have taken their own lives, despite my best endeavors. The reporter who wrote this piece is an ex-girlfriend with a grudge. The paper involved printed a retraction a week later." He looked up at me. "I swear that none of those cases was anything like yours, Kate. I have never regressed anyone to a previous life before, and I would never endanger you in any way."

I shot a sideways look at Vincent. "How old was that article?"

Vincent avoided my gaze. "I didn't look at the date when Maria showed the paper to me. I confess I was already unhappy about what Colin was doing. It seemed like tangible proof that I was right, and I admit I took it at face value."

"Never believe everything you read in a newspaper," Colin warned. "And just because you don't understand something doesn't necessarily mean it's wrong." He shrugged. "My license would have been revoked if I'd been guilty of any wrongdoing."

Vincent looked as if he was struggling for words. "Maybe we jumped to conclusions," he said at last. "But I only had Kate's best interests at heart. Please accept my apologies, Colin." He stuck out his hand, and Colin rose to his feet to accept it. The two men stood for a moment, then Vincent mumbled that he had some work to attend to. "Give me a call before you leave."

After Vincent had disappeared down the hall, Colin sank gratefully back down onto the sofa. But before we had time to settle our nerves, Dempsey gave a discreet cough.

"I need to talk with you alone," she told me as she rose to her feet. She made urgent eye signals in my direction as Colin, who seemed lost in his own thoughts, stared blankly into the fire. "I meant to tell you earlier but we were sidetracked by the article."

"Is it about Colin . . . or Cheryl?" I asked her wearily, ignoring Colin as he registered his name and looked questioningly up at me.

Dempsey's eyes went very wide at the mention of her daughter-in-law. "Cheryl," she mouthed, giving a wary glance in Colin's direction.

"He knows, Dempsey," I told her. "Colin knows what happened to Cheryl."

Dempsey sat down in the chair with a thud. "Oh my God."

"Secrets eat away at you," Colin said, and Dempsey became even more flustered. "You'll feel better now that everything is out in the open."

Dempsey snorted. "Well, since this seems to be an evening for revelations, perhaps you can tell me about this information I printed off the Internet this morning."

"May I see?" Colin rose, holding out his hand while Dempsey

fished in the pocket of her jeans and produced a crumpled computer printout, which she handed to him.

"While we're clearing the air and outing secrets, I thought I ought to show you this. It's some things I looked up on the computer as soon as the power came back on this morning."

Looking over Colin's shoulder, I scanned the printout quickly and frowned as I read it aloud more slowly, " 'Flunitrazepam . . . a drug otherwise known as Rohypnol, a powerful sedative. Rohypnol is a powerful sedative that comes in the form of a small white tablet, which leaves no taste or odor when dissolved in a drink. It creates a sleepy, relaxed feeling lasting two to eight hours. Side effects are blackouts, loss of memory, dizziness and disorientation, nausea, and difficulty with movements and speech. The drug is available in the United States only by prescription as it can cause psychological dependence. This is the so-called date rape drug.' Why did you look this up, Dempsey?"

"Cheryl took it for depression, and she overdosed on this damn Rohypnol stuff," Dempsey explained. She went to the cabinet where Vincent kept the brandy, removed the bottle and a glass, and poured a hefty measure. She swirled the amber liquid around the brandy balloon and watched it as if mesmerised. "I knew my daughter-in-law was on tranquilizers to help her sleep, to help keep her from cracking up, but I didn't know what they were—not until the morning I found her lying there with the bottle on the floor by the bed." Dempsey crossed to the armchair and sat down again, still watching the contents of the glass as she swirled it round and round. "I picked up the bottle and read the label before putting it on the bedside cabinet. I knew it was already too late for Cheryl, but I hurried to get Vincent, hoping he could do something, anything. I just couldn't believe we had lost her. When he ran in, I could see from the look on his face that it was hopeless, but he still tried to revive her. When she didn't respond, he told me to go to my room while he got Jules from next door. Later Vincent told me to stay calm and not to say anything to anyone, that Jules would deal with it."

Dempsey lifted the glass to her lips but didn't drink. She just held it there as if frozen with the memory of what she'd seen.

"Why did you wait all this time to look up the drug on the computer?" Colin was watching Dempsey with the glass.

"When they had taken Cheryl's body away, I went to look in Amber's room, but the drug bottle was gone. I assumed at the time that the doctor had taken it. Then, when Kate got so drunk at Maria's last night, it brought it all back to me. Her symptoms made me uneasy. And this morning the poor girl looked so ill, and I remember Cheryl looking just the same. I recalled the drug's name and thought I'd look it up as soon as we had the power back on." She paused to see that we were still going along with her train of thought. "If it turns out that Jules was the doctor who prescribed the drug that killed Cheryl, it would explain why he was so eager to handle her suicide so quickly and discreetly. And I wondered if there was more of the stuff in their house."

"You're not saying someone put some of this Rohypnol in Kate's drink?" Colin probed.

Dempsey shrugged. "Not necessarily. It was just the way Kate's symptoms this morning reminded me of Cheryl, that's all. If it was Jules who took the pills away with him, Maria or her son might have gotten hold of them by mistake or something. You never know."

"Doctors don't usually make a habit of leaving drugs lying around where their wives or children might find them," Colin said gently. "And even if by some chance they did, how could it have ended up in Kate's drink?"

"Oh, I don't know." Dempsey groaned. She tipped the glass to her lips.

Colin crossed to the armchair and lifted the brandy balloon out of Dempsey's hand. "You don't need this. You are strong, Dempsey, much stronger than you give yourself credit for. You've faced worse than this in your life." He put his other hand on her shoulder. "None of what happened to Cheryl was your fault."

Dempsey's eyes filled with tears, and I tiptoed away, leaving Colin to deal with a guilt-fueled, grief-stricken Dempsey. I entered the kitchen, closed the door behind me, filled the kettle, and sank onto a chair. My head was spinning, and I rubbed my hands wearily over my face. So many pieces of the jigsaw puzzle had begun to fall into place. Cheryl had killed herself with prescription drugs after the death of her daughter. Maria's husband had given Cheryl tranquilizers, but were they the same ones that had actually killed her? Either way, Vincent had covered his wife's suicide up for the sake of their surviving child, and poor Dempsey had kept the terrible secret hidden for almost two years. And there was still the mystery of Kitty and what had befallen her. Then there was the double suicide, which, according to Betty and Bill, had happened in this very house ninety years before, and of course I still didn't know the secret of my own identity.

After spooning cocoa powder into mugs, I added milk and hot water, found a tray, and took the steaming mugs back out to where Dempsey was wiping her face on a handkerchief borrowed from Colin.

"Here." I handed her a mug of hot chocolate, and she smiled her thanks, seeming much more composed as she took a sip.

"*Did Colin leave yet?*" Vincent asked when I poked my head through the doorframe to his study.

"He's been looking after your mother. Dempsey has been unburdening herself."

Vincent looked at something on his desk. "So he knows. I've done the man an injustice, haven't I? And Mom too. I was wrong to ask her not to tell anyone. I knew she was having trouble keeping it all bottled up inside. I knew she was drinking, and I did nothing."

"Why did you let your friend give Cheryl those tranquilizers?" I asked. I was standing before him with my hands on my hips. "Surely it would have been safer to have gone to your own doctor?"

Vincent brought his eyes to mine. "Jules was a respected doctor and a trusted friend. Cheryl was beside herself, and after what happened to Amber, she no longer trusted our own doctor. I was desperate to help her. I thought Jules knew what he was doing."

"Were the pills he prescribed flunitrazepam?"

"I didn't know what they were called or how strong they were. When Cheryl overdosed, Jules panicked and took the remaining pills away with him. I think he was worried there would be some sort of inquiry as to why he'd prescribed those particular pills and why he'd let her have so many."

"And you wanted him to handle her suicide discreetly, so you said nothing and allowed him to make all the necessary arrangements?" The disappointment in my voice was tangible. "How could you have kept this to yourself all this time, Vincent?" I sat on the desk and faced him squarely. "I know you've tried to bury yourself in your work, but this was such a terrible thing to have happened to you all."

Vincent's shoulders sagged, and he looked ten years older than when I had first come to this house only five days ago. "I don't know. As I said to you before, I need forgiveness from Cheryl and from Amber. I can't live with the guilt anymore."

I shivered at his words and searched his face. Was Vincent having suicidal thoughts too? What was it Dempsey had said about history repeating itself?

"I need to go back," I murmured, more to myself than to the anguished man before me. "I need to visit Kitty again and understand what happened to her and why I'm seeing her life unfold. Somehow her life is connected to this house."

There were going to be no more untimely deaths in this house, I vowed silently. Not while I was here to stop them.

chapter forty-three

$\mathcal{D}$*empsey closed her* eyes when I told her about my conversation with her son, and I thought she was going to cry again, but when she opened them, she looked determined.

"I never understood why Vincent and Jules kept the circumstances of Cheryl's death quiet. I know it would have been bad for Jadie to discover that her mother had killed herself, but when she stopped speaking anyway, I had to wonder at the reasoning behind his actions."

"Jadie's feelings were just an excuse for Vincent's cover-up." Colin was leaning towards Dempsey, his voice low so it wouldn't carry along the hall to the study or up the stairs to Jadie. "He couldn't admit what had really happened because he couldn't cope with his feelings of guilt. By pretending to the world that Cheryl had left them, he didn't have to acknowledge his culpability in not having been there when she'd needed him most."

"What are we going to do?"

"I'd like to go back and find out what Kitty has to do with all this," I told Dempsey. "I believe Vincent is still hoping that Maria's ghosts have something to do with Cheryl or Amber. Perhaps it's time I found out if there is a connection between them and Kitty."

I was lying on the couch while Dempsey tucked a blanket around me, when Vincent appeared at the foot of the stairs.

"I'd like to sit in again, if that's all right with you, Kate?"

We stared at each other uncomfortably until Colin broke the silence. "Kate tells us Jules was the doctor who prescribed Cheryl's pills. Is that right?"

"Yes. He said they would keep her calm and help her to sleep."

"You told Kate you didn't realize what they were."

Vincent shook his head. "They seemed to help, and I had no reason to doubt him."

"Did you keep the remaining pills after you found Cheryl's body?"

"No, Jules took them with him."

Colin sat back, tapping his chin with his fingertips while he contemplated Vincent carefully. "Kate wants to go back in time and see if there is a connection between Kitty and what has happened in this house in the last two years. Do you have any objections to that?"

Vincent shook his head mutely as he seated himself in the empty armchair.

"We don't even know that Kitty lived here for sure," Dempsey cautioned.

"We know that Kate's descriptions of the kind of home Kitty wanted fit this house like a glove," Colin replied as he drew up a dining chair next to the couch. He turned his attention to me. "And the name of this house, Kigarjay, is a bit of a pointer. It's a compilation of their names, isn't it? Kitty, Garrett, Jaygo. I don't believe Kitty is haunting the place, but if she did once live here, maybe there is some sort of karma at work. Maybe you didn't arrive in this place by accident. What if this is the perfect opportunity for Kitty to fix something that has troubled her through death and followed her into her present incarnation as you?" He stared at me. "Let's hope Kitty has an answer for us."

"I hope I haven't imagined the whole thing and the house was named after three different kinds of birds."

"Indeed." Colin smiled. "So close your eyes and we will see if we can find some answers."

Soon I was drifting backward through the disconcerting misty nothingness of my present life and awakening in a room that looked remarkably like the master bedroom at Kigarjay. I gazed around at the tapestries and felt a moment of peace and familiarity. But the oasis of tranquillity was short-lived as my brain clicked into place and I remembered the horror of the world I was surfacing into.

Leaping from my bed, I raced into Jaygo's bedroom and let out a wild scream of despair. His bed was empty. My little boy was truly gone.

"Tell me what you are seeing, Kitty," came the disembodied voice.

"What do you care?" I cried. "My little boy is gone and no one can bring him back."

"Don't cry, Kitty," soothed the voice. "Tell me what happened."

"Garrett was so angry with his mother for making me give our baby son away." I wept. "And she told him..." I gulped and sniffed as tears poured from my bloodshot eyes. "She told him our child hadn't died as a baby at all. He had been given away to be cared for by a couple who used to work for Garrett's family. Garrett's mother knew that if I believed he was still alive, I would try to find him, so she lied. She *lied*."

"But surely that's good news?" The voice sounded puzzled. "Did Garrett go to get him back?"

"He did—we both did. Earlier this year we traveled to Lowell and found our son well cared for and happy." I dabbed a lace handkerchief at my face and took a deep breath. "I felt bad taking him from the only mother he had ever known. It was heart-wrenching for him and for the adoptive mother, but having Jaygo back in my arms was the happiest moment of my life."

"So why the tears? You didn't leave him there?" The voice was gentle as a new wave of self-pity racked me.

"No." I fought to continue speaking. "We brought him home, and for one glorious summer we were the happiest family alive. Garrett doted on our son. Jaygo was six years old, so soft to hold and such a sweetheart. His adoptive family had kept livestock, and Jaygo had a great love of animals and wanted to work the land when he grew up. He spent hours that summer playing in the fields, despite his father's insistence that he study his books and learn his sums. Jaygo always had scraped knees and muddy hands, and Garrett would occasionally relent, carrying him piggyback around the animal pens on the farm we had bought and renovated. It was heartwarming to see them together."

"So what happened?"

"This winter the fever took him from us. Nothing the doctors or I could do would bring the fever down. I have lost everything in the world that was important to me."

"Where is Garrett?"

I snorted derisively. "He couldn't cope with his grief and has buried himself in his work. He has never been a demonstrative man, but just when I need him the most, he has distanced himself from me. I have never felt so alone in all my life."

"What about the rest of your family—your sister, Alice, and brother, Arthur?"

"Alice has become bitter and twisted. She still insists Uncle George did those things to her. She was angry with Mother for not believing her, and angrier still that she passed away while the two of them were on such bad terms over it."

"Where is Arthur?"

"He went away. Alice told me he had started drinking heavily, just like Father, and after Mother's funeral, he left."

"And where is Alice now?"

"She rents a room in the village. She keeps asking to stay here, but I haven't the time or energy for her after all that has happened to me."

"Could you find it in your heart to be reconciled with your sister?"

"How can I love anyone again? Garrett was my dearest love, yet he seems more interested in providing material comforts than showing me his emotional side. I blame myself for bringing my child to this place. Perhaps if we had left him with his adoptive parents, Jaygo would not have caught the fever and he would be alive and well, even if he wasn't with me. Sometimes the guilt is so great I wonder how I will go on."

"What if I told you that you would see your child again?"

"That is a cruel jest!" I stopped talking to gulp back tears that were never far from the surface.

"Kitty, I truly believe you will see your son again. His soul is resting in the place beyond. You will feel your child in your arms again."

"I wish that were so with all my heart. I would know him anywhere."

"You wouldn't do anything...stupid, would you?"

I shook my head. "I will wait for my time to come. Not like silly Alice, who is always threatening to kill herself. I really can't bear to hear her talking as she does."

"What does she say?"

I sighed. "She says she can't live with the shame of what Uncle George did to her, and that she would rather die than go through life with no one believing her."

"Do you truly not believe her?"

"I don't know. I can't think. How can I think about Alice when there is a space inside me that can never be filled? I wish my sister would stop pestering me for support when I am so empty and unable to give her what she craves."

"If you could wish for anything else, except the return of your child, what would it be?"

I thought for a moment or two and smiled wanly through my tears. "I know I should wish peace for Alice, but I would truly desire that Garrett and I could meet up again as we once were. I'd wish to experience the great passion we shared just that once and of which I believe we are both capable again."

"I'm going to count backward from ten, and I want you to awaken relaxed and refreshed, with all trace of sadness gone," said the voice.

"Just one thing."

"Yes?"

"Promise me I will see Jaygo again. *Promise* me."

"I promise. Now it is time to let your mind go blank. Ten, nine, eight..."

I awoke to find three pairs of eyes staring down at me.

"That was very convincing," Vincent said awkwardly. "I can

see why you and Colin have been so hooked on this hypnotherapy thing."

"How could you promise her such a thing?" Ignoring Vincent's remark, I wriggled into a sitting position, still slightly disoriented, and leaned my head against the back of the sofa to look at Colin reproachfully. "I know what's happened to me has made you more open-minded about the reincarnation thing, but you don't *know*, not for sure."

"I think I do. I think you do too."

Deciding not to pursue that line of thought, I turned my reproachful gaze on Vincent instead. "Garrett did to Kitty exactly what you did to Cheryl—emotionally distancing himself in a time of shared need."

"Are you suggesting I'm a reincarnation of Garrett?"

I shrugged, still inexplicably angry with him. "There are similarities."

"I don't think Vincent is a reincarnation of Garrett," Colin put in. "I don't believe you are soul mates, if that's what you're thinking, Kate."

"There wasn't that much chemistry between Kitty and Garrett either," I pointed out." Not in that particular life, anyway."

"I think we should stop going in circles and consider what Kitty is trying to convey to us," Dempsey added. "I don't mean the Kitty who lived then, but the enlightened Kitty who, if we subscribe to Colin's theories, is now Kate."

I turned to look at her. "I thought you didn't believe in this stuff?"

"I admit I may have dabbled in one or two things in my time and have certain opinions of what is pure nonsense and what might have its toe dipped in the murky waters of a reality we simply don't understand."

"Very succinctly put." Colin winked at her.

"All I'm saying is that we should look at the part of Kitty's life she felt important enough to share with us."

"Obviously it was her son dying," Vincent said quietly.

"Or maybe we should be looking more at Alice's state of mind?" I queried.

"Possibly both," Colin confirmed. "Perhaps the fact that Kitty wasn't thinking clearly because of her grief had an impact on what happened to her sister."

"You think Alice may have been the suicide? Betty said there were two deaths. So if one was Alice, who was the other? I just can't believe it was Kitty." I swung my legs off the couch and tested my feet on the floor. "I'm really tired; it's been a long day. Do you mind if I go up to bed and we can look at things fresh in the morning?"

"I think that's a good idea." Dempsey rose to her feet. "It's hard to believe it was only this morning you woke up with that terrible hangover."

"I've got to go anyway. Tara will be wondering where I am." Colin looked at his watch. "There will be clients waiting on my doorstep tomorrow morning, and I have to prepare my notes tonight."

"May I look in on Jadie?" I asked Vincent after Colin had collected his bag and headed out into the dark night.

He looked at me as if reading my mind. "Would that be my six-year-old daughter or Kitty's six-year-old son?"

chapter forty-four

It was hard, tearing myself away from watching Jadie sleep. She looked so peaceful with her blond curls framing her flushed face, her thumb nestling against her chin where it had fallen from her mouth. Whether what I had been recalling under hypnosis was a previous life as Kitty or a figment of my imagination, it had left me with an ache in my heart for the little boy she had lost.

Vincent leaned in the doorway to his daughter's room and watched me watching her. Eventually I pulled myself away, whispered good night to Jadie—or was it Jaygo?—and turned to face him. He closed the door softly behind us, lifted my chin with his finger, and looked deeply into my eyes.

"You know now how I feel about Jadie," he said. "It's hard to separate the love from the pain and fear of losing someone."

I nodded, watching his face in the dull light filtering up the stairs from below. "I think I understand now just how terrible it must have been to lose Amber."

"Do you hate me for lying to you about Cheryl?"

"No. I could never hate you."

"Could you feel anything more for me?"

I pondered the question, thinking back to Kitty and her un-wavering feelings for Garrett. No matter how he'd disappointed her, both physically and emotionally, she had loved him with every fiber of her being. Could I feel that way about Vincent? I wasn't sure. Convenient as it would have been to find he was my soul mate, I simply couldn't imagine myself in his arms.

"I'm sorry, Vincent. I'm just not sure we would be right for each other."

His expression hardened, and he began to turn away from me. I put out a hand to restrain him. "You don't have to be alone, you know."

He paused and looked back at me.

"Haven't you ever wondered about Tara's devotion to you and Jadie?"

Even in the gloom I could see that he was puzzled. "She's just doing her job."

"It's much more than that. She gave up her career to stay here and care for this family. She's like a mother to Jadie; she would do anything for her—and for you too.

"What are you saying?"

"That she's in love with you. Tara is in love with you—probably has been for years. I don't know how you've failed to notice."

He had fallen very still. "Are you sure?"

I grinned at him. "I'm absolutely positive. But the rest is up to you."

I stared at myself long and hard in the bathroom mirror that night. "Who are you?" I demanded, staring into those hazel eyes. Running my fingers over the partially healed cut and yellowing bruise, I wondered how such a seemingly small injury had caused such a drastic memory loss. I pushed the hair from my forehead and contemplated my features from every angle. There was no hint of auburn in my hair, but even if I had been Kitty in a previous life, our biological bodies would not necessarily be the same. I could hardly believe I was even contemplating such a hypothesis, but the possibility rolled itself around and around in my mind.

I dropped my hair back down to frame my face and turned away from the mirror. Feeling thoroughly disconcerted, I made my way to bed and pulled the covers up to my chin. I didn't want to think anymore. I just wanted to close my eyes and sleep.

I awoke the next morning to the sound of the front door banging open and voices exclaiming in the room below. I pulled on the dressing gown and, still hazy with sleep, ventured to the top of the stairs to see what the commotion was about.

Tara was lugging several supermarket bags into the front hall, and Dempsey was taking them from her and disappearing from view into the kitchen.

"The whole village is talking about it," Tara was saying loudly as she dumped another three bags through the doorway. "They found the car downstream from the bridge, almost completely submerged. Tom Smith from the garage helped pull it up. He says it looks from the damage to the hedges as if the car ran off the road. Apparently the police divers spent yesterday afternoon scouring the river for a body."

The image of a car sliding backwards on a snowy road filled my mind. I shook my head and tried to remember. I had been lost in the snowstorm . . . there was a cat on the front seat in a carrier. My eyes sprang open wide with the memory. Had the car been mine?

"Did they find anything?" Dempsey's curious voice asked from below.

"Not yesterday, apparently, but they tried again this morning, and they found a body wedged under some rocks! They're not revealing anything yet about it . . . except that it was a woman."

I sank slowly to my knees, clutching the banister for support. Ever since Colin and I failed to recover any memory of my present life, I'd had a nagging worry, a shadowy underlying feeling that perhaps I couldn't remember more than a few fragments of my most recent life because I wasn't really here at all.

If the car was mine, then perhaps the body was mine too.

"Oh God, please don't make me dead," I prayed as I huddled at the top of the stairs. It all fit—my lack of memories, my ability to flit so easily to a previous incarnation, the visions of drowning I'd had, both here in the shower and at the river's edge where we'd found Betty.

And what had Jadie said about Amber knowing I would come to this place? And then there was Maria's talk of things being inexplicably moved about in her house; even Vincent had sensed it and hoped it was the spirits of his wife and daughter. I was a ghost, a spirit, trapped on the wrong side of the veil between this life and the next.

"No," I whispered. "No!"

Dempsey appeared at the bottom of the stairs, a bulging bag still clutched in her hand. "Is that you, Kate? What's the matter?"

Gazing at her in dread, I took a great gulp of air. "You can see me, can't you?"

Dempsey dropped the bag and trotted up the stairs two at a time, coming to perch beside me on the top step. "Of course I can see you. What's the matter?"

"I heard what Tara said about the car and the dead woman. Maybe you think I'm being silly, but I appeared out of nowhere, with no memories, and now they've found an abandoned vehicle and a body. I...I think the car might be mine."

"It sounds to me like you've been watching too many horror films." She took my arm and helped me to my feet. "Come down and have a nice cup of tea while I put the groceries away."

I allowed Dempsey to guide me to the kitchen, where I slumped onto a chair and rested my elbows on the table, my head in my hands.

"You look terrible," Tara said as she bowled through the door, clutching a pack of paper towels. She made no mention of her outburst the day before, and I would have been heartily relieved if I hadn't been in such a state of anxiety. "What have they been doing to you?"

"She thinks she's dead."

"You don't look *quite* that bad." Tara opened the cupboard under the sink, wedged the paper towels underneath, and turned to peer at me more closely. "A bit ghostly white, maybe, but still breathing."

"It's not funny."

"Yes, it is." Tara slipped into the seat beside me. "You've been listening to Colin for too long. He brought me up-to-date when he came in last night about what's been going on, and it all sounds ridiculous to me."

I peered at her hopefully, glad that she was being civil again. "You still think it's all nonsense, then?"

"Let me see. You are really Kitty, back from the dead; Jadie is a reincarnation of Kitty's son, Jaygo....What sort of a name is that, anyway? And Betty was Kitty's sister, Alice, even though she was several years Kitty's junior and Betty is more than sixty years older than you. Yup, I'd say that was pretty nonsensical, but don't mind me, I'm just the hired help."

"You're much more than that, Tara," Dempsey put in, turning

from the fridge where she'd been stowing a stack of Jadie's favorite yogurts. "You're part of this family, and you know it."

Tara bowed her head before turning her attention back to me. "Just because that head of yours is empty of recent memory doesn't mean you have to absorb every bit of nonsense my brother throws at you."

"I don't think even Colin believed in all this stuff until he put me under hypnosis and Kitty materialized," I said uneasily.

Tara leaned over and pinched me viciously on the arm, making me squeal.

"Ouch! What was that for?"

"Just showing you you're not dead, kiddo. Dead people don't feel pain, do they?" She got up and went to the door. "I'm going to wake Jadie and do her physical therapy. I know she had a late night, but she shouldn't sleep in too long or her lungs will get congested."

Dempsey grinned as the door closed behind Tara. "She always was straight to the point, that one."

"Except where Vincent is concerned," I observed wryly, rubbing my arm.

Before Dempsey had time to open her mouth, she was cut short by a loud banging on the front door. "I hope that isn't Maria come to tell us the Four Horsemen of the Apocalypse are riding through her kitchen."

I smothered a laugh as she hurried out to open the front door, then I snapped to attention as the sound of men's voices filtered across the living area. Then I realized the voices were in the house and coming toward the kitchen. I only had time to run a hand quickly through my sleep-tousled hair before Dempsey was back with three men on her heels, the last of whom was Adam.

Dempsey sat next to me and took my hand protectively in

hers. "These officers have come to see you about your missing persons report."

I glanced past the two uniformed officers to where Adam was standing awkwardly in the doorway.

"They came to the farm," he said by way of explanation, "because you made the report from our address. So I brought them down here to talk to you."

"Good morning, miss. I'm Sergeant Graham and this is Officer Brent. We're sorry to bother you so early, but we're following up your inquiry. We've had quite a backlog of emergencies to clear, as you can imagine, but a new incident has come to light that we think may have a possible link to you."

"Please, sit down." I waved my hand toward the empty chairs, and they sat.

"We've found a car in the river near the bridge," the sergeant explained.

"Tara told us," I said, nodding.

"Tara never did miss out on any gossip," Adam murmured.

"Thank you. We'll take it from here, Mr. Jenkins." The sergeant turned to me again. "According to the report, you were found wandering on Mr. Jenkins's top field in a state of shock and near hypothermia last Tuesday. You had no recollection of how you came to be there." He paused to scrutinize my face, his gaze coming to rest on the fading bruise. "Was that injury present when you were found?"

I nodded.

"And you still have no memory of what happened to you?"

"No. Well, fleeting bits, but not enough to remind me who I am."

"As I said, a car has been found submerged in the river downstream from the bridge. We are still trying to locate the driver."

He took a deep breath. "So we have an abandoned vehicle with a missing owner and a 'found' person who has no recollection of how she came to travel to this area." He leaned forward across the table. "As of now no identification has been found with the vehicle, but it will be thoroughly searched and we are running the registration number through our computers. We hope an identification of ownership will soon be made."

"What about the body?"

"What do you know about a body, miss?"

"Tara said a body had been found in the river by police divers."

"And Tara might be . . . ?"

"The housekeeper," Tara said from the doorway.

She and Vincent pushed their way past Adam into the kitchen. The sergeant raised an eyebrow as Vincent held out his hand.

"I'm Vincent James, the owner of this house."

"Good to meet you, Mr. James. Can you shed any more light on what may have happened to this young lady?" The sergeant sat down again, having risen to return the handshake.

"Not really. What's all this about a body?"

"The report of the submerged vehicle came in to the station yesterday afternoon. The police officers who responded to the call requested that divers be brought to the scene, and they returned at first light today. I heard about the incident when I came on duty this morning, remembered the report of an unidentified woman in the area, and thought the two incidents might be connected. Meanwhile, the divers discovered a human skeleton, identified on the scene by our police pathologist as that of a female."

"A skeleton?" I leaned forward in my seat. "Not a recent body, then?"

"The pathologist will have to run tests, of course, but he said he could tell from the pelvis that the skeleton was female, and it looked as though it had been down there for quite some years. It was tangled in old wire and had been partially swept under a large rock. It couldn't be seen from the surface and may never have been discovered at all if the divers hadn't been down there searching for the driver of the vehicle."

"Not you, then." Dempsey gave my hand a quick squeeze.

I smiled sheepishly at her. "No, not me."

Sergeant Graham glanced from one of us to the other. "Would you have any objection to Officer Brent taking your fingerprints, miss? We could check them against the database to try to identify you and also compare them with any the forensic team might lift from the vehicle."

"No, of course I don't mind."

He glanced around the crowded kitchen. "Perhaps Officer Brent could have a little more space?"

Tara pursed her lips and headed back out into the hallway, closely followed by the unusually attentive Vincent. Dempsey remained seated in her chair and Adam continued to watch the proceedings. I opened my mouth to tell him he didn't need to wait around, I was sure he had a million pressing jobs to do on the farm, but as my eyes met his and he returned the look with his calm gaze I fell silent.

The fingerprinting didn't take long, and then the police officers were getting to their feet.

"I advise you to see a doctor as soon as possible, miss. You should have that head injury looked at by a professional." Sergeant Graham turned to Dempsey. "Would you like me to contact social services about the young lady? They may be able to find her some temporary housing until a formal identification can be made and her family located."

"That won't be necessary, Sergeant. She's more than welcome to stay here."

I smiled gratefully at Dempsey.

"Just one more thing." We all looked at the sergeant. "I'd like another word with Mr. James before I go. I gather he was the one who found her and brought her back here?"

Adam cleared his throat. "Well, no. Actually, I found her. I was checking the ewes on the top field and found her lying just off the path."

My eyes opened so wide that I thought they might pop right out of my face. I felt my heart hammering in my chest and put a hand to my throat. It was Adam who had found me and carried me here, not Vincent. Everything I had believed since I'd woken in this house had been a misconception. Suddenly random pieces of the jigsaw puzzle I had been struggling with began to fall into place.

chapter forty-five

I was still staring incredulously at Adam when the sergeant sat down again. "Then, why did you bring the young lady here and not to your own house, sir?"

The sergeant's voice seemed very faint and far away, as if I were listening to it in a dream. Adam's voice, when he replied, sent shivers of recognition down my spine.

"The lane to my top field passes the end of this drive. She was suffering from hypothermia and exposure and in danger of frost-bite. This was the nearest warmth and shelter. It would have taken an hour to get her back to my farm. I saw Vincent—that's Mr. James—out clearing the snow off his drive, and I handed her over to him. He hurried her into the house, and I knew Tara would look after her."

"Can you tell us anything more about how you found her?"

I could tell him, I thought as my hand left my throat and drifted across my shoulder to rub up and down my arm. I could recall the very scent of him, the feel of his coat chafing against my chin, the way our bodies moved in unison as he walked with me clasped hard against his chest. I could hear again the heaviness of his breathing as he struggled through the deep snow.

Blushing to the roots of my hair, I kept my eyes downcast as Adam gave a brief description of how he'd found me.

"She was wearing jeans and a thin sweater, lightweight boots . . . not clothes suitable for a walk in the snow. I remember wondering where she had come from and why she was so inappropriately dressed."

"So in your opinion she looked more suitably dressed for someone who was making a car journey than one on foot?"

"I'd say so, yes. I went back later to get the cat and looked up on the top road to see if I could spot a vehicle, but there was nothing in sight."

"A cat, sir?" The sergeant sounded confused. "What cat would that be?"

"She had a cat with her, in a pet carrier. It was hidden under her when I found her. It looked like she was trying to shelter it with her own body."

"Where is the cat now?" Sergeant Graham looked around the kitchen as if expecting the animal to materialise before his eyes.

"I took it home with me. When I realized how deep the snow was getting, I went back with my sheepdog to herd the flock down to a field nearer the farm. I collected the pet carrier en route, but I needed to supervise Lad herding the sheep across the fields, so I didn't have time to come back here with the cat. Vincent left a message on my answering machine that night asking if I'd found a cat. He said the mystery woman was concerned for the animal's welfare, so I brought the cat down the next morning."

"I see. And I assume the cat didn't have any identification on it, no name tag or address?"

"No, nothing."

"Very well, sir. Thank you for your time," the sergeant said. Then he turned to me and said, "As soon as we get the information about the ownership of the vehicle, we will cross-check it against your details and get back to you. If anything else comes to light on your end, you know where to find me."

Dempsey showed the officers out, leaving me alone in the room with Adam. I could barely look at him. I wondered if he had felt anything when he'd carried me, or whether I meant no more to him than if I'd been an injured ewe he'd found lying half buried in a snowdrift.

"Why didn't anyone tell me it was you who rescued me?" I said at last in a tight voice.

He shrugged. "It was no big deal. I handed you over to Vincent, and you seemed comfortable here when I came over the next morning with the cat."

Remembering Vincent's possessive attitude when he'd found me talking to Adam in the doorway, I wondered if Vincent had kept the truth from me on purpose. Perhaps believing I had performed some kind of miracle to make his daughter speak after almost two years of self-imposed silence had made him want to keep me to himself. Thinking back, though, I realized that he had never actually claimed to be the one who had found me up on the field; he merely hadn't said anything to the contrary. As far as Tara or Jadie or, later, Dempsey knew, he had indeed been my noble rescuer.

Adam was looking at me strangely. He peeled himself off the wall where he'd been learning and made as if to come toward me, but I pulled away in the chair, my body language echoing my anger and confusion. He stopped, suddenly awkward.

"I'd better be off, then."

"Fine, don't let me hold you up."

He hovered. "Kate . . ."

His voice sent shivers down my spine. I wanted to touch him. Every fiber of my being wanted to make physical contact with him, to see if there was anything tangible between us. Swallowing, I bit back tears of frustration. Kitty had hoped for a lifetime of passion with Garrett. I'd hoped for similar fireworks with Vincent, thinking he had been "the one," but I had been disappointed. Could I bear that disappointment again?

"Thank you for rescuing me," I said stonily. "I appreciate it."

"If you want anything, you know where to find me."

"Yes."

He turned on his heel and left the room, and I sat staring through the kitchen window into the distance where a shrunken snowman wearing a red scarf melted in the spring sunshine.

By midmorning I was in such a state of anxiety that Dempsey, who was still waiting for the return of her car and had called the gallery to say she wouldn't be in, suggested a walk with Jadie. Tara was making the most of having Dempsey there to look after her charge while she cleaned the house, and, having wrapped Jadie in sweaters, coat, and fleece-lined boots, she waved us away with something akin to relief. Vincent had headed off to the city as soon as the police had gone, and wouldn't be back until the evening.

"The police must have found out who the vehicle belonged to by now," I agonized as we tramped along a particularly muddy bridle path. The spring thaw had turned the paths into a quagmire, but Jadie was loving every squelch in the thick mud.

"Don't get too dirty," Dempsey called at one point as Jadie contemplated an especially deep brown puddle, "or Tara will never let you out with me again."

"Amber likes mud," Jadie sang as she jumped into the puddle, staining her jeans and the hem of her coat. "She likes mud a lot."

"Yes, well, it isn't Amber who will have to face Tara's wrath," Dempsey replied.

I was glad to hear them using Amber's name freely. It seemed much healthier to acknowledge that Amber was still very much alive in their hearts and memories.

"Jadie seems much happier," I observed as Jadie walked a little ahead, out of earshot.

"We've all been much happier since you came to stay," Dempsey replied. "I have to confess that, selfishly, I don't want the police to find out your true identity, because then you'll leave us, and I don't want things to return to how they were before."

"I don't think that will happen. Vincent seems to have acknowledged his grief and the part he played in what happened to Cheryl. He'll be a better father to Jadie because of it. Things will be different now, I'm sure."

"Vincent won't be happy to see you go."

"I'm hoping he'll acknowledge how Tara feels about him and forget all about me." I stopped walking. "Would you be happy with Tara as a daughter-in-law?"

Dempsey pursed her lips, contemplating her answer. "I have nothing against the girl. If she's what Vincent wants, then I'm sure we'll all get along famously, but do you think she ever will be what he really wants?"

Shrugging, I continued along the path. "Who can tell? She'd be perfect as a mother to Jadie, wouldn't she? She knows exactly how to look after her, with the CF and everything." I bit my lip, trying to keep out of my voice the panic that arose whenever I thought of leaving this place.

"Wouldn't you be jealous? I don't mean of Tara with Vincent, but of Tara being Jadie's mother? I'm thinking, you know, with the possibility that Jadie is a reincarnation of Kitty's boy, Jaygo. How would you feel to have someone else raise her?"

I avoided a particularly sticky-looking patch of mud. "I don't think it would be so bad if I still had some contact with her. If any of that was real, then it was a lifetime ago. Jadie is who she is now, though I confess I have a special place in my heart for her. It's strange because I still don't know if I have children of my own somewhere, but if I do, I can't believe I feel any more for them than I do for her."

Or for Adam, I thought miserably. Adam, who had no time for romance and who felt nothing for me; Adam, who might have been my soul mate if he'd taken the time to read the signs, to open his mind to the burst of energy I'd felt pass between us.

We watched Jadie as she inspected the hedges for birds' nests, standing on tiptoe in her mud-caked pink boots.

"And what about that business next door?" I went on, changing the subject as a lump formed in my throat. "Maria is still convinced they have a ghost."

Dempsey gave me a sideways glance. "You don't believe any of that, do you?"

I picked my way across a muddy puddle, which gave me an excuse to hide my face from her eagle-eyed scrutiny. "There was the way that article about Colin was just lying open on the table for Maria to find. And she says things have mysteriously moved from one place to another. And then there are these memories I've been having of Kitty and Garrett..." I turned to look at her. "What if one or both of them are haunting the place?"

Dempsey glanced at Jadie and lowered her voice to a whisper. "I'm inclined to believe there is a much more mundane reason for the disturbances next door. And I still want to know whether there are any more of those pills lying around. You know, the ones

Jules gave Cheryl. Maybe we should tackle Maria about it. I mean, it seems it was her husband's ill-advised actions that caused all this misery. If Maria is still anxious to deal with that ghost of hers, perhaps we could go over there and do a little snooping?"

The footpath, which had threaded between bare trees on one side and a field on the other, ended suddenly at a narrow road. Looking back the way we had come, I realized this was the path I had taken the previous week, but the scene looked vastly different without its thick blanket of snow. From the top of the hill, looking out across the road, I could see marshy lowland running down to the river, which coiled in a huge loop, flowing under a pretty bridge at the bottom of the road, then winding in a wide arc, which encompassed farmland belonging to the Jenkinses. The farmhouse itself, built on the top of the next hill, obscured my view of the river beyond, but I judged that was where Betty had gone to sit by the water and where I believed Kitty and Garrett had come ashore in their skiff all those years ago.

I wondered fleetingly how things would have turned out if I had found the farm track and ended up in the Jenkinses' farmhouse instead of at Kigarjay. I probably would never have met Colin, and therefore neither Kitty nor Garrett. Strange, I thought, how one's choice of direction colored one's life so completely.

Dempsey had taken Jadie's hand and was leading us down the road toward the bridge. In the distance I could see rescue vehicles and a tow truck moving away from the river, but as we descended the hill, my view was blocked by trees and shrubs. I remembered looking down at this bridge from the top of the hill when I'd first found myself shivering on the shoulder of the road in the snow. Could I have been the driver of the car that had plunged into the river below? Nearing the bridge, I took in the scene. The old stonework and pretty parapets made it look like something from a watercolor painting.

Dempsey checked the road for traffic, then led us across to the middle of the bridge and peered down into the dark fast-flowing water.

"I've been here before," I told Dempsey. "I'm becoming more convinced I was the driver of that car they fished out of the river."

"If that's true, then they'll soon find out who you are."

Jadie was hunting around in the bushes. She straightened up with a stick in her hand and ran to the upstream side of the bridge.

"Pooh sticks," Dempsey explained, keeping watch for traffic as her charge dropped the stick from the parapet and ran to the other side to watch it float under the bridge and reappear on the other side, "one of Jadie's favourite games."

"It looks like something is still going on down there." Shielding my eyes, I pointed downriver through the trees to where a couple of people were moving around on the riverbank. "Do you think that's where they found the body?"

"It may be. Do you want to take a look?"

I glanced uneasily at Jadie. "What if the body is still there?"

"They're bound to have moved it by now, and it was only bones anyway, not a real body."

"If you're sure . . ."

"Come on. I can see you want to. And this is the most exciting thing that's happened in these parts for many years." Dempsey set off along the riverbank with Jadie scampering along at her heels.

I followed more slowly, a host of emotions running through me. What if the car was mine? What if the body had something to do with my memories of being Kitty? Could it even be Kitty herself, or maybe Alice? I was still half afraid the body would turn out to be mine—even though I had been assured the skeleton had lain undisturbed at the river's bend for many years. It would be something of a coincidence, after all, if the car I had possibly been driving had been swept downstream and come to rest so close to the remains of a body that had been missing for the better part of a century.

A shiver ran through me. Was it a coincidence or fate?

Dempsey arrived ahead of me at the scene, where deeply gouged caterpillar tracks showed where the recovery had taken place. A band of yellow and black police tape fluttered in the light breeze, cordoning off the bank, beneath which the body must have lain trapped for so long.

There were still a couple of official-looking people wandering around taking notes and measurements, and I watched as Dempsey called to one of them and struck up an animated conversation. I cringed when she looked up, saw me, and waved me over.

"This is Professor Johnson Clarke," Dempsey announced. "He's a local historian and an expert on old bones. He thinks the skeleton had been in the water for well over fifty years, possibly longer."

Johnson Clarke, dressed in white coveralls with a red silk scarf just showing at his neck, looked to be almost a decade older than that himself, but when he turned his gray eyes on me, I could see reflected the quick mind behind the smile. He reached out a gloved hand, and I shook it warily.

"What would be your interest in this sorry business, ladies?"

"There's a good chance my friend Kate here was the driver of the submerged car," Dempsey explained. She glanced over my shoulder. "Jadie, come away from the tape. We're not allowed to touch it."

"Don't you know whether you were the driver or not?" the professor asked with interest.

"She lost her memory—we think maybe in the crash—and has been waiting for the emergency conditions to ease up to find out who she is and where she comes from. She's interested in the body too. Jadie, come away from the edge!"

Dempsey strode off to pull her granddaughter away from the water and left the professor gazing at me speculatively.

"May I ask what your interest in the body might be?"

"I . . . I know something about a family who may have lived here more than ninety years ago. Could the body have been in the water that long?"

"We won't know for sure until a proper investigation has been done—an autopsy performed and the bones dated." He narrowed his eyes at me as if thinking. "Does the family have a name?"

"I only know their first names—Kitty, her sister, Alice, and Kitty's husband, Garrett."

The old man's eyes took on an excited gleam. "The Larkspur suicide? I have been puzzling over that story for many years. What information do you have on them?" He took my arm and led me to where a beautifully restored Morris Minor was parked off the road. I watched as he opened the passenger door and lifted a yellow folder from the front seat. "As soon as they called me about the skeleton, I wondered if it might have something to do with the legend of the Larkspurs."

Peering at the folder, I echoed stupidly, "The Larkspurs?"

"They were a New England family, made rich by their textile mill until the industry started to collapse. They owed lots of money to various debtors, and they left Lowell and went into hiding. No one heard of them for many years until the son turned up near Andover and bought several properties around here." He broke off and peered at me anxiously. "Here, come and sit in the car for a moment. You've turned a nasty shade of gray."

Slipping gratefully into the passenger seat, I waited as he

ambled around to the driver's side, removed the white coveralls and a pair of plastic overshoes, and climbed in next to me. I glanced toward Dempsey and saw she was following Jadie as she wandered a little farther along the bank to throw some of the stale bread she'd stuffed into the pockets of her coat for some hopeful ducks.

"Are you quite sure you're all right?"

"Yes. Please go on."

"The legend has it that Garrett Larkspur and his wife, Kathryn, had a son who died of a fever when he was only six years old. The couple was heartbroken. He was their only child and they never got over losing him. There was a sister, Alice, who was known to be 'delicate.' Anyway, as the story goes, one day the grief got to be too much for Kathryn and she and her sister jumped from the bridge upriver from here and drowned. Garrett Larkspur never recovered from the loss. He became a recluse, hiding himself away in the family home and refusing visitors. He died a few years later—some say of a broken heart—and was buried in the local cemetery. The strange thing was that they only ever discovered one body...that of the sister, Alice. Kathryn's body was never found."

chapter forty-six

Through the car windows I watched the sunshine sparkling on the water as it flowed swiftly past. It was warm in the car, but my hands, which were gripped tightly on my lap, were cold.

"So tell me, what do you know of the Larkspur family? Very little has been recorded about them, so if you can give me some details, you will make an old man very happy." The elderly historian was looking at me hopefully from under heavy white eyebrows.

I shook my head. "I don't know much more than you do. I didn't even know their last name was Larkspur until you told me just now. I knew of Kitty, who must have been the Kathryn of your story, and I knew that she and Garrett lost their son, Jaygo, to a fever. But I can't reconcile the fact that Kitty killed herself. She was such a strong, resilient character."

Johnson Clarke had gone very quiet. I realized I had said too much. A historian dealt in hard facts, not dreamlike memories from the past. I decided to come clean.

"A psychoanalyst put me under hypnosis to see if I could re-call my true identity, and I came up with Kitty instead. I know it sounds crazy, but apparently lots of people do believe in reincar-nation and the ability to access previous lives through hypnosis."

Professor Clarke looked at me skeptically. "Was this psycho-analyst and so-called hypnotherapist a local person? If they had lived here for long, they would almost certainly know the legend of the Larkspurs."

I remembered Adam saying that he, Tara, and Colin had lived in the village most of their lives. Adam had once moved away with his mother's family, but they still considered themselves old residents of the village, not "newcomers," as they described the James family and Maria next door. Betty and Bill had certainly heard something of the legend, as it was they who had told me about the drowning. Adam might never have heard the stories be-cause he'd spent most of his childhood in the city, but why had Colin and Tara never mentioned that they recognized anything I was recalling from the old legend of the Larkspurs?

I must have looked as uncomfortable as I felt, because he raised an eyebrow. "May I ask who recommended this hypnother-apist to you?"

"His sister; she works for the family who took me in." I ac-knowledged the stupidity of this as soon as the words were out of my mouth. Once again Colin's credibility came into question in my mind.

The old man patted my knee. "Don't blame yourself. You were in a vulnerable position, with your memory gone and finding yourself dependent on the mercy of these people."

"Do you think Colin—the hypnotherapist—planted those suggestions in my subconscious brain?" I tried not to dwell on the thought that Colin may not have been telling the truth when he'd said he had been cleared of any wrongdoing.

"I really don't know. I wouldn't want to hazard an opinion. I deal in facts backed by irrefutable records and historical proof."

"It all seemed so real."

"Please don't distress yourself. The story is real. The Larkspurs were real. I can even show you Garrett Larkspur's grave, if it would make you feel better about everything."

The thought of seeing Garrett's final resting place gripped me with a strange longing. Having discovered that the man Kitty had loved so unconditionally and who had until now resided only in my deepest subconscious was real after all, I felt a compulsion to go to him. He had a body, albeit nothing more than bones by now, and under the ground, but it was tangible proof that he had once truly existed.

"Would you?" I asked. "I'd be very interested to see his grave, if you wouldn't mind showing me."

"I'm about finished here anyway." He shuffled a few papers back into the yellow folder and reached around to slide it onto the backseat. As he did so, a pencil sketch fell out and fluttered almost into my lap. I picked it up and felt a sharp stabbing pain as my chest constricted.

"Where did you get this picture?"

"It's the Larkspur brooch. It was about the only thing the family didn't sell to try to pay off their debts before they left Lowell. No one knows what happened to it, but I copied this sketch from a book in the library."

"It's Kitty's brooch! I was there when Garrett gave it to her."

He raised an eyebrow and slid the sketch back into the folder. "I don't pretend to understand these things." He looked past me out the window, obviously uncomfortable that I claimed to have witnessed something that had happened more than a hundred years ago. "What about your friends? Are they coming to see the grave too?"

I saw Dempsey and Jadie meandering toward the car. "Could I go and ask them?"

"Of course."

I hurried over to Dempsey and explained the situation to her. Her eyes shone excitedly with the news. "I can hardly believe it was all real after all! So they really existed . . . and you want to go to see Garrett's grave?"

I decided not to mention the fact that Colin had probably known the legend all along. I was trying to keep an open mind as to whether he'd planted the story of Kitty in my subconscious, because while this seemed the most feasible explanation, the memories themselves and the emotions behind them were still very real to me.

"If you don't mind, Dempsey, I really would like to go with him. If you don't want to tag along, perhaps he'll give you and Jadie a ride home on the way."

Johnson Clarke dubiously accepted the rather muddy pair into his spotless car, and we set off along the narrow lane.

I had never seen the village before—as far as I knew, anyway—and I looked with interest at the low stone walls and small cottages we passed. At a bend we encountered a tow truck pulling a battered bright yellow Ford Focus from a drainage ditch, and Dempsey let out a squeal of recognition.

"That's my car! Vincent told me he asked them to take it directly back to Kigarjay."

"You'll be going home, then?" I realized I didn't want Dempsey to go. She was the only person in the household—apart from Jadie, of course—that I really trusted.

"Now that Tara's back, there's no reason for me to stay," Dempsey was saying. "I have my work at the gallery and my own life to get back to."

"Yes, of course. But I'll miss you."

"The police have the car you were in all likelihood driving, so it won't be long before they identify you as the owner and you'll have your own life to get on with too. You probably won't even re-member any of us in a few months."

It was a frightening thought. What if it was like one of those films where the heroine woke up after being in a coma and found she had dreamed the whole thing? I sat in subdued silence while the professor pulled up at the curb outside Kigarjay, and Demp-sey and Jadie scrambled out.

"See you later." Dempsey turned to follow Jadie up the front path.

Hopping out of the passenger door, I watched her over the roof of the car. "You won't leave until I get back?"

"No. I need to pack up my things." She nodded her head toward the adjoining property. "And we have a visit to make, I believe."

I sat in silence as Johnson concentrated on negotiating the narrow lanes toward the village church. He drew the car up out-side the cemetery wall and pulled on a camel hair overcoat as I stepped out into the thin sunshine, pulling my own coat tighter. After the heated car it seemed much colder outside than it had earlier in the day. I found myself shivering again and wondered how much was due to the cold and how much to my apprehension at actually seeing Garrett's final resting place.

I realized with a jolt that I recognized the church. It looked slightly different with the cherry trees bare of their leaves, but it was unmistakably the church I had visited with Kitty and Garrett the day they had come ashore in the skiff. Johnson made his way along the cobbled path leading to the church door, then veered off around the side of the building, with me following on his heels.

"The oldest part of the church dates back to colonial times," he told me over his shoulder.

"You may think this crazy, but I recognize it. While I was

under hypnosis, I came with Kitty and Garrett to this place. It was the first time they'd been here, and they fell in love with the place. They were thinking of buying a property in the area, somewhere they would live together."

"They certainly bought property. Garrett Larkspur bought and renovated at least three properties."

"Was one of them Kigarjay...the house where you just dropped off Dempsey and Jadie?"

"It could well have been. I have the locations recorded in my notebooks. Apparently the first place he purchased was susceptible to flooding when the river broke its banks. He and Kathryn lived there only a few months in rather basic conditions while alterations were made to the bigger property just outside the village." He turned to look at me. "Do you know, I think that might have been the place they eventually settled. Kigarjay, did you call it? It sounds right to me—a compilation of their names, isn't it?"

I nodded. "Some people think it was named after three birds that nested in the area, the kite, the garganey, and the jay, but I did wonder if Kitty and Garrett called it after themselves and their lost baby son."

"Maybe we'll never really know." He stopped in the middle of the path beside a line of neatly tended graves. "The third place Garrett bought was a very run-down local farm. According to records, the Jenkinses, who were listed as the original owners, were down on their luck, and he bought them out on a whim, spent a fortune on renovations and alterations, and then sold it back to them for a token amount when his only son died."

I thought of what Betty had told me about her mother's reference to what she had called "the miracle of giving back." Perhaps she hadn't only been referring to the birth of Betty and her friend Rosemary, but to the miraculous return of the farm to the Jenkins family soon after Jaygo died. My mind went to Adam and his love of the farm. If Colin was right about us coming back to experience life from a different perspective, it would be fitting for the father to experience the joys his son had had snatched away by an untimely death.

"Garrett probably couldn't bear the memories of the place. For the short while they had their son, Jaygo loved the farm," I murmured. "The boy adored animals and the outdoors. Garrett must have already bought the farm before they had brought Jaygo home. He must have put in the paneled hallway and that ornate sweeping staircase Kitty loved so much. For the few months they were together, Garrett tried to make sure his son had a head for figures, probably so he could run the place properly one day, but the little boy died from the fever, and Garrett must have lost all interest in the farm."

Johnson was smiling at me. "Do I detect a leaning toward believing the reincarnation theory?"

"Even if Colin had fed those names and places into my head, I don't see how he could have made me see the church so clearly. He would have had to describe every detail to me under hypnosis for me to actually feel I'd been here and seen it as it really is."

The historian touched my arm. "The human mind is a lot smarter than most of us realize. Perhaps we would be best advised to keep open minds." He left the path and set off over the grass, and I hurried after him, passing older graves with moss-covered headstones and mounds with no stones at all. He came to a halt near a grave that was set back under a sprawling hedge against the far wall of the cemetery. "Garrett asked to be buried in this exact spot as close to the wall as possible."

"Do we know why?"

"It is believed that he wanted to be buried close to his sister-in-law, Alice, who is in unconsecrated ground beside the wall on the other side. Because she was a suicide, he was not permitted to bury her within the cemetery."

I looked at the lonely grave with its headstone tilted at an angle and covered in lichen. "Why did he want to be close to Alice?"

"My understanding is that he believed his wife had also killed herself. If her body was ever found, she would in all likelihood be buried with her sister, and he wanted his final resting place to be as close to Kathryn's as possible."

I kneeled to rub the lichen from the stone and gave a yelp of excitement as my fingers detected the indentations of engraving on the stone. "There's writing here!"

"Really?" Johnson dropped onto one knee beside me with a small grunt. "I thought it had eroded away years ago. Here, let me see."

I watched as he carefully scraped away the moss and let out a snort of incredulity. "Look, it's a verse of some kind."

Running my fingers over the faded inscription, I managed to decipher the words: "Garrett Larkspur: A loner in life, Abandoned in death, Alone for eternity."

Sitting back on my haunches, I dabbed at my eyes, which had suddenly watered up. "He must have been bereft, believing Kitty had committed suicide. It would have meant she'd left him on purpose." My mind went to Vincent and the extremes he had gone to, to deceive the world into thinking Cheryl had merely gone off with another man rather than having done the unthinkable and chosen to abandon them so completely.

"Perhaps he couldn't bring himself to admit she had left him so totally." Johnson echoed my thoughts. "It must have been hard to come to terms with the fact that he had not been enough for her."

"Well, I don't believe it," I said, straightening up. "I don't think Kitty killed herself, and I'm going to find Colin." I sniffed back my unshed tears and squared my shoulders. "I have to put my trust in the hypnotherapist because I need him if we are going to unearth the truth about what happened to Kitty."

Johnson got stiffly to his feet. "There's keeping an open mind and there's burying your head in the sand, my dear. We have a body fished out of the river where Kathryn was supposed to have drowned herself, and we have a grieving husband who, according to this inscription on his grave, appeared to believe his wife had committed suicide. You have to look at the facts. Think with your head and not with your heart."

We began to walk slowly back through the churchyard to the car, but all I could think about was Betty's story about the supposedly deserted house where a lone man with dark hair roamed, sparking the rumor of a ghostly figure haunting the place.

"Would you be kind and take me back to Kigarjay? I need to see Colin, but I have no idea where he lives. I can contact him from there."

The historian sighed, but nodded kindly. "Come on, then, Kate, or whoever you really are. Let's get you home."

Home, I thought as I trudged behind the figure in the camel coat. Home. Where was that anyway, but the place you felt happy and relaxed and at ease with the people around you? I thought of Kigarjay, where I had felt mostly on edge and apprehensive, and had a sudden change of heart. "May I ask you another favor?"

He paused midstride. "Of course, my dear. I'm rather hoping you are going to ask me to meet this hypnotherapist friend of yours."

"I'm afraid not. I'm asking you to drop me at the Jenkinses' farm instead. There's someone there I need to see."

chapter forty-seven

Johnson Clarke dropped me in the cobbled yard in front of the Jenkinses's farmhouse and drove away down the lane to the town, where he intended to begin a detailed examination of the skeleton exhumed from its watery grave. He had promised to call at Kigarjay later in the day to report on his preliminary findings as to the skeleton's age and an estimate of its time in the water.

I stood for a while, surveying the farm buildings in the late morning sun, and breathed in the earthy smell of animals and rich country air. I had taken one tentative step toward the dark oak front door when a dog barked behind me and I turned to see Adam come striding around the corner of the barn with Lad at his heels.

He stopped dead when he saw me. Even Lad paused with one paw raised, before trotting over to sniff at my outstretched hand. Adam and I stared at each other.

"I'm sorry about earlier," I began as he crossed the yard toward me. "I was . . . confused."

Slowly his eyes locked on mine, and he must have seen the longing reflected there, because he held out his hand to me. "Come into the hay barn. It's warm in there and more private than the house."

I eyed his outstretched hand, still nervous to make that first physical contact. What if I had imagined everything? What if he was just a farmer who had happened upon me when I was delirious with hypothermia? What if it was Vincent who was the reincarnation of my lost love? Vincent shared far more similarities with Garrett, after all. . . .

"Stop thinking, Kate, and come with me." Adam dropped his hand, turned, and walked off toward the hay barn, the dog behind him.

After a moment's hesitation I followed them, my mind churning with possibilities. Adam was standing just inside the door, where a beam of sunlight played on the stacked hay, illuminating each strand of the golden bales.

I stood before him, my knees trembling. "I need to know—"

"Shush." He slid the door closed, leaving the dog sitting like a guard outside.

Pressing my lips together, I gazed into his deep brown eyes, and the world seemed quite literally to stand still. Nothing existed but the two of us. Slowly his hand came up as if to caress my cheek, but he seemed equally unable to make that last connection between us. His hand hovered a hairsbreadth from my face, and I could feel the warmth emanating from him, leaping across the small divide to flutter against my skin, making my flesh tingle with anticipation.

"Kate." My name issued from his lips in a whispered groan.

It was my turn to reach out to him. With a fingertip I traced the rugged contours of his face, touching him so lightly I could feel the fine bristles brushing against the palm of my hand. We moved a fraction closer until I could feel his breath warm against my cheek. We smiled at each other as he took my hand and gently pressed it to his lips.

It was like an explosion. I gasped and clung to him with my other hand to stop myself from falling, and he let go of my hand so he could pin both of his arms around me, hugging me to his chest. The heat rose up between our two bodies as if sealing them together. Tilting my head back, I raised my lips to his and he brought his mouth down onto mine. In an instant I was lost in the taste and feel of him, the kiss penetrating to the very core of my being.

I knew—lost memory or no—that I had never experienced anything like it in my life. I could barely breathe, not because his lips were firmly on mine but because my lungs seemed to have stopped pumping air. I didn't need oxygen when I had this.

Adam was pulling me toward a low platform of stacked hay bales, and, without releasing my lips, he pulled me down with him, smoothing my coat off of my shoulders and running his hands up and down my body, exploring the curves and contours beneath his fingertips.

When his hands finally paused at the button of my jeans, I found myself arching involuntarily toward him, and then and only then did he release my lips to pull open the belt and loosen the zipper. Not to be outdone, I reached down and unbuttoned his jeans before peeling his coat away and ripping his shirt off over his head, revealing a tan and muscular torso.

We paused there, half-undressed, and I lowered my mouth to his chest, brushing my lips over his glorious skin until he cried out for me to stop. For a while we lay nestled against each other, reveling in the shared intimacy and catching our breath, and then he pulled my sweater off over my head and lowered his head to my throat, flicking his warm tongue over my tingling flesh until I could bear it no longer.

Urgently grabbing his hair, I drew him toward me, fastening my lips on his as we struggled out of our remaining clothing. If there had been an explosion at our first touch, it was nothing compared to the sensations flooding through us as we clung naked and abandoned in the hay, our bodies gliding unerringly into one as an eternity of longing flowed between us.

We lay for a long time together afterward. Adam had pulled his coat over us and we dozed, then lay staring with wonderment into each other's eyes.

"Kitty got her wish," I murmured.

"And what was that?"

"She wished that she and Garrett would experience passion in their future bodies."

"Do you really believe we might be them?"

"I don't know." I smiled at him. "It doesn't really matter anymore, does it? What we have now is what counts."

"What, that quick roll in the hay?"

I nudged him and laughed. "How long have you known? Did you feel something when you rescued me from the blizzard?"

He leaned up on one elbow and contemplated me with an exasperated smile. "Why do you think any sane man would venture out through waist-deep snowdrifts to take a lost cat back to its owner? I was desperate to see you again. I couldn't believe what passed between us the day I found you. I had never experienced anything like it in my life."

"You kept it pretty quiet."

"I wanted to know if you'd felt it too. But when I got to

Kigarjay and saw you awake for the first time, you were already under the impression Vincent had rescued you, and he made it very clear he wanted to keep it that way."

"Why didn't you push yourself forward?" I traced the outline of his chin with my forefinger. "I nearly got things so terribly wrong."

"I didn't want to put pressure on you. You were lost and confused and didn't know who you were. Vincent was looking after you, and I hoped you might remember in the end. I did my best to see you whenever the opportunity arose. I was itching to touch you, but every time, something happened to prevent it."

"I felt the connection when you first came to the door with the cat." I nodded, remembering. "It was as if the world had stopped turning when I saw you standing there on the doorstep, but Tara was hysterical about the cat and everything happened so fast that I pushed it to the back of my mind."

"We've found each other now." He nestled his face into my hair. "So let's make up for lost time." He drew me toward him again. Raising my lips to his, I closed my eyes and lost myself once again in his arms.

It was early afternoon by the time we walked hand in hand through the utility room to the farmhouse kitchen, where we found Betty and Bill halfway through their lunch. Betty ignored us and continued eating, but Bill glanced up and studied us closely for a moment before his face broke into a gappy smile.

"It's about time you two came to your senses," he proclaimed. "Congratulations."

"How did you know?" I asked as Adam pulled out a couple of chairs and we slid onto them.

"Apart from the fact that you're holding hands and looking

like a pair of cats that have been at the cream?" He grinned even more widely. "You've both got hay in your hair."

"Are you okay with it?" Adam inquired of him as I self-consciously brushed my fingers through my tousled locks, knocking loose several little knots of dried grass.

"I'm delighted." Bill reached a gnarled hand across the table, and Adam took it warmly in his. The old man glanced at his wife's blank face. "We both are. You were made for each other. I'm just surprised you both took so darned long to realize it."

Somewhere at the back of my mind a little voice reminded me that I had no idea whether I had the right to make a commitment to this man, to this family. Sometime soon I would find out who I really was, and then everything might change. But for now I nodded and smiled happily from Bill to Adam, hope in my heart.

"Is she staying?" Betty barked suddenly, looking at me.

"She is, Gran." Adam rose and went around the table to give his grandmother a hug. "I hope she'll be staying with us for a long, long time."

My chest knotted with anxiety at his words. I wanted to stay more than anything in the world, but aside from the question of my forgotten identity, there was other unfinished business to attend to. There was one more trip to make into the past. If Maria was right and there really was a displaced entity in her home, then it was time to bring it peace.

Betty had shuffled to her feet and was laying a plate of food in front of me. I thanked her absently, lost in thought. More likely, I mused, there was no ghost at all but only the imaginings of a woman missing her husband. I thought of Dempsey and her promise to help me find out if any of those pills Jules had prescribed were still in Maria's house, and I realized I was anxious to get on with doing a little detective work.

"Aren't you hungry?" Adam was looking at me anxiously.

I looked down at the plate and was surprised to find that I was famished. Picking up a fork, I dug in.

"When we've eaten," I mumbled, my mouth full, "would you drive me back to Vincent's?"

I felt Adam tense beside me, but I reached out and rested my hand on his as it lay gripping his fork. Immediately a shock wave of electricity sizzled between us and he grinned at me, reassured.

"If you'll give me a hand feeding the lambs when we're done, we'll go straight after."

"Thank you. I have a few things I need to sort out."

The first thing I noticed as we drew up outside Kigarjay in Adam's Land Rover was Dempsey's little yellow car parked outside the house in the narrow lane.

"You are sure you'll be all right?" Adam asked anxiously.

Leaning across to give him a lingering kiss, I assured him I would be fine and promised to call him when I was ready to leave. I had already decided that I could hardly impose on Vincent's hospitality any longer, and Adam had offered me the use of one of the spare rooms at the farm until I figured out who I really was. Watching longingly as he turned around and made his way back to the farm, I wondered with a smile if the spare room would get much use.

Tara opened the door wearing a pretty teal-colored sweater I hadn't noticed this morning, which exactly matched her eyes. She ushered me inside, and I stood in the living room, surveying the place I'd called home for the past week. Suddenly I felt like a complete stranger.

"Dempsey's waiting for you upstairs." Tara said. She turned on her heel and retreated to the kitchen without another word. Before the kitchen door swung shut behind her I caught a glimpse of Jadie sitting at the table, eating from a bowl of something I had no doubt would be highly calorific and full of nutrients. Tara was back and in charge.

I tiptoed up the stairs, paused outside Dempsey's room, and then knocked softly. When she opened the door, I saw that her weekend bags were packed and waiting just inside.

"Did you see Garrett's grave?" she asked at once as we sat down on the bed. When I nodded, she went on, "Did you feel any sort of connection? Any sense that you once knew him?"

"It was very sad, actually. There was an inscription on the headstone hidden under the lichen."

"What did it say?"

"'A loner in life, abandoned in death, alone for eternity.'"

"How awful; poor man."

"I know. It breaks my heart. He went to his grave believing Kitty had abandoned him, but I knew her, Dempsey. Even after losing her son for the second time, she wouldn't have done that. I just don't believe it."

Dempsey took my hand in hers and patted it. "And if this body they've found in the river turns out to be hers, will you accept it then?"

I shook my head. "I need to see for myself—not the remains of who she might have been, but the real Kitty. I want Colin to put me under again, one more time."

Instead of looking doubtful, she gave me a knowing smile. "You may get your wish sooner than you think. Colin called a few minutes ago. Apparently his last appointment was canceled and he wants to come over to see you. He'll be here within the hour." She got up and went to sit at the dressing table, where she reached into her cosmetics bag for a compact of blue eye shadow and began to reapply it liberally to her upper lids, her mouth open as she concentrated. "And after that, I arranged for us to go over to

Maria's. She's still anxious about that ghost of hers." She popped the eye shadow back into the bag and extracted some mascara, which she brushed onto her lashes with bold sweeping strokes.

"I'm not really sure what we're hoping to find out. Even if there are some of those pills somewhere in the house, it doesn't mean anything, does it?"

"Of course it does. I've wondered more than once if Maria is taking that stupid Rohypnol herself. Maybe she doesn't know how dangerous it is, but I think that it's very probably the cause of her anxiety over this supposed ghost. And"—she surveyed me in the mirror—"I'm still not convinced you weren't slipped some in your drink the other night.

"I can go up to their bathroom and have a good look while you talk to Maria," she said, looking in the mirror. "Sometimes a little duplicity is necessary for the greater good."

chapter forty-eight

I wondered again as I thought of duplicity why Colin hadn't told me about the Larkspurs. Had that been for the greater good too? Twice now I had been persuaded to give Colin the benefit of the doubt. I decided to run my suspicions past Dempsey and was surprised by her reaction.

"Even if Colin knew," she said as she applied lipstick, smacked her lips together, and pouted at her reflection in the mirror, "he obviously didn't connect that story with what you were telling him. I can't believe he planted Kitty's memories in your head. . . . I mean, why would he? And how? What would he have to gain from doing such a thing?"

"I don't know. Notoriety, a bigger client base, fame in the world of psychology?"

"I have a hard time believing that. Colin strikes me as honest and totally unpretentious. Look what he did for Vincent and me, getting us to accept our grief over losing Amber and starting us on that journey of grieving."

My glance inadvertently strayed to the drawer where I'd discovered the gin bottle on my first night in the house.

"And I haven't been drinking, if that's what you're thinking," she said in a tight voice. "The bottle was there only as a last resort, in case I couldn't bear things anymore. I took comfort from knowing it was there, but I haven't touched it.

"I've been thinking about reincarnation a lot," Dempsey continued. "And if Colin is right and you really have experienced being Kitty, and our souls really do continue from one life to the next within a 'family type' group, then it matters less than I thought that I was adopted into a family that was not mine by genes or birth."

I had forgotten she'd mentioned being adopted as a child. For Dempsey, however, it was evidently not something she had ever been able to put aside. But now her eyes shone with a newly discovered contentment.

"I spent so many years wondering who my birth parents were, what they were like, if they looked and acted like me. But if Colin is right about all this, then I may well have been with my rightful family all along. It's possible I have always been exactly where I belong."

Dempsey and I carried her bags down to the living area and deposited them by the front door, ready for her departure, then went into the kitchen to see Jadie and to wait for Colin to arrive.

The washing machine was whirring through its cycle in the corner, and Tara was blending something in the smoothie maker. She turned when she heard us come in.

"Hi. You're just in time for a cup of tea."

"Look what I've drawn," Jadie called over the cacophony as

Dempsey and I sat ourselves at the table, where Jadie leaned on her elbows surrounded by colored pencils and felt-tip pens.

She held up a picture of the bridge over the river where she'd played Pooh sticks that morning.

"It's very good." I looked closely at her, noticing the color in her cheeks.

Dempsey nodded her agreement. "It's lovely, Jadie."

"Amber told me to draw it. She said it was where your car went into the water."

Tara jerked around, almost dropping the teapot she was holding. "Where do you get ideas like that from?"

"Amber told me," Jadie said with a touch of defiance. "Except I've made it green and it was all white and snowing then."

Tara finished pouring boiling water into the pot and sloshed the tea into three mugs, which she plonked onto the table in front of us. "You should be more careful what you discuss in front of her. Jadie doesn't miss anything, do you?"

I tried to think back to whether we'd said anything about the possibility of my being the driver of the submerged car while Jadie had been listening.

Tara pursed her lips in obvious disapproval and placed a banana smoothie in front of Jadie, who dutifully picked it up, giving a perfunctory suck at the straw. A moment later there was a knock at the front door.

"That must be Colin." Dempsey glanced at her watch. "He's early."

"I'll go." Tara pushed me back down in my seat as I began to rise. I remembered her pushing me back down onto the couch when I'd first arrived almost a week ago, and sighed. I wish I could have told her Vincent really was all hers, but I wasn't sure how to go about it. Colin sauntered through the door behind his sister. He smiled at us disarmingly, and I found something in his relaxed demeanor infuriating, when I was in such a state of anxiety.

"How are my four favorite ladies?" he quipped.

"A bit pissed off, actually," I replied shortly.

I belatedly realized Jadie was listening and asked her to go upstairs and play with her dolls.

Colin's smile vanished. "Why?"

He pulled out a chair and sat down opposite me.

"How about the fact that you knew all along that what I was telling you was the local legend of the Larkspurs? Why didn't you tell me you knew the story? Or had you already told me all about them when you hypnotised me, and all I was doing during our little sessions was enlarging on suggestions you may have made during the relaxation exercises?"

Colin's face drained of color, and I felt my stomach tighten. So I was right; he had put those memories into my head. I realized I was not only angry at him but desperately disappointed to find that Kitty's world had been a figment not even of my, but of Colin's imagination. And if that, then what else was he guilty of?

"I tried telling you it was all nonsense," Tara said sternly. "I'd heard the legend myself, of course, but Colin begged me not to tell you about it in case it influenced what you 'saw' under hypnosis." She fixed me with her turquoise eyes. "I want you to know I was never happy about it."

"It's true." Colin kept his eyes averted from his sister's and looked at me. "I did ask her not to say anything. The more you talked about being Kitty, the more I began to realize you might be the Kathryn of the legend. But I swear I never put those thoughts in your head."

"Do you honestly expect me to believe you?"

He leaned across the table and rested his hand lightly on mine. "I hope you will."

"Did you ever actually try to find out who I really am, or did you view me as an opportunity to see how much nonsense you could feed into an empty head? You used my state of amnesia to make me your 'lab rat.'" I wrenched my hand away angrily, aware that Dempsey was looking positively sick.

"I promise you I did no such thing." Colin was looking angry now, his lips set in a straight line. "You came up with those memories without any prompting from me."

"Can you prove it?"

"Usually I make tapes of client sessions, but because of the circumstances, I wasn't able to. If you remember, I didn't know you were here when I came over in the blizzard to check on Tara and Jadie. I can't prove anything except to point out that during your very first session there were other people present in the room."

I thought back to the afternoon he had arrived, realizing the truth of this.

"But one was Jadie, who wouldn't have understood what you were saying to me, and the other was Tara, who, if I remember rightly, recommended you in the first place."

"When I recommended him, I thought he was going to help you recover your actual memories," Tara said sincerely. "But for what it's worth, although I was worried about what you were saying under hypnosis, I can't recall Colin having prompted you in any way."

I didn't know whether to believe her. I turned back to Colin.

"The second time we were on our own in Adam's parlor. You could have suggested all sorts of things to me then."

Colin shrugged. "I can only repeat that I didn't. It was stupid—unprofessional of me, even—not to record the session or to have someone else present. I was so excited about what you were recalling that my normal practices went right out the window."

"You're asking me to take a lot on trust," I told him. "First there was the article about some of your patients having committed suicide, and now this." I stared at him, wanting to believe him but knowing that even if we could verify his innocence regarding the first accusation, I would never be quite sure about the second. "Did you bring a tape recorder with you today?"

"I did, actually."

"I still don't know what to believe." The trouble was, Colin was my passport to Kitty's world and I desperately wanted to visit her again. I knew I either had to put my trust in Colin and allow him to hypnotize me again or I would have to accept that I might never find out what had happened to Kitty, Alice, and Garrett. I chewed my lip and stared into his eyes, trying to find reassurance there.

"I'm certainly not going to do anything you're not happy with," Colin told me. "I can leave right now if you want me to."

"No. No, don't go."

He peered at me. "Well, then?"

I looked from Tara to Dempsey and back to Colin. I knew he held all the trump cards, and I capitulated. "Okay. I'll let you hypnotize me one last time."

"You're sure I wouldn't just be planting suggestions in your head?"

"I'll never be sure, but I need to know the ending to Kitty's story. Can you do that for me?"

"As long as I have your word you won't come and sue me afterward?"

"I promise I won't sue you." I smiled tentatively. "Let's just go and visit Kitty one last time."

chapter forty-nine

It took longer than usual to achieve a state of deep relaxation. Every time I began to slip under, I wondered about whether I should be trusting Colin or not, or whether I was being a complete fool, and the anxiety brought me back to a state of consciousness. I'd asked that Dempsey witness the session, and she sat quietly in the corner of the living room, watching the proceedings while the fire crackled in the grate, filling the room with the smell of wood smoke.

And suddenly, like falling asleep when you least expect it during a restless night, I found I had stepped back through a door in time. Smoke belched upward as I gave the fire a despondent jab with the poker and sat back on my haunches to watch the smoke rise up the chimney. I was Kitty again, crouched miserably by the fire while the rain beat heavily against the windows. The grayness of the day matched my mood.

"Tell me what you are seeing," said the voice.

"I'm watching to make sure that the fire doesn't go out. It's raining so hard it's coming down the chimney and spitting into the grate."

"Are you at Kigarjay?"

"Yes."

"Where is Garrett?"

"He's gone to work in the city. It is almost three years since Jaygo was taken from us, and Garrett has distanced himself from me. He won't be home until nightfall."

"What time of the year is it?"

"It's springtime, but you wouldn't know it, looking at the weather."

They were gentle questions, intended to relax and disarm, but in a moment everything changed and I forgot the disembodied voice as I focused on the moment. I had heard something through the beating rain, something or someone moving about outside the house.

A resounding crash at the front of the house had me leaping to my feet. It sounded like something had been hurled against the front door. I opened the door and gave a gasp of consternation. "Alice!"

"Talk to me, Kitty, tell me what is happening," the voice said.

"It's Alice! She's wet through to the bone and shaking with cold."

Drawing her inside, I tried to close the door behind her, but she clung to the door frame, her eyes wide and wild.

"I can't stand it any longer," she moaned when I tried to coax her farther into the house, and she attempted to shake me off. "I can't bear the loneliness and the pain. I have to end it, Kitty; I have to end it once and for all."

"Stop this nonsense at once. Why do you only ever think of yourself? My son is dead and my husband is a stranger to me but I'm not screaming on a doorstep in the rain."

She turned her maddened eyes on me and gave a hysterical laugh. "You never believed me, did you, Kitty? So occupied were you with achieving your dream home and your perfect family, you never saw what was happening right under your nose!"

"You aren't well. You don't know what you're saying."

"I know exactly what I'm saying. Uncle used me, and no one tried to stop him. He gave our aunt a sleeping draft in her bedtime drink each night, and she never suspected what was happening. But Arthur knew. He knew and he put the pillow over his head to block out my screams while Uncle George held his hand over my mouth! Why do you think our brother ran away? It was because he couldn't live with knowing that he did nothing to help me!"

I felt my mouth go dry. "Come indoors and we will talk about this sensibly."

"It's too late for talk." She searched my face. "I need to know that you believe me."

I shook my head. "I don't know, Alice."

Her icy hand shot out and clasped my throat, grazing the edge of my cameo brooch against my flesh. "Tell me you believe me!"

Carefully I pried her fingers away. "Even if I believe you, what good can come of it now? If what you say is true, then Aunt Maude is not at fault. Arthur was no more than a child and cannot be held responsible for something he could not have prevented, and Uncle George has since passed away. Who should be held accountable after all this time? Forget it, Alice, and get on with your life."

"You are all I have left, and I see now that there is nothing between us. You could have saved me, Kitty." She flung the words at me and backed away, out into the sheeting rain. "There is no point to anything anymore."

"Tell me what is happening, Kitty," demanded the voice in my head. "What is the matter with Alice?"

As I listened to the voice, I watched my sister's waiflike figure disappearing into the mist and rain, and the realization suddenly hit me that this time she was really going to do it.

"I think Alice is going to kill herself."

"Are you going to try to stop her?"

The question, so calmly asked, hit me like a bolt from on high. It was as if I had awakened from a long sleep. She was my only sister, my only living relative, and I loved her. I knew I would never forgive myself if she killed herself while I stood by and let it happen. Without even stopping to grab a coat, I hurried out after her.

The rain hit me in the face, stinging my eyes. I could still make out her figure running ahead of me, making light of the mud underfoot and the twigs and branches that snatched at her clothing. Panting, I followed her along the footpath and stopped for breath as I saw her pull herself up onto the parapet of the bridge.

"Alice!"

She turned to look at me with tortured eyes. "Don't come any closer or I'll jump."

I stopped dead in my tracks and held out my hand to her. "Please, Alice. I believe you! I believe what Uncle did to you and I'm so very sorry. It wasn't your fault. Please believe me. I understand; just come down from there. The river is swollen with spring rain and the current is uncommonly fast."

For a moment I thought she was going to comply, but then her face took on a serene expression. She spread her arms wide as if welcoming her fate. "Goodbye, Sister."

And she toppled away from me, down, down into the racing water.

"No!"

"Talk to me, Kitty! Tell me what you are seeing." The voice was insistent now.

"She jumped." The words slid from my mouth as I kicked off my shoes and raced to the parapet. I was still in shock but I could see her auburn hair spread out on the surface of the water as she was swept downstream, all the time being drawn away from me, my little Alice, my dearest sister.

Climbing onto the parapet, I stared into the racing brown water and took a huge gulp of air.

"Talk to me," demanded the voice. "What are you doing?"

"I'm doing what I should have done a long time ago. I'm going to save my sister."

I jumped, and the world became cold and dark as the freezing water bit into my flesh. I tried to swim, but the current was so fierce it merely swept me on, battering me, waves of murky water breaking over my head. At the bend in the river I caught a glimpse of her and tried to shout her name, but water filled my mouth, and then my feet snagged in the weeds and my head dipped under the water, and my nose and lungs filled until I could barely breathe.

I opened my mouth to call to her but found it full of rancid water. Mud washed from the riverbanks found its way into my throat, clogging my airway, choking me.

"Alice! Alice, I am here."

And suddenly she was right before me, her eyes wide and staring, long hair fanning out around her head in a cloud. Reaching out my hand, I felt her fingers touch mine, but before I could grasp them, she was whisked away on the current. I tried to follow, but my oxygen-starved lungs felt heavy. My brain, sluggish with the cold, registered that I would never see the sunlight nor look upon Garrett's face again. I had failed—failed to save my marriage, failed to save my son, and failed to save my sister.

But I wanted to live, to lie with Garrett one more time. With every ounce of strength I had left, I clawed my way down through the icy water to where my foot seemed to be wedged under something heavy and unyielding. Tugging and pulling, I tried with the last of my strength to break free. My lungs burned until my eyes felt like they were going to explode. Desperate for air, my hand groped for the brooch pinned at the neck of my dress—the only love token Garrett had ever given me. I wrenched it free and held it to my lips in one last kiss. And then I thought no more.

"*I want you to* come back to me right now. Three, two, one. Open your eyes, Kate."

I sat bolt upright, gasping for breath. Colin was looking anxiously at me, and Dempsey was on her feet at my side.

"That was terrible." Dempsey grabbed my hands away from my throat and began to massage some warmth back into them. She turned on Colin, her voice angry. "You allowed her to experience her own death; I never ever want to watch anything like that again."

"I didn't make her do anything she didn't want to." Colin handed me a glass of water, and I extracted one of my hands from Dempsey's grasp to sip the cool liquid gratefully. "She wanted to know the ending; it was her choice, not mine."

"How do you feel?" Dempsey took the glass from me and placed it on the coffee table. "Can you get up?"

I smiled wanly at her. "I'm okay, Dempsey—more than okay. I've found out that Kitty didn't kill herself. I knew it. I just *knew* she was stronger than that."

"But she died anyway. And she died feeling like a complete failure."

"She died fighting for life," I corrected. My whole being seemed suffused with peace. "And while there are many questions about how I came to experience Kitty's story, we do know from Johnson Clarke that some of it is true." I thought through what I was going to do about what I'd seen and experienced. "I won't allow Kitty's previous life to remain a failure. One way or another she has sent me a message, and I intend to act upon it."

It was past five o'clock by the time Dempsey and I went to Maria's house next door. Colin had offered to watch Jadie while Tara made dinner, and I knew she was safe enough with Tara in the kitchen and only a shout away.

Maria opened the door to us, looking pale and anxious. "Where is Vincenzo?"

"Vincent is at work. He'll be home around seven. So how about a nice cup of coffee, and then you can tell us everything you know about what happened to Cheryl." Dempsey glanced around the room as she spoke, as if hoping she might find a suspicious-looking prescription lying in sight, or a bottle of pills standing openly on the coffee table.

"I have already told Kate what I know," Maria said nervously. "My husband tried to help Cheryl and Vincenzo."

"We think the pills your husband gave Cheryl were inappropriate and that he gave her far too many, considering her emotional state," Dempsey said as Maria walked toward the kitchen.

"If this is true, I knew nothing of it." Maria shook her head and turned to face us. "I don't know what you want from me, but everything I told Kate is true. I wasn't here when Cheryl died. Until a few days ago I was unhappy about the way my friend disappeared, but when Vincenzo explained that she had taken her own life, I believed him."

"And you don't think Jules was culpable in any way?"

Maria's expression became wary. "Jules is the father of my child. If the medication he gave Cheryl was 'inappropriate,' as you put it, then it was a mistake—but perhaps not a mistake worth jeopardizing his career over, I think." She stared at us, looking affronted. "I thought you were going to help me to hunt out this ghost of ours?"

"Kate thinks your ghost could have something to do with the couple who built this house," Dempsey said. "I'll let Kate explain. May I use your bathroom?"

"Of course. You know where it is." Maria seemed relieved to have Dempsey out of the way for a moment.

I followed Maria to the kitchen, where she spooned coffee into the percolator and pulled out a stool for me to sit on. "No one has taken talk of my ghost seriously," she complained. "But things are getting worse. There are strange smells, odd sounds like loud banging on the front door, but when I answer it, there is no one there. Things happen that I cannot account for."

"Let me tell you what I know about the people who used to live here," I said slowly.

"I will call Michael. He returned to school today and has homework to catch up on. But he will be interested to hear what you have to say."

Maria went to the foot of the stairs and called her son, but there was no reply.

"Michael! We have guests!"

When the boy still didn't respond, Maria frowned and mounted the stairs. Following closely, I hoped our hostess wouldn't find Dempsey rifling through her medicine cabinet, but she passed the bathroom and stood calling outside what I assumed was the door to her son's bedroom. Getting no reply, Maria headed along the landing and up the shallow steps to the attic room, the mirror image of the room I was using as my bedroom in Vincent's house.

"Michael must be working in his hobby room," Maria muttered. She flung open the door of the small room and marched inside, then stopped abruptly. Her son's eyes opened wide with surprise at seeing his mother, and he quickly hid his hand behind his back, the long telltale tendril of smoke from a cigarette rising from his hand toward the open window behind him.

"Michael!" Maria cried. "What on earth do you think you're doing?"

chapter fifty

The familiar smell of burning tobacco was like an assault to the senses. Visions filled my mind, of an elderly lady exhaling a cloud of blue smoke and waving the evidence away with a frail white hand.

"You're not smoking again, are you, Mom?" my mother was calling from downstairs, and I hastily opened the window in my grandmother's room to waft the smoke away.

The old lady smiled at me with a twinkle in her green eyes. We had always been close, Grandma and I. When I'd been small, she had taught me to make angels with only a piece of paper and scissors, regaling me with stories of her youth as she cut and trimmed. When she unfolded the paper, I would shriek with glee as the row of little hand-holding figures appeared. She had taught me how to play cards too.

The world was as misty white as the curling smoke, an echoing void that seemed to have no beginning and no end. My head ached and I held a hand to my forehead as I inched forward through the fog of years, my hands stretched out in front of me, blind and searching. Snatches of conversation filled my ears. Grandma telling me how her parents had waited so long for a child. How they'd taken in a baby boy, born out of wedlock to wealthy folk. Her mother's heart had been broken when after several years the natural parents had come to claim the child for their own. But Grandma had been born as a late surprise, and the story of the lost child had become a family mystery. Where had the boy come from and where had he been taken? Who had his parents been? A chill wind seemed to come from the open window. I was shivering, hurrying toward a car. Indistinct figures gathered in a doorway waving from afar as wood smoke curled from the chimney of the house behind them, mixing and mingling with the mist.

A young girl, my sister, was watching from the shadows as I left. "Bye, Emma. Don't forget to call!"

I was turning the key in the ignition with a million emotions jostling in my head. I was embarking on an adventure into the unknown, but where was I going? Wrinkling my brow in concentration, I tried to remember. Wasn't I taking up some kind of new job far from home? The patches of mist swirled and thinned still further. Of course! I was to be the head archivist at a university museum. It was what I'd always wanted, wasn't it—what I'd studied so hard for? I'd decided on a clean break. I was going to be working as a historical consultant, organizing exhibitions, assisting patrons, managing projects and people, as well as working with records in a variety of formats. And I had planned to use those resources to research and discover the mystery of my late grandma's missing adoptive brother.

As if from a great distance I saw myself glance into the packed car, trying to shrug away any lingering doubts. The university was a long way from anything I knew, but the relationship with my boyfriend was finally over. This was a new chapter—a clean start, a fresh beginning. So why did I feel like a condemned woman awaiting the executioner's block?

A cat meowed plaintively from somewhere nearby, and I shushed it. "You'd better be good, Mitsy; we have a long journey ahead of us."

Feeling again the mixture of apprehension and excitement, I recalled the moment I had turned the car south, leaving the familiar New England coastline, my parents and my kid sister waving behind me as I headed off toward a new job and a new life.

"Kate!"

I was jerked back to the present with a start as someone gripped my shoulder and shook me roughly.

"Kate, are you all right?" Dempsey was staring at Maria indignantly. "What's going on here?"

"It's Michael!" Maria cried, advancing on her son. "He's been smoking." She turned angry eyes on her son. "How could you? You know how your father hates those things!"

"Dad's not here, though, is he?" the boy shot back bitterly. "You made him leave, and now it doesn't matter what Dad thinks."

Dempsey laid her hand on my arm, momentarily ignoring the standoff between mother and son. "Are you all right? You look shaken."

"I ... I'm fine," I said, surprised to find that it was the truth. I was fine—and I had regained my memory. I knew at last who I really was and how I had come to be here.

Dempsey turned her attention to Maria again. She held out her hand, palm up, to show Maria a bottle of pills. "Did your husband prescribe these?"

Maria picked up the pill bottle, turning it over in her hand.

"Yes. These are mild tranquilizers to help my nerves. But where did you find them? They have been missing for days."

"I'm afraid there's nothing mild about these," Dempsey said. She took the bottle from Maria and stowed it in the pocket of her jeans. "I believe these pills have been contributing to your belief that the house is haunted. They've made you forget things you should be remembering, kept you in a state of anxiety, and caused you to hallucinate."

"No! Jules wouldn't have given me anything like that. When things were so tense and uncertain between us, they helped me to feel relaxed and happy again."

"They did indeed." Dempsey turned to Michael, who was staring at her, wide-eyed and drained of color. "There is no ghost, is there? Everything strange that's happened in this house was staged by you, wasn't it? Why did you try to make your mother believe the house was haunted, Michael?"

Michael glanced uneasily toward the window behind him, as if looking for a means of escape.

Maria was looking at Dempsey in confusion. "What are you saying?"

"It's Dad," Michael mumbled miserably. "I thought that if you believed the house was haunted and you were too scared to be here on your own with me, you would ask him to come back to live with us again." He backed closer to the window as his mother advanced on him.

"You mean you moved all those things when my back was turned? The odd smells and the strange noises, the newspaper article about Colin mysteriously appearing on the table . . . they were all you?"

Michael reached behind him and leaned out of the window to toss the cigarette out into space. As he did so the ancient wooden window frame seemed to bow outwards under his weight, and suddenly visions of Alice hurtling downwards from the bridge flashed into my mind.

Michael's expression turned to one of fear as he pushed against the soft rotten wood of the frame to regain his balance and the room resounded with an ominous cracking noise. Lunging toward Michael, I grabbed his flailing hands just as the window frame gave way behind him and went crashing to the ground below. Holding both my own weight and his against the yawning void behind him, I braced my legs and held on with all the strength I could muster. In my mind's eye I felt Alice's ice-cold fingers slipping from my grasp, and I clung to Michael with grim determination. History was not going to repeat itself, I vowed. Not this time.

Maria, who had been rooted to the spot, ran toward us and helped pull Michael back into the room. She scooped the shocked boy into her arms. "My poor baby," she cried. "You could have been killed!" She held her son away from her and studied his shocked expression. "We did not explain things properly to you, your father and I. You didn't have to scare me into begging Jules to come home. It was your father who decided to leave, not me who sent him away."

The thirteen-year-old didn't look much of a man at that moment, more like a frightened little boy as he hugged his mother tearfully. "You don't hate me for trying to get Dad to come back?"

"Hate you? My sweet boy, I love you more than anything else in the world."

Dempsey, I noticed, had obviously thought better of accusing the boy of spiking my drink a few days earlier, and had fallen silent. Maria looked at the gaping hole where the window had once been, then raised tear-filled eyes toward me. Over the head of her son she mouthed a heartfelt "Thank you."

The merest whisper of something brushed lightly against my

arm, filling me with a sensation of peace and tranquillity. The vibration traveled to my neck and caressed my hair as it passed, sending tremors tingling down the length of my spine.

I shivered and smiled into the nothingness. "You're very welcome."

Later that night, when Vincent was home from work, Dempsey and I told him everything that had happened.

"So Maria was taking the same pills Jules gave Cheryl?" he said in horror.

"Maria only took them occasionally to help her nerves," Dempsey explained, "but she had no idea how addictive they can become. Michael must have found them and either took them to give to his mother to make her more susceptible to the haunted house scenario he'd cooked up, or simply to experiment with them himself. We've flushed the remains of the bottle down the toilet now."

"So there was no ghost?"

I said nothing, thinking of the whisper of energy that had passed me after I had saved Michael from his fall.

"And Kitty?" Vincent asked quietly as Tara placed a huge casserole dish on the table in front of us.

"Kitty is at peace," I said quietly.

"And you?" His eyes searched mine.

"I have my memories back." I told them what I knew. "I know who I am and where I was going when the snowstorm hit."

Instead of being delighted for me, Vincent seemed disappointed. "So you'll be going home now?"

I nodded. I would be going home all right, but not to the place from where I'd come. I thought of Adam, Betty, and Bill and smiled. "Yes. I will be going home now."

After the meal and a tearful goodbye, Dempsey headed off in her little yellow car. Tara did Jadie's physical therapy, and then I went up to kiss the child good night.

Jadie curled her arms around my neck. "Amber said everything would be all right," she said. "I love you, Kate."

"I love you too, Jadie." I hugged her to me, thinking of Kitty's lost child. "Sleep well."

Half an hour later I asked Tara where Vincent had gone. "I need to get going. Adam will be here in a moment to get me, and I want to say goodbye."

"He's reading Jadie her favorite bedtime story," she said, "the one Cheryl used to read to her and Amber every night."

Climbing the stairs, I paused to run my hands over the warm wooden banister and thought how Kitty had once loved this house. The warm feeling was still with me as I stopped outside Jadie's door.

"How's my little girl?" Vincent's voice came softly back to me past the ajar door of Jadie's room. I waited silently.

"Are there really such things as ghosts?" I heard Jadie's voice, muffled and sleepy.

Holding my breath, I listened for his answer, hoping he wouldn't just kiss her and leave, still unwilling or unable to answer her difficult question—a question that had given him equal quantities of hope and despair of late.

"No, sweetheart, I don't think there are." I peered through the crack in the door to see that Vincent was sitting on his daughter's bed. He took her hand in his and kissed it. "I think when people die, they go to heaven and stay there and are happy. Are you worrying about Amber?"

Jadie shook her head and smiled up at her father. "No, silly;

I know Amber isn't a ghost because she's here, Daddy." Jadie pressed her free hand to her chest. "You can talk to me as much as you like and Amber will hear you."

Vincent stared at his daughter as if he were seeing her for the first time. I found I could hardly breathe as he pulled her to him and cradled her against his heart. Tears glistened on his cheeks before he lowered his head to Jadie's and pressed his face into her hair.

"I'm so sorry," he whispered as he hugged her close. "I'm so sorry for shutting you out. I should have been there for you, but I'm here now. I love you more than anything else in the world. You know that, don't you?"

Jadie was nodding. I didn't know if his words were for Jadie, for Amber, for his dead wife, or all three, but it didn't really matter. Vincent was saying what he'd needed to say for so long, and he at last could find peace.

two years later

The sun was shining from a clear blue summer sky as I steered the stroller over the dry lumpy grass in the field leading down to the river.

Jadie chattered happily at my side, pausing to pick up the plastic toy that baby Jay was throwing out of the stroller at regular intervals. Jadie shrieked with delight as Lad came bounding across the field to push his wet muzzle into her hand.

When I reached the bench by the river, I put the brake on the stroller, made sure that Jay was securely strapped in, and shook out the rug from the basket underneath, spreading it on the ground while Jadie asked endless questions and the baby sucked noisily on his fist.

"Does Auntie Betty like having that lady come in and look after her and Uncle Bill?" Jadie asked as she sat on the rug next to me, picking daisies from the grass around her.

"I'm sure she's very pleased not to have to work so hard anymore."

"She still likes cooking, though, doesn't she?"

"She does." I smiled. "But she lets other people do some of it now."

"Tara says that you're nuts for keeping Auntie Betty and Uncle Bill at the farm."

I nearly laughed. Tara never was one for tact and diplomacy. "The farm is their home and always will be. They wouldn't be happy anywhere else, and we are fortunate that we can afford to hire a nurse for them."

Jadie thought about that while she threaded daisies into a chain. "I hope I'll get to be old one day like them, but maybe not so wrinkly or forgetful."

This time I did laugh. As Tara had once pointed out, Jadie didn't miss a thing. I realized she was looking at me with those serious blue eyes and that her comment about growing old had not been a flippant one.

"Did you know that some people with cystic fibrosis live well into their seventies?" I asked her. "You're strong and single-minded, Jadie. I think you'll get to be very old." I reached out and stroked her long blond hair. "And you'll still be as beautiful as an angel."

She smiled into my eyes and then looked up at something in the distance. I glanced around to see a silver Range Rover bumping through the field gate and down the slope toward us.

"That's Tara and your dad with Betty and Bill," I said.

The Range Rover drew to a halt nearby, throwing up clouds of dust. Vincent climbed out of the driver's seat and hurried to the passenger door to help Tara down.

"Stop fussing." Tara flapped him away. "I'm pregnant, not an invalid."

Vincent went to the back door, where a uniformed nurse was helping Bill into a wheelchair, and handed Betty down. I could see from Betty's face she had been crying over some forgotten thing, but when her eyes alighted on the river, her face took on a serene expression and she shuffled past me to sit on the stone bench behind me.

"Is Adam nearly finished with that field?" Vincent asked, gazing at the tractor in the distance as he dragged picnic baskets and folding chairs from the back of the vehicle.

I checked my watch. "He said he'd meet us at one o'clock. The workers will already have taken their break, so they'll take over from him for an hour or so."

"Thanks for looking after Jadie this morning." Tara waddled over to her stepdaughter and admired the daisy chain. "I was able to have a good rest." She looked up, shading her eyes with her hand as she sank into a canvas picnic chair. I followed her gaze to the top of the field, where a figure in a panama hat and an open-necked shirt was making his way through the gate and heading toward us. He was halfway down the slope when Adam appeared over the rise. The two men met and shook hands.

"Isn't that Johnson Clarke with Adam?" Bill asked from his chair, which had been parked beside the bench so he could sit next to Betty. "What are they doing?"

"Johnson is handing him something," Tara murmured as she accepted a glass of lemonade from her husband, who had spread food, drinks, and glasses out on a folding table.

The two men came toward us, and on closer inspection I saw that Johnson was looking unusually casual in a pair of tan trousers, although he still wore a red silk scarf tied rakishly at his neck. He had become a good friend over the last couple of years as we had scoured the archives and pored over old papers together, our combined knowledge of history and investigative procedures making us a formidable pair. Johnson, using his skills and as swiftly and respectfully as only he could, had helped the police pathologist successfully date the skeleton that I believed had once been Kitty. Without any existing Larkspurs to check against DNA samples, they had been unable to identify the remains positively, but the date and age of the skeleton were precise enough for me to believe it was her.

"Vincent and I got a letter from Maria yesterday." Tara jolted my thoughts back to the present. "She says she's getting used to living back in the bosom of her family in Sicily. Michael is at a boarding school in Boston, near the hospital where his father works, but has found himself a Sicilian girlfriend for the holidays. He spends half the time with each side of his family."

"And family is so important," I murmured, echoing the words Maria had spoken the second time we had met. Glancing over to where Betty was watching me, I caught her eye and smiled. To my delight she appeared to recognize me and smiled back.

It brought a further smile to my lips. There was no evidence, nothing to show that characters from the past had taken an active hand in shaping this wonderful present. Betty's ramblings about visiting an uncle in her childhood had probably been picked up from my deliberations around the farmhouse table about what I'd experienced under hypnosis. She, like Jadie, had listened to everything and had confused it with her own jumbled reality.

And although it was accepted that there had never been a ghost in the house that Vincent and Tara were busy converting back into one huge property, I had my own opinions on the subject. I had never mentioned the whispery feeling of gratitude and release I had felt when I'd saved Michael from falling from the upstairs window, and even if I had, it would probably have been attributed to my head injury and amnesia. But sometimes I woke in the night with the memory of that benign presence.

I accepted a glass of champagne from Vincent and smiled as he rested an arm around Tara's shoulders. Cheryl, of course, had never been missing. Her death had been duly recorded as a suicide, and I had since seen the coroner's report to put my mind at rest. Jules, I'd heard, was no longer in private practice but working long hours in a public hospital. I hoped that what had happened to Cheryl would make him more cautious about what he prescribed to his patients in the future.

Looking up at a pair of swallows as they rose higher and higher in the cloudless blue sky, I sighed with contentment. Even Colin had turned out to be blameless. No one could ever be sure he hadn't—even inadvertently—slipped suggestions into my deep subconscious. And my own extensive knowledge of history was also cause for belief that my experiences under hypnosis had merely been dredged from my own subconscious mind.

"Here comes Grandma!" Jadie shouted, gleefully leaping to her feet and hurrying up the slope to where her grandmother was lugging a large basket of goodies toward us. I thought fleetingly of my own grandmother. I had never been able to tell her how I'd solved the family mystery of the lost boy, but I understood that wherever she was resting now, she would know.

It wasn't Dempsey, however, who held my attention. I was gazing at Adam, my heart filled with love. He was hot and dusty, and his blue jeans were flecked with hay. As he moved toward me, his tanned arms bare and muscular and his dark hair sticking to his neck, his eyes held mine. But instead of bending to kiss me, he held out a package, which he placed carefully in my hands.

"That story you told me, about Kitty's final moments, just kept bugging me," Johnson said from behind Adam's shoulder. "In the end I managed to get one of the divers to go down and take another look at the site where the skeleton was recovered. This was lying buried in the silt, exactly where you said it must have fallen."

I peeled away the brown packaging, and there before me lay

an exquisite cameo brooch, the face of a young woman in profile carved in shell and set against an amber background. The whole thing was set in a gilt rope-twist surround. Gazing up into Adam's expectant face, I found myself speechless as he took it from me and pinned it carefully to my sleeveless shirt. It dawned on me that this was a very special gift indeed. It was not only a token of his love, but proof that despite all the rationalization and reasoning behind everything I had experienced, I had accurately reported Kitty's final moments. And that was something that simply could not be explained away.

"The brooch proves the skeleton's identity as that of Kathryn Larkspur, and I thought it should go back to its rightful owner." Johnson's voice came from somewhere in the distance. "And you're the nearest thing to a relative Kitty has. Adam asked me to get it cleaned and mended." Adam drew me toward him and, as little shivers of pleasure tingled between us, I pressed myself against his chest.

"Kitty can be buried with Garrett in the churchyard now," he murmured as we smiled into each other's eyes.

With one hand on the brooch and the other entwined in his hair, I closed the last tiny gap between us. "Garrett will no longer be alone."

As Adam kissed me, I closed my eyes, listening to the murmur of familiar voices around us—Jadie laughing, our baby gurgling in delight, and the sound of the river bubbling endlessly by. I had come back to the world of the living, and I was going to make the most of every minute I had been given. Allowing myself to melt against Adam, I lost myself in his timeless embrace.

ADOPTING OUR SONS

Melanie Rose

When my husband and I adopted our two lovely sons we were fulfilling a dream that had begun when we were first married. I had always wanted lots of children, but the world seemed an unfair place when there were children in care who badly needed loving parents and a settled home life. I was a trained nursery nurse in England and had worked with children since leaving college: first in the Special Baby Care Unit of a local hospital, then for several years in a council-run day nursery for underprivileged children, and later as the play therapist on the children's ward at the Royal Marsden Hospital in Sutton.

We'd decided to have two birth children of our own and then consider adopting, perhaps two siblings, to meld us all into one large, happy family. But life—as it has a habit of doing—had different plans. After a couple of years of trying unsuccessfully for a baby, we decided to go the adoptive route right away. We registered with a church adoption society and underwent a year of intensive vetting to establish our suitability as adoptive parents.

Everything about our lives was scrutinized. Our home, our income, our extended families, and our views on parenting all came under intense examination. We went to meetings with social workers and adoption workers and joined an adoptive parents' group. The children we might be taking would in all probability have had a rough start in life. As adoptive parents we had to prove that any children we took in would have a happy and settled life with us. It was a necessary learning curve, but also an emotionally grueling experience.

When we were shown photos of our boys, brothers aged two and three years old, we fell in love with them at first sight. Visiting them in the foster home where they were living confirmed our feelings and we began to make plans to bring them home to live with us. But there were problems. One of the boys had learning difficulties and might need special education. The other had emotional problems, which included an eating disorder. Still, we thought, we were up to the challenge.

I gave up work to care for the boys and we began the slow process of bonding as a family. Like the character Jessica in my novel *Life as I Know It,* I found our ready-made family members had preconceived ideas and routines and insecurities of their own. We hadn't grown slowly together like a birth family but arrived suddenly in a situation that was new to all of us. We had temper tantrums and nightmares and we had to get used to one another's personalities. For my own part, I'd been accustomed to going out to work and had to adjust to finding myself at home, as a full-time mum.

Also like Jessica in *Life as I Know It,* I needed to learn to love my new family unconditionally, while not being sure we would be together permanently. For the first six months we lived with the fear that the boys' birth family might have a change of heart and contest the adoption. We had met their birth mother and she had made the brave decision that giving the boys up for adoption was the right thing to do, but there was always the possibility she might change her mind. At any time we could have had our new little family members snatched away and I would be flung back to my previous life.

The characters in my second novel, *Finding Home,* experience the trauma of losing a beloved child and find themselves almost afraid to love her sister, Jadie, in case she is taken from them, too—yet they find they are unable to not love her. Both Jessica in *Life as I Know It* and Kate in *Finding Home* end up making up their families from children not necessarily related to them by blood. In *Finding Home,* Kitty's son is taken from her and given up for adoption, and when she claims him back, the pain of his adoptive family echoes down the generations to form the hub of the mystery of the "lost boy" that Emma/Kate sets out to investigate.

In *Finding Home,* another character, Dempsey, says of her adopted family, "It's possible I have always been exactly where I belonged."

Going to court and having the boys legally made part of our family was one of the most nerve-racking days of my life—but also one of the best. A year later I found I was expecting another little boy to add to our growing brood and four years after that our youngest son was born. I'm often asked if I treat all the boys the same and I say no, absolutely not. They are all individuals with different personalities, and I have a unique relationship with each of my lovely sons. Looking back, I realize that we were always meant to be together and I wouldn't have missed the experience for the world.

Acknowledgments

Thanks to the following authors and institutions, whose informational fact sheets and books were of great use in the research of this novel.

"Cystic Fibrosis"—published by Bupa's health
    information team, May 2009

Cystic Fibrosis Trust—www.cftrust.org.uk

Destiny of Souls by Michael Newton, Ph.D.

"Elective Mutism"—Simple Psych
    http://easyweb.easynet.co.uk/simplepsych/mutism.html

about the author

Melanie Rose was an avid reader from an early age and found herself looking at the world around her and wondering "What if?" She began writing as a teenager, progressing to short stories and articles for magazines and newspapers. She trained as a nursery nurse and later became a play therapist on the children's ward at the Royal Marsden Hospital, continuing to write in her spare time.

She now lives in Surrey with her husband and four sons, who, along with many of the children she has cared for, provide much inspiration for her books.

For further information about Melanie please visit www.melanierose.co.uk.